Estrella Chavez Goes To Mystery School

Lesson 1: Water

L.C. Matherne

Printed in the United States of America
Magazine Street Journal
Paperback ISBN: 978-0-692-06415-3
Ebook ISBN: 979-8-9926863-0-2

For the Remundus

I am The Cosmic
This is my Scroll
You are my servant
I guide your soul
I am Water
I am Day
I am Night
I made the beginning
The Sound
The Light
From Suns
From Void
From Tongues
I am employed
I am Truth
You will know Me
By my words
Here unspooling

CONTENTS

JULY

The Tearful Eyes of Our
Lady of Guadalupe

"For what is mysticism but a song of the divine,
a swimming in the womb of God?"

Linda Chavez clicks off the *Be Here Now* radio show, bows her head, and folds her hands into her heart. "Thank you, Our Lady of Guadalupe, for this womb of God. For my girls, for the ranch, even for Victor. It's not where I thought I'd be, not what I wanted, but it's all been worthwhile—all the pain, all I've lost."

She crosses herself as Marina, her oldest daughter—a blossoming thirteen—opens the key lid to the baby grand piano and summons Bach's "Praeludium" in G-sharp minor. It's melody still bruises Linda's heart.

Estrella, Linda's 'oops' baby, a happy, fat toddler, crawls onto the piano bench next to Marina and hits random keys, making a cacophony and laughing.

"Such a light you bring, Estrella!" Marina coos, tickling her baby sister's chin. "You're everybody's favorite and already funny, like your daddy."

"She has a bit of a temper, but it seals her charm," Linda says , her eyes full of love, as the old-fashioned house phone rings. She crosses broken rays of sunlight to answer the phone. ""It's your father, no doubt, calling to see what's for dinner. I swear that man loves to eat more than he loves to breathe."

The piano goes quiet. "It's not Dad," Marina says, her eucalyptus-green eyes wide with terror.

Linda picks up the receiver.

"Pay attention, Linda. I'm going to tell you what to do."

"Who is this?" Linda hisses, her voice tight.

"We have Victor."

Linda's heart freezes in her chest. After all this time, she almost thought they were safe.

"Do what we say, and we won't kill him. We need three million American dollars. You have two days." The line goes dead.

Estrella screams, and the room darkens Sudden lightning flashes outside.

"We must call Kit," Marina says.

• • •

The quarter moon shines silver between fast-moving clouds above the ranch house that blazes with lights.

A black Mercedes sedan winds through the moonlight up the long driveway. The car stops, dust puffs from the tires. Yves Pearce, a meticulously dressed man in his early twenties, opens the back door. Kit Hamilton steps a stiletto heel onto the dusty drive.

"Thank God she's here," Linda says to Cesar, Victor's brother, who stands next to her, his eyes bloodshot from the joint he puffs. "Kit will know what to do, unlike you, who were supposed to be watching Victor. You are useless, I swear, but by some cruel twist of fate, here you are again, involved in yet another life and death situation far beyond your pay grade. And *you're* going to deal with Zandra. Why you ever married her I have no idea."

Cesar shrugs. "I *was* watching him," he replies. "But I can't be with him every minute of the day. You know he has his interests."

Linda glares at him as Kit and Yves approach. Kit, a tall, slender blonde strides ahead with her usual authority, but uncertainty pools in her blue eyes.

"Where's Estrella?" Kit asks. "Keeping my goddaughter safe is our top priority. This kidnapping could just be a trick to expose her, though I'm certain they have no clue that they're looking for his daughter. Saul has made sure of that." She takes a deep breath. "I could take a dagger and cut out my own heart for not seeing the signs. I thought we'd secured what we needed to have in place for our protection. But maybe my powers are failing. I must talk to Babatunde."

"Estrella's with Marina," Linda says. "Why Babatunde?"

"He's near the caves. He may know something." Kit replies.

"This is such bullshit," Cesar says. "You're looking for answers in a fairytale book. It's the cartel, I'm telling you."

Kit rolls her eyes at Cesar, pushing past him toward the house.

Linda stops her a few feet in front of the wrought iron front door. "Zandra doesn't know yet."

"Oh, come on." Kit's eyes land on Cesar. "She's *your* wife."

He looks away. "I'm not telling her any bad news. You tell her—it's *your* fairytale."

Kit straightens her cream silk blouse. "Well let's do this, then." She tosses Yves a bottle of Xanax from her purse. "There's liquor in the kitchen. She likes scotch."

...

Zandra Chavez reclines on the sofa, a telenovela murmuring from the TV. Her black hair is wrapped around curlers; one eyebrow drawn in on her round face. She wears a dressing gown and holds her hands out, fingers spread wide so as not to ruin her wet nails.

She looks from Kit to Yves to Cesar, who averts his gaze, and finally to Linda. "What the hell is going on?" she accuses. "Why is Miss High and Mighty Kit Hamilton here with her so-called butler? I sense death."

Linda, finding all the eyes she searches turned away, finally says, "Victor's been kidnapped by the narcos. We have to figure out how to get him back."

Zandra screams loud and long, then falls to the floor, where she shouts prayers between more bloodcurdling screams. Cesar bends awkwardly to comfort his wife. Yves takes the Xanax to the kitchen.

"Mami! What's wrong?"

Alfonso, Zandra and Cesar's oldest son, runs into the room. A wisp of mustache tickles his thirteen-year-old lip. He takes his mother's hand as Yves, like a benign wind, appears with an icy drink.

Zandra drinks it in three gulps, then turns her eyes of fury to Linda.

"How could you keep this from me? You think you're better than me, that I deserve nothing."

"Keep what from you, Mami?" Alfonso looks from his mother to Linda and back.

Linda's voice finally cracks. "Your Uncle Victor has been kidnapped by the narcos." She brushes back a tear. "I know you worship your Uncle Victor, and he loves you too, so much, but we adults need to handle the situation now. Alfonso, you take care of your mother. We'll be in the kitchen."

Alfonso stands, Zandra already passed out cold from the laced drink. "I'm coming to the kitchen, too," he says, his voice resonating from a new, low register. "I know who I am, what blood flows in my body. I am the nephew and godson of Victor Chavez, champion of the people. If anyone hurts my uncle, I will kill them myself."

. . .

"Talk to me, Babatunde. What have you heard?" Kit sits at the head of the humble Chavez kitchen table, phone to her ear.

"It is the Proletum," an elegant, African-inflected voice replies through the crackled line. "Saul is certain of it. They do not have the sword, so more demands will surely come. Expect a negotiation."

"They must have at least one of the knives to have held onto him for this long," Kit says. "I'm at the ranch. Call if you hear anything new." She hangs up the phone. "Babatunde says Proletum."

"Of course it is the Proletum," Marina says, drifting into the room.

Linda rolls her eyes and sighs. "We all agree the water needs to be pure and free, but I just can't listen to this nonsense about demonic cults and angels and demons roaming the earth. Wickedness is as old as time. There is no evil conspiracy pulling the strings of the world, just an endless struggle. It's the narcos and we know how to deal with them – pay them off."

"What's Proletum? Are they demons or angels?" Alfonso asks, taking a sip of the coffee Yves places before him.

"The Proletum is nothing," Cesar says. "You're too young to be here, anyway. Go to bed."

"I'm not going to bed. I just drank coffee." Alfonso sets down his chipped china cup and puffs out his skinny chest.

"The Proletum are the bad guys," Marina says to Alfonso, her younger cousin by two years. "Don't worry. We're the good guys and we always win in the end."

"It's the narcos," Cesar says. "You know how they feel about Victor."

Linda nods.

"And..." Cesar casts his eyes down as he makes the sign of the cross.

"What, Cesar?" Linda asks. "What do you know?"

Cesar shakes his head and sighs. "Say what you will, but I can keep a secret. If you were to cut me open right now, secrets would seep from my body with my blood."

"What. The. Hell?" Linda breaks into an involuntary shout. "Tell me everything right now, Cesar."

"But I just want you to know that, if I didn't think it could help Victor, I would never say anything because he asked me not to, and I would never betray my brother."

Cesar makes the sign of the cross a second time. Finally, he speaks. "Last week, Gabriel Estrada and Victor got into a fistfight in the city."

"Gabriel Estrada is the kingpin of the Cobras, the most evil cartel," Alfonso says. "They say he killed forty men in one night."

Cesar nods at his son, then continues. "We were at the bar, having a drink before we came back to the ranch. Gabriel walked past, and Victor stuck out his foot and tripped him. Gabriel landed face down on the grungy floor. Then Victor said, 'How's Rosanna Gomez, you piece of dirt?' Rosanna's mother found her in their yard, sliced open from her belly to her chest because she refused to marry Gabriel's brother. She was thirteen."

"My God," Kit says. "Marina's thirteen. Why are these men so wicked?"

"Me and Victor got some good punches in before we fought our way out of the bar, but it's only a matter of time. You can't humiliate Gabriel Estrada and live. Not even Victor, who has the strength of five men. But I think they'll take the money, too. Besides, you already have all the water stuff locked up I thought, years ago."

The phone rings. Linda's fingers tremble as she picks up the receiver.

"Get a pen, Linda. I'm going to tell you where to bring the money," a gravelly voice commands.

"We want proof of life." Linda presses the phone more firmly to her ear.

Heavy footsteps, grunts, and shattering glass sound through the line, then a ragged breath. "Mi corazón, I don't know these men. Don't pay them. They're going to kill me anyway."

"Victor!" Linda cries, as more shouts and crashes come through the phone.

The gravelly voice comes back, winded. "There's your proof of life. Come to Mary of Guadalupe church in Tlaxcala the day after tomorrow at 5:00. Just you, or he dies."

The line goes dead. Linda puts the phone back in the cradle, her whole body shaking.

Alfonso speaks first. "Should we call the police?"

Everyone laughs.

"The police *are* the narcos, at least on that we can all agree," Cesar says.

A wail pierces the heavy air like the howl of a dog.

"Estrella!" Marina runs from the room and returns with Estrella in her arms. Hugo, Zandra and Cesar's five-year-old son, trails behind.

"Estrella had a nightmare," Marina says. "Monsters."

Lightning brightens the room from outside. Thunder booms.

Marina holds Estrella until her screams turn into broken-breath tears. "They will kill Father either way," Marina says, breaking the quiet. "There is no reason to pay them."

...

Late in the night, almost morning, the moon sunk below the horizon, Linda cries into her pillow. Marina enters her mother's chamber and kisses her worried brow.

As she does, the room glows with a soft, pink light. A butterfly flutters through the open window. Outside, birds break into song.

"It's going to be okay, Momma," Marina says. "They can't hurt him. It's only his body."

...

The south Mexican sun, not yet fully risen, sends a gray light over the plain. Linda presses the puffy skin around her eyes, dresses, then makes her way back to the kitchen. From the corner of the window, she watches her daughters play together in the courtyard.

Marina gives Estrella a stick and some leaves to play with, then punches, kicks, and jumps. She bends her back in half, transitions until she's standing on her head, and rests there for several minutes, finally sitting cross-legged, head bowed in prayer. She chants softly. "*Shanti, shanti, shanti.*"

Estrella giggles and sits cross-legged, too, chanting with her sister.

Marina opens her partially closed eyes. "Not a word of Spanish, just flawless Sanskrit. I love you, Little Star," she says, jumping soundlessly to her feet. Estrella motions for her sister to take her in her arms. Marina pulls her up without touching her. Estrella floats to her hip, laughing with delight.

"Breakfast!" Zandra's call breaks Linda's concentration. "If you spied on your husband the way you're spying on your girls, we wouldn't be in this mess," she says from behind Linda as Marina and Estrella traipse to the kitchen.

Linda looks again. On the warming bricks of the courtyard, Estrella's stick and leaves transform into a thriving branch—every second, a new shoot growing.

•••

"I'm going to pay them." Linda says to Kit in the afternoon courtyard that's blind with sun. They smoke cigarettes together, as they have for almost two decades. "After everything Victor has done for me, I will not leave him to die at the hands of his enemies."

Kit looks to the dry, rolling hills, where pines droop in the July heat. "I'll give you the money then."

"I can't accept your money. You know that. I still have what's left of my inheritance. It's enough."

Kit nods. "What is it they say about pride coming before a fall? But whatever happens, I'll always be here for you and the girls, and the Water Trust, too. Whatever it takes, whatever the consequences."

"These are some heavy consequences," Linda says. "And they just keep coming."

Estrella toddles into the courtyard and climbs onto Linda's lap. "I want my daddy. Now."

"Her first words! And a complete sentence." Linda swallows. "This morning, I think she was flying."

Kit gives Linda a look of victory. "Very, very smart, with some highly unusual talents. And she's just getting started. You'll see. Just like we've been telling you."

"I want my daddy now!" Estrella screams, her eyes intense.

A hot wind blows through the ranch, dark clouds gather in the blue sky. Thunder rumbles, lightning flashes.

. . .

Our Lady of Guadalupe Church peeks up from the desert. A wind-battered cross fixes to its sagging roof, all its windows are broken. Linda breathes into her fear as two men with machine guns step outside the sand-beaten chapel.

"They're here. Two of them so far," she whispers into the wire she wears under her headscarf, her heart beating fast.

A man with an eye patch taps on the window with his gun. "Get out."

Linda descends, chanting silently to herself, "*Stay calm, stay calm, stay calm.*"

The man examines the empty Jeep. "Where's the money?"

"Where's my husband?"

The man pulls back the barrel of his gun.

Linda's heart spasms. *Stay calm, stay calm, stay calm.* "Show me Victor," she says in a low, steady voice.

The man grabs Linda by the neck and drags her into the church. She struggles to breathe as her dangling feet make a trail in the sand and her knees bang into the doorframe.

Inside, a naked man hangs, nailed to the massive wooden cross on the altar.

"Victor!"

He raises his bloody head from the cross. "My love, why are you here? I told you they would kill me."

"Take him down!" Linda screams.

Eye Patch Man slams Linda into the dusty wall of the church. "Show us the money, we take him down."

"Don't touch her, pendejo!" Victor shouts from the cross. He breaks one hand free from its nail—the cross sways. A man at the foot of the cross unsheathes a knife with a black crystal hilt and cuts Victor's calf muscle. Victor screams and goes limp.

Linda takes a breath and stands at her full height. "Take him down first, and then I'll give you the money."

"Put another nail, Domingo," the man with the eye patch replies.

A man in the front pew rises and puts down his machine gun to pick up a hammer and nail from the floor.

"Don't worry, mi corazón, this doesn't hurt as much as you think. Call in your people. Keep the money, take care of the girls. And remember we all are water. They can't destroy us. I will always be with you. You'll see." Victor moans as the man hammers a nail into his palm.

Linda grabs Eye Patch Man's arm and pulls him outside, running, tripping and falling as tears make a thin mud of the dust on her face. She claws at the sand to unearth a leather bag.

Eye Patch Man squats and rifles through the stacks of money, then hits Linda across the face with his gun; she collapses into the sand. "Kill him and let's go," he says into a walkie-talkie.

Gunshots ring out in the church, hundreds of them.

. . .

Blood trickles into Linda's mouth as ATVs swarm from every direction, their passengers firing machine guns. Eye Patch Man runs inside with the money and reemerges with five men, all loaded with weapons.

Linda drags herself behind the Jeep as the men shoot at each other, bodies dropping with each exchange. The shots silence. Only Eye Patch and two of his men still stand, gun smoke drifting around them.

Linda wiggles like a snake into the driver's seat of the Jeep, her hand on the ignition.

One of the shooters says, "At least we get the bonus. He said if she brought it, we could keep it."

Eye Patch raises his gun and shoots twice, killing both men. "You mean *I'm* getting a bonus. I did all the work anyway."

"The girls can't lose us both," Linda whispers through her tears. In one motion, she turns the key, puts the Jeep into reverse, and slams on the gas.

Eye Patch Man fires; one of the front tires deflate. He fires again into the engine; it catches fire. Linda runs, but he grabs her by the hair, drags her to the ground and kicks her in the ribs.

"This is how you die," Eye Patch Man says.

"You would be ugly, even with both eyes," Linda replies. "And the devil will feast on your flesh for eternity," she spits, then begins to murmur the words to Hail Mary, steeling herself for death.

Eye Patch presses the gun to Linda's forehead, it's metal still hot. "He said not to kill you, but I don't like you. You're a stupid, mouthy bitch." He squeezes the trigger.

Nothing happens.

He tries again.

Nothing.

He grunts in aggravation, then whips the gun across Linda's face a second time.

Linda hears the crunch of her own bones before the world goes dark.

* * *

Blood dribbles down Linda's cheek, her temples pound. With effort, she half-opens her right eye, the left swollen closed. A small brown eye of a puppy looks back at her. He appears to be part wolf—skinny, long tail, big paws. He nuzzles Linda's neck. As he does, a calm comes over her, a relief from the pain, the power to stand. She limps unsteadily toward the church, the puppy keeping pace at her side.

Everywhere around her, bodies, machine guns, and blood dirty the desert sands. "These men were like my family," she cries. "How will I tell their wives, their mothers, their children? *I* did this. They all told me not to, but I did it anyway."

"Linda." Cesar's weak voice summons her from the scarlet sands. He crawls out from behind an ATV, blood soaking his shirt. The puppy licks Cesar's wounds, the bleeding stops. Cesar looks at Linda. "Maybe there are angels," he says.

"Maybe," Linda replies as they enter the church.

Butterflies, songbirds, and bees flutter around Victor's bullet-riddled corpse. He hangs from the cross by his right arm, his left arm completely severed by the force of gunfire.

"Do you see the light shining all around him?" Cesar asks, his eyes bright with tears.

"All that they've been saying is true," Linda replies, falling on her knees before the cross. "It isn't about drugs, or even vengeance. It's about the water."

The puppy barks. A black Mercedes approaches through the empty desert.

• • •

The desert passes in a blur of oranges, pinks, and purples as the sun sets. Linda strokes the fur of the puppy. "I'm naming him Guadalupe," she says. "And every day that he is alive, he will remind me to believe. I will remember that all this death was my doing because I doubted, because I thought I was smarter, I knew more. I must believe it all, even the parts that I don't want to be true...about the demons. No matter who they are."

Kit's blue eyes meet Linda's in the rearview mirror. "No matter who they are," she says as Yves turns onto the long ranch road, into a cloud of toxic smoke.

Flames lick the sky.

"The girls!" Linda calls out. "The ranch! All I have left!"

Suddenly, a torrential sheet of rain pours down from what had been a cloudless sky.

Zandra and the four children stand in the downpour, watching their home burn to ash. Sirens sound in the distance.

Marina comes to the car window, water running rivers down her brow. "I couldn't stop them. I tried...the rain..."

* * *

The rain stops, the last embers burn.

Estrella and Guadalupe cuddle in the backseat of the Mercedes. For the first time in two days, Victor Chavez's young daughter sleeps.

The puppy extends his oversized paw around Estrella's curled body, opens one wolfish eye, and growls.

AUGUST

Townies

Green vines, green trees, green bushes line the muddy path. Mist dampens the ionized atmosphere; clouds make the air cool and gray. Wildness and the rich scent of water imbue the air. A bear, her fur half brown and half white, steps onto the path.

"Hello, Estrella," the bear says.

"Hello, Bear," Estrella replies.

"I am Islid." Now they are on a rocky beach, where a river of crystals bubbles and flows. "I am the keeper of these waters."

Birds, badgers, turtles, wolves, deer, and foxes emerge from the green forest beyond the banks. In the crystal river, salmon, and trout glisten. The animals sing together, making a unified, wordless song.

The molecules of Estrella's body vibrate. Her palms throb. The top of her head opens into a waterfall of crystals as the bottoms of her feet lift from the shore. Now she is flying, soaring over the forest. She flies over the ocean, over desert sands, over mountains, rivers, and jungles.

The song of the animals fills her skin as she ripples toward the stars.

. . .

Estrella wakes, reluctantly. She pets her old dog, Lupe, who sprawls out on the bed next to her, still snoring. "I just had the best dream," she says, her palms still tingling. "I was flying over these crystal waters. And there was a bear. Islid."

She takes the rosary beads from a box by her bedside and prays, as she does every morning. She replaces the beads and stretches her arms over her head. "Come on, Lupe. Time to do this."

Lupe waits for Estrella while she dresses—her usual jeans, t-shirt, and Converse—runs a brush over her teeth, pulls a comb through her hair, splashes her face with water, and gathers her long, thick hair into a ponytail. She winks at the face in the mirror. "Could be worse."

They descend the carpeted steps of the small, quiet house, Lupe leading the way. She lets the dog out the back door, then waters her plants, looking around before she touches her fingertip to a little, green bud on her potted rosebush. She closes her eyes until light streams from her finger. The bud opens into a happy, pink flower.

Estrella relinquishes the rosebud and does fifty push-ups and one hundred front, back and side-kicks, then kisses Lupe goodbye. She jumps on her bicycle and pushes hard on the pedals.

The humble houses of her neighborhood give way to ever larger homes on ever larger pieces of land. Her legs burn as she turns onto a tree-lined road, with no houses on either side. She keeps pushing with all the strength and speed she has for the final quarter mile, plants her foot, and skids to an abrupt stop in front of a white, columned, exceedingly grand mansion. She checks her watch.

"Ten minutes, forty-five seconds. Dammit! I'll get it to ten minutes next time."

• • •

Yves opens the door and sighs. "I thought you were going to start making an effort."

Estrella wipes the sweat from her face with her hand, pulls a lip gloss from her backpack, and sweeps it across her lips. "*Voila.*"

Yves rolls his eyes. "Where did this attitude come from, Estrella? You were always such a sweet child, if a bit headstrong."

"Being headstrong's better than being a wimp," Estrella replies.

Yves lowers his voice. "Kit's in a bit of a mood this morning, so keep your distance. God knows I am."

Estrella grins. "Kit's always in some kind of a mood—that's what makes her fun. Most of the time."

"This isn't one of those times," Yves replies as they pass the Picassos and O'Keefes that line the silk-papered walls, finally taking a left into the east wing.

Kit Hamilton paces her extravagant bedroom suite, headset in her ear and espresso in her hand, still wearing her dressing gown.

"Get it done, or don't call back!" she yells into the headset.

"Madame, your librarian has arrived." Yves bows, then quickly exits.

Kit examines her goddaughter. "You look like a vagrant."

"Whatever. I don't have time to dress up—I'm too busy getting perfect grades. But I put on lip gloss just for you." She tosses her backpack by the door and kisses Kit on the cheek, leaving a shiny imprint.

Kit softens with the kiss, but says, "Lip gloss or not, you look like you just rolled out of bed, threw on your brother's least attractive clothes and did nothing with your hair."

"I like my clothes. They're comfortable."

Kit sinks into a red velvet chair and takes a sip of espresso from a bone china cup. "Life is not comfortable, Estrella. We all have high expectations for you at Glouton."

Estrella groans. "This again! Stupid Glouton, the most uptight, rich kid school in the whole world. Why can't I just go to

Washington High, where all my friends are going?" She rattles off the stats. "It's ranked in the top twenty public high schools in the country, with a ninety-seven percent graduation rate. Eighty-seven percent of those graduates go to college, and forty-seven percent of those go to Ivy League schools. I don't want to go and live with the richies. They're terrible!"

Kit raises a brow. "Oh, are they?"

Estrella blushes. "Not *you*, Kit, but you know that you're basically the only rich person I've ever met who isn't fake as hell. Well, and Evan, obviously."

"Of course, Evan is down-to-earth—I've raised him to be. Just like Marc."

Estrella's heart thumps at the mention of Marcus Aurelius Hamilton, Kit's other nephew - the handsome, older one.

"So, I don't want to hear it," Kit continues. "There is absolutely no comparison to Glouton in terms of both academics and access. And I know you're excited for Mystery School."

"Mystery School is the only reason I didn't purposefully fail the Glouton entrance exam." Estrella says, to a shocked look from Kit. "How cool is Dr. Mather's theory that the vibrational waves of words and thoughts can influence matter. Like how I think the Latin words at mass do. And his whole concept of 'The Cosmic'? No wonder he got the Nobel Prize. But Mystery School is the only reason I'm going to Glouton, and if I don't like it there, I'm leaving, no matter what you and Mom say. I'm tired of you bossing me all the time."

"I took the course, as you know," Kit replies. "Like you, I had to apply and be selected—though I was a senior, and you're just a freshman. That never happens, by the way, so you will be staying in Glouton the entire four years, whatever delusions of autonomy you may be harboring."

"I wonder why it's so hard to get in," Estrella says. "The course description in the Glouton handbook calls it 'a seminar exploration of mysticism.' From what I've read, mysticism is all about transformation, and being one with God. Seems like it would be an easy class, especially because—you know..." Estrella looks around, then whispers, "...my Mayan gifts. Like Dad was a shaman and everything."

"Well, it's not easy," Kit responds. "It's incredibly difficult. And your father would want you to go to Glouton and take it seriously and not talk about those gifts." Kit continues, "Don't forget that you owe me for getting you out of that trouble at school, or you wouldn't be able to study with Dr. Mather at all."

Estrella's lips purse with shame. "I guess I regret punching Cooper Necker, but he deserved it. He was a bully, and now he's not. I'll bet Dad would be proud of me for punching a bully in his stupid, soft guts, since he spent his whole life standing up for people who couldn't stand up for themselves. But Mom sure was pissed. It's ridiculous that I'm still grounded."

Kit buffs her nails as she says, "It's time for you to act like the well-bred young woman that you are. How can anyone take you seriously if you don't?"

"I'm fourteen! I'm not supposed to be serious right now." Estrella slumps onto Kit's satin bedspread.

Kit's swats Estrella on the knees. "You're almost fifteen. This is absolutely the time to be serious. Now go sort that new shipment and then come help me with my correspondence."

"Ooh! Correspondence—we haven't done that for a while. Who are you going to be way too honest with today?"

Kit smiles. "I have a list. And please find Yves and tell him I need to see him."

Quincy, Kit's parrot, wakes from his perch in his solid gold cage and squawks, "Go to work!"

Estrella shoots the bird a dirty look. "Even Quincy tries to boss me."

Estrella passes Yves in the hall on her way to the place of her summer labors for the past three years: Kit Hamilton's library. "She wants to see you," she says. "Good luck."

...

Estrella puts up the last of the seventy-four books on art and architecture into the shelves of Kit's library—gifts from an estate in Belgium. "Why are these rich old people always dying and leaving Kit their books?" She mutters. "And I thought art was supposed to be pretty, anyway, unlike the pictures in these books."

She settles into a reading chair and checks the news, searching for some mention of Gabriel Estrada—the man who killed her father, ruined his reputation, and burned down their house. "One of these days you're going to get caught, Gabriel Estrada, and when you do, Alfonso and I will kill you," she murmurs.

But her search only uncovers the regular bad news: Water shortages throughout Asia are causing riots; thousands of people are fleeing their countries for Europe and Australia. There's a photo of a baby drowned in the sea.

Estrella's heart hurts with sympathy. "*This* is why I'm going to keep studying and get my dual JD/MBA—so I can run the Water Trust and make clean water available to everyone, like my dad."

She prays.

"Our Blessed Mother, please ask your son to help all the people of the world. Please ask him to send the people in Asia rain, and to guide all the refugees to safe places to live. Please also ask him to give Mom and Kit and Marina the strength to do their jobs, and please also give me the strength to control my temper, so I don't make any more bad decisions that keep me from achieving my goals. And please, Most Blessed of Mothers, please help Kit be happy so we can all have a nice day today. In Jesus's name, amen."

As she lifts her bowed head and crosses herself, the memory of her dream flits through her mind, making her smile. She texts an invitation to dinner to her best friend, Nadine. Nadine texts right back.

Tamales? I'm in.

Kit's disembodied voice sounds over a speaker. "Estrella, bring me *Songs of Innocence*. Blake."

"Okay!" Estrella yells back, plucking the ornate book from a row of shelves. As she does, a book falls from a shelf above and plops onto her feet as if someone pushed it.

Divine Harmony: The Life and Teachings of Pythagoras. "Hmmm," she says. "The math guy." She opens to a random page.

Perhaps the most essential of Pythagoras's teachings, outside of his realizations and practical applications of music and mathematics, is the teaching that we can communicate with animals, that animals have souls, and are our friends in another form.

She closes the book to find a pair of green, feline eyes staring into her own. Kitty-Kat, Kit's cat, sits on the shelf where the book was.

"Damn, cats are stealthy," Estrella says, recovering her balance from the shock of the cat's inscrutable eyes. "Come on, Kitty-Kat," She says. "Let's go see your mommy."

Kitty-Kat jumps down, as easy and fluid as water.

"I guess Pythagoras must've been only half-right about communicating with animals, though," Estrella says as she runs her palm over Kitty-Kat's silky back, "because you haven't said a word yet."

...

Kit lays fully clothed on top of the bed covers, smoking a cigarette. Her ruby-studded dressing table—a gift from an Arabian sultan to her grandfather, William Hamilton the First, the founder of Community Oil and the Western Railroad—holds her four o'clock martini. It's 1:45.

"Why do you shout, darling?" Kit asks Estrella, the earlier pinching edge to her voice dissolved.

Estrella smiles inside and quietly thanks Mary of Guadalupe for answering her prayer.

"Why do you use the speakers when you could just shout?" Estrella asks back.

"Because shouting isn't ladylike."

"Oh well. It should be clear to everyone by now that I'm not exactly ladylike." She glances at the stack of paperbacks on Kit's bedside table. "What're you reading?"

"I'm reading about how to break young girls of their sassiness and make them into elegant young women," Kit replies as she flips through Blake's poems on innocence. "*Priests with black gowns, were walking their rounds, and binding with briars, my joys and desires*," Kit quotes. "Maybe I should have asked for *Songs of Experience*. Lord knows Archbishop David has enough of it. I need a quote for his birthday card, and I certainly can't use that one."

"You're not even religious," Estrella says.

"Clergy make excellent political allies, because they can get their followers to do whatever they want," Kit replies, as the watch on her bony wrist lights up. "It's Senator Morales. I'm beginning to suspect he's an idiot." She puts down the book, picks up her drink, and speaks to her wrist. "Give me some good news or stop calling me."

The voice from Kit's wrist says, "This is Washington. You know there is no good news."

Kit paces the room, sipping her martini. "Fair enough. Then give me some not-so-bad-news."

"Unfortunately, I've got some not-so-good-at-all news."

"I pay you too much to hear anything like that."

"Shhhh!" Estrella hisses, eyes wide. "You know they record all the senator's phone calls!" Kit waves her off.

The strained voice from the watch talks quickly. "We didn't get the votes to pass the Alkalinity Treaty. The Privatization Wing doesn't like the opportunities for increased regulation. You're going to have to wait for the Water Trust's Species Extinction report in the spring to gather more support."

"We're not waiting." Kit's voice strengthens. "Did you use the Soledad Springs bottling rights to sweeten the deal for those greedy idiots like we discussed? Miakoda Grace is firmly on our side on this."

"You know you just referred to your own brother and several of your best friends as greedy idiots?" Estrella whispers. Kit rolls her eyes.

Senator Morales replies, "It wasn't enough. We're making some revisions and sending it back through committee. Miakoda may be Speaker of the House, but this is the Senate. We're all doing what we can."

"You mean you're giving away the farm! Grow some cojones, Senator. I'm looking at a little girl who's got bigger balls than you. Don't call again until the treaty is signed." Kit disconnects the call at her wrist and sinks into her velvet chair. "Do you see what we have to deal with, Estrella?" She lights another cigarette. "Don't tell your mother about this cigarette or I'll fire you, too. God forbid anyone has a vice. She's become joyless, your mother. She needs a man."

"Gross, Aunt Kit. She's not joyless, anyway, just busy," Estrella replies.

"We both know she's a workaholic with no social life." Kit lights a second cigarette.

"She'll have more time when that report's done. She says it's super-complicated, and, like, all the governments of the world have to work together to keep the water pure and free, but it *is* possible. Hopefully. Maybe you *should* hire another senator. A few."

"Perhaps I can hire you once you've graduated from Glouton and the university of your choice—so long as it's Harvard or Oxford. And don't be so unsubtle. You know I can't *hire* a senator. He's elected."

Estrella flops across the bed. "Why are you talking about Glouton, school of douchey rich kids, *again*? And how am I supposed to control my temper when all people do is make me angry?"

Kit blots her lipstick with a tissue. "Have you found a dress for your quinceañera yet?" she asks, menacingly.

"Aargh! Why did you remind me? My stupid quinceañera! Another thing I've argued against every chance I get. But no one listens to me." Estrella throws her arm across her eyes.

Quincy shuffles back and forth on his golden bar. "Put up and shut up!"

With a prim undertone of malice, Kit says, "I won't bring it up again, except to say that your mother, sister, and idiot aunt have been looking forward to this moment from the day you were born, and you'd do well to be graceful about it and keep your mouth closed for their sakes."

"Why is everything in my life about everyone else? Where I go to school, what I do for my birthday. What about me?" Estrella spits out the words with self-righteous fury. "Don't I get a vote?"

"No. Here." Kit tosses the *Songs of Innocence* over her shoulder. Estrella leaps off the bed, rolls onto the floor, and catches it in midair.

"Good one, Kit."

"Always be ready, Estrella. Take this, too." She hands Estrella a small jade box.

The box tingles Estrella's hands. "Look—it's chipped," she says, pointing to a ding in the green stone. "I don't want to be blamed for it later."

"I suppose that nothing so old can escape some wear and tear. God knows we're all living proof of that. Put it in with the Asian art books but keep it somewhat hidden. We wouldn't want it to get another flaw."

Estrella's almost to the door when she bumps into Marina, who glides into the room, carrying a scent of roses, her light green eyes the crowning feature of her other-worldly beauty.

Marina affectionately ruffles Estrella's hair then kisses Kit, who giggles. Kitty-Kat rubs up against Marina's leg and purrs as Quincy squawks, "Va va voom! It's Marina!"

"Evan taught Quincy that," Estrella says. "He's totally in love with you, just like every other boy and man."

Marina giggles as Kit says, "Isn't it lovely to have both my god-children here? Estrella was just putting up this little jade box, but let's have a conversation about Glouton first."

"Oh, come *on!*" Estrella slouches onto a chaise lounge. "It's bad enough I have to go there, why do we have to talk about it all the time?"

Kit and Marina share a conspiratorial look. "Hermanita, you have to go there, even though we'll all miss each other so much," Marina says. "You have to learn from Dr. Mather. He has a lot to teach you."

"About mysticism? The Cosmic?" Estrella asks as she rolls her eyes. "I've already read the books."

"And also, what to do with your..." Marina hesitates.

"...Your special gifts," Kit finishes up. "The ones we just keep between us."

"My Mayan gifts?" Estrella's voice recedes to a whisper. "But I already know I have to not get angry, even though that's impossible. And, I mean, Dr. Mather's, like, not even Mexican. How can he help me?"

"You'll have to trust us, and be patient, and you'll know a lot more by your quinceañera."

"Whatever," Estrella says. "It's not like I have a choice anyway."

"It's all going to be so much more fun than you can even imagine," Marina says. "Let's get your bike in the car and get home. I've been saving my calories all day for your tamales."

...

"Mami, we're home!" Marina places her giant Birkin bag, one of the many gifts from Kit that Linda disapproves of, on the table by the front door. Estrella tosses her backpack on the floor, kicks off her Converse, and heads to the kitchen, where she pets Lupe, then drinks milk straight from the carton.

Linda Chavez, a faint scar above her left eye, listens to a phone call through her headset. She hisses at Estrella, motioning to the carton.

Estrella wipes her lips with the back of her hand. "I was starving."

Linda puts herself on mute. "Have you seen the Syrians drowning in the ocean? Their bellies are so bloated from hunger they float like rafts. You are not starving." She unmutes and gets back to her call. "What are we supposed to do? Shoot him in the road like a dog? He's holding all the cards. We're just going to have to give him what he wants for now." She motions to Estrella with her eyes and two pointed fingers to let her know she's watching her.

A gangly teenage boy with a faint mustache and a shock of black hair sticking straight up walks in and plunks himself down on a chair at the simple wood table.

"Hugo, my good cousin," Estrella says, pulling out a bowl of masa from the refrigerator. "Help me roll? Tamales are a lot of work."

"My hands were made for coding, not kitchens."

"Don't eat one then," Estrella says. "You might be smart, but lazy doesn't eat."

A metal cylinder hovers just above the floor and floats over to Estrella; a thin metal arm emerges and pokes her on her bum. "I've been working on this robot all summer," Hugo replies. "So, not lazy, but also not a cook, obviously." Lupe feebly lifts his head to growl at the robot.

"It's too quiet in here!" Marina rhumbas into the kitchen. "Siri, play Bad Bunny." Party music fills the room. She bumps her hip into Estrella's, and pinches Hugo's nose. He swats her hand away, but not with any real irritation.

"Just because I adore you doesn't mean you can mess with me," Hugo says. "I'm grown now, you know."

"You'll always be my baby!" Marina says, grabbing him by his big ears and smothering his head with kisses.

Linda walks back in, earbudless. "Siri, turn off the music," she says, then turns to Marina. "I just got off the phone with Dr. Friedrichs about the study on algae in the Great Lakes. We're going to use it in the solutions section of the Species Extinction report. Who knew algae could do so much for such little cost? Will you reach out to Miakoda's people and ask them to update the text?" Linda trips over the robot. "What the hell is this?"

"Mr. Roboto," Hugo replies. "Just one of the many reasons they want me at MIT. Maybe I should remind everyone, again, that I'm the youngest person ever selected for graduate studies there."

"As if Zandra doesn't tell everyone about it three times a day," Estrella replies.

"So, what did Dr. Friedrichs say about the algae?"

"It can be used for fuel now, but the Trust is going to have to part with some real money to make it scalable. Once the initial investment is made, we'll make it all back and more. Now, if only we could get the Senate to give us our tax breaks. At least we've got Miakoda in the House."

"Yeah, I don't think that the tax breaks thing is working out," Estrella says, sealing up the last of the corn husks and putting them all in the steaming pot. "Kit told Senator Morales she was going to fire him."

"Kit can't fire a senator," Linda says.

"Yeah, right," Estrella replies.

Linda's voice tightens. "You just worry about Glouton and your quinceañera. Maybe being formally consecrated to Our Mother will straighten up your attitude."

Estrella looks to the heavens. "So much for my prayers."

Marina turns on *Entertainment Tonight*, her favorite show. "They're interviewing Celeste James! The internet says she has a hot new romance."

Estrella rolls her eyes. "Talk about an unhealthy girl crush. I swear you would become Celeste James if you could—you're too obsessed. Even the characters she plays. You were depressed for a week after that one girl died in that war movie. So much for a Hollywood ending."

"That anorexic girl has nothing on you," Hugo says.

"Those blue eyes and those skinny hips… Oh, is she wearing Valentino?" Marina leans in to examine the TV more closely. She settles back into her chair. "At least Nicolas likes my hips."

"What are you talking about?" Estrella asks. "Every man who's ever lived likes your hips."

"To say the least," Hugo chimes in. "Remember the day I came home from school and that old man was riding up on a white horse to propose to you? When you were *seventeen*? And even on that day, you were already on the porch with two other boys who were about to have a fistfight over you."

Linda shakes her head. "That was some day. Thank God you're finally settling down with Nicolas Salvatierra. He comes from a very good family, and he's in an influential position for us as senior counsel to Representative Grace, especially now that she's Speaker."

"Speaking of romance..." Marina pauses for dramatic effect. "Have you given any thought to who you want to be your quinceañera escort, Estrella? What about that cute boy who works with Nadine at Burger Shak? Teofimo, I think?"

"Teofimo? He ate glue in third grade," Estrella replies, making a face.

"Well, you're going to have to work with me on this, Estrella. I've been tossing out names of potential escorts for over a year now," Marina says with a pout.

"I still haven't given up hope that I can somehow get out of the whole thing," Estrella mutters to Marina. "Like, maybe I'll break my leg or something. But knowing Mom, she'd probably make me do it even *with* a broken leg. I'd have to have a complete, temporary paralysis. Even then, she'd remind me of some other girl who did it with paralysis *and* fourth degree burns or something."

"That's a negative way to think, Estrella!" Marina gasps. "Remember how important it is for you to use positive words."

"Blah, blah, blah," Estrella replies, as the front door slams and footsteps sound in the hallway. Lupe struggles to get up. "He's getting so old." Estrella gently pets her wolf-like dog. "Yet another reason I don't want to go away to school. He needs me."

Zandra Chavez ambles into the kitchen, followed by her husband, Cesar. Dorothy and Toto, Zandra's two toy poodles, bounce around her feet.

Cesar pulls out a flask from his coat pocket. "Where's Alfonso?"

"Alfonso!" Linda practically shoots laser beams out of her eyes at Zandra. "I told you; he's not welcome here. I'm done with his constant, destructive antics."

"Alfonso's trouble but he's a badass," Estrella says. "We all saw that fight on ESPN."

"ESPN 3+," Hugo retorts, then turns to Zandra. "You know you worship him. In your eyes, he can do no wrong, unlike me, who actually does no wrong."

"He's my firstborn child and the closest your uncle Victor ever had to a son of his own, may he rest in heavenly peace and one day see his enemies burn in hell. It's as if you are turning your back on your own child," Zandra says to Linda, ignoring Hugo.

"Aunt Zandra's playing the Victor card," Estrella whispers, loud enough to be heard.

"If he were my own child, I would not have let him burn down Mohammed Mossad's garage with his illegal fireworks," Linda says. "Do you remember that? Last month?"

Estrella has to bite her tongue to keep from laughing out loud.

"Of course, it was too bad about the garage," Zandra replies, "but Mr. Mossad can buy ten garages now. Thanks to Kit Hamilton, their whole house is totally renovated, and they have a new Lexus in the driveway. Mr. Mossad should thank Alfonso for what he did."

"Do you know how many favors Kit owes everybody in this town for that fiasco?" Linda asks, fury burning behind her eyes.

Zandra shakes her head in judgement. "Would Jesus hold a grudge against his oldest nephew?"

"Ohh... the unbeatable Jesus card," Estrella whispers. Hugo nods.

At that exact moment, Alfonso, his hair shaved into a mohawk, his designer t-shirt tight across his strong chest, swaggers into the kitchen. Dorothy and Toto bark with joy as he raises his chin in a greeting to everyone.

Linda eyes her nephew warily. "Estrella, get place settings for your uncle and cousin."

"How can you be such a big career woman, but be so sexist?" Estrella says to Linda. "Now I'm the maid?"

"You are a lady in this house, and these are your guests."

"They're not guests. It's Uncle Cesar and Alfonso. And I'm not a lady—this isn't 1858." Estrella slams the plates down in front of the men. "Have some forks, too, since I guess your fingers are broken and you can't get them yourselves."

The men laugh.

Linda doesn't. "All this attitude, Estrella. You need some manners to go with that brain of yours."

"No, what I need is for some equality between the sexes. Now I'm *really* glad I punched Cooper in his flabby guts."

Linda gasps. "How will you succeed at Glouton if you act as trashy as everyone expects you to? You know that everyone at Glouton will have heard the rumors about your father and the cartels before you set one foot on campus. Even though they're wrong, your reputation is all you have in this world."

"Can we pray and eat already?" Hugo asks. "I can't wait to go to MIT and finally be free from this dysfunctional family."

Linda shoots Hugo a dirty look as she leads the family in a quick prayer. Everyone crosses themselves before they reach for the tamales.

"Very good, Estrella," Zandra says, savoring her bite. "You followed my recipe. This Christmas, I'll show you the mole recipe, since your mother's too busy to cook for her own family."

Linda gives Zandra another dirty look as Hugo says, "So, are you going to ask that guy to be your escort for your quinceañera? You should already have someone, or your party's going to suck. It's a performance as much as a rite of passage. Oh my God, Marina's quince was so everything. Fire! How many likes did your dress get on social?"

"Almost a million," Marina replies.

Estrella shoots Hugo the bird under the table. "How is this still a topic of conversation?"

"We have to practice your hair and makeup for your quinceañera before you go to school," Zandra says.

"This is the Age of Aquarius, Aunt Zandra. I'm here to make a difference in the world and accomplish real things, not play dress up."

"But don't you want to look like a beautiful Disney princess for your quinceañera?" Zandra asks.

"'Gender is the most restricting form in American life!'" Estrella angrily quotes Gloria Steinem.

"You sound like a lesbian," Zandra replies. "That must be why you don't have an escort yet."

Hugo clears his throat, prompting Zandra to add, "But if you want to be a lesbian, it's okay. You do you. Like Hugo. He's gay, but we love him anyway."

"Of course we do!" Marina chirps, putting her hand over Hugo's. "He's the best of all of us."

Estrella glares at everyone as she picks up her phone. "Nadine's here."

Linda's face gets tight. "I wish you would stay away from that fast girl."

A petite, blue-eyed girl in a Burger Shak uniform, wearing purple lipstick and smelling of French fries, enters the kitchen. Her blond hair is tipped with black dye, and her ears each have multiple piercings.

"Hey, Chavezes!" Nadine says to the table. "Hello, my best friend since preschool," she says to Estrella, giving her a quick hug,

"How's your family, Nadine?" Linda asks.

Nadine replies, "Pretty good, except Dad's in a bad mood because they suspended him for that whole malfeasance of public funds thing. I guess that's what your enemies do to you when you're the chief of police. But he thinks he knows a way to get reinstated in a few weeks." She reaches for a tamale. "He's innocent. It's just a witch hunt by the city council. He's got Mayor Kaminsky on his side."

Estrella perks up at the mention of the mayor.

Nadine notices the light in Estrella's eyes. "I know the one you want as your quinceañera escort is the mayor's son, John. You think he's hot because he goes to fascist Hargrave Academy, and he's the best at sports and academics like you are." She looks at Estrella and pantomimes a giant yawn. "Boring! But everyone says he'll be president one day. I know he's got your vote because you look at his Instagram three times a day. Too bad you can't get close to him because you've been grounded all summer."

"Shut up, Nadine," Estrella hisses as everyone at the table laughs. "And Hargrave isn't fascist just because it's an elite military boarding school."

"Heil Hargrave!" Nadine replies, making a military salute. She turns to Alfonso. "So, what's going on around here tonight? Shooting off some fireworks?"

Everyone but Linda breaks into laughter again.

"I'm going to dice," Nadine says. "Colt's running a game tonight. Should be fun. I won $300 last week."

"Colt sucks," Estrella says, angrily, her face still burning. "He's been in juvie more than out since the eighth grade."

Linda meets Estrella's eyes and gives her a look that says, *I told you this girl is trashy.* Out loud, she says, "Please don't talk about anything illegal around me. I'm a lawyer."

Zandra pinches Cesar's arm. "If you go to that dice game, I will leave you and murder you in your sleep."

"Empty threats we've all heard before," Hugo mutters as he plays on his phone.

Linda stands and clears her plate. "I have work to do."

"Thank you for the hospitality," Cesar calls to Linda's backside as he passes Alfonso his flask. "Women. Just do what they say, son, and you'll live a good life."

Zandra snorts. "Then you must not be living a very good life, because you haven't done anything I've said since we were sixteen."

Cesar winks at his wife as he tips the flask to his lips.

Nadine hands her empty plate to Estrella, reaches into her pocket, and pulls out her phone. "Colt's asking if you want a spot at the game," she says to Alfonso.

"Why not? I need some spending money," he replies.

"Hilarious," Estrella says. "You are literally the worst gambler ever. That's why I can't wait for football—I make fifty dollars from you every week."

"My luck is changing, little cousin," Alfonso replies. "I won three dollars on a scratch-off last night."

Cesar says, "I haven't shot dice in years, but I used to have lucky hands. Where's the game?"

"Somewhere with a bunch of not old people," Hugo replies, without looking up from his phone.

Cesar laughs. "Then I guess this old man is going home with his wife."

"Oh, now that nobody wants you, you want to come back to me." Zandra says, a big smile on her face. "Let's go, and bring that whiskey." Dorothy and Toto follow them to their house across the street.

Nadine looks up from her phone. "They're in Colt's basement. Alfonso, you drive. They'll want your autograph; you're like a movie star around here since you won that fight on ESPN."

"ESPN 3+," Estrella says, as Alfonso grins with pride and literally flexes his biceps.

"I'd invite you, Estrella, but you're grounded," Nadine says, floating a peace sign for a farewell as she leads Alfonso out into the warm August night.

•••

Islid meets Estrella in the green, sun-dappled forest. They lift from the mossy ground, flying in time to the music: a waltz. The melody of the birds becomes a piano's song.

•••

Estrella wakes to a sticky heat. Music floats up from the piano downstairs. She runs through her rosary to the beat of a waltz in a minor key. Estrella's heart expands with the music, as she once again wishes she could've heard her mother play, but Linda hasn't touched a piano since Marina was born.

The music stops with the last of Estrella's fifty-six amens.

The front door opens downstairs, letting in Kit's raspy voice. Estrella slinks down the carpeted steps, determined to listen in on their conversation. She is convinced that Marina and Kit share a secret, because every time she walks into a room they're in, they quit talking. She stops just short of the bend in the staircase, where they can't see her.

"Are you sure about the timing?" Marina whispers to Kit. "I sometimes think we should have already told her. We talked about the 'Mayan Gift' at least. If only she wasn't so traumatized by the fire, she would be farther ahead." Marina sniffles back a tear. "I just want it to be special for her and for her to really be ready. It's so much for her to bear. But I guess the timing is perfect. It'll be a big night, and we'll all be there."

"Just a few more weeks," Kit says. "Saul will need to work with her first to get her stronger. And the Scroll came right out and said November. It tears me apart too—to throw the child into the storm like that—but it can't come soon enough. The Remundus certainly needs some celestial help. Raeesa's in over her head. If we don't take power now, we'll lose it forever."

"But taking power's not her mission, remember? It's celestial," Marina replies. "Yours too."

"My purpose is the water—the same as everyone's," Kit says. "What do you think we're all doing..."

The front door opens again; Estrella can make out Yves's profile. She silently runs back up three steps.

"Oh, hello, Yves!" Marina chirps.

"Marina. You look lovely as a Monet today."

Linda steps through the open door, sweaty from her run, and looks right up at Estrella. "What are you doing? We're all going to lunch in the city, at Per Se. Figure out what you're wearing. Hurry up." She bounds up the steps past Estrella.

"Quit lurking around, and come down here and give me a kiss," Kit commands.

Estrella slowly descends into the living room.

"Oh my God," Kit says, taking in Estrella, still in her pajamas at quarter to twelve. "You look terrible. Marina, help her."

Marina claps her hands in delight. "I've been waiting for this moment! I have the perfect outfit in mind—you can definitely pull it off with those legs. I swear they grew three inches this summer."

Marina catches a glimpse of herself in the mirror above the piano and touches up her already heavy, flawless makeup. "I actually wonder if this dress is too casual now."

Estrella rolls her eyes. "Maybe for the Oscars. Fine. You can do my makeup, but not too much."

• • •

Forty-five minutes later, Marina parades Estrella downstairs, a look of triumph animating her face.

Estrella's wavy hair is straight and falls past the middle of her back. She wears high-heels and the loose mini-dress Marina can no longer pull over her hips.

"Ta-da!" Marina sings. Kit, Linda, and Yves stare at Estrella with their mouths open.

Yves speaks first. "You are the vision of loveliness."

Linda glares at Yves as she stands on her tippy toes to air-kiss Estrella. "Who is this supermodel? What did you do with my daughter?" She smiles gratefully at Marina. "Good work, but the dress is a little short."

Kit shakes her head. "I don't know how you went from tomboy to vixen in under an hour. Shouldn't there be some sort of in-between stage? At least with Marina we saw it coming."

Estrella knows she looks good. She blushes. "I'm hungry. Can we go?"

• • •

Marina pulls a bottle of Dom Perignon from a bucket of ice; Kit hands her four glasses from the bar of her Rolls-Royce limousine.

Linda frowns. "Estrella's only fourteen."

"In France, they drink champagne from their teething rings. And Estrella's almost fifteen," Kit says, which reminds Estrella that Kit wanted to take her to Paris last summer, but Linda wouldn't let her go. She shoots her mom a dirty look.

"Fine. Just this once," Linda says. "If you're going to drink alcohol, I'd rather it be in a safe situation."

"Tastes like a sour soda. Not too bad," Estrella says, following her first taste with a longer sip.

"Be careful," Kit says. "It goes down easier than it comes up."

...

"This guy, Chef Michel, can really cook," Estrella says as she eats an oyster from Linda's plate. "We should bring Aunt Zandra here—I bet she could figure out how he does it and make some stuff at home."

"It's a bit refined for Zandra's taste," Linda says, checking her phone. "It's Senator Clay," she whispers, before pulling back her shoulders and putting on her serious face.

"Tell him we've got deep pockets for the algae credits," Kit says right before Linda taps her phone to answer it.

Everyone at the table listens to Linda's end of the conversation.

"Okay...okay...alright...I will." She hangs up. "He says he hears the board is divided. I thought you had your brother in line on this."

Kit pours another glass of champagne. "I've got the board, don't worry. Every one of them owes me more favors than they owe their mothers. And that includes my brother, Bill. I may have to make one or two more concessions—he's a tough negotiator—I wouldn't respect him if he weren't. But he's generous, and he has to think of his legacy."

Linda looks pointedly at Kit. "I wouldn't count on any generosity from Bill."

"Bitter grapes," Kit says, taking a swig from her crystal glass.

Yves motions to the waitress who's standing at attention only a few feet away. "What does Chef Michel have for dessert?"

"I'm not ready for dessert," Kit says, slurring a little. "More champagne! *I've* got Bill, you focus on the Species Extinction Report."

Estrella takes another sip of champagne. "Glad you have it all worked out, because I'm doing my internship with Bill on the for-profit side. I mean, if you just give all the water away, where will the money come from to take care of it? Marina, I know you say The Cosmic will provide, but I have my doubts." She burps.

"Oh, look who it is!" Marina waves at two men entering through the pale blue doors of the restaurant.

Estrella freezes at the sight of Marcus Aurelius Hamilton, Kit's oldest nephew.

His brown hair is longer than two summers ago—the best summer of Estrella's life—but his eyes are still brown and soft, like a cow's. Big diamond studs adorn each of his ears. Estrella's palms sweat and her heart races.

Marc and his father, Nelson Hamilton saunter across the restaurant toward the table. Estrella avoids looking Marc in the eyes.

"What? Is that you? Strella Chavez? The one and only? Wow. You look...beautiful," Marc says. "How old are you now?"

"Almost fifteen," Estrella replies, making her voice lower so she'll sound older.

"So, when we spent that summer together, you were like almost thirteen, right? *I* was fifteen then. Wild. Times change, right?"

"I'd hardly say you spent the summer together," Linda says.

"We totally spent that summer together," Marc replies, his eyes looking for Estrella's. "I spent the summer at Aunt Kit's that year because Dad was going through a divorce, and Mom was on that spiritual retreat in Costa Rica. We had so much fun, remember? You, me, Evan and your cousin, Hugo. It was awesome—horseback riding lessons and kung fu with Sifu Joseph. I got that trophy, remember? Best fighter in the class."

"I've really improved since then," Estrella replies, finally meeting his gaze. "I have my black belt now, and I've actually won that trophy twice."

"Awesome," Marc says. "Even then you were really good. Do you remember that day we went to the creek?"

Estrella opens her mouth to speak, but no words come out, though in her mind, she replays the memory. They rode their horses all the way onto the estate next to Kit's and went swimming in the creek there. They started sparring in the water, and suddenly Marc had his arms around her. Then his girlfriend called, and they had to go back.

"You know, you should check out my Spotify," Marc continues. "I think you would like it. I found this band from Nigeria this summer that's next level, and there's some brand-new Bollywood on there. A little eclectic, but I know you like just about everything. I've been in India all summer—it's like the center of the world right now—we should go sometime."

Marina gives a little giggle. "Estrella will definitely be checking out your Spotify, Marc." She winks at Estrella, whose face turns red.

"Come give me a kiss, Mr. India," Kit says. "You can walk down memory lane at school."

"You'll be at Glouton, Estrella?" Marc smiles. "Like Mark Twain says, though, *'don't let schooling interfere with your education.'* But it's a great school. I'll show you the ropes."

"I'm sure Estrella will be busy studying," Linda says.

Nelson Hamilton—a tanned, middle-aged man with hazel eyes and wavy, graying hair; a more hip replica of his twin brother, Bill—says, "Estrella, you look just like your mother." He kisses Linda on the cheek, then immediately becomes absorbed in his phone.

"What's so important that you can't be an adult and participate in the conversation, Nelson?" Kit says. "Lord knows you have no serious endeavors."

Nelson bristles. "I have serious endeavors, alright? Just maybe not ones you and Bill deem worthy. That was Melissa. She's upset about the interior decorator. They put the wrong flooring in the Malibu house."

"What was I thinking?" Kit replies. "Of course you have serious endeavors. God forbid your third child bride has to walk on the wrong floor. Or is she your fourth child bride?"

As Kit talks, Marc rolls his eyes and turns his attention back to Estrella. "So, what are you doing tonight? Maybe I can tag along. I hear there's this new comedy night at the Hotel Edison. Still kind of underground, but I know a guy who can get us in without i.d."

"Estrella's going home," Linda says.

Marina ignores her mother. "Everyone's having such fun! Wouldn't it be even more fun if we all went to a show and a late dinner? Who doesn't love to laugh?"

"No," Linda says. "It's getting late, and we have a busy day tomorrow. We have to pack."

Undeterred, Marc leans in and says, his lips brushing Estrella's blushing ear, "Wish you could stay." A tingle travels through Estrella's whole body as the small, crystal-studded handbag Marina gave her to use for the day buzzes with a text from Nadine.

John K's having a party tonight and he wants you there.

The text is followed by several emojis of various fruits and vegetables with sexual connotations. Estrella shoves the phone back into the purse.

Chef Michel stands outside the kitchen in a dress coat and pressed jeans. He nods at Yves. "I'll see you in the morning," Yves tells Kit. "Tonight, the August moon calls me into the streets."

"Maybe it's your British accent, Yves, but everything you say sounds cool as hell," Marc says, then gives Estrella's hand a little squeeze. "I'll see you in school next week. What a trip—we'll basically be living together. Life—it's full of pleasant surprises, isn't it?"

Out of the corner of her eye, Estrella notices her mother go pale.

...

"How did you convince your mom to let you out?" Nadine shouts over the thumping bass that pours from the turntables of the town's hottest DJ.

"Must've been the champagne," Estrella shouts back.

"Let's go find John," Nadine says, tugging Estrella past the crowd of teenagers lined up with little plastic cups in front of a silver keg. "This is the best you've ever looked; might as well work it."

"There's Hugo!" Estrella says. Hugo stands with a group of cool, older kids. "I had no idea you went to parties," Estrella shouts to him.

"Estrella! You look great! I didn't even recognize you—obviously Marina's work. How did you get out of the house? Oh my God, it's like Cinderella."

Estrella feels a tap on her shoulder and pivots toward the touch to find the ocean-blue eyes of John Kaminsky. Nadine nudges Estrella toward him. "Me and Colt have to go talk to my Uncle Chuck." She takes Colt's hand, and they're lost in the crowd.

John smiles. "Nadine's uncle is here?" he asks. "Kind of old for this party, isn't he?"

"She has a huge family. Some of her uncles are younger than she is," Estrella replies, realizing as she speaks that she is living the best day of her life.

"I wish I had a bigger family," John says. "Then all the attention wouldn't be on me and Matt." He leans closer to her. "I heard you're going to Glouton. Excellent school—obviously, one of the best in the world. You can make some great connections there."

Estrella nods. "I mean, but the last thing I care about is making connections with a bunch of fake rich kids."

John nods. "But they rule the world," he says, then makes a chopping motion with his hands. "Congratulations on winning the state championship this year, by the way."

"How did you know about that?" Estrella asks, silently praying with all her strength that he doesn't know she got suspended for punching Cooper Necker. She blushes with premature humiliation.

"When your dad's the mayor, you know a lot about everyone. But I pay special attention to what's happening with you. You're one cool chick, Estrella Chavez. Like your dad."

"My dad?" She searches John's eyes to see what he knows.

"Victor Chavez is a hero of mine," John replies. "He pulled together the workers of Mexico and the United States—even part of the eco-labor movement in Africa, all the way across the ocean. He demanded a better life for the laborers, the ones who make other men rich. And all his work on purifying the water. I'm all about that."

"He wasn't a drug dealer," Estrella blurts out.

"I believe he was framed," John says. "It just doesn't add up. But that's how it is, isn't it? They never let them live, the ones who really care about the people and stand a chance to make a difference."

Her phone vibrates with a text of a clock emoji from her mom. "It's 12:30," Estrella says. "I have to go home."

"I can drive you," John says. "Matt can handle the party."

. . .

They ride with the windows down through streets thick with summer. The breeze cools the sheen of sweat on Estrella's skin, the wave returns to her hair. As John pulls up outside her house, Lupe watches through the picture window.

"I want to see you again." John turns off the car.

Estrella's heart beats as if with wings. "I'm leaving for school on Monday. But I so do not want to go—now more than ever. If I were going to Washington High, I'd have another week of summer."

"We all have to sacrifice for our greatness. What's a week of summer compared to the education you're going to get?" John replies, reaching for Estrella's hand. "Can I call you? Send you texts?"

"Only longhand letters, please. I am going to Glouton, after all. Founded in 1787."

They laugh as Estrella's phone lights up with another text from her mom. She sighs and moves to open her door.

"Wait." John puts his hand on Estrella's knee, then the back of her neck. He pulls her close and kisses her.

At first, they bump teeth, but then he pokes his tongue in, and she does the same, attempting to seem experienced, though it's her first kiss. She kisses him again, leading with her tongue this time, before she floats up the porch steps, through her front door, past her anxious mother and faithful dog, and into bed, where she lies, wide awake almost until dawn, playing the day's events over and over again, and wishing it could last forever.

SEPTEMBER

The Golden Halls of Glouton

"I will never forgive you for making me come here." Estrella pushes open the car door but remains in the backseat. She, Marina, and Linda watch the bustling Glouton parking lot—the expensive luggage, the perfectly coiffed moms, the dads and their Patek Philippe watches, the hired help that trots suitcases and trunks from the cars and into the dorms.

"Don't be so dramatic." Linda says. "Do you know how lucky you are to have an opportunity to go to a school like this?" How many immigrants wish they could go to the best school in the world? You should thank God."

"Blah blah blah, I've heard it all before."

"It'll be so fun!" Marina says. "You're going to make so many wonderful new friends and you already know Evan and Marc."

Linda gives Marina a dirty look while they carry Estrella's brand-new luggage, a gift from Kit, across the green grounds and into an ivy-covered, brick building.

"So, this is where the world's most influential statesmen, scientists, and leaders of industry spent their high school days for the past 207 years. Kings, queens, presidents, and sheikhs! Before they had the power to send men into war, they went to school right here!" Marina chirps as they walk the hall toward Estrella's room.

"We're so proud of you already. Just imagine all that you'll learn here. Maybe one day *you'll* be the president."

Estrella fiddles with the simple, slender rubber and steel brace-let that adorns her wrist, a going-away gift from Hugo. The steel links serve as command buttons. The first link records audio, the second creates a sound wave pattern that vacuums the sound of the voice, then throws the voice 500 meters. The third link activates microwaves that bend incoming light waves around whatever ob-ject emits the microwaves. The light rays meet on the other side making it seem like the object has vanished.

Estrella places her fingertip above the third link. "Who wants to live with total strangers?" she asks, hesitating before the door to her new dorm. "They seem nice enough on social media, but still."

"You'll be fine," Marina says, then whispers, "Just remember to be careful with your Mayan gift. Don't get angry."

Voices come from inside the room as Linda knocks three times softly then enters, Estrella right behind her.

A tiny girl, with wooly hair hanging down to her waist, taps on her phone. An olive-skinned woman and blue-black man talk into their cell phones while two muscular men unpack several Gucci trunks.

Without looking up from her phone, the tiny girl says, "Amare, put those shoes under the bed. Be careful, Adisa, my laptop is in there. And hurry and hang the Cézanne before anyone else gets here."

Estrella clears her throat.

"Look, Amaka, it's Estrella." The olive-complected woman gets off her phone. She takes Estrella by the shoulders and finds her eyes. "Look how tall you are!" she says, pulling Estrella in tight for a hug, then quickly releasing her. "And you must be Linda and Marina." She gives them each an air-kiss. "I'm Goldie Abioye, and this is my hus-band, Babatunde." The short, round man with John Lennon glasses shakes each woman's hand. "This is my daughter, Amaka."

The tiny girl looks Estrella up and down. "You're prettier than your profile picture." She motions to the men hanging artwork. "These are my guards, Amare and Adisa Ekwensi." The men acknowledge Estrella with a nod.

Estrella nods back as she sneaks a peek at Marina, and mouths, *guards?*

Amaka says, "You can have either remaining bed. You beat Margeaux here."

Estrella picks the bed furthest away, drops her suitcase on it, and places her small aloe vera plant on the bedside table.

Linda smiles graciously at Amaka's parents. "It's wonderful to meet the couple who have donated three wells in Western Nigeria to the Water Trust."

Goldie says, "Well, who doesn't need water?" Babatunde stays quiet as his wife continues, seemingly without taking a breath. "We do what we can, but it's never enough, there's always so much more to do. It's wonderful that you're involved in the Trust, and, of course, I love Kit Hamilton. How can you not?"

Linda opens her mouth to speak, but Goldie keeps talking. "Can I offer you a Pom tea? They're delicious. We get them every time we're here. You wouldn't believe how many things we just don't have across the ocean, even with capitalism everywhere and all the delivery."

Goldie pulls three magenta glass bottles from the refrigerator as Amare and Adisa finish hanging a framed picture of tulips in a vase above Amaka's bed, all while Amaka taps steadily on her phone. Goldie keeps the one-sided conversation going.

"Can you believe how small these rooms are? We would've brought so much more. Adisa, can you move that nail to the right about three centimeters?"

Amaka looks up from her phone. "Give them a chance to breathe, Mother."

Goldie rolls her eyes playfully. "Kids. You raise them to be polite and still, they say anything they want." Linda nods in agreement, as Goldie leans closer to her and whispers just loudly enough for everyone to hear. "The one we really have to watch out for is Margeaux Prince—what a reputation! What, with the paparazzi and the scandals of her mother or her father, or both, in the papers every two weeks—"

The sound of a throat clearing from the doorway interrupts her. A thin girl with bright pink hair and a guitar on her back says in a British accent, "Good afternoon. I'm Margeaux Prince. But don't worry, I've left the scandal in London."

Goldie says, "Margeaux! Your hair is fabulous! And whatever you heard me say just now, well...you have to admit that your family is notorious."

"As is yours, Madame Abioye." Margeaux puts her single backpack and her guitar on the remaining bed.

Goldie ignores Margeaux's insinuation and says, "Like father like daughter with the music."

Estrella meets eyes with Marina who told her that Margeaux's father is a rock star, old enough to be her grandfather and her mother is British nobility, young enough to be her sister.

"Where's the rest of your luggage?" Goldie asks. "And when do we get to meet your parents?"

Margeaux reclines like a bony cat on the bare bed. "They're bringing my things round later. As for my parents, long story. I expect they'll be here eventually."

Babatunde, speaking for the first time, says, "We have to go." He pulls Amaka close. "I trust that you will study hard and take this expensive school seriously." He lets go. "Be easy on these girls, my precious daughter."

He motions to Amare and Adisa, who follow him into the

hallway; Amare gives the room a formal nod and Adisa flashes a bright smile as they go.

Goldie takes Amaka's head into her hands and looks into her eyes. "You wanted to be here, my little lioness. My heart is breaking, but I have to go now, or I'll never be able to leave you."

Amaka wipes the tears from her mother's face. "I will see you in three weeks for Parents Weekend."

"It'll be the longest three weeks of my life," Goldie says, then releases her daughter and walks bravely through the doorway.

Finally, Linda stands. "Pray your rosary," she says, kissing Estrella on her way out the door, as Estrella forces back the tears that unexpectedly spring to her eyes.

"I want one FaceTime chat a week," Marina says. "And don't just study all the time. Life is short. Enjoy it." Before she leaves, Marina pulls a long necklace from her blouse and removes the pendant: a pink, egg-shaped crystal. She mounts the crystal over the door. When she does, the room sparkles with rose-colored light for a second. "This will be a little piece of me here, watching over you."

"Finally," Amaka sighs, reclining on her silk-sheeted bed the moment the door clicks closed, "I can rule my own destiny. No longer a child, commanded by others."

Margeaux stretches out even longer. "No different for me, really. I've been ruling my own destiny since I was in diapers. This will be good, though. Regular meals. And another country, so the press won't be bothering me about my hair."

"What about you?" Margeaux asks Estrella. "You ready to set your own rules?"

"If I could set my own rules, I wouldn't even be here." Estrella flops onto her newly made bed. "I'm here to work hard, stay out of trouble, get into a good college, and make a difference in the world."

Amaka sits straight up. "What difference do you want to make?"

"Make sure everyone has pure water, like my mom and dad have worked to do." She sizes up her roommates. "And then I'll find the man who killed my father and make him pay."

After a moment of quiet, Amaka says, "I know about your father. He was a great man. I want to do what he did—organize the people." She paces the small room. "First, I will become the richest woman in Africa. All I have to do is marry a rich, weak-minded man—I have already found him—and then use the power of our combined fortunes to assemble an army of peaceful warriors, who will build schools and hospitals and protect the people from the corruption of wicked men."

Estrella narrows her eyes. "What do you know about my father?"

Amaka sits back on her bed. "That he was murdered by his enemies, and that they destroyed his reputation, and the movement he built. They said he was a drug lord; I think that is a lie. There was never any evidence of his involvement in the cartels, only conjecture. But there is evidence of the organizing he did for the people and the environment. Of course, his enemies can put forth any narrative they choose. Your father was at a disadvantage; he was a poor man. Only wealth can protect you, but not from all things."

"So that's why you have the guards?" Margeaux asks. "Hedging your bets?"

"Yes, of course. What good am I to my people if I am kidnapped or murdered?" Amaka replies.

"And you, Estrella? What will you get once you avenge your father's death?" Margeaux asks. "I can see the pure water for the world bit; that goes somewhere. But 'hatred and vengeance, my eternal portion, scarce can endure delay of execution, wait, with impatient readiness, to seize my soul in a moment.' It's a quote from William

Cowper, a poet, and a prophet of sorts." She pulls a cigarette from her backpack, opens the window, and lights up. "Do you mind?"

Estrella says, "Don't worry about my soul—you need to worry about your lungs. Nice line, by the way. My godmother, Kit, is always throwing out random quotes and poems, too."

"Smoking will make your white skin wrinkle like a golden raisin," Amaka says.

"I only have one every now and again." Margeaux blows the smoke out the window. "It's been a very long day. And night. And yesterday."

"Aren't you worried your parents will see you breaking the rules?" Estrella asks.

"My parents aren't coming. And I don't follow rules unless they suit me."

Estrella nods her head in a sign of respect.

"As for my parents," Margeaux continues, "We all had quite enough of each other in the city last night. Mum and her much-too-young boyfriend, and Dad, and his much-too-young girlfriend have blessedly left to Rio and Rome, respectively. The proprietors of Nobu decided to dissolve our party early. FedEx will deliver my things tomorrow."

"Wait. Did you just say that you and your parents actually got kicked out of a fancy restaurant last night? Reminds me of the kids back home," Estrella says as laughter rings from outside the dorm room door. Amaka opens it to find a tan, blonde, blue-eyed, long-legged fashion plate, and two perfectly put together older girls standing in the hall.

"Tatiana Duplessis," Amaka says.

The blonde girl's smile falls before it replaces itself. "For one blissful moment, I forgot you were going to school here, Amaka. Next, they'll let in chimpanzees."

Estrella's mouth drops open. "What a *bitch!*" she loud-whispers to Margeaux, then stands and joins Amaka in the doorway. "Take that back," Estrella says to Tatiana.

Tatiana looks at Estrella. "And you must be Estrella Chavez, daughter of the notorious gangster and drug dealer Victor Chavez. I thought your family lost all your money. Glouton does offer excellent financial aid for the needy. And Mexicans."

Estrella's mouth drops again. She curls her hands into fists. Amaka steps between them.

"How dare you speak to us in this way!" she says. "I will see you suffer for your racist remarks."

"I doubt it," Tatiana says as she takes another step in. "Could it be *the* Margeaux Prince? Are you smoking a cigarette? Make sure no one Snapchats that. You hardly need more bad press."

Margeaux slowly takes a drag and blows the smoke out the window. Tatiana's entourage giggles from the hall.

As Tatiana turns to leave, the pink egg above the door catches Estrella's eye. Again, it emits a pink light. Suddenly, Tatiana stumbles over her feet and falls gracelessly to her knees.

"I told you you would suffer," Amaka says as she slams the door and locks it.

"Tatiana Duplessis is my enemy," Amaka says. "When we were in Santorini for the NoAIDs event this summer, I made the serving staff give her an old fish."

The girls share a laugh, smiling at each other with the recognition of friends.

"Speaking of old fish," Margeaux says, "let's go get something to eat."

. . .

"There is Princess Silvie of Sweden. No real power, but her name carries weight," Amaka points to a plump, blonde girl with unattractive glasses who sits by some nerdy younger students in the modern dining hall. A dazzlingly handsome, older boy walks away from the Smoothie King with a smoothie in each hand. "Octavio dos Santos Kong," Amaka says. "He's got real money. Chinese-Brazilian descent, stakes in oil and cattle. He and his twin sister Nikki will be in Mystery School with us."

Margeaux follows Octavio with her eyes. "He's so hot."

"How did you get into Mystery School?" Estrella asks. "I did a project on the vibration of spoken Latin words and their effect on emotions."

"I submitted a song cycle based on Shakespeare's tragedies. I never actually thought I'd be accepted, being a freshman. Just did it for a lark, really," Margeaux replies. "And you, Amaka, how did you get into Mystery School? I'm assuming that's the reason we're rooming together—we all got into Mystery School as freshmen."

"If you bribe enough people, you get what you want." Amaka replies as she scans the room. "Look, there's Evan and Marcus Hamilton." Amaka motions to the boys with her eyes, keeping her head still. "They have enough money to raise an army." She smiles. "This kind of access is worth all of the boring hours of study." She ducks her head and focuses on her salad. "They are walking over here."

"We're friends," Estrella says. "Especially Evan. I've known him basically my whole life." Her heart beats faster as Marc approaches.

"Interesting," Amaka says. "I assumed that you would be worthless to me. I will get more information from you later."

Evan, Marc, and two older boys approach the table, trays piled high.

"Hey Strella!" Marc says, plopping down his tray right next to Estrella's. "These are my very best friends, Louis Washington and Christophe Markov. We have the whole top floor of the boys' dorms so get ready for some epic parties this year."

Louis, his hair cut close, dresses his athletic physique in shorts and Nikes, while Christophe, blond and tall, wears all black and never removes his oversize sunglasses. Estrella recognizes Christophe from DNN, the cable news channel; he's the son of the prime minister of Russia.

"Wow!" Evan says to Margeaux, his head shaking with nerves. "I'm a huge Lenny Prince fan and a musician myself. Playing the bass is one of the few activities that helps me with my high-functioning autism. Maybe we could jam sometime, Margeaux. I saw a YouTube video last year with you and your dad playing together backstage at Coachella. You're really good."

"You must invite Amare and Adisa to play," Amaka interjects. "They are the best musicians in Lagos." She motions with her head to the table next to them. "They are my guards, but I love them like brothers. They are in your dorms."

"I didn't know we could bring guards to Glouton," Marc says.

"Those of strong will can do anything," Amaka replies.

Estrella laughs. "I like you more each time you speak, Amaka."

Louis, whose eyes haven't wandered from Amaka since he sat down, says, "If I was your guard, I wouldn't leave your side for a minute."

Amaka examines him. "Louis Washington?"

"That's right, Amaka Abioye. When we're married, you can have that name all to yourself."

Amaka rolls her eyes. "Oh, please."

"Anything you please at all."

Amaka puts down her fork. "It will please me to marry Abimbola

Ojukwu, from the best family in all of Africa, who is right now studying at Oxford, and to whom I am betrothed. Not you."

Louis broadens his already broad shoulders. "That college boy's got nothing on me. I'm captain of the football team, I have the highest GPA in the school, and I've met with the president of the United States—twice. I'm chair of the National Student Coordinating Committee, and, as you can see, I'm dashingly handsome. Stick with me and we can accomplish great things together."

"*And* you are a fool." Amaka goes back to her phone, but a blush creeps into her cheeks.

"I'll bet that Ambibuju over there in England doesn't make your cheeks pink," Louis says.

"How do you like Glouton so far?" Marc asks Estrella, letting his knee fall open under the table so it brushes hers.

"It's not as bad as I thought it would be," Estrella replies, quickly adding, "I mean, everyone is really nice and I'm looking forward to Mystery School. We're all in." She motions to her roommates.

At the mention of Mystery School, everyone at the table leans toward each other.

"I'll be there too," Louis says.

"And I as well," Christophe says.

"Evan and I are in," Marc says. "Estrella, you're so smart—Dr. Mather never takes freshman. I've applied every year, and I'm still shocked I made it. My luck, though; we have a class together. It'll be the highlight of my day."

Amaka looks from Marc to Estrella with a raised brow.

"I've been a big fan of Dr. Mather since I was a kid," Estrella says, ignoring both Marc's compliment and Amaka's insinuating look.

"You know about the Vision Quest?" Marc asks.

"I've heard of it," Estrella replies, "It's hard to find much information online about Mystery School from previous students, but the one thing I do find is how much everyone loved the Vision Quest. They meet out in the woods for a weekend in October."

"It's the weekend after homecoming," Marc continues. "Do you have a date yet, Estrella?"

Estrella chokes on her fish sandwich, finally swallowing to find everyone at the table looking at her and Marc, who wears a shy smile.

"Hi, boys and girls." Tatiana and her groupies materialize at the table. She turns to Estrella. "Be careful, you don't want to eat too much at once—you might choke." Then to Christophe, "Chrissy! I've missed you! I love your t-shirt. Prada?"

Christophe stands and air kisses her as Tatiana puts her hand on Marc's shoulder. "Marc, will you pretty please drive me into the city? I left something important at the penthouse and Mother's driver is sick. I wouldn't ask, but it's sentimental."

"Whatever," Estrella mutters beneath her breath.

Marc stands. "We better go now so we can be back before they start looking for us. Nice meeting everyone—see you in class!" His eyes linger on Estrella as he follows Tatiana.

"So when should we jam, Evan?" Margeaux asks. I hear there's a room in the Media Arts building we can use. Amaka, hopefully you can make your guards available for a few hours a week?"

"Hey, Amaka," Louis cuts in, "Maybe you can teach me how to use my will to get my own musical guards at Glouton. I have a few cousins in New Orleans who would be perfect. Maybe you could teach me a lot of things." He reaches his hand across the table to hold hers, but she smacks it away.

"Can I teach you to own the deeds to all the diamond and uranium mines in Africa? Once I am married, I will oversee both my father's vast telecommunications conglomerate *and* my husband's mining empire while I unite Africa for all the people. Can you learn this?"

"I may not have diamond mines, but my heart is pure gold." Louis makes his hands into the shape of a heart and places them on his chest.

Christophe organizes the empty plates on his tray. "Time to hit the gym, Louis. Maybe this season we'll win a game."

"It is unlikely," Margeaux says. "If past is prologue, you're looking at another losing season."

"I haven't worked out since last week and I can feel it," Estrella says. "Evan, let's meet up tomorrow morning before class and spar for an hour."

"I haven't practiced all summer," Evan replies. "And I'm not that great, anyway."

"You'll do," Estrella says. "Meet me at six in the gym."

Evan's head shakes. "I mean, I really don't want to, but okay, I guess," he says, following his friends from the dining hall.

As soon as the boys disappear through the dining hall door, Margeaux says to Amaka, "Louis sure was all about you. And Marc about you, Estrella."

Amaka hides a smile. "Louis Washington is handsome. And bold. And athletic. And his grades are the highest in the school. But he has no fortune, no name. He can never give me what I want. I am only here for one reason, and that is to secure my influence in the world."

"You're too young to be so serious," Margeaux says.

Amaka puts down her phone. "If you had seen what I have—children watching their mothers get cut down in the streets by men who have nothing to live for, in a land with all the riches of the earth—then you might understand why I am so serious."

"I get it," Estrella says. She covers Amaka's hand with her own, and when she does, a pink light briefly sparkles from Amaka's crown of long hair.

...

Estrella arises from a dream of singing birds to a room still dark with the last of the night.

Margeaux sings in her sleep, the same melody as the birdsong of Estrella's dream, while, in her bed, Amaka lightly snores. Estrella takes the rosary from her nightstand and goes through her Hail Marys, then dresses silently, Marina's crystal above the door warming her as she passes beneath it.

She jogs, lunges, kicks, and punches her way across the magnificent lawns to the gym as the first hint of light breaks and builds upon that break. A nightingale whistles from a low branch, then flies with Estrella as the light grows stronger. Under a tree in the north yard—the oldest tree on campus, called Methuselah—she sees the outline of a man practicing tai chi. His grace and power cause her to stop and watch as the nightingale alights on a branch nearby.

From the semi-dark, a crow charges and, with a shriek, attacks the nightingale, knocking it from its branch. The shocked bird falls at Estrella's feet, the crow screams into the early morning sky.

Estrella takes the bird into her hands and checks for a pulse, looking around to see if anyone's watching her. "I know Marina said not to do this," she whispers as she touches the broken bend of the wing, pouring the love in her heart through her fingers. The tiny heartbeat comes back into the bird, the wing softens and then straightens. The bird flutters its rejuvenated wings and hops to Estrella's shoulder, continuing with her to the gym until Estrella enters the modern building.

Dim shadows swaddle the room that grows lighter by the moment. Estrella takes off her shoes, lays out the mats stacked against the wall, and runs through her kata: Crane, Tiger, Snake. Evan arrives after a few minutes and they silently practice together, finally finishing Dragon and bowing to each other.

"Ready to spar?" Estrella asks.

"Sort of," Evan replies, throwing the first punch. Estella blocks it with her forearm, hits him in the ribs, and kicks up to his head. She stops the kick just beside his ear.

"Point," Evan says. They continue in this way—kicking, punching, and circling each other—for several minutes, until Evan, panting, says, "I need a break." They bow. Both he and Estrella sweat. "Damn, Estrella, how are you not winded?"

"I train," Estrella replies as the door of the gym bangs open.

Marc, in baggy pajama bottoms and a t-shirt, frames the door, flooded now with light.

"I thought you were meeting at six." He looks at his watch.

"If you're early, you're on time. If you're on time, you're late," Evan says. "Remember?"

"Oh yeah, Sifu did say that." Marc does a few jumping jacks and some stretches. "Hey, Strella, how about a match? Like when we were kids?"

Estrella walks back to the center of the mat. "Are you warmed up enough?"

"I'm always ready to go," Marc says with a wink. They bow.

Evan calls out, "Be careful."

"I'll be gentle," Marc replies.

Estrella immediately flips and drops Marc on his back, where he lays stunned and immobilized.

Evan laughs at his cousin. "I meant be careful of Estrella. We're not little kids anymore. She trains."

Estrella helps Marc to his feet. "Oh my God, I am so sorry. I remember how good you were. Sorry. I thought you were ready."

Marc rubs his shoulder. "No, Estella, you are definitely not a kid anymore. But I never really thought of you as a kid, anyway; you've always been too cool for that. In fact, I was hoping to ask you—"

A huge shadow casts over them from the open door. "Good morning, boys," the shadow says in a loud, southern twang. "Young lady." He nods dismissively to Estrella.

"This guy kind of seems like a dick," Estrella says beneath her breath.

"Hey, Coach Bugsby," Marc and Evan say together, respect edged with fear lining their voices.

"Football conditioning starts in fifteen minutes. You need to put up these mats. Only football players in here now."

Estrella and Evan replace the mats together.

Coach Bugsby watches the boys with a frown. "Evan Hamilton, it's time to get serious and focus on football. You're a hell of a wide receiver. We need you on the team." Evan's head shakes involuntarily. "Don't tell me no, boy, until you hear me out. Your family has played football here at Glouton for over one hundred years, and it's time for you to play, too. It's what your father wants. You need to start taking your position in the world seriously."

"I'm tired of hearing about how great my family is, and how I don't measure up," Evan replies as Estrella puts on her hoodie and laces her shoes. "Besides, I like kung fu."

Coach lifts the volume. "Son, this isn't about what you like anymore. This is about your family name. Your bloodline. You're not a common person. And that goes double for you, Marc," he says, throwing his big voice at Marc. "Why weren't you at camp this summer? Who's going to protect Louis?"

"I'm a Buddhist now, Coach," Marc replies. "I can't participate in a violent sport. We lose almost every game anyway. What's the difference?"

Estrella lingers at the door, pretending to look for her keys in her backpack.

A blue vein throbs above Coach's left eye. "A Buddhist? A *Buddhist*? What the hell does that even mean? You're one of our best, and you're playing this year."

Marc shrugs and takes a step toward the door, but Coach Bugsby grabs his arm and puts his finger in Marc's face.

Estrella straightens up tall, and mutters in a louder whisper, "*Total* dick."

Coach Bugsby either ignores Estrella or doesn't hear. "You listen to me, young man," he says to Marc. "You go into that locker room and put your pads on. You're going to keep your grades up and you're going to play football for this team, just like your great-grandfather did, and your grandfather, and even your own father, despite the fact that he's chosen to do nothing with his life since then." Coach takes a breath and wipes away the spittle that has collected on his lips. "And you're out of shape. I saw this little girl drop you just now—violently, you fake Buddhist. You boys are playing football, you hear me? Go get dressed."

"Yes, sir," both Evan and Marc say on their way to the locker rooms.

Estrella slips out the door.

•••

"The way to Mystery School is, itself, a mystery," Margeaux whispers as Estrella and her roommates explore the many narrow passageways of Seton Hall, where the class takes place, running into one dead end after the other.

Finally, they approach a rickety, darkened staircase leading to the attic of the oldest tower on campus. Margeaux almost falls through a termite-eaten step on the way up.

A partially open door awaits them at the top of the fifty-six steps. Amaka pushes it open the rest of the way. Thirteen red velvet cushions lay in a circle on the gleaming wood floor, incense pours out the open windows that line the circular room and show off the green treetops of Glouton.

"The vibe is so peaceful," Estrella whispers. "Like church."

Three older students sit cross-legged on their cushions, their feet bare. An older girl with a black braid that brushes her knee motions for Estrella and her roommates to come in and sit. They place their backpacks and shoes on the shelf just outside the door, alongside three similar sets of belongings.

"It's too quiet in here," Amaka whispers. "It makes me nervous."

They sit next to the girl with the braid, who sits next to an exact replica of herself, but with a stronger jaw, shorter hair, a mustache, and broader shoulders. Estrella recognizes Octavio dos Santos Kong, the handsome boy with the smoothies.

A round-faced older boy with unruly dark curls has the cushion next to Octavio. His breath sounds like the waves of the ocean, his eyes are closed. Amaka pokes Estrella and Margeaux, pantomiming like she's sleeping and snoring. Estrella ignores her, but Margeaux starts laughing nervously until silent tears stream down her cheeks.

A crash comes from the stairs, and a moment later, the plump silhouette of Princess Sylvia appears in the doorway. Her book bag clangs again as it hits the floor. She plops down next to Amaka as the boisterous voices of Louis, Evan, and Christophe come from the staircase.

"Hey, watch that step," Christophe booms.

The boys suddenly modulate their voices to match the quiet of the room as they take off their shoes and sit on the cushions. Evan raises his brows at Estrella, silently asking what's going on. She shrugs her shoulders. The boy with his eyes closed continues to breathe like the sea; the Kong twins close their eyes and breathe with him.

More whispers float up the stairs. Marc, Tatiana, and a girl wearing a headscarf silently enter the room. Tatiana leads Marc by the hand to one of the remaining cushions. The girl with the headscarf gracefully lowers herself to the cushion next to Evan. Marc waves to Estrella and smiles, but Estrella pretends not to notice. Louis throws a wadded-up ball of paper at Amaka. She gives him a dirty look; he makes a motion with his hands of a beating heart.

They sit like this for a few long minutes before the round-faced boy beside the twins exhales completely and opens his eyes to look at the small, white-haired man with horn-rimmed glasses standing in front of the windows—the same man Estrella saw practicing tai chi that morning, the one who has looked at her from the poster above her desk since she was nine years old.

"Welcome to Mystery School, kids," he says. "I'm Dr. Saul Mather, your teacher." The class hangs on the Nobel Prize winner's every word. "At this moment, you don't know your true power. We have all been fed a lie here on this earth—a lie of limitation. During these afternoon hours, we will chip away at those lies that place a barrier between you and the truth of your glory." He paces the room. "There are no tests in Mystery School. You've already passed a number of them just to be able to take this course. There are no assignments, though you will find yourselves practicing what we learn outside of this room. And there are no notes here; nothing is written or recorded. What you learn here will become part of your cellular memory. You do not need to look outside yourselves for anything."

Christophe shifts on his cushion; Dr. Mather notices and says, "You will find that sitting like this becomes more comfortable with time. Patience makes all things bearable."

He resumes pacing. "This is our first Mystery School seminar with thirteen students. I usually cap it at twelve, but you are quite an exceptional crop. In fact, this is the first year I have ever selected freshmen at all, and you youngsters make up almost a third of the class. You give me hope for our battered world." He stops abruptly. "Ultimately, you are here to uncover and harness your power because each of you has something extraordinary to contribute. Of course, we all, every one of us on earth, are extraordinary, but not every one of us are the children of Kings." He lets his words settle.

"Let us not underestimate the power of a lucky birth, of the institutional access that was built for you before you were an egg in your mother's belly. That cannot be taught." He turns his gaze to Louis. "Though, not all of you won the ovarian lottery. In every epoch, some of our most powerful leaders come from humble birth."

Louis clears his throat and winks at Amaka.

"So, why you? Why this thirteen?" Dr. Mather continues, ignoring the flirtation. "Is it an accident of fate, a coincidence that you are all here now? Maybe something greater is at work." The kids adjust on their cushions. Dr. Mather looks around until his magnified eyes focus on one student. "Amaka Abioye."

She raises her hand, lifts her chin. "I am here, sir."

Dr. Mather nods. "Your paper on using Machiavellian strategies to reform African bureaucracies impressed me greatly. Though I may disagree with some of your tactics, I revel in the purity and greatness of your vision." Amaka beams. "You would do well to work with Louis Washington." Louis smiles with delight as Amaka's grin falls. "His work on organizing student bodies across the United States has the power to dramatically change the direction of national policy. In fact, there is some evidence that it already has.

"Christophe Markov." Christophe sits up a bit straighter and grooms his nascent, blond mustache with his fingers. "Your designs to modernize the Trans-Siberian Railroad are both elegant and efficient. Perhaps you will collaborate with Princess Sylvie, whose work on solar batteries has the potential to virtually eliminate acidic greenhouse gas emissions." Sylvie blushes.

"Margeaux Prince." Margeaux bites her lip. "What good is this world without poetry and song? You cannot imagine my delight, listening to the songs you wrote based on the Shakespearean tragedies." Margeaux turns as pink as her hair.

"And speaking of Shakespeare: Marcus Hamilton, your book of short stories chronicling your many adventures announces the voice of a generation. Where would we be without our storytellers?" Marc looks at the floor while Tatiana gives him a flirty punch on the arm.

"Evan Hamilton." Evan's head wiggles slightly. "So young and such a great mathematical mind. You have grappled with and might have even solved the Collatz conjecture. A mind like yours can unravel not only our tricky theoretical math problems, but perhaps also some of our humanitarian riddles, like how to finally bring peace to the Middle East.

"Zaharia Namazi." The girl in the headscarf looks Dr. Mather directly in the eyes. "How can we speak of a courage like yours? Your fearless reporting on the conditions of women in your region has already provoked attempts on your life, and yet, you persevere. You may one day require the services of Octavio and Nikki Kong."

The twins bow. Dr. Mather bows back. "You both are now masters of kung fu and jiu jitsu. You are the most fearsome of warriors, in both body and mind."

Estrella and Evan bow to the twins—the sign of greeting and respect between martial artists. Marc sees them bowing and does it, too.

"Shabad Padmanabhan. Why are you here?" The round-faced boy with the heavy breath bows to Dr. Mather. "Why would I ask back a Mystery School student? This is unprecedented." Everyone looks at Shabad. "I was so intrigued by your thesis in concurrence with my work on The Cosmic and the idea that the incantation of certain Sanskrit words can create brain waves that dissolve anxiety, that I invited you here last year. Imagine my joy in learning of Estrella Chavez's experiments showing that the incantation of certain *Latin* words can have the same effect. These experiments point to the very essence of The Cosmic. In fact, I am so intrigued by this proposition that you both put forth that I wanted to explore the power the two of you can share together."

As Estrella and Shabad share a smile, Marc clears his throat, drawing Dr. Mather's focus, before he transfers it to Tatiana.

"Tatiana Duplessis. You're here because you want to feed the hungry children. Who can deny that this is among the noblest of goals?" He looks away from her as she smiles.

Dr. Mather continues. "In these sessions, we will delve into the ultimate mystery; The Cosmic. We will explore this omniscient, connective web, primarily through breathing. It is through the breath that we access The Cosmic, the Divine, God—feel free to call it what you will." His eyes sweep over the fidgety class. "Sit up straight and breathe!"

The room quickly fills with the sound of deep, even breaths.

"In six weeks, the weekend after homecoming, we will go into the forest for our annual Mystery School Vision Quest. All the work that we do between now and then serves to prepare us for that experience."

Dr. Mather takes a cushion from the shelf by the door and joins the circle next to Shabad. He effortlessly crosses his legs into a lotus pose; his spine grows long. "Do what I do," he says. "Pull your navel toward your spine but leave air for your lungs."

The students cross their legs in the traditional position, except Marc, Christophe, and Louis, who can only stack one leg.

"Breathe," Dr. Mather commands. "In time, your hips will relax. Practice, practice, and all is coming. Eventually, this position will become comfortable. Today, for most of you, I imagine it is not. All of our great leaders—the saints, the visionaries, the mystics—they all learned to sit and breathe through discomfort. This is the first lesson of Mystery School—its very foundation—but it is by no means the easiest. Breathe in through the nose, out through the nose. Make the sound of the ocean, like Shabad. Breathe into your belly, and out from your belly. Keep your back straight and your lungs open. Relax your eyes. Breathe through your impatience and discomfort."

The room becomes a sea. Finally, Dr. Mather's voice breaks through the waves.

"Very good!" He smiles. "Excellent concentration." He stays on his cushion. The kids fidget but do the same. "Now I'll pose a question. What is the underlying concept of mystery and the mystics?"

No one says anything.

Estrella waits, silently wondering why no one else seems to know the answer, as if they didn't even prepare, despite Glouton's academic reputation. She waits another minute, then says. "The Greek word 'muo' is the root word of mystery. It means 'to shut the eyes or the mouth.' It's closely related to the verb 'mueo,' which means 'to initiate into the mysteries.' The closed eyes and mouth in this context don't signify blindness or muteness, but secrecy and silence, and the order not to reveal the secrets of the initiation and revelations that one has received. The essence of mystery and mysticism is silence."

"Quite right, Estrella," Dr. Mather says. "Silence."

The class is completely silent for several moments until Louis raises his hand and says, "But, sir, I fear silence will be too challenging for Amaka. It's not fair. You can see that a little lion like her must roar."

Amaka seethes. "And yet you are the one talking. Maybe *you* need to practice silence before—"

Dr. Mather strikes a gong next to his cushion three times.

"Class dismissed."

...

"Why are you so happy?" Amaka asks Estrella, the dining hall buzzing around them with the sounds of hungry Gloutonites. "What is that little smile that pulls at your lips?"

"What do you mean?" Estrella replies.

"It's because she distinguished herself in front of a Nobel Prize winner," Margeaux says. "Who knew you were studying Greek over the summer?"

"No, that is not a smile of academic achievement," Amaka says. "That is a smile of love. Tell me now or I will learn it another way. It is futile to resist."

Estrella hesitates. "Okay, but if you tell anyone, I swear I'll kill you."

Margeaux and Amaka nudge closer to Estrella.

"Marc asked me to homecoming after class, that's all. It's not a big deal."

Amaka raises her eyebrows. "So, the rumor that he was with Tatiana is false. She must have disseminated it herself."

Margeaux sighs. "Figures you and Amaka have boys falling all over you and I'm the ugly stepsister."

"What? No way," Estrella says. "I think Evan likes you. I mean, he does like lots of girls though."

At the table next to them, the older of Amaka's guards, Amare, sits at attention, his serious eyes taking in the room of teenagers, while Adisa, the younger brother, eats heartily as he absentmindedly drums a rhythm with his fingers on the tabletop.

"I can only imagine that your guards will grow painfully bored here," Margeaux says, dabbing her fries in mayonnaise.

"They are happy to be bored," Amaka replies, between bites of salad that she eats with onyx chopsticks she pulls from her Chanel purse. "All the men in their village were executed, the women raped and taken as slaves, the boys forced to fight for a barbaric army. Only they escaped. My mother found them at a refugee camp one hundred kilometers from their village. Adisa's feet still bear scars from the blisters."

Estrella's eyes brim with tears. "Tonight, I'm praying the rosary for them and for forgiveness for ever feeling sorry for myself."

"Now they are my family," Amaka continues. "Last year, my father arranged for them to train with the Navy Seals. They can disappear in a room full of people, swim for three minutes on a single breath, and make a man unconscious with one touch. Yes, they are here to protect me, but they are also my brothers. I would kill for them, as they would for me. Also, they are taking business classes online through Boston University. We will all have diplomas when we leave Glouton."

Sylvie and Zaharia approach the table with their trays.

"Hey, fellow Mystery Schoolers!" Estrella says. "I swear I feel like we've known each other for years, even though all we did was sit and breathe together."

"I feel the same!" Zaharia replies.

"Me too," Sylvie says, joining the table.

Zaharia quietly prays over her plate of rice and chicken before she picks up the hot sauce and covers her food with it. "They really are not the best cooks here," she says.

"Could be worse," Princess Sylvia says, cutting into her steak and potatoes.

"Why are we talking about food?" Amaka pushes her plate away. "We are in a world crisis now. Everywhere, people are suffering, starving, dying of thirst. *They* can talk about food. We, among all the masses, can do something about it. The actions we will take—this must be our discussion."

Margeaux rolls her eyes. "I adore you already, Amaka, but you are far too serious. What about fashion? Can we talk about that instead? Or cute boys like Octavio, for instance? Or cute girls like Nikki?"

"Oh, they are cute," Sylvia says, nodding her head and chewing.

Zaharia says, "You are right, Amaka. We have no time to waste. Have you heard of Raeesa Gajani?"

Amaka shows Zaharia her phone. "This is her Twitter feed. I am always following her."

"I've heard of her," Estrella says. "She's a big advocate of the Water Trust, and a bunch of other causes."

"I will intern with her this summer," Zaharia says.

Amaka's eyes grow wide. "She is the greatest champion of women in the world, and she speaks for equality between all the people of the earth. As a woman, a Muslim, a Yoruban, and a Jew, I am inspired by all she does."

Now Zaharia's eyes widen. "You are a Muslim and a Jew? How many times a day do you pray?"

"Because my mother is Jewish, I am officially a Jew, but we are not observant, so I only pray when I want something, though I do keep kosher. My father is Muslim and Yoruban but practices no religion. Like Raeesa, I see the dignity in us all, no matter our religion."

Princess Sylvie wipes her mouth with a napkin. "It is very dangerous, what Raeesa Gajani is doing. My mother saw her in Davos. She slept for twelve hours every night. Outside of Switzerland, she is afraid to sleep. Every moment of her life she is afraid someone will kill her. Or worse."

Zaharia sits taller in her seat. "If we want to see the world change, we must be willing to pay the price."

"One day they will all pay the price for their wickedness," Amaka says. "When I have my army, they will see what it is like to be afraid."

• • •

The smell of earth and water; a pleasant chill in the breeze. The liquid green forest wraps around Estrella.

Islid picks blackberries from a bush. "Soon, winter will be here, and I will sleep. In the long sleep, we are transformed."

• • •

Estrella's phone dings, waking her. It's an email from Dr. Mather. The subject line reads "Transformation."

> *Estrella Chavez,*
> *You will train with Octavio and Nikki Kong from 6:00 to 7:15 a.m. at the gym each morning for the rest of the school year, beginning today.*
> *Dr. Saul Mather*

• • •

Estrella checks Twitter on the dark path to the gym.

The Financial Times: "Algerian Water Crisis Leads to Exodus of Country's Poorest—Tensions Mount at Border."

The World Economic Forum: "Droughts in Asia Lead to Food Shortages and Riots as a New Leader Rises in Indonesia, Former General Su Bang Bang." The link leads Estrella to a video of a small man in a uniform standing before a sea of men and women who chant his name. The subtitles read "*Revolution! We must take back what has been stolen from the people. Drag them out, cut them down, show them what happens to the educated elites who steal with a smile.*"

"Damn," Estrella mutters as she jogs across the pristine green grounds of Glouton, passing its magnificent buildings. "Talk about educated elites—thank God Su Bang Bang's not here." As she jogs, her nightingale dancing above her head, she prays for all the poor people of the world who need food and water.

Too late, Estrella notices the shadow from the corner of her eye. Like a panther, Nikki Kong pounces just outside the door to the gym and slams Estrella to the ground, ramming her knee into Estrella's chest. Her left arm pins Estrella's elbow to the grass, her right fingers thrust just in front of Estrella's eyeballs.

"Good one, Nikki," Estrella wheezes.

Nikki leaps off Estrella and bows. "Pay attention."

Estrella limps into the gym, where Octavio practices Dragon kata with two swords. As soon as she's in the door, Nikki tackles her again, shaking her head as she backflips away from Estrella's prone body. "How did you not see that coming?"

"You ladies ready to stop playing around and fight?" Octavio calls from the center of the room.

Estrella rolls to her knees and mutters, "It's going to be a long day."

• • •

Estrella hobbles into her empty dorm room, breathing in the luxury of a moment alone. She feels her ribs to make sure they aren't broken as her phone buzzes with a text.

Let's Zoom. I want some intel.

Estrella smiles, opens her laptop, and clicks the Zoom link. Quincy perches on Kit's shoulder, a cocktail fizzes at her side. Off-screen, Yves murmurs bets on a horse race.

"Why haven't you called me?"

Estrella stumbles for a reply, unable to tell Kit that she had forgotten all about her.

"Don't bother with an excuse—You're young, I'm old," Kit says. "I didn't call my grandmother for half a year and then she died, and the remorse still haunts me—keep it in mind. So how are you holding up? I know you must hate it there."

"Okay, you were right, and I was wrong. I love it here." Estrella relaxes back onto her bed and settles in for a chat.

"How's Mystery School?" Kit asks.

"All we've done so far is sit and breathe," Estrella says. "It's my hardest class though."

"Ah yes, sitting and breathing...I remember it all too well. Good for you." Kit takes a sip of her drink. "Keep at it—you want to be prepared for the Vision Quest."

"Yeah, it'll be right after homecoming." Estrella smiles at the mention of the dance.

"Homecoming?" Kit stares at her with expectant eyes. "Are you going?"

Quincy stops shuffling and looks right into the camera.

"Uh, yeah, I guess." Estrella says as she curses herself for bringing it up.

"You guess? Do you have a date or not?"

Estrella swallows, her face growing red. She places her finger over the laptop power switch.

"Who is he? Yves! Estrella's got a date to homecoming. I'm about to find out who it is. So, who is it?"

"Someone from Mystery School." Estrella looks away.

"Oh wonderful," Kit says, in a tone that means *stop stalling.* "Anyone I know?"

"Marc." Estrella replies, unable to say Kit's own last name to her.

"Marc who?" Kit asks, but then her eyes widen with recognition and implication. "Oh. My Marc? Marc Hamilton? Is there another Marc in your class?"

Estrella says, "No, I mean, yeah. I mean, yes, your Marc."

Kit sits and breathes for a moment before she says, "That's wonderful, Estrella."

Estrella recognizes the sound of Kit's fake voice.

From the other room, Yves asks, "Well, who is it?"

Kit yells over her shoulder, "I'll tell you later."

Estrella counts her breaths during the awkward pause, like in Mystery School.

"Have you told your mother?" Kit asks.

"That I'm going to homecoming?" Estrella asks.

"That you're going with Marc."

"Um, not yet." Estrella avoids looking at the monitor.

At that moment, thank God, Amaka sails in for a change of clothes—her third of the day.

"Amaka!" Estrella practically yells with relief. "Come say hello to Kit Hamilton."

Amaka smiles wide at the screen. "Your work on the Water Trust and your way of seizing power from idiots inspires me to study."

"How charming you are!" Kit says, clearly flattered. "Babatunde must be proud."

"My father has many reasons to be proud," Amaka says. "I am happy to have formally met you." She blows a kiss to Kit, waves to

Estrella, and leaves with her cheer uniform in a Gucci duffle bag.

"She's lovely," Kit says.

"Margeaux is cool, too. You'd like her. She's actual royalty. A few of the kids are." Estrella silently rejoices in the conversation's turn away from homecoming.

"Well, her mother certainly is a piece of work, but I suppose that's par for the course." Kit says, unafraid of shameless gossip. "Dr. Connie says you haven't met with her yet. You know I told her you would schedule a tea."

From Kit's shoulder, Quincy caws, "Dr. Connie needs a cocktail!"

"Oh, come on!" Estrella huffs. "I have less than no desire to meet with the principal. She seemed nice enough in orientation, and I kind of remember meeting her at your house when I was a kid. You two just smoked cigarettes and drank whiskey and laughed while you shouted out the names of people you wanted to see burn in hell." Estrella's voice takes on a slight whine. "Plus, don't I need an appointment or something? What would we talk about, anyway?"

"You are an elegant young lady, groomed in the art of conversation. You should be able to chat with my dear friend over a cup of tea." Kit takes a sip of her fresh drink. "I'll set the appointment and text to confirm." Then Kit asks, in a softer voice, "Have you happened to see Coach Bugsby?"

"What a jerk!" Estrella sits up straighter. "He yelled at Marc and Evan because they don't want to play football."

"Some people are more passionate than others," Kit says with a satisfied smile. "Especially someone with Mike's...virility. So, are the boys going to play football?"

"Yeah," Estrella sighs. "Our first game is this weekend."

"Well, how can you fault a man for getting what he wants? It's such an attractive quality." Kit's phone rings. "*Ciao!*"

Estrella's screen goes black as she picks up her own phone to call her mom with the homecoming news before Kit does.

...

The principal's office at Glouton couldn't be more regal: plush armchairs, mahogany desk, Tiffany lamps, oriental carpets. Extravagant silk drapes dress the large windows that overlook the sprawling lawns. Ms. Tempest, the assistant to the principal, ushers Estrella into the room and motions for her to sit in one of the leather chairs that face the massive desk.

Estrella mentally curses Kit as she checks her phone to find nothing much on it. She takes three sections of her disheveled hair and begins to braid it, making it halfway through a fishtail when the door opens.

A short, fat woman with gray, bobbed hair enters the room. She laughs a husky laugh, turns back to the reception area, and drawls, "Well, if you can't make a monkey jump then you better give him a banana. Wisdom of the ages, Ms. Tempest. Say, you gonna bring us some tea? Make mine a coffee. Wait a second..." She turns to Estrella. "You want coffee or tea?"

"Coffee, please." Estrella sits up taller.

"You heard her—make it two coffees. Put it in the tea set, though, so we can look proper. Hey, don't skimp on the scones. And bring enough butter this time, and cream. I don't want my mouth drying up and I'm sure Ms. Chavez doesn't want hers drying up either." She walks a few feet into the room before she turns back again. "And call that Goldie Abioye. Don't email, just pick up the phone and call. I don't care if it's the middle of the night in Nigeria. Wake her up and tell her we are truly out of closet space in the dorms. We can't store whatever Givenchy collection she thinks her daughter needs. This isn't the Oscar Awards; it's high school." She waddles toward her desk. "Hell, I'd put them in my own closet for a new chem lab. Mention that discreetly."

Estrella puts out her hand. "Nice to see you again, Dr. Anderson."

Dr. Anderson shakes her head. "What are we, doing business? I've known you since you were a baby. Give me a hug for Chrissake." She throws her plump arms around Estrella. "Look at you! Kit said you were pretty just like your mother. Poor woman—talk about a twist of fate. Go ahead and sit."

Dr. Anderson keeps on. "Pretty is as pretty does, though, and don't forget it. They got a line of pretty girls long enough to make a chain around the planet. That whole chain of them's worth about fifty cents. You're here for your smarts, Estrella. How do you like Glouton so far?" Dr. Anderson's rheumy blue eyes are curious and friendly.

Estrella politely replies, "Glouton is a great school. I like it a lot." But as she speaks, she's wondering about the twist of fate Dr. Anderson mentioned about her mom. She almost opens her mouth to ask if Dr. Anderson meant the fire and what happened with her dad, but she stays silent.

"I'm relieved to hear it," Dr. Anderson replies. "Kit said you'd rather contract the plague than attend, but I guess it's charmed you."

Estrella reddens, silently cursing Kit for always telling her business to the exact people Estrella doesn't want to know about it. Ms. Tempest carries in a silver tray loaded with cookies, scones, and coffee. "That smells delicious," Estrella says, her mouth watering.

"Here, fix yourself a plate," Dr. Anderson hands Estrella a delicate porcelain plate, a scone already in her jaws. The two women go about buttering their pastries and adding cream and sugar to their coffee. "I remember the first time I ever had coffee, Estrella. It was in my bottle. My grandma fed me coffee and condensed milk for the first three years of my life. Thought it would help me sleep, of all things. You think I'm not addicted?"

Estrella nods and chews, a look of bliss on her face. "These are the best scones I've ever tasted. Where do you get them?" she asks. "Do they sell them on campus?"

"Ms. Tempest makes them every morning, just for me," Dr. Anderson says. "I had to fire my personal chef a few years back for being a loudmouth traitor, and while we were looking for a replacement, Ms. Tempest stepped in. I give her a bonus now to make these."

"She deserves it," Estrella says, between bites.

Dr. Anderson dusts crumbs off her desk. "Let's cut to the chase. I'm a busy woman and so are you." She holds Estrella's eyes with her own. "Anything you need, I'm here for you, alright? You need some money, you ask me. You need a shoulder to cry on, here's mine. I know what it's like, being from the other side of the tracks and getting thrown into *their* world. Trust me. The only reason I'm not collecting welfare in a trailer in South Carolina right now is that my momma used her beauty and wits to get what she wanted. If she hadn't run away from my daddy to Atlanta and managed to marry one of the Coca-Cola heirs—probably through some sort of blackmail for all we know—I wouldn't be here today. I've been on the outside my whole life. Don't get me wrong, I've made some great friends: Kit primary among them. And you know what? I'm one lucky son-of-a-gun, and so are you. We get to be in a place that actually appreciates our ideas and our drive. One of the best places in the world. Sky's the limit for you now, Estrella. But I know it can be hard, all the same."

She hands Estrella a card from her desk drawer. "Here's my personal cell and email. Text me, call me, whatever. And don't worry about me taking sides with what's going on between Kit and your mom. I'm staying out of it. I like spending time with you, Estrella. You're a great conversationalist."

Ms. Tempest opens the door a crack. "Your four-thirty is here."

Again, Estrella's lips part to ask Dr. Anderson about her comment, but again declines to give voice to her questions, and instead says, "I like spending time with you, too, Dr. Anderson. I can see why you and Kit are such great friends."

Dr. Anderson hugs Estrella again. "Be strong, child. Be strong."

. . .

"Is there something going on with Mom and Kit?" Estrella Facetimes Marina the minute she's outside Dr. Anderson's office.

Marina frowns. "Who told you that?"

"Dr. Anderson, my principal."

Marina giggles. "Isn't she so funny? I *love* her! You know her mother married one of the Coca-Cola heirs and then divorced him and took half of everything. She has a real rags-to-riches story. Maybe Celeste James could play the mom in a movie about it."

"Whatever," Estrella replies, rounding the corner toward her dorm. "Is there something wrong or not?"

"Of course not! They're best friends. You just focus on making friends and having fun."

"Something's not right, I can feel it," Estrella says. "If you won't tell me what, I'll find out another way, so you should just tell me now. Anyway, I love you, goodbye." She pushes open the door to her room, flops onto her unmade bed and feels the crinkle of paper. She pulls a handwritten, stamped envelope from under her. The return address is from Harrison, Virginia.

Amaka watches as Estrella reads the letter to herself.

Dear Estrella,

I was going to text, but I remembered that you were at Glouton, and would prefer a longhand letter, so here it is.

Life here at Hargrave Academy is pretty good, except that it's a military school, so we have to wake up at the crack of dawn and make our beds and say 'yes, sir!' all the time. After this year I plan to never make my bed again, though I suppose I'll be back in the make-the-bed, yes-sir game once I get to West Point.

I've been thinking about you since I dropped you off at your front door. I wish we could have kept on driving.

How is life at Glouton? I hope you find the curriculum challenging, and that you're making good friends. The one saving grace of Hargrave is all the friends I've made.

Please keep me in your thoughts until we can see each other again over the holidays. I'm already looking for opportunities to get you back out on the dance floor.

John

Estrella's heart beats fast as she re-reads the letter.

"Who sent you a letter?" Margeaux asks as she returns to the room, guitar strapped to her back.

"A cute boy from home," Estrella says.

Amaka raises an eyebrow. "How many cute boys do you need?"

"Oh, you mean Marc?"

"Yes, your homecoming date," Amaka replies. "The one you share every meal with, who sends you texts all day long, and who looks at you with his big, lovesick eyes. Marc Hamilton."

Estrella reads the letter again. "But, I mean, it's the Age of Aquarius, and Marc hasn't even kissed me yet, and maybe he really does like Tatiana for all I know. It's probably best to keep my options open."

. . .

"Wake up!"

Margeaux and Estrella sit bolt upright in their beds, Estrella's iPad and books crashing to the floor as she reflexively jumps into a defensive kung fu stance, while Margeaux throws the controller to *Game of War* across the room.

Amaka stands in the center of the room in a Gucci sweat suit and limited-edition Nike's, her makeup flawless, her hair elegantly piled atop her head. ""It's football season—the first game starts in two hours. We must have breakfast now so I can be on time for warm-ups." She stays rooted to her spot while Margeaux and Estrella roll out of their beds. "You are moving too slowly. Hurry."

"Have you considered exploring your codependent tendencies?" Margeaux asks as she pulls on her clunky Doc Martens. "Plenty of people just go and eat breakfast all by themselves when they're hungry."

Amaka narrows her eyes. "Would you have me walk alone through the entire campus like an outcast?"

"What about Amare and Adisa?" Margeaux replies.

"I must pay for my companions?" Amaka asks. "Have I no friends?"

Estrella laces her Converse. "All right, let's go."

Amaka surveys her roommates. "You will not dress?"

Estrella shrugs. "That's the benefit of sleeping in your clothes."

Amaka sighs. "You will never succeed in life if you do not prepare properly for important events."

Estrella picks a sweatshirt off the floor. "Breakfast before a football game is an important event?"

"Every breakfast with the children of the most powerful families in the world is an important event," Amaka replies.

...

The September New England afternoon sparkles blue from the sky. Estrella opens her face to the sun and closes her eyes. Next to her, Margeaux wears a wide hat and dark sunglasses to shelter her fair skin.

"Maybe this will be the year they win," Estrella says. "Glouton might be the top school for academics, but it sucks at sports. Washington High, my hometown school, is almost always the state champion. I love football. Every Sunday me and my family watch the Patriots. Except my mom. I have a Tom Brady poster on the wall opposite Dr. Mather."

"Who's Tom Brady?" Margeaux asks. "And why do you call it football? They hardly use their feet."

"Look!" Estrella points to Amaka, who shakes her pom-poms and leaps into the air, landing in a split as hundreds of phones flash.

The first quarter goes well; Louis throws a touchdown pass to Evan in the second quarter, which sends the Glouton crowd into a frenzy.

"This could be the year that Glouton finally wins it all!" Estrella shouts over the roar of the crowd.

St. Albis responds immediately with a touchdown, then another. The score at halftime is 17-10, St. Albis. "Dammit," Estrella says to Margeaux. "We suck."

"I am entirely uninterested," Margeaux replies. "Wonder how Real Madrid did against Manchester? *That's* a game I'd like to see."

St. Albis begins the second half with a kickoff return for a touchdown and then a two-point play. 25-10. St. Albis scores the next points as well: a field goal followed by another field goal. 31-10, St. Albis.

Margeaux yawns. "The St. Albis kicker's quite good, isn't he?"

Estrella says, "At least we're holding them to field goals," just as the St. Albis cornerback snatches the ball from the air and returns the interception for a touchdown. 38-10, five minutes left to play. St. Albis puts their freshmen on the field.

Coach Bugsby shrugs his shoulders on the sideline.

"What would Kit say now if she saw Coach Bugsby like that, utterly defeated?" Estrella asks as her phone buzzes with a text from Amaka.

Meet me in the locker room in ten minutes.

Estrella nearly puts up her phone but decides to send a text to Marc.

Do not dwell in the past, do not dream of the future, concentrate the mind on the present moment. —Buddha

• • •

"Thanks for the Buddha quote," Marc says to Estrella in the dining hall vibrating with the low energy of defeat. "It just wasn't our day to win."

Amaka says, "It hasn't been Glouton's day to win since 1953."

Louis shakes his head. "Where's the drive, the passion? Let's have some faith! Next week we'll win." He turns to Amaka. "And where's *my* heartfelt text? I saw you out there, looking cute in your little suit. I saw you watching me. Where are my words of encouragement?"

Amaka puts down her phone. "I wasn't watching you; I was watching the game that you lost. And it's called a uniform, like you have. But here are some words of encouragement—keep studying. Your future is not in the NFL." She goes back to her phone. "My split has over 1,000 likes on Instagram, and 3,200 shares on TikTok. People are so easily entertained."

Marc's phone vibrates. "It's Tatiana. She's too upset about the game to come down. She wants me to bring her a cheeseburger, no bun." Estrella stares at him until he adds, "She's one of my best friends. Who else can she ask?"

"She could've asked me," Princess Sylvia points out, from across the table. "We room next door to each other."

Marc looks to Estrella's angry face for permission.

"Do what you've got to do," Estrella says. "Me, I'm going to study. Like Amaka says, none of us are destined for the NFL."

She tosses her tray into the bus tub on her way out the dining hall and sends a quick text to John.

Thinking of you!

. . .

A deep hunger wakes Estrella at midnight. She lies in bed and listens to her stomach grumble for half an hour, images of toast, hummus and chocolate dancing behind her closed eyes.

She slides out of bed and tiptoes down the hall, her mouth-watering. A slice of moon illuminates slivers of the shadowy kitchen.

"There it is!" she whispers, spying a carton of hummus that Zaharia made behind a box of condiments and a carton of milk.

She grabs the container, takes a fork from a drawer, says a one-second prayer of thanks, then rips off the lid. Large black flies buzz from the Tupperware and swarm her face. She frantically swats at them as her stomach heaves. The flies affix themselves to a window where they writhe and buzz.

A lilting laugh sounds behind her.

"You look like an idiot, spazzing around like that." Tatiana lounges at a table in the shadows, eating a mound of steak tartar with chopsticks. "I felt like a midnight snack. You, too?"

Estrella tries to stop shaking as her hands clench into fists. A streak of lightning illuminates the window of flies.

Tatiana licks her plate clean before she puts it in the dish rack.

"Aren't you going to wash that?" Estrella's heart rattles her chest with each thud.

"You wash it."

A fly buzzes from across the room and brushes Estrella's lips as Tatiana steps closer. "Marc Hamilton is mine. Let's come to an understanding about that. I was born to be with him. You're out of your league."

Estrella lengthens her spine and broadens her shoulders, stepping into Tatiana's space. "*He* asked *me* to homecoming the first day of school. Talk to Marc if you have an issue. Probably he thinks you're ugly."

Tatiana squares Estrella. "He's just using you for one of his stories. The exotic brown girl from a bad family—he'll get tired of you just like all the others. And I'd hardly say I'm ugly. Quite the opposite."

"You sound insecure." Estrella bumps Tatiana with her shoulder. "I would slap you right in your ugly face, but I'm not letting you ruin my future." Estrella steps away, takes the unclean plate from the rack, breaks it over her knee, and puts the pieces in the trash. With one swat of her slipper, she kills all the flies on the window, scooping them up with a paper towel and throwing them in with the plate.

Tatiana smiles tightly. "Aren't you just the good little Mexican, cleaning up everyone else's mess? That's all you're doing for Marc: giving him a place to sow his wild oats. You're getting it out of his system for me. Thanks, chiquita." She spins on her heel and slithers into the dark, empty hall.

Estrella eyes the broken plate in the trash. She imagines taking a jagged piece to slice Tatiana's head from her neck.

• • •

The room at the top of the fifty-six stairs fills with the breath of thirteen Mystery School students and twenty Mystery School parents. The adults sit on cushions behind their respective children. Kit Hamilton sits behind her nephew, Evan, whose parents are absent.

Dr. Mather emerges from his side door.

"Distinguished parents of Glouton, this is what your children are doing for several hours each week. As some of you are graduates of this seminar, you know this already."

Dr. Mather scans the room, then brings Fyodor Markov, Christophe's father and the prime minister of Russia, another cushion. After a second scan, Dr. Mather brings extra cushions to Sameer Namazi, who sits with his wife Leilah behind Zaharia. Neither man can easily cross his legs. He also brings one to Dixon Duplessis, who fidgets on his pillow, his knees practically up by his ears. Dixon sits behind his daughter, Tatiana, and his willowy ex-wife, Susan.

As Dr. Mather brings Dixon the extra pillow, Estrella recalls reading an article in *The Post* about how Dixon's considered the most desirable bachelor in the world right now, and decides that it must be for his money, because it's certainly not for his looks.

Only Linda and Marc's parents, Nelson and Mia, sit comfortably on their cushions, knees open wide, their breaths deep and fluid. Marc told Estrella they both do yoga: typical Californians.

"We won't be here for the full three hours that your children endure thrice weekly. This is an abbreviated class, for your benefit," Dr. Mather says.

"Oh, thank God," Goldie says from behind Amaka. "I haven't sat this long in one place since that conference on human rights at the UN four years ago where they just droned on and on and never let you leave. My legs fell asleep, and it took them over two hours to wake back up. Nightmare." Babatunde, next to her, shakes his head imperceptibly. Amaka puts her finger to her lips to quiet her mother.

"I remember that conference," Kit rasps from across the circle. "Nightmare is right. By the end, I didn't care if we all got sold into slavery. I just wanted it to end." Kit and Goldie share a chuckle over the memory.

"Let me interrupt," Dr. Mather says, "Before we find ourselves engaging in a politically incorrect conversation here in class. We'll have that conversation at the Gala Saturday night." The parents laugh as he continues. "In reality, of course, this weekend is a construct. For all you know, we could be practicing witchcraft in here." The parents laugh again. "Even if we are, the numbers don't lie; Mystery School graduates go on to attain the highest levels of personal and professional success, and who doesn't want that for their child?"

Lenny Prince's iWatch sounds as Margeaux hisses, "Dad!"

"So sorry," the small, slim man with windblown hair and dark sunglasses says in a thick, East London brogue. "We're negotiating the Re-Re-Union Tour. I told them not to call."

"Hey, you do what you've got to do for rock 'n' roll," Dixon Duplessis says in his heavy New York accent. Fyodor Markov guffaws in agreement.

Behind his twins, Peng Kong says in broken English, "It's only rock 'n' roll, but we like it."

Raquel Kong puts her fingers to her husband's lips, and with a sultry Brazilian inflection whispers, "Shh—we aren't supposed to talk."

Dr. Mather, a grin in his eyes, says, "It's true that we don't usually talk in Mystery School, but you are the financiers of this operation, and can have your run of the place today." The parents smile with pride. "In fact, let's wrap up. Do you have any questions for me before we set out for the great city of New York to participate in what is called 'the greatest gala of the season' for a reason?"

Kit says, "It certainly is—I've made more deals there than in any boardroom." The parents nod in agreement.

Jia Padmanaban, who sits with her husband, Gaja, behind their eldest son, Shabad, lifts her hand. "I have a question. Maybe you could tell us, finally. What is the meaning of life?"

All the parents—even the stony-faced Madeleine and Gustof behind Sylvia, Louis's elegant mother Marie Washington, the handsome and wry Bill Hamilton sitting with Kit behind Evan, and the poker-faced Linda Chavez—burst out laughing.

Fyodor Markov's serious voice breaks the laughter. "We're old enough now to know that it's not what we'd once hoped it would be."

• • •

Kit reclines on Estrella's bed in the small dorm room and checks emails on her phone while Margeaux and Estrella pack overnight bags.

"We will meet in the city the night of the Gala," Amaka says. "All of my outfits are planned, including accessories. Amare and Adisa, take my bags." Goldie air-kisses everyone, the room carrying the scent of her perfume as she and Amaka chatter down the hall, Amare and Adisa trailing them with their suitcases.

Linda closes her laptop, revealing the "chicana" sticker Hugo stuck on it. "I have to make a phone call to Senator Clay—talking points for the Energy and Environment Committee. Then just a quick email to Miakoda, and I'll meet you at the car. Estrella, remember to pack your gi for your classes with Sifu Chang."

"Already in there," Estrella says. Like I would forget my gi for my invite-only kung fu intensive with the Kong twins. I am so ready to be tested for my first stripe on Sunday." She holds up her forearms that are covered in bruises. "The Kong Twins are no joke."

Linda shakes her head. "I've had to make peace with your hobbies, but I still worry about you doing all that fighting."

Margeaux pulls a silk cloth-covered deck of oversized cards from a drawer beneath her bed. "You never know when you'll need to consult the tarot," she says, putting the cards in her suitcase.

Kit looks up from her phone. "Do you read tarot?"

"One of Father's girlfriends showed me how to read them a few years back. I find them helpful, though they didn't predict that Mother would show up unannounced in the dining hall an hour ago and engage in a horribly embarrassing, pill-fueled screaming match with Father in front of all of my friends and their parents. Though, with Mars in opposition to Saturn, perhaps I should have seen it coming."

Kit fixes her attention on the pink-haired teenager. "Yes, we are under a trying aspect this weekend to say the least, but Venus is in Libra, so that could help soften some of the tension. How fascinating that you are so informed."

"You know I think that's devil worship," Linda says.

"I don't know," Estrella says. "Kit read me something once about Scorpios and it did kind of fit me. And Marina goes to get her cards read about once a week and plans her outfits by the phases of the moon."

"I wish she would go to mass instead," Linda replies, her serious face absorbed in her screen.

"Would you like to ride with us into the city and join us for dinner?" Kit asks Margeaux. "Unless you have other plans?"

"I did have plans to dine with Mother, but seeing as how she took her driver and fled the scene, and Father took his driver and fled after her, I think it's safe to assume that my plans for both the evening and my transport to the city have opened up. Thank you, Ms. Hamilton, for your gracious invitation."

"Call me Kit. We'll look at the cards before dinner."

Estrella latches her suitcase. "I'm ready when you are, Pink. Let's go see the city."

• • •

"Zip me." Linda examines herself in the mirror with a frown while Estrella dutifully zips up her mother's elegant evening gown. "I'd rather have my teeth pulled than go to this excuse to show off how rich and important you are, but this is my lot in life."

Marina, wrapped in a silk robe, her hair in curlers, turns on the stereo in Kit's Upper East Side living room. Frank Sinatra's clear tenor rises from the speakers. "Perfect music for tonight! Think about all the eligible men around your age Mami, or even a little younger, who will be there. You need love!" She smothers Linda with kisses.

Linda pushes her away with a shake of her head and a smile. "I do not need love, and certainly not from any younger man," she says as she re-examines her profile with a confident eye.

"Where do you and your friends want to go tonight?" Marina says to Estrella. "Let's make it someplace fun. If I'm your chaperone, it has to be the best time ever."

"One place we're definitely not going is to the big party Tatiana's having at her family's penthouse. None of the freshmen have been invited. Amaka found out about it. No way. I hate that girl. Flies follow her."

"Flies?" Marina asks as Estrella gets a text from Marc.

Going to Tat's early but let's meet up later.

"Don't worry about it," Estrella replies to Marina, tossing her phone to the thick-carpeted floor and immediately picking it back up. She texts Marc.

Have fun.

She throws her phone back down, picks it back up, and blocks him. "Definitely not meeting up with him later," she mutters beneath her breath. "Like I'm second choice."

"Who are you texting?" Marina asks.

"No one," Estrella replies.

"I know it's Marc," Marina says as Estrella receives a text to her and Amaka from Margeaux.

I know a place. Let's go here.

There's a link to an all-ages club/coffeehouse.

Estrella texts the link to Marina from the sofa. "It was Margeaux."

"What about that party?" Marina asks.

"Who cares about a stupid party hosted by Tatiana of House Slytherin?" Estrella replies. "All I want is a mellow night out with my friends. And then ten hours of sleep. Every muscle in my body aches from Sifu Chang's classes. Just one more to go tomorrow, and

I get my stripe. If I keep up at this pace, I can compete in the world championships in two years. Sifu Chang's a trip—I swear he's quoting to us from that old TV show, *Kung Fu.* Like from an episode I just saw a few weeks ago."

Kit drifts into the room, her gown understated, her jewels not.

Quincy caws "Don't leave me!" from her shoulder when she puts him in his cage.

"I wish Margeaux hadn't pulled the Moon card, but at least it wasn't Death." Kit says as she presses a link on the slim band that circles her left wrist between rows of diamonds. She silently mouths into it, and suddenly her voice saying "Yves, we're ready. Bring the car," sounds loudly from across the house. "I love this thing," she says. "I recorded my entire D.C. dinner meeting last week, and no one had any idea. Hugo is a genius."

"Literally," both Estrella and Marina say together as Yves appears in the living room, keys in hand, suit crisp, hair impeccable.

Kit puts her burner phone and her gold cigarette case in her jewel-encrusted handbag. "Alright, Linda. Let's do this."

• • •

Estrella relaxes her aching muscles back into her chair while Margeaux, Amare and Adisa tap their feet to the rhythm of the music that travels from the stage of the Nuyorican Poets Cafe.

Marina leans close to Nicolas, her boyfriend. "This is so nice," she says. "It's easy to be your chaperone."

Hugo flops heavily into an empty seat at the table, removing his motorcycle helmet. "Who knew driving a motorcycle in Manhattan traffic would be so fun," he says. "Not. So not. Thank God I'm alive. The ride from Boston was a thousand times less stressy. I need a latte."

Nicolas motions to a waitress as Estrella yawns.

"How can you be tired?" Amaka says. "Listen to this music. Even in the clubs of New York, they are singing of revolution."

"The only revolution I'm interested in right now is the one I plan to make when I roll over in my sleep," Estrella replies. "That bed at Kit's is so soft. Sifu Chang looks all weak and skinny, but he's even tougher than the Kong Twins. I'm so worn-out. Let's go." She pushes her chair back from the table.

"I just got here," Hugo says. "Be polite and entertain your guests."

"Really," Margeaux chides. "It's not our fault you can't keep up with your kung fu mates."

Estrella flips Margeaux the bird. "You have no idea—you can't even run a lap around the track."

"Look, here's Evan!" Margeaux jumps up from the table.

Evan, Marc, Christophe, and Louis approach from the small door.

Marc pulls a chair from a neighboring table next to Estrella. "You blocked me?"

"No," Estrella lies.

"Yes, you did," Marc says, smiling. "I'll forgive you if you admit it." He nudges closer, until he meets Estrella's downcast eyes with his own.

"Whatever," Estrella finally says. "How was your party?"

"Not as wonderful as being here with you," Marc replies. "How's Sifu Chang?"

"She's exhausted and just about to go home to sleep," Hugo says.

Estrella dirty-looks him. "I'm staying for a little while," she says. "For my guests. But yeah, Sifu Chang is no joke."

"I'm Christophe Markov." Christophe extends his hand to Hugo. "And you are?"

Hugo blushes. "I'm Estrella's cousin."

"Is that your bike outside? I noticed the helmet. I have a great interest in all things transportation." Christophe sits next to Hugo, and the two fall into immediate conversation.

"Nicolas Salvatierra?" Louis asks. "I think you work for a hero of mine, Miakoda Grace." He turns to Amaka. "You look beautiful tonight. Won't you join Mr. Salvatierra and I in a scheme to reform the world in our own image? I know you have a suggestion or two."

"Of course I have a suggestion," Amaka replies. "We can begin with Speaker Grace's position on the role of the African Assembly in eco-affairs."

"Man, that was some Uber ride," Marc says to Estrella as Amaka clicks off suggestions. "I almost had to die to get to you. As soon as we got in, the driver said he was 'angry, very angry,' because Uber was threatening to take away his permit to drive because 'they say when I get angry, I drive dangerously.'" Marc puts on the driver's New York accent. Estrella forces back her smile. "This guy's driving like a maniac, honking his horn, weaving in and out of traffic—just getting *pissed* talking about how angry he is that they want to take his permit for his anger issues. We literally had to jump out at the only red light he stopped for and run the last several blocks to the cafe. He's getting a bad review. 'Entertaining but dangerous.'"

Estrella laughs then firms back her lips. "I'm sure you'd give a better review to Tatiana's big, upper-classmen party."

Marc takes Estrella's hand in his own. "So jealous, and for no reason."

"I'm not jealous," Estrella replies.

"Then come back to the party with me later."

Marina removes her lips from Nicolas's neck. "Estrella's not going anywhere tonight after this. She's testing for her stripe tomorrow, and I've got to get the new Louboutins at Barney's first thing. Enjoy her while you can, Marc."

"I always enjoy the time I spend with Estrella," Marc says, as Estrella's cheeks burn.

Marina's phone buzzes; her happy smile falls. She whispers into Nicolas's ear; he nods and motions for the waiter to bring the check. "It's time to go," Marina says to Estrella.

Estrella pulls Marina aside. "You're always trying to get me to go on dates, and now I'm kind of on one, and you're trying to wreck it for me?"

Marina drapes her jacket around her shoulders. "We're going now. It's Alfonso. He's got a problem. A big one."

"Figures. All Alfonso does is cause problems. He used to be so cool," Estrella says, irritation creasing her brow.

Marina turns to Amare, her smile brightening the dimly lit room. "You're so big and strong. Would you mind coming with us for just a little while? I would appreciate it so much."

"Of course," Amare replies with a gentlemanly bow, then taps Adisa on the shoulder, cutting short Adisa's conversation with Evan about Miles Davis. "Take the girls home," Amare says to his brother. "I'll text you."

Amaka looks away from Louis for the first time in an hour. "Where are you going, Amare?"

"He's coming with me," Marina says. "I may need his help. He'll be back in no time. Hugo, you're coming, too. Estrella, I'll see you later. Adisa's taking you home."

"This is bullshit!" Estrella whisper-yells to Marina. "How come Hugo gets to go with you? Because he's a boy?"

Hugo, who has been inching ever closer to Christophe, whines, "Why do I have to go? Where *are* you going anyway? We were just solving all the problems of fast fashion with the concept of endless-ly reproducible fabric."

"The Bronx," Marina replies. "You might need to talk to Alfonso. You know he listens to you."

"The Bronx? To talk to Alfonso? No, thank you. *Hell* no," Hugo says. "Alfonso can die for all I care. I'm so over him ruining my life. I'm going to a party with Christophe and his friends."

Christophe smiles at Hugo, who smiles back.

Marina gives Hugo a rare, serious look. "We don't have time for drama right now. Let's go."

Hugo hesitates, his gaze pinging from Marina to Christophe and back. "Dammit!" he finally says. "You know I can deny you nothing, Marina." He hands Christophe an old-fashioned calling card and says, "Stay in touch."

"Oh, so now Hugo's Mr. Cool Guy all of a sudden and I have to go home like a little kid?" Estrella sneers.

"Twenty minutes ago, all you wanted to do was sleep," Marina replies, motioning with her eyes to Marc and making a kissing gesture with her lips.

"This is bullshit," Estrella says to Marina. "I'm going."

"I've never been to the Bronx," Marc interjects. "I'll take a ride."

Marina looks to the heavens for guidance, then rubs her flawless brow. "Marc, Estrella will see you at school. Estrella, you're going home. Amaka and Margeaux can spend the night if you want. You're not getting involved in this. Not yet."

* * *

"Zaharia says that there are over three hundred people now at Tatiana's penthouse." Amaka throws her phone onto the sofa in the cozy den on the second floor of Kit's brownstone. "I can only imagine the access such an event could provide."

The band's performance from the cafe livestreams over the Sonos as the girls spread out over Kit's kitchen bar. "No one would ever notice we were even there," Margeaux points out. She and Amaka exchange a glance.

"I'm thinking it too," Estrella says as she texts Marina.

Marina's reply comes back within a minute:

Just another hour!

"In Marina time that means at least two hours. Let me text Hugo to be sure."

His reply comes even faster.

We'll never leave!!! I hate Alfonso. We'll be lucky to all stay out of jail tonight.

"If we take an Uber and stay only long enough to make five important contacts, we can be back in ninety minutes," Amaka says.

All three look to the ceiling, listening for Adisa, who's in a guest suite on the fourth floor.

"He is a sound sleeper," Amaka says.

• • •

"Okay, this is it," Margeaux says. "Not quite what I expected, though. Edgier."

The street is dark and deserted. No signs of a party. The Uber drives away.

"This is not it," Amaka argues as the single streetlight overhead makes a sound like an angry bee and burns out, leaving the girls in a pitch black.

Margeaux looks at her phone. "Oh. My bad—my finger must've slipped. I entered East 191st Street instead of 19th Street. I should've suspected once we passed the park. No harm, we'll just get the Uber back. You know, they say New York has become one of the safest cities in the world."

A low rumble cuts through the dark.

"Who is there?" Amaka calls out.

The clouds part, and the half-moon illuminates the street. The rumble turns into a growl that comes from a pit bull; its teeth bared. The five men with the big dog don't look friendly, either.

Estrella steps in front of her friends. "Can we help you?" She puts on a brave face.

"We're about to get raped and murdered," Margeaux whispers.

Amaka nudges Estrella and murmurs, "Your kung fu—do it now."

Estrella mentally assesses that she can take maybe two of the men, but there are three more men. And the dog and all its teeth to consider.

A man with a teardrop tattoo on his cheek steps in front of the dog. He holds a gun. "Give us all your shit."

Amaka and Margeaux breathe heavily behind her. Estrella fights the urge to throw up as she silently prays to Mary of Guadalupe for a miracle, then takes her wallet from her backpack and hands it to the man with the gun. "Give them your money," she instructs the other girls.

Estrella recalls the first lesson of her training in kung fu—avoid conflict first and fight only when all other options fail.

Amaka and Margeaux hand their wallets to Estrella, who has to force her hands not to shake as she passes them to Tattoo Face. The dog lunges at her, getting so close she can feel its spit on her thigh.

"You have our money. Now go," Estrella says.

The men don't move. Neither does the gun.

"Where is the Uber?" Margeaux whispers through her tears.

"I said give me *all* your shit. You can start with that watch, pretty girl," Tattoo Face says to Amaka. "And you, with the pink hair: give me that ring."

Margeaux fiddles with the small emerald ring on her right hand. "It's been in my family for eight hundred years."

"Give it to him," Amaka hisses as she divests herself of a diamond-studded Rolex and the enormous diamond studs in her ears.

Margeaux cries as she hands Estrella her ring.

Estrella only wears the slender bracelet Hugo made for her. She hands it over as she silently curses herself for not thinking to somehow use it to help them.

Tattoo Face steps closer. He touches Amaka's hair, then pushes her into the bricks of the dirty building behind her and begins to unbutton her blouse.

Amaka jams her knee into Tattoo Face's groin. He screams out, high-pitched, and his friends laugh. He cocks back his arm to punch Amaka, but Estrella blocks his punch with one of her own and then snaps back his head with a spin kick. He drops to his knees as his gun clatters along the broken sidewalk.

Four more guns point at Estrella.

Tattoo Face crawls to his gun and rises slowly. "Take all these bitches."

"Not today." Nikki Kong's calm voice cuts through the momentary silence before a knife slices the air and plants itself in Tattoo Face's shoulder. His gun jumps from his hand again. Nikki snatches it before it hits the ground and fires a bullet into the thug next to him. He drops his gun; Nikki grabs it, too.

Estrella back handsprings at the criminals, her final rotation knocking the third thug over like a bowling pin. Amaka points the gun that skids toward her at the fourth man. Nikki shoots the fifth man's gun out of his hand, leaving a bloody hole in his palm. The dog launches itself at Nikki. She flips into the air, and the dog slams into the bricks, knocking itself unconscious.

Estrella, Nikki, and Amaka train their guns on the battered thieves. Margeaux sinks to the dirty ground, her body shaking uncontrollably.

Estrella looks to Nikki, wondering where she came from. Nikki keeps her eyes and gun locked on the battered men and dogs.

Amaka approaches the man who holds her jewelry, her gun clutched in her steady hands. "Get on your knees," she says. He does. She cocks the gun and holds it to his forehead. "Return our jewelry and our wallets."

His hands shake as he hands the objects to her. Nikki shoots each man in the knee. The men release a chorus of howls while Nikki empties the guns of their bullets, then wipes the guns clean with her black jersey blouse. She lets the guns clatter to the street.

"Get in the car," she says.

"What car?" Estrella asks.

An Uber pulls up.

"This never happened," Nikki says as she runs off into the night.

• • •

The Uber driver makes a turn onto Broadway, where groups of tourists laugh along the late-night streets of Midtown Manhattan.

"How in the hell did Nikki Kong find us?" Estrella whispers. "I'm finding out tomorrow, I know that much. No way that was a coincidence." A familiar face on the street catches Estrella's eye. "Holy shit!" She pushes Margeaux and Amaka low into the seat, as she peeks out one eye.

Through the candlelit windows of a Fifth Avenue hotel lounge, Estrella's mom and William Hamilton sit together on a piano bench. Linda's fingers run over the keys as Bill moves even closer to her. Nelson Hamilton and Marie Washington, Louis's mom, sit forehead to forehead at a far table, and at the bar, Dr. Mather, Kit, Coach, and Babatunde congregate. Also at the bar, Senator Clay and Dixon Duplessis are in animated conversation, waving their hands as they talk, while Goldie and Dr. Anderson smoke cigarettes at a corner table, both their mouths moving at once.

Estrella and her roommates stay ducked down until the Uber pulls up to Kit's brownstone. "That was close," Estrella says, as they creep to the kitchen, where they gather around the marble breakfast bar. "If any one of the adults at the bar looked out the window into our Uber at that exact moment, we would've been busted."

Footsteps clack though the foyer.

"We're home!" Marina's cheerful voice dances through the shadowed mansion. She glides into the kitchen with Amare, Nicolas, Hugo, and Alfonso.

Alfonso heads straight to the refrigerator. "There's nothing in here. Hey, baby brother, why don't you hit up Uber Eats?"

Hugo taps on his phone. "I hate you and I hope you starve to death."

Alfonso laughs.

Adisa comes down in his pajamas. "Did I hear Uber Eats? Try the Thai food restaurant on 74th." He sleepily regards Amaka and her friends. "Sorry about your boring night."

Estrella, Margeaux and Amaka exchange glances. No one says a word.

...

Boxes of Thai food spread out over the coffee table in the den upstairs. The girls speak in whispers.

"Was she following us?" Margeaux twists her emerald ring around her finger.

"Why?" Estrella asks.

"Maybe it has something to do with Mystery School," Amaka replies. "Who knows what's really going on in there."

"Maybe she was in the area," Margeaux says, then, "Nah."

"Thank God she *was* there," Estrella says.

"We could've died," Margeaux says.

"Next time, *I* will determine our course," Amaka says, her eyes pointing at Margeaux.

"It was an honest mistake," Estrella says. "It could've happened to any of us."

"Not me." Amaka replies. "I have never made a mistake. By a miracle, Nikki Kong appeared and saved us. We are safe now, and we have our jewelry, and those men will never be the same again. From now on, they will think twice before they judge who is mighty and who is weak." She puts her hand over Estrella's. "You showed courage. I will not forget."

"Forget?" Margeaux says. "Only in a case of PTSD, perhaps. I will always remember how brave you *both* were. And, until the end of my days, I will sing a song of gratitude and praise for Nikki Kong, no matter how or why she found us there."

...

Sifu Chang bows; Estrella and ten other students bow back. Estrella can hardly bend to bow, she is so sore from both her training to test for her stripe, and her fight with a street gang a few hours ago.

She sneaks a glance at Nikki Kong, who shows no emotion whatsoever, her face placid as a deeply frozen pond, eyes entirely focused on Sifu Chang.

Black robes flowing, his wizened face radiant, Sifu Chang speaks.

"Now you are true martial artists. The true martial artist is not motivated by emotion or desire, but by the attainment of moral excellence. From the crane, we learn grace and self-control. The snake teaches us suppleness and rhythmic endurance. The praying mantis teaches us speed, the tiger, power and tenacity, and from the dragon, we learn to ride the wind."

He is *paraphrasing Kwai Chang Caine from* Kung Fu, Estrella says to herself. She saw that episode just last week.

"To be one with the universe, you must find your true path and follow it." His robes follow him as he glides across the room. "So, what is your path, you wonder. Why are you here? The mind is a fertile garden. It will grow anything you wish to plant. Do wars, famine and disease exist? Do lust, greed and hate exist? They are man's creation, planted by the dark side of his nature. Madmen ruled by fear—they hold the same seeds you do. Look at the landscapes of terror they grow from the seeds they sow. We have no good without an equal capacity for evil. So, what do you wish to plant? What is your purpose here?"

Sifu Chang holds them all in his magnetic gaze. "Fear is the only darkness. It will knock on your door; it will wake you at midnight. It will ask you to plant its seeds. A clear conscience never fears midnight knocking. So, we must know this, for our conscience to be clear: what is my purpose? Why am I here?"

OCTOBER

Vision Quest

Breath like the ocean fills the room. Estrella counts her breaths—inhale, exhale, belly expands, belly empties. She peeks out from one partially closed eye. Marc and Christophe's knees finally fall open in a true lotus pose, and everyone's backs are perfectly straight—quite a change from the first class five weeks ago.

She looks instinctively to her left.

Tatiana's crystal blue eyes stare straight at her. Estrella cannot look away. Her temples begin to pound, her circulating blood sounds like a pile driver in her skull. The blue of Tatiana's irises becomes darker, the sounds in Estrella's brain louder.

Estrella gulps in a breath; the taste of metallic blood surges into her mouth. She shakes uncontrollably, a sheen of sweat breaks out on her forehead. She tries to call on the name of Jesus, as she's done to ease her childhood nightmares of evil, but the words don't come. She can't scream, can't move.

Like a voice from a well, words sound inside her mind. *Shanti, shanti, shanti. Peace, peace, peace.* The pounding in her temples calms and she stops shaking. Waves of peace soothe her stomach, her breath deepens.

The gong rings three times.

"Alright, kids, come on back. Be here now. Open your eyes." Dr. Mather puts down the mallet that struck the still ringing gong. "Today we're going to take the second half of class to begin discussing one of the primary mysteries of Mystery School. We'll get to that in a minute. First let me say, good job! You have successfully sat here and done nothing, three days a week for five weeks, three hours at a stretch, just sitting and breathing. Do you know how hard that is? It's basically you and the Dalai Lama who can do it. Take a moment to acknowledge that you all have strength of body and mind that was heretofore unknown. Maybe there's more to come. Who knows?"

The Mystery Schoolers share smiles of pride.

"Good, we're all acknowledged. Let's move on," Dr. Mather says. "Today we're going to begin a discussion, which we'll approach from many different angles throughout our academic year, and which you'll keep exploring for the rest of your lifetimes, whether any of us wants to or not. We're talking about what might even be *The* Mystery. We're talking about good and evil."

A prickle of excitement moves through the class.

"Okay. Thoughts, anyone?"

"Who is to say where good begins and evil ends? It's all so relative, isn't it?" Tatiana says, folded gracefully on her red pillow.

Amaka bursts out, "Me! I can say what is good and what is evil. It is good to feed a hungry child. It is evil to steal food from a hungry child. It is good to heal a broken man. It is evil to beat a man until he breaks. Even idiots can see this."

Tatiana fake smiles at Amaka.

"Maybe it's not so simple," Octavio says. "What if the child lives a miserable life of poverty and depravity? Isn't it better to take his food and give it to someone who has a chance to contribute something to the world? And the broken man: what if he beats his wife and makes everyone around him miserable? How can we draw simple lines in a complex world?"

"It has to do with intention," Louis says. "Like voodoo. The power is there, and you can do anything with it. But you have to make a choice. Do you want to cast a light spell or a dark one? I'm with Amaka. We know the difference, but maybe we lie to ourselves about the choices we're making."

"The lies we tell ourselves, that's the evil," Christophe says. "If you're going to beat a man, don't tell yourself it's because he's a lout when really it's because you want to take his money and his wife."

"Is it good and evil, or just karma?" Marc asks. "The Buddhists say we work it all out in the end. We live each life and learn a little more each time. Eventually, we all get there, though we suffer along the way."

Zaharia quotes the Quran. "'It is possible that you dislike a thing which is good for you, and that you love a thing which is bad for you. But God knows, and you know not.' Baqarah 2:216. "We must give ourselves completely to God. Only then can we be free from evil."

"What if you don't believe in God?" Evan asks. "I don't. I don't even see good and evil; I see ethics. We all have to live by a certain moral code. We probably all want to do so-called evil, at least sometimes, but we play by the rules so we can all get along."

"Are you saying that good and evil is a question of managing the drives of our primal human nature?" Nikki asks. "What about the equally powerful drive to kindness? Don't we arrive again at an essential duality?"

"There is no duality. The many forms that God takes are but illusions—a game that God plays for its entertainment. We are all one pulsing goodness. It is when we lose our connection to the oneness that we hurt ourselves and others," Shabad says.

"Evil comes from pride," Princess Sylvia says. "Thinking that we're better than anyone else. Pride gives us an excuse to be cruel to one another."

"It's a slippery slope, isn't it?" Margeaux asks. "You're just doing your job, trying to make a decent living, and the next thing you know, you've ordered twenty tons of poison to be dumped into the sea because it's company policy."

Estrella speaks. "It's the devil. I've felt him in my dreams. He makes us do the horrible things. He tells us the lies. Only God can protect us from him."

• • •

"Hey, um, Nikki?" Estrella lengthens her steps to catch up to Nikki, who glides across the Glouton greens seemingly unhurried.

Nikki faces Estrella, her face unreadable.

"Um, yeah, well," Estrella says, as she looks around. "I mean, like, what happened the other night? Thank you, of course, but... Were you just in the neighborhood or something?"

Nikki remains still for a solid minute as Estrella shifts her weight from one foot to the other. Suddenly, Nikki gets very close, almost pushing Estrella backwards. "If your sister had done her job, we wouldn't be having this conversation. All I will say is that prayer is powerful. Especially coming from you. And now the conversation is over. Never speak of this again. To anyone." Nikki turns her back and glides away.

• • •

"That's all she said?" Margeaux asks, the dining hall filling up around them. "I wonder what she meant about Marina. And the prayer."

"I did pray for a miracle that night," Estrella whispers. "But I have no idea what she means about Marina. I definitely think we should keep this to ourselves. Nikki Kong scares me."

"Of course we will keep this to ourselves," Amaka agreed. "We participated in a crime, though our cause was just."

"You scare me a little, too, Amaka." Estrella says. "I really thought you were about to pull that trigger."

Amaka smiles. "There is power in fear."

"Charming," Margeaux says. "Chem Lab has me afraid. Thank goodness Evan's been tutoring me. But off I go." Margeaux pushes from the table.

"I'm going that way," Estrella says as she gathers her plates. "You coming, Ms. Machiavelli?"

Amaka wipes her chopsticks clean with a baby wipe she pulls from her purse, and motions to Adisa, who sits at the next table. He rolls over the case that holds her laptop and books. "I am no Machiavelli," she says. "I am a Medici. I am not the writer of the book—I am its subject."

• • •

"Sukha!"

"Gaudium!"

"Joy!"

"Alegria!"

The filtered water in the dish before Estella and Shabad organizes itself into beautiful structures under the microscope, like crystals or snowflakes. The Mystery Schoolers burst into merry laughter.

"Okay, so when we said the neutral words like dog, dish, Saturday, school, the water molecules didn't do much. But now, with the Sanskrit and Latin words for love, peace, joy, and beauty, the water almost dances into these beautiful shapes—even in English and Spanish. Frickin' awesome!" Estrella says as she sips on an iced mocha that makes her sweat a little.

Shabad takes a long drink from his reusable water bottle.

"What's up with all those bad dreams you have about the devil?" Shabad asks. "Pretty intense, what you said in class yesterday. You've got to stay more focused on the positive."

"Why? I'd rather be honest," Estrella replies.

"Because The Cosmic is good—that *is* the truth. You need to know that. Especially you."

"What do you mean?"

"Because…" Shabad looks deeply into her eyes, then takes another drink. "Because you're too young to be so jaded." He looks away. "Like Zaharia. She's a year older than you, though. Do you talk to her?"

"Yeah, she's awesome. She and Amaka are really close—they're both pretty militant about politics and they both basically worship Raeesa Gajani."

Shabad lights up. "Wow. So cool. Like, she has so much depth, like how she quoted the Quran? And her eyes are so beautiful."

"Oh—you *like* her. I'll tell her how awesome you are," Estrella says. "You should ask her to homecoming."

"But I'm a Hindu. I mean, I don't care about that, but maybe she does. I know my mom does."

"Whatever," Estrella says. "I'll find out. It would be her loss if she's too into her religion to go out with you."

Shabad smiles. "Alright, let's get back to it. Time for the bad words."

"*Odium!*"

"*Dvesa!*"

"*Krodha!*"

"*Ira!*"

Shabad and Estrella gleefully shout out the Latin words for anger and hate. Estrella shouts one in English. "Cruelty!"

The pretty shapes of the water scatter into chaos.

"Wow," Estrella says, to Shabad, who shares her look of sorrow. "It's painful to watch that."

"See what negativity does," Shabad replies.

The growl of a Jaguar breaks the silence.

"Marina!" Estrella says, gathering her things. "My sister. She's taking me home for the weekend so we can plan my stupid quinceañera." Estrella looks out the window; Marina blows her a kiss. As she does, the water molecules in the dish transform from their chaos into new, beautiful shapes—like crystals shining in the sun.

...

Lupe pokes his head out of the open back window, his tail wagging so hard and fast it smacks against the leather seats like a bass drum. Estrella touches the tip of her nose to his. "You look so old," she says to him, petting his gray head.

"He *is* thirteen," Marina says. "Pretty old for a big dog. Anyway, are you ready to plan your quince? Pull up the spreadsheet."

Estrella pulls out her phone and opens an elaborate Excel document that includes columns for guests, flowers, catering, the dress and the cake.

"Mrs. Ruff is making the cake, right?" Estrella asks. "I can taste that almond flavor just thinking about it. You asked for extra icing, right?"

"Of course!" Marina replies.

Estrella tosses her phone into the backseat next to Lupe. "Then I'm good—you guys can figure out the rest."

"But you're coming home to plan it," Marina says.

"Whatever. I just want to come home. I need some rest."

Marina laughs, a twinkle of windchimes. "I'm sure you're exhausted from all of the fun you're having with your friends."

"It isn't all just fun and making friends, though Margeaux and Amaka are, like, definitely my best friends. And my friend from Mystery School and kung fu, Nikki Kong. Do you know her?"

Marina's happy face falls for a second. "I don't think so. Why do you ask?"

Estrella considers the consequences of telling Marina about the night in the Bronx. Estrella and her friends could get into serious trouble for sneaking out, and Adisa could get into even worse trouble, since he was supposed to be in charge. Estrella bites her lip. "Just, I thought maybe you knew each other, no reason."

"No, never met her," Marina replies, avoiding Estrella's searching eyes. She turns up the music, and the highway flies by, leading them back home.

• • •

"I've got hot tea inside. Zandra made some cookies," Linda says as she hugs Estrella with all her might. "You grew since Parent's Weekend, I swear!"

A car drives fast up the street with loud death metal blaring from its speakers. It screeches to a stop in front of the Chavez cottage.

Nadine jumps out the passenger door. "Bye Colt." She leans back in the open window, makes a V with her peace fingers and sticks her tongue through. "See you tonight!"

Linda rolls her eyes and sighs in disgust. "Why does she have to be here?"

"She's Estrella's best friend," Marina says, overly cheerfully. "Now where are those cookies?" She ushers Estrella, Nadine, Linda, and

Lupe through the front door of, where, for the next forty-five minutes, they discuss Estrella's quinceañera, until Estrella noisily pushes her chair back from the table. "I can't take anymore! Who cares? We'll just have the mass, have a dance, cut the cake, and go home."

"And what about the flowers, and the guest list and the transportation, and the party favors?" Linda says, her voice just below a yell.

"What difference does it make?" Estrella shouts. "It's not like my dad will be there to put the shoe on my foot!"

The room gets silent.

"You know your uncle Cesar is so honored to take your father's place," Linda says, her voice softening.

Estrella's heart rate slows. "Whatever. He'll probably be drunk like he's drunk every day of his life."

"Will Uncle Cesar be able to handle the bizarre and suspiciously sexist task of putting a high-heeled shoe onto his niece's foot, or will he have a drunken epic fail?" Nadine puts on a sports-announcer voice as she reaches for another cookie.

"Really?" Linda says. "You're going to make fun of my culture and my family under my own roof?"

"I have an idea!" Marina chirps. "How about just one item on the list, and we can finish the rest of the agenda tomorrow before you go back to school?"

"Fine," Estrella says. "Better than watching Mom and Nadine fistfight."

"What about your escort? I know you've made some friends in Mystery School." Marina's light green eyes sparkle with insinuation.

Nadine chuckles. "That's right, Estrella—you got guys all over the place. John Kaminsky for the hometown crowd and Marc Hamilton for your fancy friends. You could have a band called Estrella and Her Apostles. Me, I'd go all in on the billionaire. Honestly, you're wasting time. I'd be pregnant with his baby already."

Linda glares at Nadine before she turns her laser eyes on Estrella. "I thought you were just going to homecoming with Marc as friends."

"We are. It's not like we've even kissed yet."

The front door bangs open. Dorothy and Toto, Zandra's little dogs, precede Alfonso, who holds hair clippers. "Marc Hamilton? Kit's nephew? Such a douchebag," he says, as he sits heavily down at the table. "I heard he got too stoned and crashed his brand-new car the day he got it. Can't handle his weed."

"You're the douchebag!" Estrella shouts.

Alfonso puts on an English accent. "Please, father, may I borrow the Learjet? I smoked so much weed that I can't tell my head from my ass and now I'm late for polo." He laughs at his own joke.

"That's not true!" Estrella shouts. "Where did you hear that?"

"The Internet," Alfonso replies. "You're supposed to be so smart but you don't have my knowledge, little cousin."

"Enough!" Linda snaps from the head of the table. "Stop instigating, Alfonso. Why are you here?"

"I need Marina to tighten up my hawk." He checks his phone and suddenly strides back toward the door, dogs following. "Give me a minute."

Linda rolls her eyes, then turns them to Estrella. "I thought John was your boyfriend. He's a very nice boy. I see his mother at mass. She told me John asks about you all the time. I swear he could be the president one day."

"He's not my boyfriend, Mom. I don't have a boyfriend, I'm not even fifteen yet. I think I'm going to play the field for a while so when I settle down, I know I've had my fun," Estrella says, looking to her mother for a reaction.

A look of sheer horror takes over Linda's face. "Your father would roll over in his grave if he heard his daughter talking like a common whore."

Marina's permanent smile dissolves. "I think that's a bit over-stated, Mom. Dad was pretty open-minded, as you know, and Estrella has a right to explore her options. It shows her strong spirit. Not like me, falling in love all the time, like a fool. She has her own mind."

Linda glares at Marina before she turns back to Estrella. "You listen to me," she says through gritted teeth. "Either you have no boyfriends and no dates, or John Kaminsky. My daughters are good Catholic girls, who wait for marriage. If I hear anything else about Marc Hamilton, Mr. Party Boy, I will take you out of Glouton immediately. I don't care what Kit or anyone else says."

Marina looks at her feet as Nadine stifles a laugh. Both she and Estrella know that Marina hasn't waited for anything in her life except the season's new Chanel bag.

"Whatever. I can have as many boyfriends as I want," Estrella says, ensuring she gets the last word on the matter. "Anyway, I asked John, but he can't get the weekend off from school, so Hugo can do it, or Alfonso," She checks her phone for more information about Marc's weed accident.

"Definitely Hugo," Linda and Marina say together.

...

Estrella's wide-open bedroom window lets in the fresh October breeze and the sunset that melts across the New England sky. Estrella and Nadine lie together in Estrella's single bed.

"So, you've got to like one better than the other one. Who is it? Future President or Rich Party Boy?" Nadine asks.

"He's not a party boy," Estrella replies. "He's a Buddhist, and he's funny, and he volunteers once a week to be a Big Brother for some kid in juvenile detention. They work on writing together."

"I guess the answer is Marc? I told you, you should get pregnant with his billionaire baby and be set for life."

"Gross, Nadine. He hasn't even kissed me yet, anyway. We almost had a chance in the city during Parent's Weekend, but then Marina had to go do something with Alfonso and..."

"And what? What happened in the city?" Nadine asks.

"You better not tell anybody," Estrella says.

"You know I'm loyal," Nadine replies. "Despite all my other qualities."

"Margeaux entered the wrong address for a party, and we ended up in the Bronx and there were these guys with guns and a dog. I thought we were going to die—I never prayed so hard in my life. They robbed us and then one of them was going to do something to Amaka, but she kicked him in the balls, and he tried to punch her, but I blocked his punch, and then all of the sudden this senior girl from class, Nikki Kong, showed up and she kicked all their asses— even the dog. I mean, I did help too. And then when I asked Nikki about it, she wouldn't tell me anything except how Marina didn't do her job watching me and that my prayers are powerful.

Nadine listens with her mouth hanging open then says. "Holy shit! Thank God you guys are okay. You mean, this girl, Nikki, just shows up out of nowhere? And why did Marina leave you?"

"Yes, exactly, I'm telling you—Nikki showed up out of nowhere, like she was following us. Marina had to go and break up a fight with Alfonso and some politician's son. But that was the only thing Nikki said, that Marina should do a better job of watching me. I didn't even know she *knew* Marina, and Marina says she doesn't know her, but I think Marina's lying to me. And the thing about me and the prayers."

From downstairs, Linda's voice rises into the room. "You know this isn't what we had planned for over twenty years now!" A moment of silence, then, "He's lying to you. You know who he is! You're the one who told *me*. Privatizing even one more part undermines all of our work." More silence, then Linda's barely tempered scream. "You're going to regret this, Kit. On your deathbed, this decision will be the one that haunts you."

The phone hits the kitchen wall.

"Damn, I didn't know she got pissed like that," Nadine says.

"She doesn't," Estrella replies, her heart pounding.

"You think it's about the Water Trust?" Nadine asks.

"Probably. My principal told me that my mom and Kit were having a disagreement about something. They'll work it out. They've argued before over the years, but it's always turned out okay."

"If they can't figure it out, we're all screwed," Nadine says. "We all need water, not just the rich people. But you know how rich people are. They always get what they want, no matter what."

· · ·

Crisp leaves crunch beneath Estrella's Converse. Magnificent reds, oranges and yellows stretch from the trees, the air carries the scent of apples. She revisits the angry words between her mom and Kit. "Please help them, Mother Mary of Guadalupe," she murmurs as her phone vibrates: a text with a link from John.

Thought you'd find this interesting. Keep your eye on Speaker Miakoda Grace. I hear she might run for President.

Estrella recognizes the women in the photo from a fundraiser Kit and her mom made her attend last year. The article discusses the combat mission that cost Miakoda one of her legs, her role as the first-elected female chief of her tribe in Washington state, and the eco-legislation she has been championing as the Speaker of the House in congress, including her work with the Water Trust.

"Hmmm," Estrella says to herself. "Kit made a good investment by fundraising for her."

Another text—this one from Marc.

Where are you?

She jogs up the library steps for their private, semi-weekly study session as a cheerful bird whistles from the branches of Methuselah and the sun beams through the crystal blue sky.

Marc smiles when she approaches. "Just in time to work on Latin." He holds up a Starbucks cup. "Your favorite—extra whipped cream."

Estrella pushes send on a message back to John, a happy face emoji, then tosses her book bag down next to Marc.

"*Salve!*" She says as she takes a sip of whipped cream. "*Gratias tibi.*"

"*Enim, Domine.*" Marc replies.

Estrella face turns puzzled. "Latin is open to a lot of translation because it's such an old language, but you literally just said, 'For, Lord.'"

"Anything for you, is what I meant. It was the closest I could get," Marc replies as he puts his hand on Estrella's knee and gazes into her eyes. He leans toward her; his eyes begin to close. Estrella closes her eyes too, ready to feel the touch of his lips.

"There you are!" Tatiana's throaty voice rings through the quiet library.

Estrella opens her eyes to find Tatiana and Christophe standing before them.

"Hey Tat!" Marc says. "Wassup Tophe? We were just studying Latin. Come help us brush up."

Christophe and Tatiana join them while Estrella angrily flips through her books.

"*Auribus teneo lupum!*" Christophe announces, as he pinches the tops of each of his ears.

Estrella looks up from her books and smiles. "You have a wolf by the ears, Christophe? Sounds dangerous."

From out of nowhere, a fly buzzes straight into Estrella's eye. She awkwardly swats it away as Tatiana laughs. Estrella stands up from the table to leave, fighting the urge to thrust her fingers into Tatiana's long, white throat.

Marc grabs her hand. "Where are you going so soon?"

Tatiana takes Marc's other hand and looks into his eyes. "Remember the Trevi Fountain in Rome? Your dad found that adorable man to take us all around. What were we, like twelve? He said Trevi came from a Latin word. Wasn't it beautiful? We jumped in together with all our clothes on, even though we weren't supposed to."

Estrella pulls away from Marc. "'Trevi means 'from the Tigris.' That's where they got the stones for the Fountain: the Tigris River," Estrella says, taking big steps away from her billionaire classmates.

"The Tigris River. That's where I'd like to drown Tatiana," she mutters to herself as she sends John another text—three big hearts.

• • •

Glouton's humble chapel sits on the outskirts of campus. Estrella searches the empty chapel, dollar in hand, to buy a candle and pray. She looks for the holy water to touch to her forehead, but sees none, so she makes the sign of the cross, curtsies, and walks to the front of the church.

"No candles here, either—what kind of church is this?" Estrella mutters to herself. "And no knee benches in the pews? Oh well."

She kneels on the cold floor and prays. "Dear God, please be with my family and all my friends. Please help the whole world, the animals and the water." She chants *pacem, veritas, spero, gratia*: the Latin words for peace, truth, hope and grace.

She is almost finished with her prayers when the image of blue eyes and blonde hair closes up her heart. "But not Tatiana. *Fata* on her. *Fata*. Doom. Let her doom please be that she misses homecoming. Just for one night, I want Marc all to myself. Amen."

. . .

"What is on your face?" Amaka, sashaying out of the bathroom in her flowing purple silk robe, stops short at the sight of Estrella.

Estrella touches her face then looks in the mirror. "Holy shit!"

Pus-filled, red blisters burst from her face and neck.

Amaka steps away from Estrella. "You must see a doctor now. You look contagious." She goes back two more steps. "Who wants that all over her skin for homecoming? How will you heal in two days?"

"It looks like chicken pox," Margeaux says, taking a look. "I had it when I was ten."

"Oh good," Amaka says, visibly relaxing. "I had them when I was a baby. I hear they are very painful if you get them when you are older."

Estrella scratches her skin as she pulls on a hoodie and dark sunglasses. "I'm going to the infirmary. Maybe there's a pill they can give me that'll make the spots go away before homecoming."

"I'll come with," Margeaux says.

"Do not let anyone see you," Amaka says. "Hurry."

. . .

"Chicken pox," Nurse Nolan says.

"I was right!" Margeaux says. "Maybe I should consider medicine instead of music. Much more helpful of a calling, isn't it?"

"You can't do a thing about it," Nurse Nolan continues. "Go back to your room and rest. You'll have to email your teachers for your assignments. It's good your roommates have already had it, or you'd have to be completely quarantined. Still no leaving your room for ten days."

"Can't I take a pill or get a shot or something?" Estrella asks, scratching her neck. "What about Homecoming?"

Nurse Nolan laughs. "I'm sorry, but you can't be near anyone for the next ten days. Let your professors know to send your assignments." She holds open the door for them.

Estrella holds back tears on their way back to the dorms as Margeaux says, "Could I be the next Medical Medium? Like Bill himself says, '*It is not in the stars to hold our destiny but in ourselves.*'"

"Bill who?" Estrella asks, irritably. "Whoever he is, I could choke you both right now. The stars, or God, or probably actually Satan— that's who gave me these horrible, itchy spots on my face."

"Bill Shakespeare," Margeaux replies, when suddenly, Tatiana stands before them, radiant from her daily run, her skin flawless. "That looks awful, Estrella," she says. "What is it? Chicken pox? And with homecoming this weekend. Don't you just wish it were me?"

. . .

Bright red blisters cover Estrella from head to toe. "Why do they call this the chicken pox?" she moans to herself. "It should be called the dragon pox, or the raging, fire pox." She slaps her hands to stop them from scratching, then cues up another Bruce Lee movie on her laptop—the fourth one in a row.

Makeup and hair dryers litter the room from an hour earlier, when Amaka and Margeaux dressed for homecoming. Estrella gets another box of cookies from the mini fridge.

As she reaches into the box, she focuses her swollen eyes through the window. Marc, Tatiana, Christophe, and Evan walk across the quad together, dressed in their homecoming clothes.

"What a dick!" Estrella says through her blistered lips. "Just because I told him to go without me doesn't mean he needed to go with her!" She bursts into tears and picks up the phone to call Marina. As soon as Marina picks up, Estrella tells her the whole story through her tears.

"That Tatiana sounds awful, hermanita," Marina says, her voice soft with sympathy. "But you have to remember that men are kind of dumb and some girls are just mean. You deserve better." She listens to her sister's sobs until Estrella's tears are dried streams on her cheeks.

Finally, Estrella says, "Put the phone near Lupe's ear so I can talk to him. At least I know he loves me unconditionally.

Marina hesitates. "Um...Oh, honey, I don't know how to tell you this..."

"Tell me what?"

"We had to put Lupe down last night. He was ready."

"What do you mean, put him down?"

"Lupe's gone from the earth, but his spirit is with you now more than ever."

Estrella sobs renew mercilessly. "You...You killed my dog?"

"We didn't want to upset you," Marina replies. "You're already missing homecoming. Lupe's spirit is still alive, hermanita. He'll always be with you. I promise."

Nicolas' voice filters through the phone. "Marina, I'm starving! Let's go or we'll be late."

"Just go to dinner," Estrella says, "I know it's your one-year anniversary. You've been gushing about it on Facebook all week. Have fun." Estrella throws the phone on the bed.

Images of Lupe and Marc swim through her mind as fresh tears stain her cheeks. The room grows dark with early evening shadows. She checks her phone. Nothing.

She falls into a deep sleep.

· · ·

The bear, Islid, lifts her blood-darkened muzzle from the carcass of an elk. Nearby, a wolf paces, waiting. An orange moon illuminates the pines. Islid roars at the wolf, who moves backward but continues to pace around the carcass.

An owl flies in low and says, "I'm trying, but who knows where he might be." *Estrella steps closer to the owl. The owl looks at her sideways.* "You've got your intel, but it's not complete, obviously; maybe the activation hasn't happened yet, but I know he's not here, not yet anyway, and I'm looking at Estrella right now, so she's still safe, and the boys under control. You've got the Trust, what more can we do? Maybe you're reading too much into the cards tonight. It wouldn't be the first time."

Estrella reaches out her hand to the owl.

· · ·

Estrella's fingertips touch the glass of her dorm room window. She blinks her sleep-swollen eyes, looking past her reflection in the glass. Dr. Mather's eyes look into hers. He drops the cellphone he holds.

"Somnum!" he shouts, waving his hand.

Estrella flies from her feet and slams into the wall.

. . .

Wolves run through the forest in a pack. One of the wolves is Lupe. He licks Estrella's palm, then rejoins his pack.

Dr. Mather descends from the midnight sky; an ocean manifests in the distance. A whale opens her mouth, Dr. Mather walks in. Crystal rain-drops fall from the purple sky. Estrella collects the crystals in her palm, washing her face with them. Voices call from the forest behind her. The ocean fades, the forest disappears. A dull light shines.

. . .

"Estrella! Estrella! Oh my God! She is dead!"

Amaka's voice wakes Estrella from her dream.

"Did you see the wolves?" Estrella asks, touching a bump on her head. "And all the crystals? Where's Dr. Mather?"

"She is alive, but her brain is damaged," Amaka says. "I have seen this before."

"'Wolves?" Margeaux asks. "*Wolves play over her back and live in her crystal womb...*'—it's a line from the Vaska Popa poem I read just this morning. Bizarrely apropos." She joins Amaka to help Estrella off the floor. "And I've no idea where Dr. Mather might be, he wasn't at the dance." Margeaux looks at Estrella more closely. "Holy shit! Your chicken pox is completely gone!"

Estrella touches her face. "No bumps!" she says, then hobbles to the bathroom mirror. The raging, pus-filled sores are gone. Not even an outline remains.

Amaka says, "This is Yoruba witchcraft."

Margeaux says, "Alien visitation."

"Why was I on the floor," Estrella asks, "and how did my chicken pox heal so fast? I had this dream—I was washing my face with crystals. I think Dr. Mather was there. I can't remember. Oh my God, I hope I don't have brain damage. There were the wolves and this whale and Dr. Mather. And Lupe."

Estrella bursts into tears. "They put Lupe to sleep!"

Louis pushes in the door and pokes his head in. "Amaka, are you alright?" He steps all the way into the room. "Strella, what's wrong?"

"Leave us alone," Amaka says. "Estrella has lost her beloved pet."

"I'm so sorry, Estrella," Louis says. "I just wanted to check on Amaka. She had a bad experience at homecoming."

Estrella dries her eyes. "Wait. Amaka, your hair is messy, and your makeup is smudged. That's weird."

"Amaka's date went too far. Louis had to pull him off her," Margeaux says.

"I could've handled it myself," Amaka says. "Just one text to my guards inside."

"Well, he had your hands pinned and you couldn't send that text," Louis replies. "Maybe next time you and Mr. Oxford Abuser can just go it alone." He turns to leave, but steps back into the room. "You know, Amaka, a man in love can only take so much abuse." He straightens his tie.

"Then it is not true love," Amaka replies.

Louis sighs. "I hear you. And I'm still here. You looked beautiful tonight, Amaka. The prettiest I've ever seen. Sorry about your dog, Estrella." He walks out the door.

Margeaux breaks the silence Louis left behind. "Quite a homecoming I'd say, what with the impending sexual abuse, the broken-up fistfight between Louis and Ambibijo, or whatever his disgusting name is, and then finding Estrella passed out on the floor with no spots. And her dream and my poem of crystals and wolves."

...

The morning sun breaks through the autumn chill. Estrella, her twelve Mystery School mates, and Dr. Mather file past Mrs. Franks, Glouton's bus driver.

"This is it! The Vision Quest," Sylvie giddily whispers to Estrella, as the bus takes a left and then a right into the forest.

"I can smell the trees," Estrella whispers back. "There it is!" A large, sturdy cabin sits at the end of the dirt road.

The students are up before Mrs. Franks opens the door.

A floor to ceiling stone fireplace stretches the length of one wall in the main room of the cabin. The boys go to one of the bunk rooms, and the girls drop off their backpacks in the other. They do all this in silence, then meet back in the main room where the fireplace yawns open, gray and cold. The Mystery Schoolers sit, cross-legged in front of it, shivering. They breathe and shiver, their collective breaths like clouds in the large room. Estrella clenches her fists to keep her fingers from going numb.

Finally, Dr. Mather rises and speaks.

"Well, class, here we are. Sink into the truth of this place. It's cold. You're hungry. The forest that surrounds you is vast and dangerous. We brought no provisions, though we do have running water. All of your phones are back at Glouton, and there's no service here anyway. Everything we need to survive this night is in these woods. Now go. In addition to the list of herbs I gave you, you'll want to gather some firewood, too, as well as any other food you can find." He holds up a box of matches. "And we have fire, should you bring us anything to light." Twenty-six eyeballs look greedily at the matches.

Stiffly and silently, the students venture out into the forest. Estrella hoists her empty backpack onto her shoulder and studies her list. As Amaka passes her, she whispers, "All of this, I do for my people. I have already broken a nail, and there is not even a mirror in the bathroom. Now, I brave these woods. I will return victorious." Her petite frame disappears into the woods.

Estrella watches Margeaux disappear into the oranges and reds of the autumn forest—a pink bird. The fallen leaves and pine needles crunch beneath Estrella's feet as she picks juniper berries, edible mushrooms, nettles, wild geranium, and yarrow root. She stumbles into a chestnut tree laden with fruit. "Awesome! My prayers to St. John Gualbert of the Forest worked!" She picks the nuts off the tree's lower branches. "Now I can make something really good."

She reaches for a big, furry chestnut on the earth below the tree. The forest floor cracks. She looks into a pair of gold, slanted eyes.

A skinny young wolf holds its ground before her.

The wolf comes closer. Estrella feels a flood of love in her chest, like she's meeting an old friend. She reaches out her hand.

The wolf comes closer, then gazes beyond Estrella to where Margeaux approaches. The wolf's tail disappears into the forest.

"A wolf! Like your dream and the poem," Margeaux says.

An animal scream cuts through the quiet. Estrella doubles over in pain.

"Are you alright?" Margeaux asks.

Estrella straightens. "Yeah. That was weird."

"I'm lost," Margeaux says. "Glad I ran into you."

"You're a genius when it comes to some things, like music and poetry, but you have one messed up sense of direction. "

"No, I don't…" Margeaux begins to say, but is stopped short by Estrella's incredulous look. "Oh, you're right. Couldn't tell my left from my right until I was thirteen. And, of course, that episode in the Bronx."

"That was an honest mistake," Estrella replies, putting her arm around her roommate. "Luckily, I've always had an excellent sense of direction, so follow me." They hike back to the cabin together, their backpacks brimming with the treasures of the forest.

Amaka approaches when they near the campground, twigs sticking out of her hair. She dusts off her Dolce and Gabbana jeans. "If this is what I must do, then I must do it." She takes a package of wet wipes from her back pocket. "Nature is a nightmare. I think a spider landed in my hair. Find it and take it out."

Estrella laughs, then searches Amaka's perfect bun of hair when Tatiana, Octavio and Evan emerge with a young deer strung on a large branch. The ends of the branch rest on Evan and Octavio's shoulders; the deer's throat hangs open. Blood colors the tree limb where the doe's ankles and hooves are tied to the branch. Evan and Octavio smile widely. Their hands are stained with blood.

A knife, its blade wiped clean, shines from Tatiana's belt. "Put it between those two trees. Like a hammock," she tells the boys.

Dr. Mather, his backpack stuffed with apples and green herbs, enters the clearing. When he looks at the elegant shape of the hanging deer, his shoulders drop, as if in defeat.

Estrella observes the deer, the blood, Evan and Octavio's bright smiles, the knife. Her shoulders droop as well.

Marc and Princess Sylvia approach, each with heavy backpacks; Sylvie sees the deer and bursts into tears. Amaka takes her hand and guides her to the cabin.

Evan practically floats over to his cousin. He points to the deer. "Tonight, we feast!"

Marc shakes the hand that Evan offers him. "Wow. I never saw you as the hunting type."

Octavio cuts skin from flesh, the wet, slicing sound echoing through the clearing.

"Actually, Tatiana killed it—she's such a badass—but we tracked it together." Evan wipes his hands on his jeans. "Want to help us dress it?"

Marc looks at Estrella. "No thanks, man. Buddhism. I'm a vegetarian now."

Evan laughs. "That's ridiculous. It's the food chain. We're at the top. And some Buddhists eat meat." He saunters off to help Octavio. "I can't wait to tell my dad!"

Christophe unites with the group, three rabbits hanging from his belt.

"I'm not a Buddhist or a vegetarian," Louis says, joining Evan. "This is like staying the weekend with my country cousins." He rubs his hands together gleefully. "I thought we were going to starve. I'll help you dress it, Evan, and I'll help you eat it, too."

• • •

The flames of the fireplace flick shadows on the Mystery Schoolers. Dr. Mather incants, *"Shanti, shanti, shanti."* Outside, a waterfall splashes into a river. *"Shanti, shanti, shanti."* The licks of fire inside harmonize with the bubble of water, making one sound.

Each breath carries Estrella deeper into the void. She is not sleeping, nor is she awake. The herbal tea they drank after dinner relaxes her muscles. The rhythmic pulse of her heartbeat is a drum.

•••

Her father, Islid, the wolf cub, crystals, water, a whale. Estrella holds a pink crystal sword; she effortlessly flies above the clouds, where Marina floats next to her. Sunlight and water descend from Estrella's crown, flow from her fingers. Dr. Mather swims in the blue, cold ocean. On the shore there is an elephant, the shape of a star radiating from her forehead. Margeaux and Kit sit at a table, playing cards with a monkey, a lavish garden blooming around them. Shabad and Nikki meditate cross-legged on a carpet of crystals with Babatunde, Amaka's father. Sylvie picks a flower. Marina points over there.

Human-shaped, glowing red lights approach from across the sea. Pure evil emanates from the molten bodies who brandish black crystal swords and knives. The drumbeat of Estrella's heart quickens as the evil red bodies multiply. Now there are thousands of them. They advance, a cockroach army, leaving landscapes of fire, drought, and blood.

Estrella, a river of blood flowing beneath her, mounts the wolf and rushes forward, into the evil, her sword outstretched.

•••

Estrella flutters open her eyes. Around her, the cabin fills with starlight. Fireflies, butterflies, bees, and doves fly in through the cracks of the windows and flit around the room. "I am dreaming?" she asks herself as she levitates a few inches off the ground and keeps rising. Dr. Mather positions his hands over Tatiana's head, and murmurs a few words, then leaves the ground, flying up next to Estrella. He reaches into a pouch on his side and anoints her forehead with oils. Shabad, Nikki, and Sylvie fly from their seats, circling Estrella. They become transparent, their forms dissolving and leaving behind bodies of clear crystals, like sunlight through the crest of a wave. Estrella looks at her hands; they are crystals too.

Suddenly, Estrella becomes the night sky. Below her, the wolf howls, the night birds sing, the waterfall tinkles like a piano. The river roars, the stars shine with more light. She can see the whole earth. Rain falls in the deserts. In the vast oceans, the remaining whales sing together, their sonic waves waking the men and women on submarines, who laugh and spontaneously hug one another.

She blinks, and she's back in the cabin.

Dr. Mather, Shabad, Nikki, and Sylvie are on the floor, cross-legged, clothed in their human skin. The cold floor pierces through Estrella's jeans.

The starlight dims, the fireflies, butterflies, bees, and doves fly back out the window.

"Fiat voluntas Dei."

Dr. Mather's words wake Estrella from her dream.

"You have your visions," Dr. Mather says to the Mystery Schoolers. "Now go to sleep."

•••

Estrella wakes first. Alone, she goes into the fresh, earthy woods.

"Great time last night," she hears someone say.

"What?" Estrella asks, turning toward the voice to find a chipmunk peering back at her.

"You heard me," the chipmunk says. *"What a party."*

From a nearby branch, a bluebird sings, *"Cloudy today, rain tomorrow!"*

"What. The. Hell?" Estrella asks as, in the far distance, a mountain lion says, *"Breakfast,"* then a squirrel screams.

Estrella freezes after each step she takes, after each voice. "Have I lost my mind?" she whispers to herself. "Is this how it happens? Schizophrenia? Maybe I'm having one of those dreams where you think you wake up, but you're still sleeping." She pinches herself, hard. "Ouch!" she says, the red marks inflaming her skin.

She reaches for a pretty stone. It zooms into her hand, as if her fingers were magnets. She tosses it away, then reaches for a stick. It, too, zooms up to her palm. Then another stick. A whisper sounds inside her mind. *Agape*; the Greek word for love.

The yellow eyes of the young wolf look into her own. She reaches to him, he nuzzles her palm. "*Agape*," Estrella replies as her heart expands.

Footsteps crunch through the leaves behind her. The wolf runs, his gray fur winding through the woods.

"Wow! Was that a wolf?" Marc asks.

Estrella nods, her eyes still following the beast.

"Estrella, can we please talk? I mean, this is getting out of hand—you've been blocking my calls since homecoming."

Estrella drops the stick in her magnetic hand. "Uh, yeah, I guess," she says as she keeps her ears trained on the sounds of the forest.

"Look, I *swear* that Tatiana is just a friend. I just walked over to the dance with her. I didn't even dance with her, or anyone. I didn't even dance by myself. I missed you the whole time."

"Oh, yeah, Homecoming," Estrella says.

"Yeah, Homecoming. I missed you the whole time. I've been missing you. Like, I really, really like you. All I do is think about you. But you need to give Tatiana a break. I can see from the way you look at her that you don't like her. And I get it—she can be a lot. But she's had some pretty traumatic stuff happen in her life. She almost drowned when she was six; it's a miracle that she's still alive." Marc keeps on. "And don't tell anyone, but when she was ten, she accidentally killed her shooting instructor during a lesson. She's pretty messed up from it. It was horrible—can you imagine?"

Marc puts his hands on Estrella's shoulders. "But forget her. I like being with *you*, Estrella. It's not just because you're beautiful. It's like you're my closest friend." He throws his arms around her in a hug. "And I know the trauma you've experienced too when you were a baby. And I *never* want you to feel unsafe or abandoned ever again in your life. I will always be here for you, I promise."

"*Agape*," Estrella says, returning his embrace. "I understand. We're all just doing the best we can."

He hugs her tighter, then takes her hand. "*Agape*—that's like brotherly love," he says. "I'll take it. For now." Their fingers entwined, they return to the cabin grounds.

The first person they see is Tatiana.

Her blue eyes are red, her skin a dirty green, her hair slithering black snakes, spiders, and worms. She smiles, flashing corroded yellow fangs.

Estrella looks to Marc, but he doesn't seem to notice that Tatiana is a monster. "What's up, Tat?" he says, inching closer to Estrella, and tightening his clasp on her hand.

Tatiana ignores him, and says to Estrella, "You look different, Estrella. Not the same person you were, are you? I guess that goes for all of us. This Vision Quest has been a pretty intense experience, don't you think?"

•••

Estrella scans the bus on the ride back to Glouton. Tatiana licks her thick gray lips with her long, cracked tongue. Estrella looks away, her eyes finding Dr. Mather. His eyes shine like crystal moons, like in her vision. He winks at her! She quickly looks away, to the left. Mentally acknowledging that she's hallucinating and telling herself to keep her cool.

Marc scoots closer to Estrella on their shared seat. "So now that we're best friends again, don't you want to ask me to your quinceañera?"

"How do you know about that?" Estrella asks, removing her hand from his.

"Amaka."

Amaka puts on her headphones and looks out the window.

"I'll deal with you later, Miss Big Mouth," Estrella says to the back of Amaka's head.

"It's too late now—the damage is done," Marc says, smiling. "You either have to invite me or have a good reason why not."

"Okay, you can come," she sighs, "but it's going to be weird, and my family is crazy, so don't say you weren't warned."

Louis moves to the row in front of him, pulls Amaka's speaker from her ear, and says, "Want to be my date?"

"No."

From the back row Christophe says, "Your family can't be any weirder than you are. And your cousin, Hugo, is nice."

Everyone laughs, which makes Estrella feel loved somehow.

"Okay, you're all invited. You too, Mrs. Franks. My mom wants me to invite more people anyway. Marina had like four hundred people at her quince."

Amaka practically stands. "Four hundred? Ha! For my bat mitzvah we had more than a thousand guests. Billie Eilish performed. Vera Wang personally designed my dress."

Estrella laughs and chatters with her friends about celebrities and other light matters the rest of the bus ride back to Glouton, choosing to temporarily forget the voices of the animals, Dr. Mather's fingernails, and Tatiana's slimy tongue.

. . .

"Do you think Dr. Mather drugged us or something? It's clear something happened to us at the Vision Quest," Margeaux asks from her perch on her messy bed.

"So what if he did?" Amaka replies as she brushes polish on her nails. "I am not complaining."

"Why would you complain? I just watched you do seven backflips in a row at the football game. That Glouton just won," Margeaux replies.

"Yeah. It's like they're a different team all of a sudden," Estrella chimes in, putting down the cookbook Zandra sent her. "Louis threw, like, a fifty-yard pass that Evan actually caught in the endzone, and Christophe jumped four feet straight up off the ground to make an interception. So maybe there was some sort of natural steroid in the tea? Mixed with natural Adderall?"

"And look at this," Margeaux says as she picks up her guitar. She runs her fingers over the strings, eliciting beautiful sounds. "I've been struggling with this piece the whole semester, and I've been able to perform it flawlessly since the night we returned."

"And Octavio aced his chemistry midterm even though he's been failing the class," Amaka says. "Quite unusual."

"And I read a whole hundred-page chapter on Stoicism in like fifteen minutes," Estrella says, then whispers, "And yesterday, in Mystery School, while I was meditating, I felt my bottom rise up off the pillow. Within a second, I was cooperating with gravity again, but that was super-weird."

Amaka raises her eyebrows. "You were levitating?"

"Just for a second. In my vision too—I was levitating, really, I was kind of flying, and so were Dr. Mather, Nikki, Sylvie and Shabad. It was like I had two visions. In the first one, there was the wolf cub, and this evil army, and a whale, and Kit and Marina were reading these cards with a monkey. Then it was like I woke up but I didn't, and that's when they were flying and I became part of the sky, and saw the whole world, like, all of it, all at once. And when I went out into the forest the next morning..."

"Yes?" Amaka says. "What happened the next morning?

"...I kind of pulled a stone and a stick toward my hand, like with magnetic suction," Estrella replies. "And I heard the animals talking. And Tatiana looked like a monster."

"Hmmm," Amaka replies. "Perhaps you are hallucinating."

"I saw a whale and a map, too!" Margeaux exclaims. "And Kit was there, reading tarot cards."

A chill raises the hair on Estrella's arms.

"It all started before the Quest, I swear," Margeaux continues, "With your dream about the wolves and the Popa poem, and your spots disappearing! It all puts the 'mystery' in Mystery School, doesn't it?"

Estrella nods, then asks Amaka, "What was your vision?"

Amaka studies Margeaux and Estrella for a full, silent moment before she replies, "Victory."

Estrella and Margeaux wait for the rest. "Victory about what?" Estrella finally asks.

"I keep my visions to myself." Amaka pulls on her Prada puffer. "Shall we go to dinner?"

* * *

"Congratulations on winning your first game," Amaka says to Louis. "Your performances were unusually excellent."

"And all your backflips," Louis replies. "You've really taken it to a new level."

"The piece you played for us on your guitar was very advanced," Zaharia says to Margeaux. "I thought you had been struggling with it before...the Vision Quest."

Everyone makes eye contact as they eat.

Marc clears his throat. "My vision was so beautiful," he says. "Trees. All these trees."

"Mine was beautiful too," Zaharia says. "But it was more a feeling of love than a vision really. And Raeesa Gajani—she was there."

"I dreamed of my future wife," Evan says. "She was so pretty. I think she's foreign."

"You would dream of a girl," Estrella says to him.

"I saw prisoners being set free," Louis says. "All of them, redeemed. Pretty cool."

Christophe growls and raises his hand like a claw. "Bears, wolves, and water, so much water. All the water, or more ice, like crystals."

Margeaux says, "More wolves and crystals. And me, I visioned a whale and Kit Hamilton, of all people."

"Our visions are irrelevant compared to what has happened to us," Amaka whispers. "We are all thinking it: we were drugged with an unknown chemical compound and now we are superhuman."

Everyone leans in closer.

"So, I have thought," Christophe whispers. "And we need to find the compound and patent it."

"Really?" Louis says, "You think we were drugged? No way. No way a drug like that could be kept under wraps."

"Maybe we just got to the next level, you know, with all the meditating and stuff," Evan looks around to make sure no one at another table is listening.

"I myself am sure that's what it is," Zaharia says. "All drugs have side effects, and I feel none. Just more power, more focus."

"You don't feel them yet, you mean," Marc says.

"Exactly what I was thinking," Estrella says. "The worst may be yet to come."

Shabad whispers, "We were not drugged. The same happened to last year's class—it is an effect of our training. But we must remember our most important lesson—as always, silence."

Everyone at the table pulls away from the circle, mouths closed.

. . .

The gong rings out three times.

Thirteen sets of eyes look at Dr. Mather.

"Silence," he says. "Silence, as we know, is the essence of Mystery School. Silence is the foundation of any powers we may perceive in ourselves. Silence is the glue that binds us. Silence alone secures our direct connection to the Divine. Silence reveals the deepest of mysteries. As we grow more powerful, we come to learn that this silence must extend even to the thoughts we think, for there are those who may be yet more powerful and can access our unspoken words. With enough breathing and silence, you may become one among them."

Dr. Mather waits for his words to settle, then continues. "In my many years of teaching this course, I have not always successfully trained my students to be moral, but I have always trained them to be silent. All except one student: Mike Hammersmark. He was a talker."

The class waits for more.

"Okay, that's it. Class dismissed."

. . .

By the time Estrella makes it to lunch with Amaka and Margeaux, she knows all about Mike Hammersmark. "He graduated from Glouton twenty-five years ago. Went to Yale," she says.

"But then he died," Margeaux replies.

"The best information was in a *New York Times* article. His Yale roommate found him dead in his bed one morning. The autopsy couldn't identify a cause of death," Amaka says. "The headline of the piece was titled, "*Yale Student Dies of Mysterious Causes.*"

• • •

Pure-bright sun blinds Estrella as she comes out from mass. "Not much of a mass," she thinks to herself. "No incense, no Latin, no kneeling. But the minister does call for peace and understanding, and who can fault that?"

Ever since she learned about Mike Hammersmark, Estrella's been praying for the strength to keep her mouth closed.

Her phone lights with a text from Alfonso.

Got him.

There's a link to an article from the *Associated Press*:
"*Drug Lord Behind Bars, Awaiting Trial.*"

Gabriel Estrada is still in Mexico, but he's going to be extradited to the U.S. in four months.

"Hah!" Estrella whispers. "Now Alfonso will kill him, and I can watch and say, like in *The Princess Bride*: 'My name is Estrella Chavez. You killed my father. Prepare to die.'"

She closes her eyes to say a quick prayer, "Dear Mother Mary of Guadalupe, please give me forgiveness in advance, for me and Alfonso both, for when he avenges the death of my dad." She reflects on the young minister's words from the church service just moments ago, from the Psalms. *"The Lord is gracious and compassionate; slow to anger and rich in love."*

"Good news, Little Star." Tatiana materializes in front of Estrella.

"Were you waiting behind a bush?" Estrella asks, the peaceful feelings from church abandoning her. "And don't you have some children to frighten somewhere?" Estrella steps around the tall, slender blonde.

Tatiana moves back in front of her. "My daddy's going to be the president. He's announcing it tomorrow. Soon he'll be the ruler of the entire world. Isn't it wonderful?"

Estrella recalls the oversized man from Parents Weekend, who she's seen on TV. He owns the Mets and about half the real estate in New York. He'd always seemed like an idiot to her. He recently made a comment about the inferiority of "the darker races," which didn't go over at all well with his baseball team whose darker players outnumber its lighter ones by a factor of three.

"Good for you," Estrella says, determined not to let Tatiana bring down her mood. She again tries to step around the creamy-skinned fashion plate.

Again, Tatiana blocks her path.

"You know, my daddy loves me more than anything in this world. It was my idea for him to run. I know he can win. He's what the people need. They're tired of all the boring, old politicians like the ones the Water Trust controls. The people want a change. They deserve it."

"The election is over a year away, so we'll see what the people want, and I highly doubt that it's your douchebag dad."

Tatiana looks down into Estrella's eyes. "You can remember today as the day that the first crack appeared in the armor you think protects you—you, Kit, Marina, your mom, and all the rest of you."

"I can take a lot, but no one talks about my family," Estrella says, raising a finger to push into Tatiana's chest. But this time, Tatiana steps out of the way.

• • •

"Nadine!" Estrella's hometown best friend shimmies out of an Uber with Ramon, the quinceañera dance instructor.

"So, this is Glouton," Nadine says, looking around the grounds. "I don't see the lives of the most rich and powerful people on the earth forming, but I did just get here. But look at that tree!" Nadine points to Methuselah, whose branches flicker with the golds and reds of autumn. "That's the prettiest one I ever saw."

"Are we done with our appreciation of nature class?" Ramon asks. "Let's get this dance taught. I have a quince in Queens to-night, and I still need to shine my shoes."

• • •

"Where are you going? Are your feet made of lead? You must lead with your heart. Your legs are your heart, your arms are your heart." Ramon passionately corrects every misstep of the young dancers.

Margeaux, Evan, Amaka, Louis, Christophe, Sylvia, Zaharia, Shabad, Nadine, Octavio, Estrella and Marc, the members of Estrella's last-minute court, awkwardly prance around the Glouton gym, trying their best not to laugh.

"As embarrassing as this experience is," Estrella whispers to Nadine, "I know my actual quinceañera will be far more humiliating."

• • •

"Why does Nadine get to dance with Octavio? Who decided that?" Margeaux asks Estrella back in the dorm.

"My mom thought since you and Evan are friends, you'd want to dance together."

"Please let Mum know that, in the future, I prefer Octavio Kong whenever he is an option. For any reason," Margeaux replies.

"He is hot." Nadine blows a strand of green and blond hair from her forehead. "But Colt Holloway is hotter. So are his friends. They're coming up tonight, so you can get an eyeful."

"I hope to God I didn't hear that right," Estrella says. "What do you mean they're coming up here tonight? Not Colt Holloway and his thieving friends. He's such a dick. I don't even know why you stay with him."

"I love you, Estrella Chavez, but you're too serious," Nadine says. "You need to have some fun."

"We can't do anything fun here," Estrella says. "This is Glouton. They have really strict policies about going out, and we need permission for guests."

Amaka, towel wrapped around her head, emerges from the bathroom. "What guests?"

"Some of Nadine's hot friends. We're going to have a bit of fun tonight," Margeaux replies.

"No, we're not." Estrella glares at Nadine. "Uninvite the boys immediately. What did you think we would do anyway?"

Nadine replies, "Christophe and Tatiana are hosting a Day of the Dead party in Christophe's room. You have to wear black. I need to borrow something."

"Girls aren't allowed to go into the boys' dorms after six without permission," Amaka says.

"How did you know about this event and I didn't?" Margeaux asks. "I'm usually the first to know about a party."

"Octavio said you all were too young, but I told him we're older than he might think, if you know what I mean," Nadine suggestively waggles her brows.

"I know exactly what you mean." Margeaux replies as she rifles through her closet and pulls out black clothes.

"I don't know why I'm watching you pick out clothes for a party we're not going to," Estrella says. "I'd rather walk on broken glass than go to any party Tatiana is throwing. And I don't want to get into trouble, which we will if we go tonight."

"I am not going to jeopardize my hard-won opportunity at Glouton by breaking rules," Amaka says. "Though, I *do* have a black Givenchy jumpsuit I had tailored just this summer."

Margeaux looks Estrella up and down with a calculating eye. "Maybe we could ask Alexis. Estrella, haven't you been helping her with her calculus homework? Time for payback. Our resident assistant is known to be easily blackmailed and bribed."

"I'm not asking Alexis for anything," Estrella replies. "Because we're not going."

Nadine tackles Estrella to her bed and sits on her. "Oh, come on! What else were you going to do? Study? It's Saturday night. Day of the Dead. You always have a big party back home."

Estrella pushes Nadine off. "I thought we'd watch a movie and hang out. And only study for a few minutes," Estrella hears the boredom of her plans as she speaks them. All three girls look at Estrella—they hear it, too.

Estrella sighs and walks out the door to the left, toward Alexis's room.

...

Nikki Kong's straight black hair, free from its braid, falls past her knees in a silky sheet. As she ushers the freshman into Christophe's senior suite, Nadine says, "You must be Octavio's sister. I can see the resemblance, but you're even more gorgeous than he is."

Nikki smiles—the first Estrella's seen. "You must be Nadine. Thanks for the men." She winks, motioning to Colt and three older boys—*not* dressed in black, despite Nadine's instructions—who drink cocktails with Tatiana and Marc.

Estrella silently prays that no one goes to jail or gets kicked out of school tonight. She almost prays that Tatiana will fall off her barstool but remembers the chicken pox.

Octavio and Christophe make drinks for three senior girls; Evan sits at a card table with Louis and more seniors. Motown plays on the stereo, the lights are low.

The girls stand in the middle of the room for a moment, unsure where to mingle first. "I think I'll let Octavio pour me a whiskey and then let's check out your men," Margeaux, the most used to partying, says to Nadine. "I heard Christophe's father had to pay handsomely for his son to have a bar in his suite. Might as well make it worth the investment."

"I fold," Louis says as soon as he sees Amaka. He tosses down his cards then crosses the room. He tries to kiss Amaka's hand, but she yanks it away before his lips touch her skin, so he bows instead. "Imagine my gratitude and surprise to see my little black dove here before my very eyes. What can I do to make you more comfortable? You look stunning, by the way."

"The jumpsuit is Givenchy, of course it is stunning," Amaka says. "If you want to make me comfortable, you can get away from me."

"I cannot believe how rude you are to Louis, and that he still likes you anyway," Estrella says.

Louis just laughs. "I'll start with getting you a glass of water. So, I'll go away, but I'll come back."

Marc makes eye contact with Estrella as he quickly rises from the bar, leaving Tatiana with a sour lemon look on her face.

"I can't believe you're here." He tries to kiss Estrella on her cheek, but she turns her head away, and he kisses air.

"I had no idea there was a party," she says. "You never told me."

"You said you were going to hang out with your friend. And I didn't think you liked to do things like this. You know—you're very focused on your studies." Marc touches her hair, "Don't be angry with me."

"If you don't want me to be angry, you shouldn't piss me off so much."

Marc smiles. "Note taken. Can I offer you a drink? I mix a mean cocktail."

Estrella's phone buzzes with a text from John.

Thinking of you. Sweet dreams.

"Who's that?" Marc glances from Estrella's phone into her eyes.

"My mom," Estrella lies, looking away. "I'll have a really small drink, thank you."

Tatiana's raspy laugh sounds from the bar.

"Actually, I'll just have water," Estrella says. "Better keep my wits about me tonight."

. . .

"Straight flush." Nadine lays her cards on the table. "Ha! And you thought I was bluffing."

Nadine and Tatiana have piles of chips in front of them. Amare and Adisa, who joined the party at ten, watch from the periphery.

Adisa inches his chair closer to Nadine's. Estrella can tell he likes her. Colt can tell, too; he's glaring at Adisa.

"You are one hell of a poker player, I'll give you that," Tatiana says as Nadine scoops the chips toward her open purse.

Octavio takes ten hundred-dollar bills from his wallet and gives them to Colt. "You're right, she won three hands against Tatiana. How is she at football?"

"Not bad," Colt says. "I know a guy in the city if you want to make some moves tomorrow. Five hundred minimum. Straight win-lose, no spread."

Margeaux opens a window and lights a cigarette. "I'm tired of the humiliation. I'm out. I've lost over seven hundred dollars in the last hour—even daddy will question that."

Louis pushes away too. "Defeated by a couple of blondes. You girls are wily."

Evan sways when he gets up.

"Don't give him any more drinks," Christophe says to the room as he pushes away from the table, too.

"We better go," Estrella says. "Alexis gave us a midnight curfew."

"What're you talking about? Things are just getting good," Nadine says, counting her money.

Tatiana sneers at Estrella. "Too bad you little girls have to go back to your house mommy."

Amaka gives Tatiana a dirty look as she joins Estrella by the door.

Margeaux closes the window. "I suppose I have to show my face to my house mummy. Anyone have a mint?"

Christophe gives her an Altoid.

"Alexis has to see your face, too, Nadine. You're not getting me into trouble tonight." Estrella turns to Colt. "Shouldn't you be heading back with your friends?"

"They've had too much to drink," Nikki says from the corner of the room, where she and Colt's friend, Leon, are absorbed in conversation. "They can stay here tonight."

"Where can we all meet up later?" Nadine puts back on the high heels she kicked off earlier.

"It is the Day of the Dead. I know where we can have some real fun." Tatiana holds up a small plastic bag.

Marc examines the baggie. "Are those what I think they are?"

"Yep," Tatiana says, popping one in her mouth. "Mushrooms. Hallucinogens." She looks at Estrella. "From the Latin, *hallucina-tions*—to wander."

"I'm out of here," Estrella says, heading toward the door. "Meet me in the hall," she says to Nadine. She and Amaka immediately leave the room; drugs are mandatory suspension. They wait in the darkened hallway until Nadine and Margeaux join them.

"We're meeting in the graveyard outside campus." Nadine says. "We're going to give the dead their day."

...

"Is that what it's like, being a senior here? You just do whatever you want?" Margeaux asks, back in their dorm room.

Everyone else on their floor is asleep. Nadine and Margeaux stand by the door, ready to leave for the graveyard.

Estrella seethes. "I swear, I will kill you Nadine and never, ever speak to you again if you get caught. And you suck, too, Margeaux. I can't believe you're going to a cemetery to do mushrooms with my worst enemy."

Margeaux justifies her disloyalty. "It's not just Tatiana. All the cute boys will be there, too."

"Neither the living nor the dead will cause me to be suspended from the school I spent the past eight years relentlessly studying to get into." Amaka puts on her sleep mask and climbs into bed.

"Oh, relax," Nadine says with a roll of her eyes. "Nothing's going to happen. This place is like Disneyland. Pay your money, ride the rides." She and Margeaux each swallow a mushroom. "Let's go talk to the dead."

...

Bodies float from the blood-soaked sand of the bright, blinding desert. Their eyes glow red, and red light shines through the bullet holes that articulate their rotted flesh. They march through the church doors.

On the altar, a robed priest holds a hunting knife. He cuts the head from a deer, throwing its spasming body to the floating dead, then rips away the skin to drink the blood and eat the muscle down to the bones.

"Necare, necare, necare," the priest incants. He wipes the bloody knife on his robes as the shadow nailed to the cross behind him screams. The priest laughs, a feminine jingle of bells. "Come on, Nadine, it's not so bad."

The priest pulls back the hood of her robe. Tatiana's pure blond hair tumbles out.

Nadine slides off the cross, holds the ears of the deer, and looks deeply into its voided eyes. "A time to every purpose under heaven," she says.

...

Estrella bolts up from bed. She clutches her heart and checks her phone. It's 4:07 a.m.

The doorknob turns. Margeaux and Nadine creep into the room, their eyes glassy. They smell like night wind.

"Where have you been?" Estrella hisses.

Margeaux falls onto her bed as Nadine climbs in next to Estrella. "Talking to the dead. They got a lot to say."

NOVEMBER

Quinceañera

or

You Never Know When Death

Comes to You—or How

"Oh, Mary, my mother, present my offering and my life to the Lord, be my model of a valiant woman, my strength, and my guide. You have the power to change hearts; take mine then and make me a worthy daughter of yours. Amen." While Estrella recites her prayer at the altar, she peeks out from the corner of her eye.

Marc sits listening three rows from the front of the cathedral, just behind her family. Estrella smiles, replaying the memory from last night, when he showed up under her window, in a sombrero, singing off-key in Spanish with the traditional mariachi band.

From her other eye, Estrella steals a glance at Kit as Latin floats from Father McGuinness's lips. Estrella touches her throat, where the delicate, gold heart that Kit gave her right before mass rests on her clavicle. It opens into a locket, but there's nothing in it yet. Kit told her not to remove it—ever. She said it would keep her safe and be a reminder of how much Kit loves her.

When she gave it to her, she also said, "I must tell you something very important later, about the library and some other things. About your father, and Dr. Mather, and Mystery School. Find me as soon as you can get away. I need to be the one to tell you." Estrella turns her eyes as far as she can without moving her head. Kit checks her iWatch discreetly.

Mass proceeds until Linda crowns Estrella with a tiara, one of the few family heirlooms to survive the fire, and Cesar puts the high heels on his niece's feet, a job meant for his brother.

Father McGuiness presents Estrella to the congregants.

Now she is a woman.

· · ·

Colorful streamers, flowers, balloons, candles, and crepe paper butterflies saturate the grand ballroom of Kit's mansion. The music is loud, the punch flows.

Estrella hugs Marina, tears brimming in Estrella's kohl-lined eyes. "You did an awesome job! Why was I so against this? It's been one of the best days of my life." Tears bloom in Marina's eyes too.

Across the room, Nadine points out various members of Estrella's family and friends from the neighborhood to Amaka, Margeaux, Sylvie and Zaharia. Estrella tunes her ears toward them, using a power she's developed since the Vision Quest.

"There's Nicolas Salvatierra," Nadine says, pointing to a man across the room who talks with Kit. "He's from one of the fancy families in Mexico, like Linda was before she married Victor Chavez, and her momma disowned her."

Estrella huffs beneath her breath, "Great—stupid Nadine Bigmouth telling everyone all my family secrets." Estrella listens harder.

"He works for Senator Allister Clay," Nadine continues. "You know, the one who got caught with those strippers?"

Estrella's phone buzzes with a text from John—an emoji of a dancing cowgirl—as her ear catches a throaty laugh. "Tatiana! Why in the hell did I invite her?" She mutters as she moves to stand by Zandra and her friends from bingo to discreetly watch and listen to Tatiana, Christophe, Louis, and the Kong twins, who hang around by the punchbowl.

From her side eye, Estrella notices Kit and Marina approach and introduce themselves to the group. "You must be Estrella's friends from Mystery School!" Marina says. "So nice for you all to come for Estrella's big day!"

When Marina turns to Tatiana, a look of surprise strikes them both. "Don't I know you from somewhere?" Marina asks.

Tatiana holds Marina's gaze. "I can't quite place it, but you do look familiar."

"She runs the PR and marketing for the Water Trust," Kit says. "She's amazing. She put together the entire "Only Water Can Quench Our Thirst" concert in Central Park this past April. She was able to get all the stars to participate and raised over $170 million."

Tatiana says, "A working girl. Noble. I'm sure your father would be proud that you've been able to build a life for yourself, after everything that happened."

Marina's radiant smile almost falls. "Idle hands are the devil's workshop, they say, and *I'm* the one who's proud and blessed that my father gave me so many gifts of spirit. Again, so nice to see Estrella's friends. Have a ball! Kit, I'm going to the ladies room to powder my nose."

"I have to go too," Tatiana says, following Marina.

Estrella excuses herself from Zandra and her bingo friends and moves toward a big flower arrangement outside the bathroom where she pretends to check her phone.

"Do you have to wear Spanx with that dress?" Estrella hears Tatiana ask Marina.

"I should've known that you would slither your way into the party," Marina replies. "You've kept yourself well-hidden, but I'm watching you now. We all are."

"Oh, you can't possibly. And shouldn't you be keeping your eyes on Estrella? We're all watching *her*." Tatiana clicks away on her Jimmy Choos.

"What the hell does *that* mean?" Estrella asks herself as Marina exits the bathroom and alights her worried eyes on Estrella.

"There you are!" Marina says, again all smiles. "Come meet some members of the board. You'll be their boss one day."

"What were you and Tatiana talking about?" Estrella asks as she follows Marina.

"Nothing," Marina replies, as she presents Estrella to a trio of old, fancy women. "And here are three of the best members of the Water Trust!" Marina says, leaving Estrella with the women, and gliding off into the crowd.

As Estrella chats with them politely, she tunes her ears back toward Tatiana, who's head-to-head with Octavio.

"Marina Chavez is the most beautiful woman I've ever seen," Octavio says. "I must know her, or I will die."

Estrella glances his way while she smiles and nods at a tiny woman in a royal blue pantsuit. Octavio's hand trembles and sweat breaks out on his forehead.

"She already has a boyfriend, and you're too young for her anyway," Tatiana says.

"True love recognizes neither rivals nor time," Octavio replies.

Hugo approaches in his tux. "I'm stealing the honoree," he says, then guides Estrella away from the little old ladies, and toward Tatiana, Octavio, and now Christophe. "You have to come with me. He's here—your friend Christophe."

"No way," Estrella replies. "I hate that girl Tatiana—I wish I never invited her! Next time I'll be ruder. Except then Ms. Franks, the bus driver, wouldn't be there, and it looks like she's having a ball." Ms. Franks, wearing a glamorous dress, laughs and drinks with Zandra. "Why do you need me anyway? You already know him." Estrella looks for Marc.

"*Please*? I don't want to do it alone." Hugo leans in. "I swear, I think he may be the actual love of my life. Like I even did a novena, and you know how I feel about the Catholic church."

"If you prayed for nine days, who am I to hold you back from true love? But you owe me. Bigtime." Estrella puts on a fake smile as she nears Tatiana's group. "You guys remember my cousin, Hugo? Nice to see everyone." She avoids Tatiana's eyes.

Within seconds, Christophe and Hugo are consumed in a conversation. Estrella is about to slink away when Alfonso ambles up.

His bow tie hangs open around his neck, his first buttons are undone, and his jacket is gone. He stares at Tatiana for an entire minute. "What's your name, Blondie?"

Hugo breaks away from Christophe, a stressed look on his face, "Tatiana, please ignore my brother. He has no manners, and he has a tendency to cause trouble."

Alfonso steps closer to Tatiana. "Trouble doesn't bother her. She likes it."

Tatiana eyes Alfonso up and down. "How would you know what I like?"

Adisa's rich voice booms from the bandstand. "May I have your attention, please! Tonight, we pay homage to the woman of the hour through hip-hop and song." He raises his glass. "To Estrella Chavez!"

The lights dim as Amare strikes the bongos. Margeaux jumps onstage with a classical Spanish guitar, then Evan picks up a stand-up bass. All of a sudden, Marc is there beside Estrella. He takes her hand and leads her to the dance floor.

Adisa sings and raps a slow song about true love, heartbreak, and redemption, about the light that "shines, shines, shines—a sun, a star, Estrella!"

Estrella can't contain her emotion. "How am I so lucky?" she asks as she dries her tears on the shoulder of Marc's tux.

"And now," Adisa says, the music settling like clouds around the guests. "We limbo!"

The lights lift; the DJ gets back to work. Alfonso and Cesar bring out the long skinny bamboo stick. Christophe goes first, Hugo right behind him. Soon everyone is bending backwards.

What begins as a battle to the finish between Cesar and Christophe is put to rest when Amaka lowers the stick to just a few feet off the floor, bends back in half, and dances through. The crowd goes wild as Alfonso and Cesar lift Amaka onto their shoulders and parade her through the room.

"Hey, let's go get some air," Marc says, escorting Estrella through the side doors of the ballroom. They step into the November night, where the black cold swallows them, the party glittering like a planet on the other side of the door. Before Estrella's eyes have time to adjust, Marc's arms wrap around her back and waist, and his lips find hers.

"I've been wanting to do that since that lunch at Per Se." He kisses her again and pulls her closer, his hand at the small of her back. "Did you get the roses?"

Estrella melts into him. "My house smells like a flower shop."

"Fifteen dozen—a dozen roses for every year," Marc says, kissing her neck.

Estrella recalls the two dozen roses John sent her, but quickly puts it out of her mind. "I hope we can do a lot more of this," she says to Marc, "now that I'm a woman."

Marc massages her neck, nibbles her ear. "Every day for the rest of our lives." He kisses her again, this time their tongues touch, like a dance—they fit perfectly together.

"Dad wanted to be here, but he got stuck in Baha with the storm," Marc says, between kisses. "He told me about how they all hung out together on your ranch in Mexico—your dad, Aunt Kit, even Uncle Bill. He really liked your dad. Check this out."

Marc takes an old, faded photograph from his tux jacket. "It's of my dad and your dad," he says. Seated between the young men, a toddler holds an infant in a baptismal gown. The toddler wears a tiny suit; the infant is plump, with a full head of jet-black hair. "That's us!" Marc says. "Can you believe it? That's the first time we met, when you were baptized. Pretty wild, huh?" He wraps her up and squeezes her tight. "You were meant to rest in my arms all your life."

"This is the best day of my life," Estrella whispers from Marc's strong shoulder. "All of this, everything, is perfect. Everyone is here—you, even my dad, my mom, Marina, Kit." Estrella lifts her head. "Oh, shit, Kit. I was supposed to talk to her about this locket and my dad and Dr. Mather or something."

Marc moves his hand to Estrella's hip bone. She leans into his touch. But an image of Kit won't leave her brain. "I have to go." Estrella kisses Marc quickly on the lips and moves to go inside, but Marc pulls her back into his warm hug.

"Stay with me," he murmurs, but she pushes him away.

"I've got to talk to Kit," she says, drinking in Marc with her eyes then suddenly seeing an image of him at Christophe's Day of the Dead party. "We're going to take a bunch of mushrooms."

Marc sighs. "I'm never going to live that down, am I?"

"Nope."

The moment Estrella steps inside, Marina grabs her with one hand and takes a glass of champagne from a passing tray with the other. "I can't let you out of my sight for a minute. It's time to cut the cake. Were you just making out with Marc, you bad girl? Good thing John couldn't make it, or you would never have a minute to yourself." Marina laughs and kisses Estrella's forehead as Marc sneaks in behind them, straightening his bow tie.

"Wait a minute," Estrella says. "I need to see Kit about something."

Estrella passes the videographer who interviews Evan in a cordoned-off section of the ballroom, then Alfonso, who feels-up Tatiana's bottom while they dance. She looks toward the drink table for Kit—but only sees Octavio, who is looking right at Marina, his hand over his heart and the pain of love in his eyes.

Estrella keeps scanning. Dr. Mather and Dr. Anderson talk, their arms crossed, in a far corner of the ballroom; Yves walks in from outside. A scream cuts through the sounds of celebration.

"Call 911!"

• • •

Estrella runs toward the scream, reaching the patio just ahead of Marina.

Zandra's hands cover her ears as she screams out hysterical, steady shrieks—like a car alarm. Linda kneels in front of Kit, who's slumped in a chair. She slaps Kit's face repeatedly, yelling, "Wake up. Wake up!"

A smashed glass glimmers on the patio stones, a trickle of blood drips from the corner of Kit's lips. Marina runs to grasp Kit's wrist, feeling for a pulse, as she murmurs a prayer.

Dr. Mather and Yves arrive next. Yves takes Linda's hand and gently pulls her away. Dr. Mather stands motionless with brimming eyes. Estrella cannot move. Zandra keeps screaming.

Evan and Mark are among the first wave of guests to run onto the inky patio. They, like the others who soon follow, fall into a shocked, crippled silence when they see Marina ministering desperately to Kit's stiffening body. Wave after wave of guests run from the lights of the party into the wall of silence.

Estrella doesn't realize she has been repeatedly chanting the word "no" until Dr. Mather puts his arm around her and guides her from Kit's body and into the surrounding circle of quinceañera guests.

The thrumming music stops inside; sirens wail. The crowd makes a path for the chief of police, his deputies, the EMTs, and the firemen. The patio illuminates wildly with the strobe of the siren lights.

Chief Morten, a tall man shaped like a bowling pin, throws his big voice around. "Stand back," he shouts to his deputies and the EMTs. "This is a crime scene, and not to be disturbed. Who found the victim?"

Linda steps forward.

"You found this woman here?"

"Yes," Linda replies in a steady voice.

"And no one else was with you when you found her?"

"Just me." Linda doesn't mention Zandra.

The chief paces the patio and comes to a stop in front of Linda. "And what is your relationship to the victim?"

"She is my best friend."

"That's all?" the chief asks Linda. "You share no other connection?"

"Why is he talking to my mom that way, like she's guilty?" Estrella whispers to Dr. Mather, her fingers balling into fists.

Nicolas steps out from the circle of spectators. "Your line of questioning seems to indicate you think Mrs. Chavez is a suspect, and we haven't even ascertained that a crime has been committed."

Chief Morten and Nicolas challenge each other with their locked eyes. The chief looks away first, then begins pacing around

Kit's lifeless body, taking notes on a pad of paper he pulls from his pocket. Sounds of weeping mix with the whispers of the crowd, who shiver in the November cold.

Amaka, her almond eyes taking in every detail, steps forward and points to the back of Kit's coiffed head. "What is that? I can see it from here, and you did not even notice it."

The chief, after donning protective gloves, pulls a tiny black crystal dart, its tip bloody, from Kit's neck. He frowns at the tiny girl. "And who are you, exactly?"

Amare and Adisa step out of the shadows. Amare says, "She is Amaka Abioye. She is entrusted to us."

The chief makes a note on his pad and then addresses the quinceañera party as a whole. "Clearly the party's over. Give your statement and contact information to one of my deputies before you go. Rufus, put on some gloves and pick up that glass."

The gangly young man at his side proceeds with his orders.

As Ms. Franks, the Glouton bus driver, pulls her bejeweled shall around her shoulders and loads into one of the rented party vans, Estrella hears her remark to another of the guests, "One minute, we're under the limbo bar and the next, we're face-to-face with death. Today it was Kit Hamilton, but tomorrow it could be any one of us. Once again, life has exposed its fundamental hitch."

• • •

"It's freezing in here!" Amaka pulls out the elegant Dyson space heater she ordered on the first chilly day, back in October. "Margeaux, you have again left the window open for your nightly cigarette." She warms her hands as Margeaux closes the window. "People were not meant to live in weather suited for polar bears."

Estrella bursts into a fresh round of tears. "Kit loved polar bears! She even dressed up as one for Halloween the year I turned seven."

"Let it all out," Amaka coos, throwing her arms around Estrella. "She was a great woman. Your tears glorify her."

Margeaux awkwardly strokes Estrella's hand. "Can I get you anything?"

"Get her a tissue," Amaka replies. "Quickly, before she stains my coat."

As Margeaux hurries to the bathroom, Estrella lifts her head from Amaka's small shoulder and wipes her tears and nose with the sleeve of her hoodie. "Why didn't I call her more? I loved her so much!" She buries her head back into Amaka's shoulder just as Margeaux brings a wad of toilet paper that Amaka places between Estrella's tears and her Dolce and Gabbana puffer.

"Why would anyone want to kill Kit?" Estrella blows her nose on the tissue and slumps against the wall behind her bed.

"Don't be naive," Amaka says as she makes her way to her own bed. "She was the wealthiest woman in the world, and a powerful political force. Who *wouldn't* want to kill her for any number of reasons? That is why I have guards. Her guard, Yves, should have stayed closer to her."

"Like Amare and Adisa stayed close to you the night in the Bronx?" Margeaux says. "A guard can only protect the willing."

A soft knock sounds on the door. Margeaux opens it. "It's Marc," she says.

Estrella walks out into the hallway, where he holds a single rose. Without a word, he kisses Estrella's eyelids, her tear-stained cheeks, her quivering lips.

"I wish I would've spent more time with her," he says as Estrella wipes a tear from his cheek. "You and Evan are so lucky—you got to see her every day. Just, with Dad, you know, traveling..." Marc leans against the hallway wall and stares into space.

"Have you seen Evan?" Estrella asks. "He won't return my texts. I feel so bad that it happened at my quinceañera. I hope he doesn't blame me in some kind of way."

"He's isolating. But I'll kick in his door if I have to. They were so close. Kit was more of a mother to Evan than Evan's own mom, you know, especially after…"

"Kit told me about how she cut her wrists after his twin died in his crib," Estrella says. "Bill found her. So sad."

"She blamed herself—you know, the baby was the one to carry the family legacy and all that—William IV. Very sad. No wonder Evan's isolating."

They are silent for a moment. "How's your mom doing?" Marc finally asks.

"I know it's hard on her, but my mom never shows her feelings," Estrella says. "Only strength."

• • •

Mary of Guadalupe opens her arms; her robe of roses becomes the sky. Below her, in the desert, the cross on the whitewashed shack catches fire. The fire grows, blazing across the bloody sands. Flames overtake Islid, Lupe, the wolf, Estrella's father, Kit. Everyone burns. Estrella calls to the heavens for rain, receiving only the sound of her echo.

• • •

Estrella wakes, thirsty. She checks the news on her phone while Amaka and Margeaux sleep, trying not to think about her dream.

The Economist has an article on how, because of the long drought, fresh water will run completely dry in the southwestern United

States within ten years, creating tens of millions of water refugees. The entire economy could collapse.

"Can the Water Trust even help with that?" Estrella whispers to herself. She knows they do a lot by keeping the wells and aquifers they own free for people, but they can't make it rain. Estrella drinks the cold water from the mini-fridge guiltily.

Amaka rouses. "You speak of the Water Trust. I have learned from my father that several members of the board have shown an interest in selling off significant land holdings to Water Corp, the Trust's private arm. And that was before Kit was murdered. What's stopping them now?"

• • •

Thanksgiving at the Chavez cottage misses its usual noise. Estrella makes tamales, Linda prepares a turkey, and Marina sets the table just like every other Thanksgiving, but tears fall into the masa and onto the china. Music doesn't play in the kitchen. Appetites are thin, conversations brief.

Linda, Marina, and Estrella wash dishes and tidy the kitchen while they discuss Kit's memorial service the next day, and the reading of the will. They, Dr. Mather, Dr. Anderson, and Yves are the only non-Hamiltons to receive invitations to the reading.

As Zandra hands Estrella a dish to wipe and put in the cabinet, she says, "I hope those two detectives don't come back here and take you downtown again, Linda."

"What do you mean?" Estrella asks.

Linda glares at Zandra. "Not tonight, Zandra."

"Not tonight, what?" Estrella says. "Are you a suspect? Did they question you?"

Marina takes Estrella's hand and leads her to the kitchen table. "Don't worry about this. Nicolas is working with the police and it's all going to be okay. You just stay focused on school and your friends and having some fun."

"Fun?" Estrella spits. "Like that's ever going to happen again. How can I have fun when my godmother was murdered at my quinceañera, and my mom is a suspect?"

"I need you to be strong, Estrella," Linda says, the scar above her left eye more pronounced than usual against her tired skin. "Things may only get worse."

...

"Is this a funeral service or a celebrity fashion show?" Estrella whispers to Marina as she studies the dense crowd of incredibly well-dressed mourners. She recognizes virtually everyone in the immense Upper East Side church from either Kit's house, social media, or DNN.

Linda, Marina, Estrella, Nicolas, and Yves are in the row behind Kit's family. Zandra, Hugo, and Cesar sit behind them. Alfonso has refused to go to any funeral since Victor's.

Dr. Mather delivers the first eulogy, as he is the Nobel Prize winner and therefore the most dignified guest. He can hardly restrain his tears as he speaks of Kit's dedication to the Water, her great love for her family and friends and her generosity. He is followed by a stream of international political leaders, clergy, and her brother, Nelson, who just cries, and has to be escorted down from the altar by Marc.

Finally, Bill Hamilton takes the podium. "I'll keep this brief," he says, "Because Kit hated events like these, and if she were here, and how I wish she were, she would've left an hour ago." Everyone in the crowd chuckles. "I'll share my feelings with a quote from her absolute favorite—William Shakespeare: *In black ink, my love may still shine bright.*" He sighs, wipes a tear, and regally retakes his seat.

. . .

"I'm Rose Ellis, Kit's estate attorney. This is Gretchen Pierre." The woman dressed in sensible shoes and pearls motions to a younger woman dressed almost identically. "Kit was my favorite client and a dear friend. This is one of the most horrible things I've ever had to do. We're all devastated, so let'**s get through this." She reads from the papers before her. "Kit leaves $4.12 billion in cash and stock to each of her nephews, Marc and Evan Hamilton. These funds will be put into trusts administered by their parents until their twenty-first birthdays."

"Great," Evan grumbles. "More money I can't spend."

His father hisses, "Evan!" and glares at him. Evan shrinks into his chair.

"She's also left Evan Spring Hall, her primary residence. It will be formally deeded to him on Evan's twenty-first birthday. Until then, Yves will manage the property. Evan, Kit has also left you Quincy, her parrot." The clouds that have covered Evan's face for two weeks break.

"Kit willed Lucy and Elvis Hamilton $200 million each in cash and stock, to be placed in trusts that they will also be able to access on their twenty-first birthday." Lucy and Elvis are Marc's little twin half-brother and sister from his dad's second marriage, who live in California with Marc's mother. Estrella has never seen them, and Kit never mentioned them much.

"Dr. Saul Mather," Rose Ellis says to Dr. Mather, who looks small on his folding chair. "Kit leaves $250 million in your name for the research arm of the Mather Foundation for Science and the Arts. She stipulated that it go to the foundation's continued research into The Cosmic and to the MIT water purification program." Dr. Mather nods.

"Nelson, Kit has left you Lewis and Clark's compass." The assistant brings Nelson a box. He smiles. "Bill, Kit has left you the Jackson Pollack piece *Number 16*. Gretchen will make arrangements with you for its delivery." Bill nods solemnly at Gretchen while Ms. Ellis continues down the document in her hand. "She has also left you each a portfolio of non-Water Trust stocks left to her by your parents, currently valued at $56 million per portfolio, and her shares of stock in Hamilton Tower, to be divided between you equally."

The attorney continues. "The contents of Kit's treasured library, including all the books, maps, and other artifacts will be moved from her residence to Glouton Preparatory School, where a wing has already been built for the collection. Dr. Constance Anderson and Estrella Chavez have been named the collection's co-executors, with Dr. Anderson and her staff managing the administrative duties and Ms. Chavez managing the installation itself."

Dr. Anderson winks at Estrella, whose lips part in surprise.

Gretchen brings a large envelope to Estrella. Even through the thick paper, Estrella can make out the shape of the gigantic key to the antique card catalog.

"Estrella and Marina Chavez," Ms. Ellis says. The young women hold their breaths. "Kit has left you each a trust of $400 million as well as a comparable sum in stocks, primarily in the Water Trust's private arm. Estrella's inheritance will be structured as a trust, to be administered by her mother until she turns twenty-one."

Everyone looks at them. Estrella's eyes widen. She was expecting a piece or two of jewelry and enough money to get her through college, and a payment on a house for Marina—not a fortune each.

"Also, she left you both quite a few pieces of jewelry. You will each receive a list of the pieces, and Yves, as the appointed custodian of her personal affairs, will make arrangements with you to receive them." Yves stays stone-faced as Ms. Ellis turns to him next. "Yves, Kit left you $1 billion and the same amount in Water Trust stocks, as well as her cars and the remainder of her art collection. You will also be given the information for a bank account in Switzerland. She said you are familiar with its contents."

Yves nods.

"Finally," the petite attorney says. "Linda Chavez."

All eyes fall on the thin, well-bred woman with the scar above her left eye.

"Kit has named you guardian of the Water Trust. You will have ultimate power and discretion over the Trust's hundreds of billions of acres of land around the world, the natural water sources on them, and the rights to the water. Of course, you must report to the board, as Kit did, and your vote will carry final authority, as did Kit's."

Linda's mouth tightens slightly as she sits taller.

Suddenly, Bill stands and looks right at Linda. "You know that this is never going to happen, right?"

Linda stands, too, and faces him. "I wouldn't be so sure about that, Bill. There are forces even more powerful than you in this world, and you shouldn't underestimate them."

He laughs. "You mean like Victor? Powerful like him? I see the forces you think can destroy us."

Estrella's jaw hangs open in shock.

Bill nods to the room, straightening his two-thousand-dollar black tie. "Come on, Evan."

Evan reluctantly follows his father out the door, his eyes downcast, his head low.

Estrella looks to her mother. "Victor? Does he mean Dad?"

...

"We're not talking about this." Linda tightens the belt of her gray trench coat on the dreary street outside.

"That's bullshit, and you know it," Estrella says. "I deserve to know what Bill Hamilton meant about my dad."

"Estrella!" Both Marina and Linda say, looking around to see if anyone overheard Estrella's profanity.

Linda gets close to Estrella, meeting her eyes, daring a challenge. "We are not talking about this now," she says. "And maybe not ever. That's it."

Estrella considers throwing a fit, but she's dressed up in heels—it would be too juvenile. She resolves to shut up and wait instead, and to find another way to learn why Bill and her mom had a fight about her dad right there in the lawyer's office. "Okay, Mom, you win. For now."

Linda almost breaks into a laugh, her eyes softening with love, before she says, "Damn right, I win. Now, find Yves and let's go."

...

Estrella knows exactly where to find Yves—having an illicit cigarette around the corner. When he sees Estrella approaching, he stubs it out, pops a mint into his mouth, and strides toward her. "Will you join me to fetch the car?"

"I could use some silence anyway," she says, as they walk wordlessly toward the garage.

After a block of snaking through the streets of downtown Manhattan, Yves stops and faces her. "Estrella Chavez, I am now your butler. I am at your service, for the rest of my life or yours. On your quinceañera day, Kit asked me to swear on my mother's grave that, should anything happen to her, I would pledge myself to you."

"The day of my quinceañera?"

Yves nods as the moving bodies of the street flow around Estrella and Yves like a river around stones.

"Even though having a butler is totally bizarre, and the fact that Kit made you swear it to her on the very day she died is creepy, I guess...okay. Thank you. I don't really need a butler, but I am grateful for you."

"You will need me, Estrella. Sooner than you know."

• • •

John Kaminsky blows on his hands to keep them warm, a dozen yellow roses sitting next to him on Estrella's front porch swing.

"Look, how sweet!" Linda says, climbing out of the backseat.

"So cute!" Marina coos, following Linda.

Estrella, up front with Yves, sits frozen for a minute before she says, "Oh shit, I totally forgot about John."

"Seems like a nice young man," Yves says. "And handsome."

"He is." Estrella replies, "But I really just want to get into my pajamas and go to bed. It's been a long day." Her phone buzzes with a text from Marc. It's an emoji of a star and the words, '*shine on.*'

Estrella looks from Yves to John on her porch and considers asking her new butler if he will break up with John for her.

Yves, as if reading her mind says, "I'm afraid I'm useless in matters of the heart."

John smiles, his bright blue eyes and sandy hair catching the slice of sun that cuts the heavy clouds. Estrella sighs as Yves opens her door.

John takes Estrella's hand and scoots closer to her on the swing. "Did you get the flowers? Sorry I couldn't be there in person. And I'm so sorry about Kit. She was a great woman."

"Oh, yes, I did get them. They were very nice. And thank you about Kit."

John leans in for a kiss. Estrella closes her lips as they connect with his.

"It's so nice to see you, but could we maybe talk tomorrow? I'm really tired," Estrella says.

"Of course." John hands Estrella the flowers. "I'll call tomorrow."

As he leaves, Estrella's phone buzzes with another text from Marc: A hundred hearts.

•••

The scent of coffee calls Estrella into the kitchen. She places the roses in the sink while she pours herself a cup, adding an extra big scoop of honey and extra cream.

"Put those in a vase!" Linda's shouts, already pulling a vase from a top cabinet. "That was very sweet of John, wasn't it? So thoughtful."

"Yeah, well, I need to break up with him. It's too much trouble, having two boyfriends."

"What do you mean? Marc?" Linda frowns as she arranges the flowers. "I thought you were just friends."

"Not really," Estrella replies. "I thought you were going to tell me why Bill Hamilton said that my father was weak in front of everyone at the lawyer's office."

Linda sits across from Estrella. "Look honey, he didn't mean anything by it, he's just a very serious businessman. Your father kept him from making a lot of money back when we established the Trust, and now he thinks I'm doing the same. With Kit gone, we have to be careful around the Hamiltons, and that means Marc and Evan too. Blood is thicker than water. They may seem like they're your friends, but they won't be there for you when you need them most."

"Oh great," Estrella says, "So now, not only is Kit dead, but I can't even execute my master plan—get the internship with Bill, get a dual M.B.A. / J.D. from Harvard, connect the Privatization and Free Water sides of the Trust, and make clean, fresh water available to everyone in the world for a minimal cost. Or date Marc, who I really actually like?"

She reaches into the refrigerator, uncovers a foil dish, scoops a serving of tres leches into her palm, and chews it right in front of her mom with her mouth open.

"Estrella! Act like a lady!"

"No!"

Estrella's phone lights with a text from Nadine.

I'm on my way.

Estrella texts back.

don't come.

The doorbell rings. Estrella hears Nadine talking to Marina in the front room.

"Estrella, come see Nadine," Marina sings. "She brought macaroons."

"So, she's trying to bribe me," Estrella mutters, the image of Nadine taking mushrooms with Tatiana replaying in her mind.

Estrella slowly goes to the front room, holding onto her anger, but when she sees Nadine, her blue eyes so full of sympathy, Estrella breaks down in tears.

"I know you never want to see me again, but I'm your best friend and you need me," Nadine says, holding Estrella while she sobs.

Marina looks lovingly at the two, takes the box of Estrella's favorite cookies to the kitchen, steals three for herself, and walks past them on her way upstairs.

...

"I never did get to tell you about that night in the graveyard, with Marc and Tatiana. Our talk with the dead."

The wooden kitchen table is littered with tiny macaroon papers, the dark outside tucks in around the cottage. Estrella leans in.

"It was pretty trippy, and not just because of the mushrooms." Estrella's lips tighten at the word; Nadine quickly keeps going. "Tatiana actually summoned a spirit."

"What?" Estrella's stomach curdles, the same way it does when she dreams of evil.

"It was almost like red smoke. I don't know if anyone else saw it; they weren't really there, kind of like they were in a trance. She asked the spirit something in, like, Italian and this voice in my brain said 'kill, kill, kill,' but it wasn't my voice. I pretended I was in the trance, too. Tatiana kept talking to the spirit, then she clapped her hands, and it went back into the earth. Everyone woke up and started laughing and cutting up like nothing happened! I asked Colt about it later and he said I just had a bad trip. I didn't think it was *bad*, but it sure was interesting."

Estrella recalls the dream she had that night, about Nadine and Tatiana and the deer. And the words Tatiana spoke—necare—to kill. She shivers.

"Who exactly was there?" she asks.

"Everyone from the party except Louis, Nikki, Amaka and you. You know who's cute? Adisa. Oh, I guess his brother wasn't there either."

"Adisa asked about you, but I told him you had a boyfriend."

"Why did you do that?"

"Because you do, even though he's a total asshole and I wish you would break up with him. And he was actually there that night you met Adisa, remember? You invited Colt even though I told you not to."

"Whatever," Nadine replies. "How was the funeral?"

"Long and boring. Kit would've hated it. Except Bill Hamilton, her brother, had a good quote. But now I guess he has to be my enemy because my dad and my mom kept him from being even richer."

"Probably for the best," Nadine replies, popping an entire macaroon in her mouth. "Well, what did she leave you in her will? Tell me it's that 1964 convertible Jaguar I've seen her drive around here. That car is fine."

"She left me and Marina each $200 million," Estrella says, as Nadine chokes on her macaroon. "Well, actually, $400 million, but half is in stock. And she left me her library."

Nadine jolts up from the table and looks around wildly. "What the hell are we doing here? Let's go shopping. Where's your laptop?"

Estrella laughs. "I'll buy you anything you want when I turn twenty-one. That's when I get the money."

"Holy shit," Nadine says, sitting back down. "You're rich."

• • •

Estrella scans the handwritten pages of cream-colored linen stationery from Kit's envelope. One of the pages is a list of books and poems. She glances over the titles, then reads the letter several times.

November 10th

Dearest Estrella,

I encourage you to read these books as soon as possible. They are the missing pieces of your education, and now that I'm gone, you'll want to become educated very quickly.

Sadly, we didn't have the time I wish we had together. You must know that you are here for a reason. I have faith, even though I won't see it with earthly eyes, that you will fulfill your purpose, and the world will be a better place for it.

You have also received a key to the card catalog box. DO NOT LOSE IT. It is the only one and it cannot be replaced. As you know, we have an entire wing already built for the collection at Glouton—don't let them give you any less. If you run into problems, Dr. Anderson will be helpful.

It hurts my heart to write this letter; it's not fun to contemplate one's own death, as I'm sure you can imagine. Know that I love you desperately.

Love Eternally,
Kit

The Canterbury Tales—Chaucer
Beyond Good & Evil—Nietzsche
The Iliad—Homer
The 48 Laws of Power—Greene
War & Peace—Tolstoy
Endymion—Keats
Ulysses—Joyce
The Bhagavad-Gita
The Koran
The Bible
The Yoga Sutras

"The missing pieces of my education?" Estrella asks. "I just got to high school. And why would Kit be contemplating her death the day before she actually died? The same day she made Yves swear he'd be my butler if anything happened to her?" A shiver lodges in Estrella's chest. "Oh my God, Kit knew."

Estrella bursts into tears as Linda's voice comes through the heating vent.

"How about some evidence?" Linda says. "Like a fingerprint, or a witness? They need more than just a motive. And I'm certainly not the only one with that." A moment of silence. "They can't have a witness, because I didn't kill her." Linda's firm voice is tinged with surprise. "How can anyone think I would kill my best friend?"

Estrella closes her eyes and breathes deeply: in through the nose, out through the nose. Her belly rises and falls several times.

When she opens her eyes, she knows what she must do.

Find the real killer.

. . .

Midnight's tiny stars shimmer through Estrella's bedroom window. Dressed in her sweats, the covers pulled over her, she listens for Marina's light, quick steps dancing up the stairs, then Linda's slower gait a few minutes behind her.

The door opens. Linda creeps in, kisses Estrella's forehead and closes the door behind her. Then Linda closes her own door across the hall.

Estrella awaits their sleeping breaths—or, in Marina's case, the snores—before she throws back her covers and tiptoes to her window.

The patio below is farther than she realized. The only other exits, the front and back doors, require her to pass by the bedrooms. She opens the window, the cold air hits her. She crosses herself, suspends for a moment from the windowsill, her body stretched long, her legs reaching toward the ground. "Please God, let me be strong enough to do this," she whispers, then takes a deep breath and lets go.

She lands effortlessly and silently as a panther. Energy vibrates through her cells, like the morning after the Vision Quest.

Silence and the black of night surround her—only a few lights shine from the porches of the neighborhood. No moon. She decides to jog the five miles to Kit's house, instead of taking her bike, as the bike might be faster, but easier to spot. She clings to the shadows as she runs, pushing her speed. Her heart hardly registers the exertion, and she reaches the gates to Kit's estate in less than twenty minutes, without even breaking a sweat.

The mansion looks lifeless, void of any color except the yellow crime scene tape stretched in front of the patio outside the ballroom, opposite the wing that houses the library. Estrella checks for a sign of the police but finds none. The lights in Yves's quarters in the back, above the kitchen, are out.

"Yves," Estrella mutters, "My butler—how ridiculous. I should just ask him to get me the books from Kit's list, but he does have a motive too. And I just know those books are clues. Why else would she want me to read them? And I know exactly where to find each and every one."

Estrella assesses the twelve-foot gates. "Why not?" she murmurs, then backs up several yards, runs and jumps over the fence, landing in the groomed gardens outside the library. She smiles as she dusts her hands on her sweats, then catches her reflection in the glass doors. "Oh well," she whispers. "If I look like a thief, I guess it's because I am one."

As she pulls the key from her pocket, she notices the shiny new lock. "Dammit! Did the police change the locks? What about the keypad code?" Fear sweeps her belly. "*Are* the police still here?"

She pulls into the shadows, where Kitty-Kat approaches and rubs against her leg. Estrella distractedly reaches down to pet her when Kitty-Kat looks her straight in the eyes and says, or more sings, "*I know the new code, Kitty-Kat does. Estrella's not alone.*"

Estrella gasps.

Another voice, this one coming from the trees, calls, "*Use your hand to open the door.*" A white owl stares at her with startled yellow eyes.

Estrella's hand throbs. She holds it in front of her face to find it glowing with pink light. "What. The. Hell?"

"*Use it!*" The owl hoots.

She waves it around the door handle.

The door creaks open.

"*Seven, four, four, seven, one, one!*" Kitty-Kat sings. Estrella punches in the code, and the panel beeps in recognition. She follows Kitty-Kat into the familiar room.

"*Shh. Look far away,*" Kitty-Kat whispers.

Something slithers along the shelves on the opposite side of the vast wing. Estrella holds her breath and clings to the shadows as Kitty-Kat leaps across the room.

Books hit the floor as Kitty-Kit attacks, making feral screams. Estrella strains to see who it is without being discovered herself, but the shadow—a person, probably a man— neither short nor tall and cloaked in black clothes and a ski mask—runs out the open door and onto the grounds of the estate, fast. Very, very fast.

Estrella recognizes the titles of the intruder's dropped books from the list Kit gave her. "Who the hell else knows about the booklist?" she asks herself as she picks up the books. "Maybe the lawyer? She seemed so normal. Or maybe her sneaky assistant? I'll be doing a little research on Ms. Rose Ellis and Ms. Gretchen Pierre." She plops down in her favorite chair in Kit's bedroom and begins reading.

She flips through *War and Peace*, the book with the most interesting title, but after three minutes closes the book. "This is already boring," she says. "Maybe Kit didn't leave a clue in here."

Kitty-Kat jumps onto her lap. "*Hide, hide, says Kitty-Kat, Kitty-Kat.*"
Estrella lunges behind the thick silk drapes and holds her breath as the loud sounds of a person bumping into furniture and walls gets closer. The silhouette of a man's body appears in the doorframe of Kit's bedroom.

Estrella recognizes him from the funeral and her lunch in August at Per Se. It's Nelson Hamilton, Marc's dad.

He tumbles into the chair where Estrella was just sitting and begins crying inconsolably. Acohol fumes seep from his pores through the drapes where Estrella holds her breath.

"I should've done more," Nelson sobs. "I should've stood up to him, Kit. For you, for us. I'm so sorry. I'm so sorry." He sobs and mumbles for several more minutes before he passes out in the chair.

Upon the sounds of his snores, Estrella slinks out from behind the curtain, silent as any other shadow lingering in the house. She pulls the books to her with the invisible suction of her pulsing hands, then follows Kitty-Kat out the back door.

The owl hoots from her tree as Estrella puts the books in her backpack, pulls her hoodie over her head and takes a final look back before running into the night.

DECEMBER

Days of Darkness

"All right, student body, we've got to talk about this head-on. We're dealing with death here." Dr. Anderson addresses all 591 Glouton high-school students from the stage of the auditorium.

"Let's face it. We can't escape the necessity of death and the pervasiveness of evil. We can only accept the truth of their power. I know that sounds bleak—it is. This is the world we're born into. That's why we cry instead of laugh when we get squeezed out into it."

"If she's trying to console us, she's not doing much of a job, is she?" Margeaux whispers to Estrella. "We'll all leave here alcoholics if she goes on anymore."

"Yet we have to live; that's our duty on this earth. And when you find yourself in one of those fleeting moments of joy between the inevitable sorrows, celebrate it! Because our days are numbered, folks. When you wake up tomorrow, you've got one less than you had this morning." Dr. Anderson continues while the assembled students stare morosely at their principal. "If you need any more emotional support, you can make an appointment with Dr. Ludwig through the counseling office. We're here for you, young people. You're dismissed. Go Owls! Let's win that state title!"

...

Estrella counts the stacks of boxes in front of her—seventy-four. She mentally calculates how long it's going to take her to put all the books into the empty shelves that define the rows of Kit's wing of the library. "If you don't start, you can't finish," she says to herself as she puts in her AirPods.

An image drifts into her mind: Marc's soft lips brushing her neck. The sound of footsteps falls behind her. She turns to see Marc with a sly grin on his face and a latte in his hand.

"I just kissed you with my mind. Did you feel it?" he asks as he hands Estrella her cup, sipping from his own.

"Yes," Estrella replies. She sends him an image of her own—the nibble of her lips on his ear. "Do you feel that?"

Marc touches his ear. "Mystery School is awesome. He leans in to kiss Estrella, just as two senior girls shuffle past, whispering the words "inheritance" and "suspect."

"Those girls suck," Marc says. "Don't pay attention to any of that. Kit loved you and Marina, that's why she left you that money. And my Uncle Bill and your mom will figure out what to do about the Trust." He wraps Estrella in a hug.

"What about your dad?" Estrella asks.

"What about him?" Marc replies between his kisses.

Estrella looks around, then whispers, "I saw him when I broke into Kit's over Thanksgiving—he was really upset."

Marc takes his lips from Estrella's neck. "You did?"

"To get the books—I think there might be clues in them about who killed Kit. I'm so scared my mom's going to go to jail."

A throat clears. Estrella and Marc look up to see Evan and Tatiana. "Maybe she *is* guilty, Estrella," Evan says.

"Evan, that's out of line," Marc says. "I know you don't have a filter or whatever, but Estrella needs our support."

"All the evidence is against her," Evan replies. "And now all the sudden her mom gets the Trust, even though it should be a Hamiton. And her whole family got rich from it too."

"Let her alone," Tatiana says. "She's been through so much. Justice will prevail, I'm sure. Marc's little brother and sister will be alright without the money that your Aunt Kit should have given to them. Marc was just talking about that, weren't you Marc?"

"What?" Marc replies. "I think you heard me wrong."

"What did you say?" Estrella asks him.

"You might not remember, you were pretty high," Tatiana says. "No matter. It'll all work out for the best." She takes Evan's hand. "Let's order that star to name after Kit."

As soon as they're out of sight, Estrella turns to Marc. "You go and get high and talk shit about me behind my back? To Tatiana?"

"Come on, Estrella. I only smoked like, three puffs and I never said anything about you, I promise. I would never say anything like that. You know how I feel about you. Tatiana was high too—she's misremembering."

Estrella's heart races, her palms seat. "Whatever, stoner. Go and get high with Tatiana. I need to get back to work." She takes a stack of books and starts shelving.

Marc takes the book from her hand. "Estrella! You're acting crazy. I know you're going through a lot, but she was my aunt, you know. It's hard on me too."

"You barely were ever even around her," Estrella practically spits.

Marc's eyes harden. "You know what? I think you need a little space right now. Text me when you've calmed down. And maybe stop breaking and entering or you'll be the one going to jail." He strides from the shelves, leaving his coffee behind.

Estrella stands alone in the silence of the library, cursing herself for her cruel words and remembering what her mother said about blood being thicker than water.

...

"Imagine light. Breathe light. *Be* light. Darkness is the infinite pull of gravity. Struggle against it." Dr. Mather leads the class in meditation.

Estrella breathes into her belly, imagining light filling every cell, but then her mind wanders, to the image of a glass of water next to a glass of blood. The water is clear, the blood deep and dark.

...

Cold wind blows from the North; Estrella claps her mittened hands together and tightens her scarf, her breath making a cloud through the fabric.

"This is it," Margeaux says, through her ski mask, "the state championship. Quite a different level of athleticism since the Vision Quest. Do you think there are Mystery School graduates all over the world, keeping their physical prowess secret?"

"Mike Hammersmark," Estrella hisses.

"No need to be so pissy," Margeaux replies. "Just because you don't have the courage to apologize to Marc."

"He needs to apologize to me," Estrella retorts as Louis throws a long pass into the end zone. Evan leaps to catch it, just as the clock runs out.

"Oh my God! We've won! I love this American football!" Margeaux throws her arms around Estrella as all the faculty, staff and alumni who have watched their team lose for the better part of a century scream and cheer.

Nadine texts Estrella.

We'll have better luck next year!
See you at the party.

•••

Lights wrap the bare branches of Methusaleh, mirroring the stars in the inky sky above Glouton. Octavio plays DJ for the hundreds who gather on the frosty green where Nadine and Colt chug the funnels of beer they brought for a Washington win.

Estrella shares hot tea from a thermos with Sylvie on the outskirts of the noisy revelers. Marc's voice flits through Estrella's mind.

I miss you.

She turns to see Marc, Christophe and Louis approaching. Marc makes eye-contact with Estrella as he pours a beer into a red plastic cup.

Estrella focuses her thoughts on Marc's mind: *I miss you, too.*

"Let's talk," Marc says, taking Estrella's hand and leading her beneath Methusaleh.

"I'm sorry," Estrella says, a tear behind her eyes, as Marc wraps her in a hug. "I just feel so emotional all the time, but why did you have to talk about me with Tatiana? And you smoke too much weed."

Marc kisses the top of her head. "I swear I didn't talk about you with Tatiana, not anything negative, I promise. But she is my friend, Estrella. And I like to let go sometimes with, you know, a little mind-altering substance, but I promise it will never cause us any harm. I care about you so much. You're all I think about."

Estrella wipes her nose. "You're all I think about, too. I mean, I do have a lot on my mind right now. I miss Kit so much, and every-one thinks my mom killed her."

"Well, *I* don't. My dad says your mom and Kit are closer than sisters. Don't listen to the haters, Strella. And it's okay that you're feeling so emotional. So am I. Margeaux says it's because we're water signs. And you especially, she says, because you're a Scorpio."

"You talked to Margeaux about us? She never told me."

Marc laughs. "Don't hold it against her—she just cares about you. Let's go back and celebrate our big win. Amaka wants a group photo."

"Where did all this alcohol come from?" Zaharia asks, joining Marc and Estrella. "I am surprised that Dr. Anderson isn't more aggressive about stopping this."

"She did say to enjoy every moment between the inevitable sorrows, or something cheery like that," Estrella replies.

"Raeesa Gajani's having a press conference!" Shabad approaches, breathless. "Su Bang Bang's army has attacked six soft targets and embassies throughout Europe and Africa. Thousands have been killed." He takes out his phone and shows it to Zaharia and Estrella.

Raeesa Gajani, a woman around Estrella's mom's age, sits in a plush chair, a fire burning in the hearth beside her.

"She's at an undisclosed location for her own safety," Shabad says, as Raeesa speaks from the tiny screen.

"*We, the true followers of Allah, denounce Su Bang Bang and his so-called caliphate. This man is a snake, and like a snake, his head must be cut from his body. We encourage the leaders of the world to stand against Su Bang Bang, to make him a dead man walking.*"

"That's right!" Zaharia shouts at Shabad's phone. Her teeth chatter.

"You're cold," Shabad says, taking off his coat and placing it around Zaharia's shoulders.

"Think he likes her?" Marc whispers into Estrella's ear.

"And here is what Su Bang Bang has to say," Shabad says, pressing the link. Su Bang Bang, a little man in an army uniform, stands behind a podium.

"I declare victory against the evil West and its educated elites. More strikes will come. Now, the world will see the power of the East. Of Allah!" His legions of followers chant his name.

Zaharia almost shakes with fury. "A man so wicked and cruel cannot speak the name Allah."

Princess Sylvia joins them, sadness in her kind eyes. She takes Estrella's hand. "Meditate with me."

"Okay," Estrella says, too surprised by Sylvie's request to deny it. She and Sylvie hold hands and breathe. Estrella feels every cell in her body tingle with love.

"Now. We must go now!"

Estrella opens her eyes to find Amaka before her, her eyes wild, Louis and Margeaux trailing behind her. Amaka grabs Estrella's hand, pulling her toward the dorms.

"It's her father," Louis says. "His company headquarters was one of the targets."

• • •

"Thank God, he had the stomach flu," Amaka says to her mom over Facetime. "Though over seven hundred of his employees were killed in the attack."

Estrella texts Louis the news as Margeaux hands Amaka a cup of hot tea.

"But what if he hadn't had to cancel that meeting?" Goldie cries, her face a river of mascara tears.

"My father has been spared," Amaka says, her voice strong. "He is favored by the gods and our ancestors. But Su Bang Bang must pay for what he has done. We must seek justice."

Amaka says goodnight to her mother and closes her laptop, then turns to Margeaux and Estrella. "Su Bang Bang calls on the name of Allah, but men like him never do anything for God, only for gold. So, who paid him for this? What riches does he have to gain? The gold he seeks—that is the head we must cut from the snake."

Estrella checks for more news. The president, Paul Phillips, offered support for the attacked nations. Miakoda Grace put out a tweet:

Su Bang Bang: Public Enemy #1

A few minutes later Dixon Duplessis tweets:

America needs to stay out of it—not our problem.

"The leadership of India says that it has no position on Su Bang Bang's caliphate, and China's party leader says that Su Bang Bang must be sanctioned," Estrella reads from her phone to her roommates. "Oh, look. Christophe's dad, Fyodor Markov, put out a tweet, too: *Su Bang Bang's Caliphate will continue to do business with Russia. We must stay above politics in matters such as these.*"

Estrella puts down her phone as if it had bitten her. "Matters such as these? Killing innocent people? How could business be more important than that?"

• • •

"Today, class, we're talking about money." Dr. Mather sighs as he steps away from the circle. "Let's hear it."

Amaka speaks first. "Finally, we get to the bottom of it all. This is what everyone is after. This is the power, the root of evil. Money is the god everyone wants to worship."

"Money is not the god *I* want to worship. It's greed, not money itself, that is the sin," Estrella says, her voice almost a yell.

Evan mutters, "Exactly."

Dr. Mather calls him out. "Please elaborate."

Evan's head begins to shake. "Lots of good people have lots of money. Lots of bad people are broke, and vice versa. Money is just a tool. If you're ethical, all the money in the world won't change that. But if you're not, you'll do almost anything for money, like killing people you call your friends."

Estrella's hands curl into fists, her head turns away, unable to look at the boy she once called a friend.

"But don't people do the bad things they do because they *don't* have money?" Zaharia asks. "It's much easier to behave ethically when there is a roof over your head and food on the table. When we see others who have so much, and yet we have so little that our children cry out from hunger, is it not understandable that we might resort even to violence for the money that will give us relief? Money, for many, is not a question of ethics, but of desperation."

Sylvie pushes her glasses higher on her nose. "In my country, we make money available to everyone, so no one has to be desperate. No one has too much, and no one too little. We do, statistically, have the lowest rates of violence in the world, so maybe there's something to it."

Christophe speaks next. "And what of all the smaller violences we inflict on ourselves for money? How many artists take jobs at hospitals and banks for the money? That is a violence to the soul. Even those of us who have money mutilate ourselves with our worry over how to keep it and who wants to take it from us. Yes, money is wicked. But we know no other way."

Estrella looks at the floor as Christophe speaks. Her thoughts go to his father, who puts business interests above mass murder.

"What is money, really?" Shabad asks. "Could it be an illusion? Maybe there is another way. Maybe our violences simply express our attachment to the things we think we desire."

"I'd like to follow Shabad's question," Marc says. "*Is there anoth-*er way? Can we have a world without money? Would a new system of trade still make slaves of us all? In some strains of Buddhism, they have a word: bhogasukha. It refers to the happiness that comes from sharing one's wealth. If this could be our collective focus, imagine how wonderful the world would be."

"You're only saying that because you haven't gotten your inheritance yet," Tatiana says. "Money is precious and should be guarded with your life. It's very hard to come by, and most people don't have it. When you do have money, you see that it's wasteful to go around sharing it with everyone. How do you decide who to give it to? Are they worthy? Probably not. Most people will do or say anything for money. Those entrusted with it have a responsibility to keep it close. The last thing we want is money falling into the wrong hands." She looks at Estrella.

"Careful that you don't sound cynical," Margeaux says. "Personally, I love having money to do whatever I want, whenever I want. I don't know why I came to the earth so lucky. Though, you do see unhappy rich people all the time. Would they be happier if they gave it away? I don't know."

"Of course not," Octavio says. "How can anyone be happy without money? Only money can buy wine."

Nikki cuts in. "The earth gives us wine. The grapes grow for free. All we have to do is pick them. All that we need is here already."

Louis gets the last word. "Where I live, there are no grapes growing for free. There are cement sidewalks where children murder other children every day for money. Ethics? They can't afford them. Attachments? What, to the shacks they struggle to pay for when, less than a mile away, folks live in mansions? Those with more do have a responsibility, Tatiana, you're right. *My* question is, is the responsibility to hold onto what they have, or, like Marc said, to give it away?"

•••

Estrella sits on the floor outside Dr. Mather's office, waiting for her end-of-semester meeting with him when she gets a text from Amaka.

> I excelled in my meeting. Dr. Mather asked me to levitate a paperweight, which I did easily. Then he told me that there is strength in humility, whatever that is supposed to mean.

Christophe smiles at Estrella when he walks out, followed by Dr. Mather.

"Your turn, Estrella."

•••

Fifteen minutes into Estrella's meeting, and Dr. Mather hasn't said a word. Estrella focuses energy into her fingers in case Dr. Mather asks her to levitate the paperweight, but Estrella says nothing, as she considers that silence could actually *be* the test.

Finally, Dr. Mather speaks. "Did Kit talk to you? At your quinceañera? About your father and your powers? We had intended to speak with you."

"You mean, like my Mayan healing gift?"

Dr. Mather nods his head. "Yes, but anything else?"

"We didn't get a chance to talk," Estrella says. "But, I mean... the Vision Quest...like, things have changed since then. But I did heal a bird earlier this year. And I levitated. Can I talk about this?" Estrella looks around.

"This is a safe space," Dr. Mather says. "But this is the *only* safe space. Remember that." He looks intensely at her through his thick glasses. "Your powers are greater than those of your peers, Estrella. And, unlike your peers, you've always had them. Like your father. But, since the fire when you were very young, you've gone backwards. It was the trauma—it weakened you."

"The fire? It weakened my Mayan gifts?"

"Yes. But they should have begun to return, especially after the Vision Quest."

"Marina says I have to be loving and not get angry or I'll lose my gift. I try, but it's really hard."

Dr. Mather smiles. "Yes, it is hard to be loving, and love does fuel your power source, but there's more than that, Estrella. What was your vision about? What about the animals? Was it just that bird, or is there more? Look into my eyes."

In Dr. Mather's eyes, Estrella sees an elephant, then a whale, then the bear from her dreams. "Islid!" Estrella says, as a soft knock sounds from the other side of the door.

"Hey, Dr. Mather. It's Evan."

Estrella looks at her watch—her final technically ended ten minutes ago.

Dr. Mather runs his hand through his diminishing hair. "We'll talk again soon," he says. "Until then, keep quiet about these things, as you have. I can't stress this enough, Estrella. Your words aren't safe right now, not until we know more—neither are mine. What happened to Kit...we have to be silent as stones."

"When can we talk again?"

"When the time is right. Pay attention to your dreams. I can reach you there. For now, that will be our only way. Just keep breathing, meditating. Experience the sorrow you feel for Kit, but don't let it weaken you. And remember to watch your anger as well. I know none of this is easy, but you're doing great." He raises his voice. "Come in, Evan."

Evan enters, all smiles, until he sees Estrella. "Oh, if it isn't the murderess's daughter."

Estrella launches to her feet, her palms suddenly burning with heat. "You know that's not true. Take it back," she says. Lightning flashes through Dr. Mather's office window.

"You and your trashy family can take it back to jail or to Mexico or to hell or wherever you want," Evan shouts. "Just stay away from me and my family!"

Estrella leaps across the room in one step and throws a punch. Evan ducks out of the way as she aims a spin kick at his head. "I'm going to knock your wobbly head off your greasy shoulders!" Estrella shouts as Dr. Mather steps between them and easily blocks Estrella's kick.

"What are you doing?" Dr. Mather says. "Kit loved you both and never would have wanted this kind of ill behavior from you—especially not toward each other. You must be patient and compassionate. Remember that you are on the same side." He shakes his head at Estrella, who looks down in shame.

"Forgive," Dr. Mather says, "and all will be made whole."

Dr. Mather's words soothe Estrella—her palms cool.

"Evan, I know you're upset," Estrella says, "but my mom loved Kit more than almost anybody in the world. Don't you see that?" She bows, recalling Amaka's text about strength in humility.

But Evan's eyes remain cold as coffins.

• • •

Holiday greenery, bells, and a banner proclaiming Glouton the state football champions deck the dining hall. Louis gulps some water to wash down his mashed potatoes. "Man, I can't wait to get back home and eat some real food. The first place I'm going when I get off the plane is to Guy's Po-Boys for a fried shrimp sandwich. Then I'm going past my auntie's—she's making yakamein. We're having a catfish fry the next day. Heaven! And then the Christmas gumbo?" He rubs his hands together in glee. "The thought of the next three weeks has been getting me through the past three months of this food."

Estrella nods in agreement. "I gave my Aunt Zandra a list of several dishes I plan to eat over the holiday. She's the best cook."

"What a child." Amaka looks at Louis with disgust. "I'm surprised you didn't say what toys you want Santa to bring you." She takes a bite of the same salad she eats every day. "Over the holiday, I am stealing a file from my father's business partner, Franz. It contains information on the labor violations Pan-West has committed since 1997. I am building my case, bird by bird."

Marc laughs. "That sounds like a nice, relaxing holiday. I'll be thinking of you while I surf those big waves out in Fiji with my dad. Can't wait to see what that will be like—you know, since the Vision Quest."

"Well, I have an audience with the queen," Margeaux says.

"Do you mean the *actual* queen of England?" Louis asks.

"Yes, it is impressive, isn't it? Father's being knighted, of all things. Perhaps now Grandmother will let him sit with her at Wimbledon."

"I'm figuring out who killed Kit," Estrella says. "It certainly wasn't my mom, like Evan thinks." She glances at him across the room where he and Tatiana share a table with Christophe and a few football players and cheerleaders.

"A noble goal," Amaka says. "I pray you will succeed."

"The Kong twins are already gone," Marc says, "and it looks like Shabad and Zaharia are getting closer." He motions to the couple, their heads bent together in the far corner of the room. "Shabad said he might tell his parents about her. They're planning to arrange a marriage for him—they've got an astrologer coming in and everything."

"Perhaps that is for the best," Amaka says. "Romantic love leads to problems."

Louis looks at her with a face full of love. "Girl, you are a case. You want to know what I want Santa to bring me? Amaka Abioye, under my tree with a big plate of catfish for us to share. We could put a little meat on those bones and get started on some romantic love and all the problems it brings."

• • •

Scents of cumin and coffee waft up the stairs to Estrella's little bedroom, where she re-reads the letter from Kit for the hundredth time. "Why would she write this letter at all? She wasn't sick and she was still relatively young. She *knew* someone was out to get her. And whoever it was, was there at the quinceañera."

Estrella places the letter on her bedside table and picks up her rosary.

"Please, dear Mary of Guadalupe, please give me a sign, point me to the real killer." She touches each of the beads, says, "Amen," then reaches for the spreadsheet under Kit's letter.

The spreadsheet of all the quinceañera guests was Amaka's idea. Name, access to victim, motive and suspicious qualities columns line the top of the four pages. Estrella closes her eyes and points her finger at a random name. She opens her eyes to find her finger on a blank space at the end of the second page. "Okay, Our Lady," Estrella says, "I guess you don't know, either."

She opens her phone to the file of the 4,000 photos of the event she's compiled so far, and the copy Marina made of the videographer's footage before she gave it to the police. She scans the pictures of the happy crowd, looking for something not quite right, when a group text comes through from Nicolas, Marina's boyfriend. It's to her, Marina, her mom, and Yves.

> The poison dart that killed Kit mysteriously vanished from the police station's evidence chamber. The breach of security could be grounds for a mistrial, should things ever go that far.

"That's good news!" Estrella says to herself, putting down her phone and picking up the book of poems from Kit's list. A dictionary page with the word "Pythagoras" marks one of the poems.

Tears fight to get out from behind Estrella's eyes. The memory of slender, bejeweled fingers ripping a page from a magazine to keep her place in a book flits through Estrella's mind.

Her eyes scan the poem by Keats: "Ode to a Nightingale."

"Like my nightingale at Glouton!" Estrella coos—the one she healed with her Mayan gift that Dr. Mather knows about, and that she can never discuss. She reads the words, re-reading two lines over and over.

> *My heart aches, and a drowsy numbness pains*
> *My sense, as though of hemlock I had drunk.*

• • •

"Are you ready?" Yves puts his hand on the doorknob as Estrella slings her book bag over her shoulder.

"I guess so, but I hate this, and they've been here all week. When will they leave?"

"Now that the interest in Su Bang Bang's attacks has subsided, I suppose we'll be dealing with the press for the majority of the holidays—it tends to be a slow time for the news cycle. The unsolved murder of the richest woman in the world is a gift-wrapped story they can rip apart."

Estrella looks through the peephole at the disheveled cameramen and the perfectly made-up reporters on the front lawn. "Let's do it."

Cameras flash and microphones thrust toward Estrella. "Is your mother guilty? Did she kill Kit? Is that Kit's car?"

Yves opens the passenger door on Kit's (now his) Rolls Royce for Estrella. Neither responds to the press's rabid inquiries.

Nicolas comes out of the house behind them. "Please don't bother the child!"

"I'm not a child," Estrella grumbles from the backseat. "He said the same thing last time, too, but the whole point of my quinceañera—the absolute worst day of my life, from now until the end—is that I'm an official adult. I get his reasoning, though."

Marina emerges from the house, all smiles, as a hundred cameras flash. She carries a tray of coffee and cookies. "It's so cold out here," she says. "This will warm you up." She distributes steaming wax paper cups and offers the tray to each member of the assembled press. "How are Kaitlyn and Kaffan?" She asks one of the cameramen.

"They love her, just like everyone else," Estrella says. "She's already learned the names of everyone's kids, and she's working on setting up one of the reporters with a boy she knew from high school."

Yves nods in assent. "If only your mother could charm them as well."

Linda, swaddled in sunglasses and a headscarf, plows through the flashes of bulbs and shouts of, "Did you kill Kit for the money or the power?"

Nicolas opens the car door for her, and she slides in next to Estrella.

They drop Linda off in the city, at the Water Trust offices, where another fervid pack of reporters awaits.

...

Check this out.

Estrella taps the link Nadine texted her. It's from the Eagle News. Estrella reads the text to Yves on their drive back from the Glouton Library.

While Linda Chavez is the prime suspect in Kit Hamilton's murder, there are some who claim that the heiress isn't dead at all. We're hearing that she's alive, with her young lover, on the private island she owns in the South Pacific. Will she emerge or stay on her private Love Island? Either way, you'll be the first to know.

Yves chuckles "She doesn't own an island. That's Nelson. A case of conjecture usurping research."

An unmarked police car leaves the Chavez cottage just as they're pulling in.

"At least our friends in the press are taking Christmas Eve off." Yves says as he opens the door for Estrella, revealing a front yard absent of the press that mobbed them earlier.

"Not this friend!" A middle-aged photographer jumps out of the bushes and blinds Estrella with a camera flash before he sprints into a car in front of Zandra's house across the street.

"I hope you get frostbite on your dick!" Estrella shouts after him.

Alfonso, Hugo, Cesar, and Zandra, all bundled in their coats for the twenty-yard walk across the street, burst into laughter at Estrella's curse. Together, with Yves and Estrella, they cross the threshold of Linda's home into what used to be the Chavez family's traditional Christmas Eve.

...

"This Christmas sucks," Hugo whispers to Estrella. "It was bad enough having to go to mass, but bringing the priest *here*? Is he going to stay all night?"

"I know, I feel like a senior citizen," Estrella whispers back, as Father McGuiness places a wafer on Linda's tongue.

"Please stay for dinner," Linda says to the priest. "Estrella, put an extra setting at the head of the table, our place of honor."

Estrella glares at Linda, then goes into the formal dining room cabinet for the fancy plates.

"And you can even stay for breakfast!" Zandra says. "It's a tradition Linda's family had back in Mexico, back when she was rich, before she got pregnant and married a servant, and her family disowned her." Linda death-stares Zandra as her sister-in-law continues. "Actually, you *are* rich again. Of course you may go to jail for murder. If it were me with all that money, I would give almost all of it to the church." Zandra crosses herself, batting her eyes at Father McGuinness.

Father McGuinness looks at the floor and coughs as Linda pulls out her checkbook. "I was going to send this to the Parish office, but seeing as you're here now, please accept this gift." She tears off the check. Zandra strains her neck to see the amount, but Linda folds the check and hands it to the priest who doesn't look at it.

"What about the rest of the gifts!" Marina chirps, draining her fourth glass of champagne. "Why wait?"

She takes extravagantly wrapped gifts from beneath the tree and distributes them. Linda opens a gift certificate to the most expensive spa in the world, Zandra tears open her package to reveal a top-of-the-line air fryer, and Caesar opens the box to a 125-year-old bottle of hand-crafted scotch.

Alfonso rips open a box to reveal a sweater with an abstract design. "It's the new Gucci!" Marina chirps as Estrella unwraps a pair of Chanel sunglasses. "They'll look so good on you!" Marina says with a kiss upon Estrella's forehead.

"Thank you," Estrella replies, simultaneously praying to St. Anthony that she won't lose them, like her last six pairs of much less pricey sunglasses.

Estrella passes around the little potted plants she made for everyone. "I would've given better gifts," she says, looking at Linda, "but I still don't get much allowance, even though I once again got straight-A's."

"And finally," Marina says, "here's your gift, Hugo!"

"Everyone knows Hugo's your favorite," Alfonso says, then affectionately ruffles Hugo's hair. "You got a multi-millionaire in your pocket, baby brother! Work it!"

Marina hands Hugo a little box with a bow. He opens it to find a single key. He clicks it, and a beep sounds from outside. Everyone rushes to the window where a gleaming white SUV sparkles under a dusting of fresh snow and silver moonlight. Hugo breaks into tears of joy. "It's the all-electric Range Rover! My dream car!"

"You only live once!" Marina says, hugging Hugo. "We control so little. Let's enjoy what we have today."

"I'm ready to enjoy the day," Alfonso says. "Where's my car at?"

"When you win your fight, you can buy all the cars you want," Marina replies. "And you know Hugo's my favorite."

Estrella pretends to cough as she says under her breath, "You're going to get your ass kicked on national TV."

"No, I'm not," Alfonso replies.

"Have you seen the guy?" Estrella asks. "Total badass and way bigger than you and if you were serious, you wouldn't be drinking Kahlua and cream and eating your seventh big piece of fudge."

Alfonso pops another piece of fudge from the candy dish into his mouth. "Training is for nerds."

"So, this is our family," Linda says to Father McGuinness. "We're far from perfect, but we know how to eat." She extends her graceful arm, guiding the priest toward the Christmas table.

• • •

"Nicolas, come hold my hair," Marina wobbles off the back steps, grabs her boyfriend's hand and drags him around the corner of the house. "Oops! I had too much champagne."

"It almost feels like a normal Christmas," Alfonso says from the back steps where he sits with Estrella, as the night grows gray with morning, "now that Marina's drunk." He takes another puff on the joint he's smoking like a cigarette and swallows the rest of the whiskey in his glass.

Estrella shakes her head in disgust. "You know my friend, Nadine, bet two thousand dollars on you to win? That's all of her savings from Burger Shak. You should at least take it seriously. Plus, two nights ago, I heard you ask Marina to lay ten million dollars on you to win. I didn't hear her answer, but I'm praying it was a hard no, but even if she said yes, it's not too late to pull out. You know the Krusher beat his last opponent so badly that he literally almost died."

"Yeah, I know that," Alfonso replies. "That's how I got the fight; no one else would take it."

"Well then you need to put down that bottle and pick up a jump rope."

Alfonso laughs as he finishes the bottle. "Don't worry about me, I'm a beast. I'm winning, I promise you. I have a good strategy." He lights another joint. "You saw Gabriel Estrada's going to be arraigned in the city? First week of January. I'll be in the front row of the courtroom. Then it's just a matter of time."

"Father-murderer," Estrella says. "He deserves every bad thing you're going to do to him." She lowers her voice so Marina can't hear her. "You need me there?"

"I need you to stay in school and get good grades. It's what your dad would've wanted. What I do, I do for you, too."

Estrella spontaneously hugs Alfonso. "Even though you've been a total dick for, like, five years, you're still my favorite cousin."

Alfonso hugs her back with his non-joint hand. "We're the most like him."

Marina stumbles up and slurs, "I'm so drunk, hermanita! I love you so much. I would die for you—in a second." She plops straight down on the snowy concrete and throws her arms around her baby sister. "Don't worry, hermanita. Mom's not going to jail. Nicolas is going to make sure of it. They won't get her."

"I think we should all go to bed," Estrella says, a vomit-wet piece of Marina's hair grazing her cheek.

"No! I'm waiting for breakfast. Help me up, Nicolas." Nicolas dutifully pulls Marina to her feet. "Where's Hugo?"

As if on cue, the universal beep of a remote car lock echoes through the still morning air. Hugo strides around the side of the house. "It rides like a dream!"

• • •

Mary of Guadalupe shines with crystal prisms of rainbow light. She levitates above the hard, gray ground. The fragrance of roses permeates the air.

Islid snores in her cave, her belly full with her unborn cubs. Estrella looks to her right, finding the yellow eyes of the wolf from the Vision Quest. The wolf becomes Lupe, becomes her father. He points.

A path of roses.

They follow the roses through the dark cave, emerging onto a rocky beach, where Dr. Mather levitates in lotus pose and Kit shuffles a deck of cards, dealing them to Marina. Babatunde, Amaka's father, flies in on a carpet of clouds. Shabad, Nikki, and Sylvie wash in on the crashing waves. All but Kit are made of crystal. A whale calls from deep in the ocean.

"You are the code and the key. All that is not love is a lie, all that is given is received," Dr. Mather says, placing his palm on Estrella's forehead. A wave gathers force out in the sea. On it ride monsters, glowing red. Dread turns Estrella's stomach.

The monsters tumble onto the shore. Babatunde pulls a sword from the clouds and offers it to Estrella. The red monsters carry black crystal knives.

Estrella's nightingale flies from the clouded sky and lands on her shoulder. "Seventy-four!" it sings in her ear.

Estrella raises her sword.

. . .

Estrella's eyes open all at once, completely awake. She looks at her bedside clock. 7:40. "Weird," Estrella says, rubbing the sleep from her eyes, her hands tingling, like she's still holding the sword. "He said to pay attention to my dreams, but what did it mean?" She picks up her phone and sends an email to Dr. Mather.

When can we talk?

From downstairs, coffee entices Estrella's nose. She looks out her window onto the gray and yucky New Year's Eve Day. The heater blows dry air on her. She closes her eyes. "Maybe I can get back into the dream. Maybe the monsters won't be there this time, and I can ask Dr. Mather what he means about the key and the code. Or maybe I'll ask Amaka's dad. Bizarre." She fluffs her pillow and closes her eyes.

Her phone lights with a text. It's a photo of Amaka holding *The 48 Laws of Power.*

Thank you for my holiday present. My favorite is *Law 27.*

Estrella reads the law from the book on her bedside table: "Play on People's Need to Believe to Create a Cultlike Following." Estrella laughs and replies with her personal favorite:

Law 15

"Crush your enemy totally—best law ever," Estrella says to herself, kicking off her covers, and following her nose to the coffee downstairs.

· · ·

Marina sits at the kitchen table in complete hair and makeup, dressed in a Versace tracksuit. Linda's still in her robe, looking tired even though she just woke up.

Estrella gives her mom a big kiss. "Love you, Mom."

"Love you, too, honey," Linda smiles. "You're up early."

"Did a dream wake you?" Marina asks.

"Uh, yeah, actually."

"I hope it was a good one." Marina's looking right at her. "I love dreams about animals. And water. I had a dream like that last night."

"It was kind of like that," Estrella says, holding eye contact with Marina and wondering if they had the same dream.

"Still no word about the jewelry," Marina says, glancing away. "I can't believe they're making us wait until next year, even if next year is tomorrow. It's been too long."

"We need that bracelet," Linda says. "Estrella, you're sure she recorded a conversation in D.C. with Senator Clay?"

"I don't know who she recorded. She just said a meeting."

"It has to be him—that's who she met with in D.C."

"Isn't his son the one..." A glare from Marina shuts Estrella's lips.

Marina told her that it was Senator Clay's son, Don, who was the reason she had to go and help Alfonso that night during Parents Weekend. The senator's son lost some money to Alfonso in a dice game, then freaked out and pulled a gun. Marina told Estrella not to say anything about it.

Linda perks up. "Senator Clay's son, Donald, who what? Got a stripper pregnant? Was found with a pound of cocaine in his father's yacht? Fell down the stairs, dead-drunk in front of President Phillips during the last inauguration?" Linda laughs. "What an idiot."

Marina gives Estrella a *you just got lucky* look.

Estrella's phone lights up with a text from Nadine.

Fight night!

"Like everyone else in America, all Nadine wants to talk about is this fight," Estrella says.

"Someone in the press figured out that Alfonso is my nephew, and now it's all over social media and the news—he should thank me for the publicity," Linda says.

"When we went to get our nails done yesterday, all the reporters were out there asking if we thought he could win," Estrella says. "No, he can't, but I didn't talk to that pack of dickless jackals, but I wanted to say, 'Only if he hits him really hard like this,' and punch one of them right in the flapping jaw. Especially that main one, with the soul patch covering up his double chin."

"That's not nice, Estrella!" Marina gasps. "It's just their job. They're very good people."

"Whatever," Estrella replies as she receives a text from Christophe.

I'll be there with Tat. Tell Hugo to remember our bet.

Hugo walks into the kitchen. "Marina, where's that Augustinas Bader facemask? Christophe's going to be at the fight, and I need to glow."

"He says to remember your bet. What is it?" Estrella asks.

"As if I could forget," Hugo replies, falling into to a chair and applying gel from a jar that Marina brings him. If Oleg, the Krusher, wins, I'm going to bow before him and proclaim my devotion to Russia. If Alfonso wins, Christophe will bend a knee to me and swear allegiance to Mexico. Either way, I win, because I get to be near Christophe. I've been practicing announcing my loyalty to Russia in Russian, since obviously Alfonso is going to get Krushed," Hugo laughs. "But I think Alfonso's crushing on your gorgeous friend, Tatiana. He knows she'll be there."

"How can he even like her?" Estrella asks. "She's a horrible, horrible person. Besides, she's still a minor. And she's definitely not gorgeous." The image of Tatiana at the Vision Quest, in the form of a monster, turns Estrella's stomach. "Especially if you drink enough herbal tea."

Alfonso saunters into the kitchen, pulls a glop of the gel from the jar and puts in his mohawk. "You talking about your friend, Tatiana?" he asks. "Like I care about the law or her personality. God wrote my name on that girl's ass, little cousin. She's mine."

· · ·

"Aren't you freezing?"

Nadine squeezes into the backseat of Nicolas's Cadillac SUV next to Hugo and Estrella. It's seventeen degrees outside, and she's wearing platform stilettos and a mini dress.

"Why are you wearing that?" Estrella asks, pulling her puffer around her. "You're going to freeze your ass off."

"I want to look good," she replies. "Where's Yves?"

"He sent a text earlier saying he would be of no use to me tonight, as he was already through his first bottle of whiskey. If it were a normal year, he and Kit would be indulging in their New Year's Eve tradition of playing cards quietly at home. It's one of the few nights Kit doesn't like to go out. 'New Year's Eve is for amateurs,' she'd say." Estrella fights back a tear, noticing that Nadine and Marina's eyes meet in the rearview mirror as if they share a secret. Before Estrella can ask about it, Nadine takes out her phone; loud party music fills the car.

"To Kit Hamilton!" Nadine shouts. "And all the amateurs out on New Year's Eve! Let's get this party started!"

· · ·

Spotlights roam the packed audience at Madison Square Garden. Hugo, standing tall and handsome in his tux, scans the crowd for Christophe. "I'm so happy that I made the effort to look fabulous today, because the press is *everywhere*. They don't even know where to focus their cameras, there's so much fabulous in the house. I mean, look at the storylines—there's Oleg, the peerless Russian champion, against Alfonso, the undefeated Mexican American with the troubled past and the newsworthy family."

He gestures dramatically to Marina. "But then there's Marina, the movie star beautiful daughter of a nefarious, murdered father and murderous mother (innocent until proven guilty isn't much fun for the media), and Tatiana, the movie star beautiful daughter of a bachelor tycoon who might be president. Everyone burns with star power, but none more that the dashing Hugo and the Russian president's son, Christophe, who worships Hugo—oh my God, it's like I'm writing a movie, and it's going to end with an epic sex scene."

"Whatever," Estrella says, laughing. "This is pretty cool though. Even if Alfonso gets killed tonight, he did make it this far, which is awesome. Madison Square Garden—it's a big deal."

"There they are!" Hugo tugs on Estrella's sleeve. Christophe sits ringside with Tatiana on the other side of the ring.

"Oh look!" Nadine says. "It's your friends." She's already weaving through the seats, Hugo following closely behind her, before Estrella has a chance to say no.

"I hate you both so much right now for making me go near Tatiana, but at least *I'm* a loyal friend," Estrella growls as Nadine and Tatiana hug and chat like two old friends. Christophe and Hugo immediately fall into conversation, just like at Parent's Weekend and Estrella's quinceañera.

Estrella seethes, standing on the outside of the group, blinded by camera flashes that capture her growing irritation. Finally, the announcer bellows his greeting to the sold-out arena, the lights lower. Estrella, Nadine, and Hugo go back to their seats.

Alfonso comes out first: the challenger. His fight music is a Latin-American hip-hop, death metal mash-up. When he disrobes, Estrella gasps. A life-size tattoo of her father's face looks out from Alfonso's rippled back. "When did he get that?" she whispers to Marina. Oleg, the undisputed champion, enters to a polka, with an entourage carrying several gaudy belts. He is the crowd favorite. Chants of *Krusher* and wild applause ring through The Garden.

The first round is a horror show. Oleg does what he wants to Alfonso. Hits to the body and a precise hook to the head drops the challenger within seconds. The crowd erupts. Alfonso gets up in two counts, smiles at the champion and opens his arms wide, taunting him and asking for more. Oleg is happy to give it.

The next rounds are just as bad. Worse, even. Blood drips from Alfonso's left eye and fills in the cracks that the Krusher's fists have etched into the skin over his nose. Twice more Alfonso hits the canvas. Both times he jumps back up, grins, and opens his arms to his opponent.

"If this is Alfonso's strategy, it's not a very good one," Estrella says, grimacing as Alfonso takes another fist to the face. "He looks like a butchered bull."

Marina sits serenely, clapping every time Alfonso springs back to his feet.

"If you made that bet like Alfonso wanted, you're already on your way to losing your fortune," Estrella says.

Hugo gasps when the Krusher lands an audible body shot on Alfonso's ribs that drops him again. The sight of his older brother being brutalized wipes his happy smile away, replacing it with tight, worried lips.

Nadine screams, "Get the hell up and fight him, for Chrissake!"

Estrella takes a peek across the arena at Christophe and Tatiana. Christophe looks like a proud father, watching his fellow countryman own the ring. She expects Tatiana to look as imperious and imperturbable as always, but Tatiana is pale, her usually icy eyes melted with worry, her forehead wrinkled.

Alfonso is up against the ropes now on Tatiana and Christophe's side of the ring, taking one blow after the next—to his head, his kidneys, again to his head. He drops to all fours; the referee begins the count for the fourth time. Alfonso raises his bloody head to Tatiana, who is almost tearful. Estrella focuses all the power of her ears to hear him say, "Don't worry, Blondie, I got this."

He rises at the count of seven, pounds his chest with his gloves, bounces on his toes, and meets his opponent in the center of the ring. With one punch, Alfonso knocks the champion out cold.

• • •

"That was quite a performance," Marina says to Alfonso in the greenroom after the fight. She and Zandra tend to his wounds while Cesar, already stinking drunk, sings the Mexican bullfighting song between shots of whiskey.

Alfonso smokes a joint and drinks whiskey straight from the bottle. Amare sits next to the newly crowned middleweight title holder.

"Amare?" Estrella does a double take when she sees him. For the first time in four months, she speaks directly to Amaka's older guard.

"What are you doing here?"

Amare smiles widely and proclaims, "I am anointing the champion!" He pours a bottle of champagne over Alfonso's head. "Babatunde congratulates you on a brilliant fight."

"Babatunde?" Estrella says to herself, remembering her dream. She checks her phone, which vibrates from one text after the next of fireworks and boxing glove emojis, but nothing from Dr. Mather.

Christophe and Tatiana enter, and the room quiets. Tatiana fixes her gaze on Alfonso, who takes another puff and a swig and gazes back at her.

Christophe walks up to Hugo and gets on one knee. "Viva Mexico!"

The room erupts into cheers as Cesar's phone blasts mariachi music, and Marina uncorks another bottle of champagne.

•••

"I'm freezing!" Nadine shivers with Estrella outside the arena. Finally, Colt and an older man appear. The man wordlessly hands Nadine an envelope and dissolves into the crowded streets.

"Payday!" Nadine says, as Colt takes several of the bills from the envelope.

"My cut," he says. "I know a guy who can get some Ketamine."

"What?" Estrella asks. "Don't bring any of your trouble near me. I have a future."

"What's that supposed to mean?" Colt says as Nicolas and Marina emerge from the venue hand in hand.

"Let's just walk," Marina says. "Getting a cab will take longer. Hi Colt. You look nice tonight." Marina pats Colt's cheek.

He blushes. "You always look nice, Marina. Can I carry your bag or anything?"

"I've got her bag," Nicolas says, as they make their way to the ball drop. They arrive just in time.

"Ten, nine, eight, seven..." As Estrella chants with the throng, a man in a business suit bumps into her. "Oh, excuse me," she says, looking up at him, and finding a pair of red eyes. The man laughs, licks his scabby lips with a thick gray tongue, and stomps on her foot, hard.

"Be careful, little one. The fun is just beginning."

Estrella blinks and the man is gone.

"Did you just see that guy?" She asks Nadine, but Nadine's sloppily French kissing Colt. Estrella turns to Marina, but she's elegantly French kissing Nicolas.

"Great. I'm hallucinating and no one even cares," she says to herself as she stares off into the crowd, where her eyes meet John Kaminsky's, before he closes them to kiss a pretty girl with red hair.

Estrella looks away, flushed with humiliation, as John finishes the kiss and walks toward her. He shakes Nicolas's hand, kisses Marina's hand, and bro-hugs Colt and Nadine. Finally, he faces Estrella. The rest of the group steps away, pretending to be interested in a man dressed in a Batman costume.

"Heard your cousin beat the Russian," he says coldly.

"Who's your girlfriend?" Estrella asks accusingly.

"Are you seriously fronting me about some girl when you took that douchebag Marc Hamilton to your quinceañera and lied to me about it?"

Estrella inhales sharply. She did lie. She told John that Hugo was her escort. She silently curses herself.

"I guess now that you're at Glouton, you have a new set of standards. Good luck with that." John returns to the pretty girl.

"Go to hell, you piece of shit!" Nadine yells at Colt.

"You go to hell! Maybe you'll see Alfonso there, you're so obsessed with him anyway!" Colt yells back.

"All I said was that he looked good when he won that belt, which he did, and now I have $32,000. I'll be happy to spend eternity in hell with a winner."

Colt makes a fist and charges toward Nadine, then stops, turns, and stalks off into the crowd.

"Dick!" Nadine screams.

Nicolas looks around. "I hope no one we know saw that. It would be bad for my brand. I think it's time to go," he says, heading back toward the parking garage.

Estrella's phone rings; a collect call from the Metropolitan

Corrections Center. It's Yves. He slurs so badly that she can barely understand him.

He is still incoherently drunk when they get him from jail just after four in the morning. He and a group of men were picked up for bare-knuckle fighting down by the East River, not too far from where Estrella, Amaka, and Margeaux were almost killed just a few months ago.

• • •

Estrella snuggles into her warm bed as the sun rises through icy windowpanes. She can barely feel her fingers when she reaches for her rosary on her bedside table; like her toes and nose, they're still numb from cold.

She replaces her rosary beads to check her email one last time. "Dr. Mather!"

The email is brief.

> *...Listen to me; Keep silent and let me speak...listen to me;*
> *Keep silent and I will teach you wisdom...*

Estrella Googles the quote—it's from the book of Job. "Who better to sum up my whole life right now?" she moans. "So, in other words—no. No, I can't get an answer when I want one, I'll just have to be patient and quiet and wait. Stupid Mystery School."

Estrella types her New Year's resolutions into her phone, as she has for the past two years.

She keeps the same resolutions from last year: She will continue to excel in school and kung fu, putting her on track to be valedictorian and national champion.

But she adds two more.

She will find Kit's murderer; her mother will not go to jail.

And, whether she's supposed to be silent or not, she will figure out what it is Dr. Mather is teaching, *really* teaching, in Mystery School.

JANUARY

Gray Wind

"I was victorious in my quest," Amaka says, proudly displaying an SD card. "It proves my father's business partner guilty of many financial violations. I will give him an opportunity to make amends for his transgressions when the time is right. *Law 35: Master the Art of Timing.*"

Louis's smile falls when Amaka adds, "I have also formed a most profitable alliance with his son. He has more money than a king and is as dumb as a horse." She pulls out her phone, puckers her lips, and takes a selfie. "Let him remember me."

Louis looks away.

"Well, I had that audience with the queen," Margeaux says.

"Of England?" Christophe asks, his usual expression of boredom replaced with interest. "Even my father cannot get an audience."

"Father was knighted," Margeaux says. "What a shame that I left my stockings tucked into the back of my knickers when I left the loo." She flashes a photo that her mother took, and everyone bursts out laughing. "I think St. Augustine had the right words for it when he said, '*Do you wish to rise? Begin by descending. You plan a tower that will pierce the clouds? Lay first the foundation of humility.*'"

Marc, tan from his holiday in Fiji, approaches the table. "What's so funny?" He puts his hand on Estrella's shoulder as he sits. When he looks into her eyes, she feels the sensation of lips brushing her neck. Estrella looks down, the blush burning her cheeks.

"Margeaux met the queen in her knickers," Christophe replies.

Marc's phone buzzes. "I got to go," he says, grabbing Estrella's hand. "Let's talk later tonight. I missed you."

"Look at Marc, all hearts and flowers," Louis says, as Marc leaves the dining hall. "He likes you, Strella."

"Estrella has no time for romance," Amaka says. "She is on route to claiming her place as valedictorian and her destiny is running the Water Trust, not entertaining spoiled boys who have to leave lunch to buy drugs."

"What?" Estrella looks at Amaka, then at Louis, who looks away.

"It's only weed," Christophe says.

"Thank God someone's got a connection on campus," Margeaux chimes in, then catches Estrella's glare. "Not that I would ever indulge."

Estrella sighs. "No wonder he has a B- average. Anyway, I've got to go study for physics. I'll be in the library in Kit's wing if anyone needs me."

As she heads out of the dining hall, Piper, one of Tatiana's super-model henchmen, walks into her.

"Did you just literally body check me?" Estrella stands taller.

"What are you even doing here?" Piper says. "You don't belong. Your dad was a greasy drug dealer, your mom's a murdering thief, and you don't belong here. And Marc's just using you. As soon as you give him sex, which you will, because that's what poor girls do for rich boys, he's leaving you. He told me so himself, in Fiji. We were all there for Christmas—Tatiana, too. Bet he didn't tell you, did he? Because he's playing you. Have a nice day." Piper saunters off, a crooked smile on her puffy, expensive lips.

•••

"She said *what* to you?" Amaka pets Estrella's hair while Estrella sobs. "I will ruin her. She will wish she had not been born." She picks up her phone. "I have unfollowed her on every platform. It is just the beginning of my campaign."

"It's not just her, it's everyone. They all think my mom killed Kit and my dad was a drug dealer. And Marc's got a drug problem and he's just using me for sex because he's rich, and he spent Christmas with Tatiana."

Margeaux brings a cup of tea from the teapot that sits on the mini-fridge in the dorm room. "How can he use you for sex when you've barely kissed? And I'd hardly say he has a drug problem. Now Christophe, or Octavio may be of some concern, but not Marc, not really. And he would be a fool to tell you that Tatiana was in Fiji—just look how upset you are."

"Louis told me that Marc told him he likes you very much, but that you broke up with him in the library, but now you are back together, but Marc is afraid he will upset you because you are fragile and overly jealous of Tatiana," Amaka says.

"*Louis* told you?" Margeaux asks with mischievous eyes.

"He tells me everything I want to know," Amaka replies. "He is under my power."

Estrella lifts her head from Amaka's shoulder and wipes her eyes. "I am not jealous of Tatiana, and I'm not fragile, either! Once I prove who killed Kit, everyone will know the truth." She bursts back into tears. "But I don't have any leads, no clues, nothing! And I keep hallucinating, ever since the Vision Quest. Some strange man with red eyes and a lizard tongue stepped on my foot on New Year's Eve and almost broke it, and Dr. Mather says he has something to tell me about my dad, but he won't talk to me about it, and I just want to know what's going on. Maybe I'm losing my mind."

Amaka gently pushes Estrella from her shoulder and looks her in the eyes. "You are not losing your mind—you have the highest GPA in our class. We may still be having effects from the Vision Quest, but we can manage the negative ones and exploit the positive. And we will help you in your search for Kit's killer, because we are your true friends. Forget Marc, he is weak. I sense a bend in his bones. You are strong, and you will persevere. Dr. Mather is playing mind games with us—our strategy must be to do what he says, which is easy—maintain silence. It is likely that he knows nothing about your father and is testing your triggers. Ignore him."

She motions to Margeaux. "Bring us all some tea, and Estrella, get that spreadsheet. There is a killer, and we will find him. Or her. Or them."

• • •

Estrella steps out from the shadows as Marc rounds the corner from his trig class.

"Strella!" Marc jumps back. "You scared the shit out of me." He laughs. "What are you doing over here? Usually, you're on your way to Literature."

"Um, well…" Estrella suddenly feels like an idiot. "I just wanted to talk to you."

Marc smiles. "Okay. I was looking forward to catching up at dinner tonight, but we can talk now. You alright?"

"So, you know I didn't ask Kit to leave me that money. And my mom didn't kill Kit."

"Right. I know you didn't ask for any of this. I'm trying to be here for you." Marc steps closer.

"Then why didn't you tell me that Tatiana was in Fiji?"

Marc rolls his eyes. "You're too jealous of Tatiana, that's why I didn't tell you—you're upset enough as it is. She's just a friend anyway and I barely saw her in Fiji—she left to go to Alfonso's fight in New York. I actually think she kind of likes him. I mean, she would never admit it because..." Marc looks away.

"Because what?"

"...well, you know, just, he's not really her type."

"I guess I *do* know! You mean because he's a dirty, wet-back Mexican."

Marc gasps. "Estrella! That's not what I meant. Just, you know, socially, they're from different backgrounds."

"Piper was right. A rich boy like you just wants one thing from a girl like me!" Estrella's voice comes out just a decibel shy of a scream. "Sorry that we're from the wrong social background for people like you and Tatiana!"

"You're taking things way out of context, Estrella. I'm on your side, remember? Even though all the evidence is against your mom, I'm still standing up for her to all my friends. Truly, I think it was Yves. And I know you're seeing other people anyway, like that guy, John."

"Who told you about him? Was it Margeaux?"

"It doesn't matter who told me, but it looks like they weren't wrong. I was hoping it was just a rumor."

"You never even asked me to be your girlfriend," Estrella shouts, drawing the eyes of passing students. "Probably because you're just using me for sex!"

Marc half-laughs. "What?"

"But you can forget it now! I will *never* have sex with you. I'm going to do it with John instead. At least *he's* from my same social background." Estrella turns on her heels. "You're dead to me now!"

...

"Zaharia said she heard you scream at Marc that you were planning to have sex with John." Margeaux slumps down by Estrella in their little nook of Kit's wing of the library. "And she's not the only one. Everyone's talking about it."

Estrella throws her head into her hands with a groan. "What's wrong with me?"

Margeaux pats Estrella's back. "You may be more fragile than you realize from all the traumas you've been experiencing of late. And, as I've been saying for some time, you *are* a Scorpio."

Estrella looks up. "Whatever. And why did you tell Marc about John, anyway?"

Margeaux looks away. "I don't think I did, did I?"

Before Estrella can reply, her phone buzzes with a text from Alfonso.

The arraignment is delayed.

"Great. So, not only are me and Marc 100 percent nothing, that father-murderer, Gabriel Estrada, gets to stay in Mexico. Life hates me!"

Margeaux shakes her head. "Who but a Scorpio would live for such vengeance?"

"Alfonso," Estrella replies. "It's what we lower-class people do."

"Come now," Margeaux says. "Marc doesn't think of you like that. He truly likes you."

"Whatever," Estrella says again, aiming her hand at *War and Peace*, attempting to suction the book toward her. It barely budges. "Before Kit was killed, I could have pulled that to me—you know, from the Quest. I'm getting so weak." She runs her fingers through her hair and a small clump of it falls out. "Great. I'm literally falling apart." Estrella bursts into tears.

Margeaux picks up *War and Peace*, her green eyes filled with tears of sympathy. "I'll help you—don't worry. I've been meaning to read this book anyway. Leo Tolstoy, I command you to tell us who killed Kit Hamilton!"

"There's no clues in there," Estrella sobs. "Just all those tiny words."

Margeaux opens to a random page. "What's this?" She shows the page to Estrella. A penciled star and two exclamation points mark the margins of an underlined paragraph.

"It's a list of seven virtues," Margeaux says. "Discretion, obedience, morality, love for mankind, courage, generosity, the love of death. That last one's a bit odd."

"The love of death?" Estrella tastes the salt of new tears. "That's a virtue? To see death after death, and then die ourselves? And we're supposed to be happy about it? Why would God even put us on the earth then?"

Her phone lights with texts from Amaka:

Piper now has only six followers. My wrath is quick and precise.
Sign this petition.

The petition is a signature gathering campaign to set free Raeesa Gajani, who has been arrested on undefined charges in Iran. Neither her family nor the press knows where she is being held.

As Estrella signs it, notifications from the BBC roll in.

Su Bang Bang has made a formal alliance with Russia.

"Look at Christophe's father shaking hands with the little dictator," Margeaux says, peering over Estrella's shoulder.

In the comments on the photo, the one from presidential candidate Dixon Duplessis is most prominent.

Happy to see guys with some balls on the world stage. America should be in on their alliance.

Among the many tweets responding to Dixon Duplessis's comment—most expressing horror that two warmongering, genocidal dictators have joined together, and that a current presidential candidate, though a complete long shot, praises them—is one from Tatiana.

Finally, a presidential candidate who says what we're all thinking. So proud of my #daddyforpresident

"I *hate* her," Estrella hisses.

"I wouldn't say I hate her," Margeaux says, "but I don't love her politics."

Estrella looks from her phone to the darkening windows. A chill infiltrates the shadows of the library. She checks the Water Trust feed to find more bad news.

Though ice storms whip the Glouton campus weekly, on the opposite coast, droughts officially enter their fifth year. Water instability has caused the price of groceries to creep up again last year in the more affluent nations. In the poorer countries, lines form for handfuls of rice. Water riots have broken out in Argentina.

Violence attends.

•••

"Today, we'll discuss love, the remedy to Evil's oldest strategy, division. Go." Dr. Mather steps away from the circle, and lets the class work it out.

"'If music be the food of love, play on.'" Margeaux quotes Shakespeare. "Though, 'the course of true love never did run smooth,' so there's that."

"What is better in this world than love, whether the river runs smoothly or not?" Octavio asks. "From the caress of a mother to the kiss of a lover, we live for love."

"Love is overrated," Tatiana says. "People like to trot it out for greeting cards and to make sense of their ultimately selfish motives, mostly for survival and security. Perhaps we should be discussing need."

"She is right," Amaka says. Estrella almost gasps in shock—it's the first time she has agreed with Tatiana on anything. "Love is used like religion or a drug: to make you see the world for what it is not. This is not paradise; it is a battle."

When Marc speaks, Estrella's heart jumps before she turns her eyes away. "Excuse my language, but I'm going to have to call bullshit here. Amaka, you of all people must know what it is to love. Your mission in life is to help people you don't even know. What's in it for you? Nothing but hard work and some appreciation if you're lucky. No, I think we are as driven by our compassion and love as we are our desires for food and shelter."

"Are you speaking of love or justice?" Louis asks. "Let's say that romantic love is simply a disguised need for security and procreation. Let's say a mother's love is a mask for mere species survival. Why will we instinctively help an old lady cross the road? A feeling comes over us and we want to give of ourselves, for no real reason other than because we know, deep inside us, that it's right. And what is right is just. Is the essence of this love an instinct for justice? And then what of the other love, the kind a man feels for his soon-to-be wife?" Louis winks at Amaka. She rolls her eyes.

"Confucius called this ren. We feel good when we act altruistically. It is the highest of ideals." Nikki says, then returns to silence.

Shabad nods his curly head. "In Hinduism, we have two kinds

of love. Kama is pleasurable love. This refers to the desires, the wishes, the longings, the romantic love, the lust. For many Hindu schools it is the third goal in life, after virtue and success. Then there is prema: elevated love. This is the highest form of love. It makes us give love and not expect anything in return, as in Louis's example of the old woman on the sidewalk. It is as strong as the need for air. It is with us always."

"The Prophet Muhammad is reported to have said, 'You will not enter paradise until you believe, and you will not believe until you love one another.' If you have not felt love, then I am sorry for you. There is paradise here. We know it because we love." Zaharia and Shabad share a shy smile.

"Back to religion," Christophe says. "Truly, the opiate of the masses. These doctrines you are trained to follow keep you docile, so the strong can take the power they desire. Justice? Love? I say vengeance and lust."

"What about friendship?" Sylvie asks. "We may be too young to really understand love, but we know what it's like to be friends. We haven't been indoctrinated into being chums. It just happened. We feel it and it's real. The world can't be all so bad as you think if we have each other."

"Your friends can betray you." Evan speaks. "Even the truest love can be taken from you. What's the point?"

Estrella looks right at Evan when she says, "In *my* indoctrinated religion, we believe forgiveness is the highest form of love. We're all sinners, but we are forgiven by God's mercy." She quotes from the book of Peter: "'*Above all, keep loving one another earnestly, since love covers a multitude of sins.*'"

...

"All that talk of love," Margeaux says, shuffling through her Tarot deck. "And here in the middle of January, when we're all frozen." She pulls out a card and shows it to Estrella and Amaka, who study on their respective beds. "The suit of Cups symbolizes water—you know, my cup runneth over—and in the Tarot, as in other places, we find water symbolizing love. It is all quite the mystery."

"Whatever," Estrella says. "Love sucks. Evan's still being a total dick. He whispers, 'your mom's a murderer,' every time he passes me in the hall, and it looks like Russia and Su Bang Bang's Caliphate are about to invade Pakistan, which could lead to a nuclear war."

"It's all everywhere else in the world, isn't it, and not anything to do with a certain Marcus Aurelius Hamilton, who despite all your words of forgiveness, remains dead to you?" Margeaux asks, as a knock sounds on the door.

"Whatever," Estrella replies, opening the door to Sylvie and Zaharia.

"Ready for our Mystery School study date?" Zaharia asks, planting herself onto Amaka's bed, twisting her legs into lotus. Sylvie sits cross-legged on Estrella's bed.

"I will," Amaka replies. "Guess. It is a number. I am broadcasting it now."

They all sit in silence, attempting to read Amaka's mind.

"Seventy-four!" Estrella and Sylvie both shout.

Amaka nods. "I am growing stronger in my ability to place whatever information I choose into the minds of others."

"I'll go next," Zaharia says. "A person." She closes her eyes.

All four other girls shout at once, "Shabad!"

Zaharia's eyes flutter open, her face flushes.

"And we were just speaking of love," Margeaux says.

"But we are only friends!" Zaharia replies.

"Yeah, right," all the girls say together, giggling, when Amaka announces," The phone is about to ring. Bad news."

Estrella's phone rings. Marina. Ice grabs Estrella's heart as she answers.

"Hermanita, I have to tell you that there is a chance that they might arrest Mom."

"What do you mean?" Estrella's heart pounds so loud she can hear it.

"The prosecution says they have a witness, a guest at the quinceañera."

"Who?" Estrella asks, her palms getting hot. What sort of traitor was on that guest list?

"We don't know yet. But I want you to be prepared, just in case. But don't worry."

"Oh, okay, I won't worry." Estrella replies sarcastically.

"I mean it, hermanita. She's going to be alright. It's all going to be alright; I promise. The darkest hour is just before dawn. Have you had any more dreams?"

"What do you mean?"

"Like, about me or Dr. Mather?"

"No."

"Well, you're going through a lot. Get some rest and pray to Mary of Guadalupe. Most of all, you have to have faith, Estrella. Faith that in the end, love will win the day."

Sylvie takes the phone from Estrella, who stares out into space.

"They have a witness," Estrella finally says. "I have to figure out who killed Kit, or my mom is going to go to jail." She pulls on her heavy coat and heads to the library.

. . .

"Please, Virgin Mary of Guadalupe, please help me find who killed Kit so my mom doesn't go to jail and whoever did it can burn in hell forever, especially the so-called witness. Amen."

Estrella shifts from one uncomfortable position to another in the gloomy, winter shadows of the library. She reviews her reading list for the night, another Keat's poem: *Endymion.* She gulps the rest of the Red Bull in her hand, then guides her finger along each line.

Estrella rubs her eyes and re-reads the page. The words "eternal spring" have been highlighted. "Why would Kit mark up such a beautiful, rare edition for no reason?" Estrella whispers. "This must be a clue!"

Dr. Anderson clears her throat. Estrella looks up and notices that her principal's hair is longer, and she looks slimmer.

She sits on the floor with Estrella. "I've lost thirty pounds. Can you see it? What a difference. Six weeks ago, I would never have sat down on the floor like this because there was no chance I'd be able to get myself back up off it. Crying shame, how you let yourself go and you don't even notice it's happening until you wake up one day and you can't see your feet past your belly. I'll be at my goal weight by graduation."

"You look great, Dr. Anderson," Estrella says. "You're growing out your hair, too?"

"My body, my hair. I'm making big changes, Estrella Chavez. "Losing one of your best friends will really put the fear of God into you. How are you holding up?" Dr. Anderson takes a longer look at Estrella and winces.

Estrella knows she looks like a zombie, but she lies and says she's fine.

Dr. Anderson looks Estrella right in her eyes. "You're gonna be alright, champ. You just gotta have faith." She easily jumps to her feet. "I feel like a four-year-old, I swear. Light as a bird and strong as a monkey already!"

Estrella hugs her principal. "Thank God for you, Dr. Anderson."

"If you need anything, and I mean anything at all, you know my cell. You're going to get through this, I promise you." Dr. Anderson walks a few steps and turns back. "Keep me posted on your progress with the books and try to get some rest."

Estrella listens to the squish of Dr. Anderson's Nikes recede across the library.

. . .

"Eternal spring? *Endymion?* Keats? Of course, I know about him. *'Here lies one whose name was writ in water.'* You know he was born on Halloween: a Scorpio, like you." Margeaux puts down her console and takes off her headphones. "We'll resume tomorrow," she says to Evan, with whom she plays Game of War nightly. "Do you have the book?"

Estrella hands the big, old, ornate book from her backpack to Margeaux, who turns the pages as if each one is a fragile, beloved child. "Page seventy-four," Estrella says. "That's weird. I just realized that's the same number that came up in a dream I had over Christmas."

Amaka sweeps into the room, peeling shiny, black, faux-leather gloves and a perfectly fitted Saint Laurent trench coat from her tiny frame. "I am now an actress. Soon the entire world will know my name."

Margeaux puts Keats aside. "Do tell."

"The new drama teacher, Bianca Wilder—great-great-granddaughter of the world's most lauded director, Billy—spent over forty minutes begging me to take the role of Titania in the spring play, *A Midsummer Night's Dream.*"

"What do you mean she begged you?" Estrella asks.

"On her knees. She watched my Instagram and TikTok like they were movies while she was in rehab. She says she has never seen a more natural star. Of course, she is right." Amaka braids her long hair and removes her makeup with special cloths and soaps that cost more than Estrella's entire yearly allowance. "Glouton will become known as a premier arts school once we have released this reimagining of Shakespeare's greatest comedy in Cannes—I told her we must film it if she is to have me as the star. The dramatic arts will balance out my college applications, and all the world will see a black woman as a queen."

All three girls get a text from Louis at the same time.

I've just been cast as Oberon in the spring play. I get to be King to my Queen.

Amaka rolls her eyes. "What a fool," she says, but Estrella sees the shadow of a smile on Amaka's perfect lips.

"Have either of you read the play?" Margeaux asks.

"I will memorize every word," Amaka says, Googling the CliffsNotes.

"Just remember it's a comedy." Margeaux goes back to Keats.

"Of course it is a comedy. It is make-believe. Real life is not funny, and it is not entertaining. It is a blood war. You are winning or you are dead."

"I wouldn't have put it as eloquently, but about life, Amaka, you and I definitely share the same mind."

· · ·

"Kit was like a mother to me, and my closest friend."

Finally, Yves speaks. Estrella hasn't heard from him since New Year's Eve. He and Estrella drink tea in the dining hall. He brought Quincy to Glouton for Evan.

"I think I lost my mind when I saw her there, but I am sorry for letting you down. It won't happen again." Yves looks her in the eyes. "I swear I will honor Kit's wish until the day I sleep in my grave. I am here for you, Estrella. Always."

They sit another moment in silence before Estrella asks, "Did you talk to Evan?"

"Not about anything significant," Yves says.

"He hates me. He thinks my mom killed Kit."

"He is experiencing emotions he doesn't know how to process," Yves says. "Be patient with him."

"Who do you think did it?" Estrella asks Yves. "I mean, on my spreadsheet, my mom has the most cross-vectors, but if it wasn't her, then who?"

Yves takes a sip of tea. "Who else is on your spreadsheet?"

Now Estrella takes a sip of tea. "Marina, you, Senator Clay. Me."

"Why the senator?"

"Just a hunch for now."

"I have found hunches to be more effective than evidence at times," Yves says. "Kit certainly believed in them. And she believed in you, Estrella. She always thought you had excellent instincts. And certain gifts."

Estrella looks into Yves' eyes, trying to discern if Kit told him about her Mayan healing gifts, but cannot read him.

"The prosecution assumes that Kit's killer was there, at the quinceañera," Yves says. "But so often what we most need to see is just outside the frame." He finishes his tea, straightens his suit, and bows to Estrella. She instinctively bows back and walks him out to the parking lot, where he jumps into Kit's 1964 convertible Jaguar to drive back to Kit's magnificent estate.

...

Margeaux turns a page of *Anna Karenina.* "This Tolstoy's quite the storyteller. Of course everyone says so, but after I read your copy of *War and Peace,* I need more. I thought I would be too young to appreciate it, but I was so very wrong."

"Who cares about that?" Estrella replies. "I'm trying to solve a murder. Of my Godmother."

Margeaux closes the book. "Alright, I'm here to assist."

"So, here's where I'm at: Marina and I are still waiting for Kit's jewelry. We should have gotten it already, but the state is dragging its feet. I know that bracelet Hugo made for Kit must hold a clue. Maybe it even reveals the killer, especially if it's Senator Clay. He just looks like a killer—you can just see it on his face. Smug, like he poops roses."

"Well, that's not much to go on, but I suppose if the bracelet has some sort of information, that could help." Margeaux eyes her book longingly.

Estrella pops open another Red Bull. "Oh look! Amaka made a mark on the spreadsheet next to one of the entries at the very bottom of the list! Mrs. Franks, the bus driver." Estrella looks closer. "It says, *Research further—she was too well dressed for her station.* Okay, so that's totally classist. But maybe. I will resort to being a horrible person right now if that's what it takes, because my mom does look the guiltiest. She has the biggest motive, and she and Kit were arguing a lot there for a while, and apparently everyone knew about it. And she was there with the body. And now there's a witness who says they saw her commit the act. But maybe the witness just mis-remembered. I learned in psychology class that people's memories can lie to them. But what *did* this witness see? Because all I can see is the memory of my mom slapping Kit's frozen face. But that's not murder. And my mom could never do that. Right?"

•••

For the first time since the quinceañera, on the darkest, coldest day of the dark, cold month, Evan walks up to Estrella in the hall between classes. Estrella smiles at first, before she sees the dark, cold grin twisting his face.

"Your evil mom is in jail, where she belongs. That's what you get for murdering my aunt and stealing from our family. Justice prevails."

Estrella freezes before she yells to his retreating back, "Come back here, liar!"

"He must be lying," Estrella mutters to herself. Her breath becomes ragged as she opens her phone to call Marina. Her phone rings with a call from Marina.

"Hermanita," Marina says, crying, "you have to stay strong."

•••

The door to the chapel creaks open, blowing in the ice storm that rages outside.

Amaka and Margeaux pull Estrella from the cold floor, where Estrella made a shrine out of branches to St. Anthony of Padua, Liberator of Prisoners. Amaka puts her little arms around Estrella, Margeaux takes her hand.

"The DA was able to execute the warrant based on the combination of her motive and her fingerprints on the back of Kit's neck, right by where the missing crystal dart went in. And of course, the witness. No bail. They say she's a flight risk," Estrella sobs. "Marina said that William Hamilton will take over the Water Trust. My mom's in jail!" Estrella's wail and coughing tears fill the cold room. She looks down at the cracked screen of the phone in her hands. "I threw my phone against the bricks of the library on my way here. I couldn't answer any of the texts."

"Marc told us he thought you would be here," Amaka says, guiding Estrella to her feet.

"We all love you so much," Margeaux says. "And we're all here for you."

"Not Evan," Estrella replies, wiping a new stream of tears.

"Do not worry about him," Amaka replies. "He is tainted by his Hamilton blood."

Together, the girls walk from the chapel and through the bitter, gray wind, back to their dorm, where Marina's crystal glows with a pink light that warms the room.

Margeaux gives Estrella a Valium. Estrella washes it down with the steamed milk Amaka brings from the kitchen. Her roommates guide her toward her bed.

• • •

Mary of Guadalupe shines bright as the sun through dense, gray clouds. The wind stills. Estrella's nightingale lands upon her shoulder, a rose in her beak.

"Fidem!" She cries as she flies away.

FEBRUARY

Maps of Africa

Fidem. Estrella mulls the word in her mind—the Latin word for faith. Complete trust. "Despite my current reality," Estrella says to herself as two officers pat down her, Nicolas, and Marina then pass them through to a large, windowless room occupied by mostly women and children.

As soon as they find seats on dirty plastic chairs, Marina closes her eyes and prays. From nowhere, a fresh breeze swirls through the room. Estrella's heart rate slightly slows; the anxious and weary people around her visibly relax.

"Number 74," a guard calls from behind a counter.

Estrella looks around, surprised to hear the same number again—the one from her dream. Nicolas shows the guard the little paper with the number printed on it. "Follow Officer Coates," The guard says, motioning to a woman with tired eyes.

They follow her through a cinder block corridor to a dismal room where they face a scratched Plexiglass window. Behind it, Linda wears an orange jumpsuit. Her roots are growing in gray and her face shows the wrinkles Botox has held at bay.

Tears form in Estrella's eyes, but she's determined to stay strong for her mom. She swallows her tears.

No one says anything for a minute.

"Did the board vote to table any decisions until after my trial?" Linda finally asks Marina.

"By three votes," Marina says. "You still have some sway there, at least for now."

"We're pushing for things to move quickly," Nicolas says. "I'm coming back tomorrow with the team, and we'll go over the strategy with you."

"Bring Miakoda with you. We need to discuss the Species Extinction Report," Linda says. "Its release is our most important priority. I'm worried the for-profit arm will try to stall her. And her coming will show I still have sway inside Congress." Linda turns her loving eyes to Estrella. "How's school?"

"How's school?" Estrella repeats back, wondering if she could use the power in her hand to suction out the window that separates them and pull her mom through, leaving only the task of taking out the three guards.

"Estrella?" Linda's voice brings her back to the present.

"I still have straight As," Estrella says, because she knows that's what her mom will want to hear.

"I know you're worried about me, but you have to be strong. No one can see that what's happening to me is affecting you. Hold your head high. Just stay away from the Hamiltons until this is over. For now, they are our enemies."

"Don't worry, Mami," Estrella says, "They're dead to me."

Linda nods. "Good girl. Don't forget that we're the ones with the power now. I'll be out of here soon, I promise. Have faith."

"I put a bunch of money in your prison account," Marina says, "so you can buy off whoever you need to stay safe."

"I've already made a few friends," Linda says, a look of pride lighting her eyes. "But I don't know how long I can keep the Trust together from behind these walls."

"This is how they do it," Marina says. "They divide us."

A guard taps Marina on the shoulder. "Time."

• • •

The dreary landscape flies past the window of Nicolas's Suburban.

"Prison is the worst place," Estrella says, "and we just left Mom there, maybe for the rest of her life." Estrella tastes panic in the back of her throat. "It cannot happen."

Nicolas clears his throat. "Well, I have some good news, Estrella. You know that we might have grounds for a mistrial since it's taken so long for the autopsy."

"You don't need to talk to me like I'm a little kid. Of course, I know—I'm about ready to take the damn bar exam myself. I've learned so much about the law these past two months."

"Okay," Nicolas says. "No need to use profanity." He and Marina exchange a glance before he adds, "They're releasing the report to the public tomorrow. We received it today."

Estrella sits forward until the seatbelt pushes into her neck. "What did it say? Why did you wait the whole drive to prison to say anything?"

"We didn't want to upset you with too much at once," Nicolas replies.

"I'm upset that you didn't tell me," Estrella challenges.

Marina gives Estrella a *behave yourself* look through the rearview mirror as Nicolas says, "Curare was discovered at the site of the wound in the back of Kit's neck, and in her digestive tract. It's listed as the cause of death."

"What's curare?" Estrella asks, already Googling it, as Nicolas replies, "It's a plant poison from the Amazon basin. It was once used as an anesthetic."

"Well, then this is a break in the case," Estrella almost chirps. "The police can trace that, right? It can't be too common. Cross-check all the people at the party, see who received a package from South America."

"My team and the police are doing that now. Hopefully, some connection will emerge. Then it's just a matter of discrediting their witness, Barbara Franks. The DA released her name to us, along with the toxicology report. We're still not sure who invited her. She's the bus driver at Glouton, so maybe she came with someone from your school."

• • •

"Why would you invite the bus driver? Do you know her or something?" Nadine pops a bubble of the bright pink gum she chews as wind and sleet attack the Chavez cottage. The childhood friends lounge on Estrella's ruffled, little-girl bed.

"I don't know what got into me. I was just trying to be nice." Estrella replies. "So stupid! My big mouth—inviting everyone on the ride back from the Vision Quest. And I thought Tatiana was the one I didn't want to invite."

Estrella phone lights with a text from Amaka.

I knew the bus driver was guilty of something. My intuition and intelligence grow by the moment.

Nadine laughs. "Your friend Amaka's a trip. Definitely not afraid to own her truth."

Estrella's eyes flit across the Wikipedia page on curare. Her stomach weakens as she reads the words aloud to Nadine.

"*Curare keeps the victim conscious until the very end, but all the neuromuscular processes are immobilized. Kit knew she was dying,* but she couldn't even cry out for help. She felt herself die, one piece at a time."

• • •

The red army surrounds Linda, who is tied to a post, naked. They whip her until the leather rips open her skin, then her muscle.

In the end, she is only blood.

• • •

Estrella wakes, screaming.

Marina and Nadine hold down her thrashing limbs that still live in the memory of her dream.

• • •

"Fear. Just free associate." Dr. Mather gives the floor to his students.

"As Jews, we are taught to fear God," Amaka says. "I fear no one else."

"'Those who believe, and do deeds of righteousness, and establish regular prayers and regular charity, will have their reward with their Lord: on them shall be no fear, nor shall they grieve.'" Zaharia quotes Allah. "Funny, I do these things and still I find fear grasping my heart."

Christophe speaks. "It's true. We are taught to be brave, to be men, to be strong above all, and always in the face of fear. Fear is assumed. And then there are the fears you cannot face."

Marc clears his throat to speak. Estrella looks away, trying not to notice that the blue sweatshirt he wears compliments his skin. "The Buddhists think that fear is the root of our ego and our restlessness.

235

We should examine fear and ask where it comes from. What sensations do you feel when you're afraid? What kind of thoughts race through your mind? Awareness is the antidote to fear." Marc sounds only half convinced.

"But where does fear come from?" Octavio asks. "*Why* are we all afraid? It seems like fear was born with the earth."

"You're afraid because you have good reason to be afraid," Tatiana says. "Life is dangerous."

"Is it death, then?" Margeaux asks. "Is the fear that we'll die one day? Isn't that what drives our ego and our restlessness, knowing that it will all end?"

"But it doesn't end," Shabad says. "Death is an illusion. We inhale and exhale. We live, we die. Fear is the blindness that does not see the truth."

"Death seems pretty real to me," Evan says. "Maybe I'm just blind. And is no one going to mention the amygdala, which literally rules our perceptions of and responses to fear? Everyone's so focused on all this spiritual stuff when it's the brain that actually controls everything."

Sylvie pats Evan's hand. "And there are fears not just about death, but fears about living, too. Like the fear of public speaking. And for sure the brain is involved in all our fears."

"Fear is a survival mechanism. The weak feel it most." Nikki says.

"And people will use fear to make you think you're weak. Most of us don't even know how strong we are because we fear we're not," Louis says. "Think of the woman whose boyfriend abuses her. She could get a group of her friends together to beat him senseless with cast iron skillets, but she doesn't. Why? He's convinced her that she's weak by sowing the seeds of her fear."

All eyes turn to Estrella. She says nothing.

. . .

"Valentine's Day at Glouton is just as stupid and awkward as in middle school, the kids here just have more money," Estrella says as she kicks off her shoes and flips through the *Laws of Power* while Amaka dresses for the dance. "So, you've got another guy flying in on a private jet to be your date?" Estrella asks Amaka. "Why do I feel like Margeaux and I will have more fun staying in?"

"Because it is a convenient lie you can tell yourselves," Amaka replies, going through the motions of her lengthy makeup and hair routine.

"Can you believe Shabad gave Zaharia those bracelets? Those rubies are flawless. He must be serious," Margeaux says. "And Alexis said that she heard that Nikki Kong's room is overflowing with red roses from a secret admirer. Wonder who that might be? She has a whole secret life, doesn't she? Unlike her brother, who's got everything on his Insta. The whole world knows he flew to Paris for the weekend on the Kong family's private jet to serenade his latest infatuation—a runway model."

Estrella glances at a velvet box with an ancient, carved jade bird and a poem inside. "Well, he's keeping his options open, because before he left, he asked me to give this box to Marina. He said, 'My body will be in Paris, but my heart is with her always.' What a player."

"Is your cousin Hugo coming?" Margeaux asks.

"Yes," Estrella snorts. "Unbelievable. Such a traitor. He's going in a big group with Tatiana, Christophe, Marc and Evan, and some other kids. But he's so into Christophe that I'll forgive him. This time. He owes me so many favors."

"You should be going to the dance," Amaka says. "You will look anti-social. Not attractive."

"I'm going with Law 36 from *The 48 Laws of Power* instead," Estrella replies, then reads from the book she holds. "*Disdain things you cannot have: ignoring them is the best revenge.*"

"What is it you can't have, then?" Margeaux asks. "Is it one of the stoic philosophers? Like Marcus Aurelius?"

Estrella gives her a dirty look as her phone lights.

It's a TikTok of Louis and his date, Miss Teen USA, a big, blonde girl from a wealthy cattle-ranching family in Nebraska he met at the White House Young Leaders Gala over the summer. They're practicing a dance. Estrella laughs. "Cute!"

"You are watching Louis' TikTok?" Amaka says, glancing away from her phone. "I'm sure he did meet that giant at the *White* House. But I smell a rat. I've asked Amare to compile a dossier on this supposed Miss Teen USA. Let's see what she's really up to. Everyone has something to hide. More than that cheap spray tan can cover." Amaka covers her shoulders with a cape dotted in Swarovski crystals. "My date has arrived downstairs. Adisa will walk me down, as you both are denying your responsibilities tonight."

"Responsibility to go to a dance?" Margeaux asks.

"Yes," Amaka replies. "The work of school is only partially academic. We must cultivate our social connections if we are to put this education to any use in the world." She dabs perfume on her wrists and neck, then opens the door for Adisa.

Adisa's bright smile lights the room dark with February. "Tell your friend Nadine, I want her to be my Valentine," he says to Estrella.

"She already has a boyfriend," Estrella replies. "You met him."

"For now," Adisa chuckles. "Who knows what tomorrow will bring," he says, trailing Amaka down the hall.

"Want to hear my new song?" Margeaux picks up her guitar and strikes an angry chord. "It's called 'I Hate You, My Valentine.'"

"I'm feeling that sentiment, Pink." Estrella says. She reviews Kit's daunting booklist. "Murders don't just solve themselves," she says, slinging her backpack over her shoulder. "I'm off to work."

Margeaux aggressively strums away.

"Hey, Pink, why don't you come and help me with this? Pleeease? You love this stuff. She's even got Chaucer on the list. You're always talking about Chaucer and Beowulf and Shakespeare, as if all literature was written by white guys before Stonehenge."

Margeaux puts down her guitar and sighs. "Oh, why not? Misery loves company."

. . .

"Look for clues." Estrella hands Margeaux *The Canterbury Tales*. The library's LED lights cast a dismal glow.

"I have no idea what kind of clues Chaucer has for us, but I'll stay open to the possibilities. Maybe the Knight did it," Margeaux replies, settling into a corner nook of the library. "English literature, my great consolation. Let them all dance and romance their night away. I am happy with my truest love." She opens the book.

. . .

Margeaux stands and stretches, wiping tears of laughter from her eyes. "Absolon's kiss does it to me every time," she says. "I'm off to the loo."

"I love how you call the bathroom the loo. British people are so classy." Estrella re-focuses her eyes on *War and Peace*, and all its words. She plans to read every one of them this time and not just flip through. "Why can't every book be *The 48 Laws of Power*? It has good information in there, actual stuff you can use, like Law 15. Crush your enemy totally." Estrella mutters, smiling as she recites her favorite law. "From what I can tell so far, *War and Peace* is about a thousand people whose names I can't pronounce going to dinner parties."

"Look at this!" Margeaux stands in front of her, holding an old, tattered atlas. "It fell right off the shelf in front of me." She opens the massive book for Estrella. "Have you ever seen anything so amazing?"

She glances over Margeaux's atlas. "Cool, an old map of Africa."

"Africa? It's a map of the galaxies or something. Can't you see all these planets? And these look like stars, or galaxies. I've never seen anything like it. They're all swirling around. It's beautiful."

Estrella returns to her book, silently cursing Leo Tolstoy.

"Surely you see this," Margeaux says, pushing the atlas closer to Estrella. "These planets are floating in midair, right off the page!"

Estrella looks at the tattered Atlas, then warily at Margeaux. "Did you go off to the loo and get stoned or something? I don't see anything but a map of Africa."

Margeaux frowns. "So..." She closes the book and opens it. "And here they remain—a kaleidoscope of stars. Am I losing my mind finally? The stress of living such a precarious life has come to break me down?" She opens and closes the book again. "Or what if I've been slipped a bit of LSD, or mescaline? God knows it wouldn't be the first time." She looks around the vacant library. "No. Definitely not drugs. Everything would look different. So, it's a psychotic break then."

Estrella puts down her book. "Look Pink, I don't see the stars, but you don't hear animals talking, so maybe the Vision Quest just affected us all in different ways. Like Amaka's getting really good at reading minds. If you see something, I believe you. I just don't see it myself."

Estrella's phone rings; the book closes itself.

Margeaux and Estrella exchange a wide-eyed glance.

"It's Marina," Estrella says as she answers.

"I'm engaged, hermanita!" Maraina holds her finger, bearing a gigantic ring, up to the phone. The half of Nicolas's head that's in the shot shows his proud smile. "I wish the timing were better, but we didn't want to wait any longer. If we wait for everything to be perfect, we'll be waiting forever. Of course we'll wait for the wedding until Mom gets out, but at least we can start planning." Marina looks lovingly at her new ring. "It was so beautiful! He got down on his knee and everything, right there at Le Bernardin. Will you be my maid of honor?"

"Of course!" Estrella replies. "I mean, I already knew I would be, and I knew this was coming, but I'm so excited and happy for you!"

"Wait, why aren't you at the dance?" Marina asks.

Estrella's face falls. "I couldn't stand the thought of watching Tatiana with Marc and Evan, and besides, there's too much work to do, you know, on the case. So, I'm at the library looking for clues and Margeaux's looking at..." She side-eyes Margeaux. "Old maps of Africa."

Marina is silent for a moment, her light green eyes blink twice. "Old maps of Africa? Can Margeaux read them?"

"Um, yeah, I guess." Estrella and Margeaux's eyes connect again.

Marina brightens back up. "That Tatiana's awful! Greedy. All she wants is money. Best to stay away from her and pray for her greedy soul. It must be terrible, living with all that greed and ugliness."

Estrella snorts. "It's Tatiana who'd best stay away from me. I'm not praying for that witch. Ever."

"Try sending her love," Marina says. "She won't know what to do."

Estrella rolls her eyes. "I'm hardly going to send love to that bitch. You're always sending love to the least deserving people. If there's a triple homicide, you're praying for the killer. Give the phone to Nicolas, so I can congratulate him."

Estrella tells Nicolas she couldn't be prouder to have him as a brother, even if he does treat her like a kid.

After Nicolas clicks off, Margeaux keeps exploring the maps of Africa in amazed delight, while Estrella flips through a few pages of Tolstoy, then drops it to the floor and opens another of the books on Kit's list. She randomly opens the *Bhagavad Gita* to its second chapter: "*Samkhya Yoga* or *The Eternal Reality of the Soul's Immortality.*"

A picture and a letter fall from its pages!

The photo shows Linda with William Hamilton. Both appear to be about eighteen years old. They smile; their arms circle each other. Mountains and a lake frame them. On the back of the photo, someone has handwritten the words "*Eternal Spring.*"

Estrella hurries to unfold the letter.

> *Climbing Vine*
> *October 1st, 1938*
> *Dearest William,*
> *I hope that life in the city is treating you fine and that the Kesey-Smiths aren't making you dine with them too often. I miss you terribly, of course. I send this missive to alert you to a few important developments here at Climbing Vine.*
> *Scarlett broke her foot falling from an apple tree. She is confined to bed and is a terrible patient, as you can imagine. Thankfully, we found a wonderful young nurse, and she has been administering all the love and patience Scarlett needs right now.*
> *Incidentally, the apples are delicious and plentiful this year. I have sent you a bushel to share with your city friends.*
> *Perhaps you could invite Mr. Philip Gregory to enjoy them with you. I have learned from his wife Martha that they own a piece of land in Mexico that they are anxious to sell.*

The land is mountainous, just outside of Mexico City, and it includes a large lake and a spring. Let's make them an offer for it. This would be a wonderful addition to our investments for this year. Between the Russian holdings, the Canadian parcel, the Norwegian springs, and now this lake in Mexico, our water interests will be flourishing by the spring.

Do keep in mind that the key that I gave to you for safekeeping should remain close to you always. The Great Tabernacle will be arriving soon from London, and the key is our only means of opening it.

The new Map Reader is accompanying them. His name is Mr. Clancy Cotton. Father Ferdinand says he could read them from the first—he stumbled upon them during a tea with Lord Penniston. I hope he's a pleasant fellow. We need him desperately now that we have lost Mirielle.

I've made arrangements for him to stay with you. Expect him in the third week of October. Give him the room closest to the library. We don't want him to waste a moment of time. He will know where else to look for water, and when we can expect an attack. Father said Cotton saw a star far on the horizon, a Newly-Born. Let us pray it will be one of ours.

You must keep young William away from Mr. Cotton, and from the Tabernacle. Though he is our son, I fear that our prayers have not been heard by The Cosmic. He grows redder, his powers increase. This is a most horrible truth, but we must bear it. His placement is superb, as seen from their side. This earthly body betrays me. No matter who he may be, I love him just as much.

I assume our children at Glouton are doing well, though I haven't heard a peep. Perhaps I'll receive a letter this week. I only hope it's not from the headmaster again. Nelson and

Marc do give him a run for his money, just like their father did, by all accounts. I wait anxiously for Christmas when we can all be together at last. Perhaps the holiday will soften our William's heart. Please bring Mr. Cotton with you, and the Tabernacles.

Love always,

Katherine

P.S. Elmer misses you terribly. Every day, he sits on his pillow by the door, waiting for you.

Estrella and Margeaux read the letter over and over. "It's from Kit's grandmother to her grandfather. They reuse names more than us Mexicans."

"Could this be the Great Tabernacle?" Margeaux points to the card catalog. "It is a boxy shape." She reopens the atlas. "Do you think I'm like Mr. Cotton? Are these the maps she meant?"

"Maybe." Estrella reads the letter again. "'He grows redder.' Reminds me of the red army from my vision. And those demons surfing the wave in my Christmas dream." She shivers, recalling, but unable to say aloud, the dream about her mother. "What do you see in there?" she asks Margeaux, who is transfixed by the map.

"A line of planets...or stars...or something," Margeaux replies. "They spiral back to a sun. Each one has a name—at least, I think those are names." She takes a closer look. Her eyes gloss over, and she stares at the map for several minutes before she abruptly snaps out of her trance. "I see your name, Estrella. Right here."

. . .

"Honey, you look like a refugee." Dr. Anderson sips a thick green drink behind her enormous desk. "Can I get you one of these? Ms.

Tempest makes a mean smoothie." Dr. Anderson pushes a button on her desk. "Ms. Tempest, will you make another smoothie?" She sizes up Estrella. "And put extra stuff in it."

"Thank you for giving me permission to see my mom in jail," Estrella says, but she's only half in the room—the other half is back in the library.

Dr. Anderson's hand reflexively moves to her chest. "My God, Estrella Chavez, I give you permission to do whatever the hell you want. My heart's breaking just looking at you. Dammit, God is one cruel S.O.B." She reaches across the desk to cover Estrella's hand with her own. "I feel responsible for you, now that Kit's gone and your mother's all locked up in jail with common murderers and thieves. I would literally do anything for you at this point."

Tears gather behind Estrella's eyes as Ms. Tempest enters with the smoothie, sets it in front of Estrella, and silently leaves the room. Estrella wipes the few tears that have made their way through and reaches for the smoothie. "It does taste good," she says, taking another swallow, then asks Dr. Anderson what she's been wanting to ask her since the last time they met in this office, and especially since she saw the photo fall from the *Bhagavad Gita*.

"How well did you know my mom? When she was younger, I mean."

"Not too well. I met her through Kit and William in college, back when they went to the ranch in Mexico for the summers. William the third, that is—it's a long line of lineage if you know what I mean. I got to go once for a long weekend, one of the best weekends of my life. Talk about a wild crew. Man, was your mom beautiful, let me tell you what. Smart as a whip, too. Never wasted a word. You gotta admire that in someone." Dr. Anderson stops to sip her green drink.

"William?" Estrella asks. "Evan's dad?" She recalls that younger version of him in the photo: his arms wrapped around her mother, both of them smiling in the summer sun, his posture practically daring someone to hurt the thin, raven-haired young woman in his embrace.

"That's the one. Kit's brother. Well, the one who actually lives in reality, not the one living out some pubescent fantasy, running from his problems, trotting the globe like it's Disneyland."

"You mean Marc's dad?" Estrella asks, remembering the night she broke into the library.

Dr. Anderson nods. "He and his son are like two peas in a pod. That Marcus Aurelius Hamilton better watch out or he'll end up just like him, living lazy off his money, an easy target for women with big titties and sharp claws."

An image of Marc with that kind of girl hits Estrella right in the solar plexus, but she remembers that he's dead to her. She wants to ask more about her mom and William, but the lifetime of training she's received, that insists she shouldn't talk about family business, kicks in. Instead, she focuses on the person sitting in front of her. "You're looking great, Dr. Anderson."

Dr. Anderson jumps up from her desk and does a burpee on the spot. "Yeah, I'm down another ten pounds. Quit smoking, too. Talk about addiction. I couldn't very well be toting that body around and do what I've got to do here. I don't know how I did it for so long."

"I'm impressed. Your transformation makes me want to train a little harder. I've been slacking—I'm just so tired all the time lately."

Dr. Anderson slurps the last dregs of her smoothie. "Be easy on yourself, child. In time you'll get your energy back, don't worry. So, how's it going in the library? Find anything interesting?"

"Um..." Estrella considers the letter from Kit's grandmother, the photo of her mom and Bill Hamilton, and Margeaux's map of Africa. She decides not to mention it, at least not today. "Just some old books and letters and stuff. Pretty neat, though." Estrella says, then asks. "Do the words 'eternal spring' mean anything to you?"

"Doesn't ring a bell, except for the line from Keats. What a poet. I almost said I'd ask Kit about it. Isn't that something? Just a reflex."

"I know! I want to ask Kit so many things. Mainly, does she know who killed her?" Estrella says, revisiting the image of blood trickling from Kit's nose and ears, the smashed glass, Linda kneeling in front of her, and Zandra's car alarm screams.

Ms. Tempest pokes her head in. "Dr. Anderson, your three o'clock has arrived."

Dr. Anderson hugs Estrella. "Keep me posted on the eternal spring thing. We will get your mom out of jail, I promise you—even if we have to break her out!"

"I'm way ahead of you on a jailbreak," Estrella says.

Dr. Anderson chuckles, hugging Estrella a second time. "I'm looking forward to an eternal spring break myself, I can tell you that." Dr. Anderson says as she walks Estrella to the door. "You got any plans?"

"Not really. Just working on the library, seeing my mom...," Estrella remembers who she's talking to, "and studying."

"Well, that sounds about as exciting as watching ice get made in the freezer, but you know your own mind."

Estrella exits into the sunny outer office and runs smack into Tatiana, getting close enough to catch a hint of perfume on her silk blouse. Her nose gets a second whiff. She catches an undertone of rotten meat.

"Hi, Estrella. How's life been treating you?"

"As if you don't know," Estrella mutters. "And you need to take a bath. You smell like shit."

"Ms. Duplessis, you can go in now," Ms. Tempest says.

Tatiana gives Estrella the finger as she gracefully slides into Dr. Anderson's office and closes the door.

...

The gloomy clouds of February sneeze out specks of cold rain.

"Thank you for taking me to visit Mom," Estrella says to Yves. "I can't wait to get her out of there. True, the place is super-secure, but every system has its weakness."

"That's what I've always found," Yves replies, keeping his eyes on the icy road. "Kit's been visiting me in my dreams."

"You have dreams? I can't even picture you asleep, you're so proper. Except of course on New Year's Eve." Yves winces as Estrella, hoping to sound more polite, says, "What was the dream?"

"Dreams," Yves replies. "Four of them so far. She wants me to see Margeaux."

"Margeaux? Why? Kit barely even knew her."

Yves glances at Estrella then returns his eyes to the road. "Kit had quite a lot of faith in you, Estrella. She believed you are here to accomplish great things. But her message was clear; I'm to give Margeaux some books. They're currently in Switzerland."

A little splinter of envy spikes Estrella's heart.

"Will you arrange a meeting when I return?" Yves asks as he pulls into the driveway of the Chavez cottage. "I've chartered a jet for Geneva. I leave tomorrow."

...

"We got the jewelry!"

Kit's favorite ten karat sapphire necklace dangles around her long neck, jewel-encrusted bracelets drape from her arm like a sleeve. Diamonds, rubies, and emeralds cascade from her ears.

"And look!" Marina guides Estrella to the kitchen table, push-es aside the architectural plans for the Versailles-like family compound she's having built, and lays the bracelet Hugo made for Kit in the center. "The recording, receiving and light-bending device! Nicolas brought it over this morning. He swears he hasn't listened to anything yet, but he'll want a copy soon. There's almost a hundred hours of material."

Estrella presses the first link. Kit's voice, raspy as ever, says, "Check, check, check, one-two, one-two." Estrella presses the bracelet to her heart, silently thanking God, Mary of Guadalupe, Saint Anthony, and Jesus himself. "This bracelet could literally free Mom from jail." She strides to the kitchen counter. "If there's a hundred hours of material here, I'm making a cup of coffee."

• • •

The first three hours don't reveal anything about Kit's murder, but they are highly entertaining.

Apparently, Kit used the bracelet to record her thoughts on any number of subjects, from her analysis of the most recent *Game of Thrones* episode, to why she really does prefer Mozart to Beethoven—she doesn't care what Alex Ross at *The New Yorker* says—to why fruit and nut trees, are the salvation of the earth, both for their potential to drink CO_2 emissions, transforming something acidic into something alkaline, as well as to fuel the people of the world with "really a delicious, simple and slimming" food source.

The highlight of the first hours of the recordings is when, in the midst of a rant about how much she can't stand Dixon Duplessis (recorded just a few days after he announced his run for the presidency), Kit shrieks in terror.

"A mouse! Oh my God! Help! Yves! Help!"

There is a sound of scuffling, more horrified shrieks, and Yves's voice, both trying to soothe ("It's alright Kit, I've got him, you can get down now.") and breaking into uncontrollable laughter ("No, I know there is nothing funny about this.").

Marina and Estrella laugh too, tears streaming down their cheeks. It's the first time they've had a belly-tightening giggle since the quinceañera, when Kit told them an unrepeatable dirty joke about a priest and "his flock" right before Cesar led Estrella into the cathedral.

Just as they dry their cheeks, the front door opens. Zandra, Cesar, Alfonso, Hugo, and Zandra's little dogs bustle into the kitchen, laden with plates of hot food. Nadine arrives an hour later, her homing instincts for Zandra's cooking as sharp as ever.

Estrella soaks in the familiar feelings, her family's laughter nourishing her like a soup. Everyone shares an unspoken pact not to talk about Linda, Kit, or the Water Trust. Even sorrow needs a rest.

MARCH

Patience, Fortitude,

and Andy Warhol

"Look, Kit, it's time to privatize the Trust's holdings in the west, particularly the northwest region surrounding the Colorado River. Let's develop the oil resources that you damn well know the people need out there."

"Can they drink the oil, Senator Clay?" Kit replies from the bracelet. "They're already in a drought out there."

"Kit, I appreciate all you've done for me, but I'm going to have to block the tax breaks for your clean water and energy technologies if you don't meet me in the middle on this."

"In other words, you've got a better offer. I can only guess from who."

"You're being unreasonable, Kit."

"That's Ms. Hamilton to you, your former benefactor. If you need anything more, I'm sure Tom here can do it for you. I'm surprised he's not already under the table getting started, subservient as he is." Kit snaps her fingers. "My coat, please. The recording beeps off.

"Wow. Kit was such a badass," Estrella says to herself from her dorm room bed where she listens to Kit's bracelet. "And apparently funding Senator Clay until basically right before she was murdered. And his friend Tom, maybe? Whoever that is." Estrella

251

moves Senator Clay to the number three position on her Excel spreadsheet of motivated suspects. Right after her mom and Yves.

"Why does everyone dress so casually these days?" Kit's voice shocks Estrella. The recording is still playing. Estrella checks the digital time stamp. Parent's Weekend. The recording beeps off and beeps on again. First, the sounds of a party—music and the rumble of many voices—then a Brooklyn accent Estrella knows very well.

"She's so much like Victor," Dr. Mather says. "Nikki says she's one of the best fighters she's seen, already strong enough for the unlocking. But we still can't see her, so neither can they. Are you sure she's the one?"

"Wait. Are they talking about *me*?" Estrella puts the bracelet right next to her ear.

"Am I sure about any of this?" Kit replies. "You just take care of your end. I'm watching the Scroll."

"*Are* you taking care of your end?" Dr. Mather sounds almost angry. "Half the assets are still private. We planned to have well over seventy percent by now."

"Don't be forward about my money," Kit snaps back. "I don't care *who* you are. Maybe you aren't who I think you are anyway. Maybe I'm the one being fooled."

The sound of the party gets loud and then soft again when a door opens, then clicks shut.

"Oh, hello, Bill. We were just talking about my contribution to Dr. Mather's water purification program at MIT. You should think about giving." Kit sounds rushed, caught.

Dr. Mather laughs. Beep.

The recording beeps back on. Horns honk in the background. "My dear Margeaux," Kit says, causing Estrella to sit up and hold her breath. "You see what you get for your gift. A very short lifetime of wondering who you can trust."

The dorm room door bangs open. It's Margeaux: headphones on her ears, pack on her back, hair pink as ever. "Hey Star, what's new?"

Estrella discreetly pushes the bracelet under her pillow. "Nothing. Just homework," she replies.

•••

"I see that the prosecution started calling witnesses," Amaka says as the girls make their way to the dining hall.

"Marina says every enemy my mom never knew she had is coming out of the woodwork to establish motive," Estrella replies. "Her own secretary, who's been to our house several times, and who I actually thought was cool, suddenly says she never trusted my mom, and that all my mom ever wanted was Kit's money and power. And they haven't even gotten to the star witness yet—Ms. Franks. Why did I ever invite her?"

Zaharia and Sylvie join the group, puffs of breath filtering through their scarves.

"Have you heard?" Zaharia asks. "More bombings in Europe, more innocent victims. Su Bang Bang's Caliphate claims responsibility. What a dick he is—such an obvious Napoleon complex."

"Mmmhmm," Sylvie nods. "Like Chirstophe's father. I have noticed that throughout history, some men look for power in violence, making up for their shortcomings."

"The world always underestimates those of slight stature," Amaka says, stretching herself up to her fullest height.

From behind the girls, Adisa throws a snowball at Amare, who simply says, "Cut it out."

"Amare's so handsome, isn't he?" Margeaux whispers to the group of girls, who giggle in assent. "But he's quite serious. Poor Adisa."

"Why are you always worried about what other people are doing?" Estrella snaps at Margeaux. An edgy silence penetrates the group.

"And how are you feeling these days, Estrella?" Zaharia asks.

"All the traumatic incidents in her life are causing her to fray," Amaka replies. "Do you see that little bald spot on the back of her head? She's so stressed now that her hair is falling out."

Estrella subconsciously touches the spot.

Amaka continues. "And she's becoming angry for no reason and taking it out on the people she loves most. She yelled at me yesterday because I asked her to keep her shoes on her own side of the room."

"I'm right here," Estrella says as the girls enter the dining hall.

"We are all so sad for you!" Sylvie says. "Please know that you don't have to be alone. We are here for you. You don't have to spend every night by yourself in the library."

"I accompany her sometimes," Margeaux says, taking on a dramatic tone. "It's like watching a detective at work. She obsesses over the night of her quince—Ms. Franks at the bar with Zandra, Amaka under the limbo bar. She examines each frame of memory like she's rewinding a movie. But what is just outside her periphery? What can she not see? And then there are all the books on Kit's list, and the map of..."

Estrella and Margeaux share a look. They haven't said anything yet to Amaka about the map of Africa.

Amaka catches their look. "What are you keeping from me?" She doesn't have a chance to ask twice as her eyes follow Estrella's.

John Kaminsky rises from his seat at a table on the outskirts of the room. He walks to Estrella. The girls all file off to a table.

"John. Hey. What are you doing here?" Estrella asks, her face red, her palms sweating.

"Can we talk?" John replies, taking Estrella's tray back to the table where his own tray rests.

"Uh, sure," she says, feeling the eyes of the dining hall following her. "Is everything okay? How did you get in here?" She silently curses herself for looking so bad. She hasn't washed her hair all week because she doesn't want to see more of it swirl down the drain. The bags beneath her eyes are bigger than an old Greek man's, and she's still wearing the clothes she worked out in this morning—the same clothes she slept in last night.

John doesn't seem to notice. He smiles, his liquid blue eyes holding her embarrassed gaze. "Everything's fine. Hargrave gave me a weekend pass for my dad's fiftieth birthday party, and I managed to sweet-talk your principal into letting me meet you for lunch."

"Yeah, Dr. Anderson's awesome."

"So," John says. "I really like you. And I'm really sorry for how I acted over New Year's. I just wanted you to know that. You're going through enough already without having me add to your stress." John takes Estrella's hand.

Estrella stops breathing. "Please wish your dad a happy birthday from all of us," she says, reverting to the manners that Linda and Kit relentlessly impressed upon her from the moment she started talking and saying "impolite" things.

John ruffles her hair affectionately. Estrella stiffens with mortification; her hair is so greasy he could use it to moisturize his hands. But then he caresses her shoulder and tilts his head toward her. They share a slightly awkward laugh as John leans in for a kiss. He's stopped by the sound of a clearing throat. Marc's standing right in front of them.

"Will you introduce me to your friend?" Marc asks.

John stands, extends his hand, and introduces himself, calm and solid as a tree. "I'm sorry for the loss of your aunt. She was a great woman."

Marc, disarmed by John's kindness, shakes John's hand and thanks him for his condolences. Not one eye in the dining hall looks anywhere but at the confrontation happening on the outskirts of the room.

"Will you walk me out, Estrella?" John asks.

Estrella can feel, like humidity, the eyes of Marc watching her and John leave.

. . .

John leads Estrella beneath the leafless branches of Methusaleh.

"You know I can't compete with guys like Marc Hamilton. I don't have their money, and I never will. I don't know which clothes look right. I can't talk about all the places I've been, rub shoulders with celebrities, or whatever they do. I'll probably never know all that much about wines or cheese or polo. I'll always have to work. And I want to work every day, for my family and for my country." He touches the tiny gold heart resting against Estrella's clavicle. "I know you're going through a lot right now; I know we're young, and I know you have so much more on your mind than me, or any boy. But I'm here for you. Whatever you need, just let me know. And when you're ready, I hope we can do a lot more of this."

With those words, John places his warm, dry hand on the small of Estrella's back, draws her into him, and kisses her. This time, their teeth don't touch.

His kiss is almost as good as Marc's.

. . .

"John came to visit me," Estrella says, forcing a smile for her mom, who looks skinny and tired behind the plexiglass.

"That's great! He's such a well-mannered young man. And devout." Linda's eyes light, lifting her whole face.

"I wish the prosecution would stop presenting all these witnesses," Marina says. "All these Water Trust employees and board members, who paint you like a jealous, bitter, cruel woman who does anything to get what she wants."

"Only part of that is true," Linda says. "And I draw the line at murder."

. . .

Marina unlocks the door to the empty, darkened cottage.

"I'm just going to bed," Estrella says. "I'm not hungry."

"Are you sure? We can get order from Jade Buddha, your favorite. You need to eat." Marina holds Estrella in a tight embrace. "You're still growing."

"I'll be alright," Estrella replies as she pulls her heavy legs up the stairs. She checks her phone for the news as her eyelids drop and lift, drop and lift. She reads a headline from the BBC:

In Pakistan, another country Su Bang Bang's Caliphate now claims as its own, a thousand college professors have been hung for "intellectual disobedience."

The photo shows a street of corpses.

. . .

The frozen waters reflect the shadows of the pines, the only trees that keep their foliage. The ground and sky blend into a single gray, snow covers the riverbanks. Islid pulls Estrella into her, curls around her, makes Estrella her cub.

Estrella falls into a second sleep, floating away, over the ocean, above mountains. Now she is in a cluster of trees, a full moon lighting the lush forest. A fire blazes in a clearing. A leopard lies before the fire, its legs bound. Estrella instinctively moves to untie him, but a rough hand pulls her back. Estrella turns to find the trunk of an elephant, her forehead bearing the mark of a star.

"It is too dangerous," the elephant says, "They have the knife."

Men and women, naked except for their painted masks, circle the fire chanting, "Necare, necare, necare." One woman beats a drum. The chanting gets louder.

The leopard screams and spasms, his eyes wild. A man kneels and holds the leopard by the neck. His other hand holds a black crystal knife. The chanting intensifies as the man slices the leopard's throat. He cuts deeper into the neck, severing the head and holding it high.

The eyes of the leopard go cold.

The masked cup their hands, forming a line to drink the blood that drips from the leopard's head. Their lips red, they rub the blood into their bare skin. The man sheaths the black crystal blade.

• • •

Estrella wakes with a gasp. Tears wet her pillow.

She goes to Marina's room, where her sister sits up in bed, holding a rosary, her face also wet with tears.

"I can't bear this world sometimes," Marina says through sobs. "Reality here is so far from the truth. Where is the light, the truth?"

• • •

"What is truth?" Dr. Mather asks.

The Mystery Schoolers remain silent.

"The Quran has much to say about truth," Zaharia finally says. *"Nay, we hurl the truth against falsehood, so it knocks out its brains, and lo! It vanishes.* Truth will always defeat lies because truth is one of the names of Allah. Truth is God himself."

Estrella perks up. "The Bible says that Jesus is the truth and the way and the light, so maybe God *is* truth, since at least two religions see it that way." She recalls Marina's teary words about truth and light, and her nightmare. Her eyes cast down.

"Again, religion. We could scour history and not find any institutions so full of lies." Christophe sighs. "Truth is what the powerful want us to believe. Whoever holds the power holds the truth. We have a saying in my country: '*tell God the truth, but give the judge money.*'"

"Yes, truth's a tricky thing, isn't it?" Margeaux says. "*The instruments of darkness tell us truths, win us with honest trifles, to betray's in deepest consequence.* That's from the Shakespearean religion."

Evan's head shakes as he speaks. "That's all crazy. Truth is what you can see with your own eyes. Truth is evidence, proof. That's why we have the scientific method—we prove what is true so there can be no doubt."

"But science doesn't know everything. In science, we are only discovering pieces of the truth. Perhaps one day we *will* find a God at the center of the universe. Human knowledge may still be in its infancy." Sylvie's high voice pierces the still air of the classroom.

"*The truth is not always beautiful, nor beautiful words the truth.*" Nikki's quotes the Tao Te Ching.

"Yeah, all this about science and evidence, I don't buy it because, as they say, appearances can be deceiving. We must all decide what is true with our own hearts," Octavio says.

"You make too narrow the enormity of truth." Amaka confronts Octavio. "And you deny the power of the absolute. Like Zaharia and Estrella said, truth is a name we give to that which is most mighty."

Louis immediately follows. "Amaka's right. It's like that African proverb: *Truth is like a fire: you cannot cover it with dry leaves.*" Amaka stifles an approving smile.

"But you can put out a fire with water," Tatiana says. "Where there is one force, there is another. Truth is no more powerful than a wave. We just see what we want to see, do what we want to do, and convince ourselves it's coming from the heart, or from God. But truth is a lie. Life is a jungle. And in a jungle, the leopard always eats."

"Om." Shabad chants the primitive sound that embodies all.

"So that leaves only one of us," Dr. Mather says, after the calming of Shabad's chant.

"Mark Twain had this to say about truth," Marc says, a look of sadness in his big, brown eyes. "*Truth is mighty and will prevail. There is nothing the matter with this, except it ain't so.*"

...

"Truth," Estrella mutters to herself as she reviews the email Nicolas sent her summarizing the week's court proceedings. "Yeah, right."

The prosecution produced what they say is evidence about the curare: packages from northern Brazil that have been tracked to the Chavez cottage. Curare comes from northern Brazil.

In his cross-examination, Nicolas got the detective to admit that packages have also been tracked to Kit Hamilton's mansion. In fact, both residences received packages from northern Brazil regularly.

"Wait a minute," Estrella says out loud, prompting Margeaux, who's reading the map of Africa on her bed under the moonlit window, to say, "What's that?"

"I've actually opened packages from Brazil at both Kit's house *and* my house. That's where they get their anti-aging superfoods. They're bright green. Ironic, when you look at it in a certain way."

Estrella's phone rings.

"Who's calling you?" Amaka asks, emerging from the bathroom, smelling like a garden. "I sense something of importance will be revealed."

It's Yves.

"I've returned," he says. "I must see Margeaux."

· · ·

"It's called the Tarts & Voyeurs, because everyone's making out all over the place," Margeaux says from her sprawled position on the library floor. "The fabled Freshmen Arts & Culture Weekend, a Glouton tradition, led by Dr. Anderson and policed by Coach. As if young Gloutonites have never set foot in a museum in New York City, when, in fact, several have entire wings in their family name."

"There's no freshman I want to make out with," Estrella replies, mentally deciding when to break the news to Margeaux about meeting with Yves.

Margeaux nods. "Nor I. If only Octavio was a freshman..." She squints at the map of Africa. "Dammit! I can't read anything today. I swear there were names here last time." She closes then opens her eyes.

"It seems like my powers come and go, too," Estrella says. "The high point was probably right after the Vision Quest, before my stupid quinceañera. I *knew* I didn't want to have that party." She pauses, the words she wants to ask at the top of her throat. "So, um, you know Yves, Kit's well, actually *my* butler?"

"You mean the British Clark Kent?" Margeaux replies. "Clearly not born of the upper classes, yet like nobility in every facet of accent, manners and dress? The one who's top of your suspects list? I've taken note."

"Um, yeah. So, apparently, he had a dream that Kit said she had something for you, and so Yves went to Geneva for it, and now he has to give it to you. I mean, I don't know why he couldn't just give whatever it is to me, and I could give it to you, but whatever—it's all past me now."

Margeaux replies, "Kit's been visiting my dreams, too. She told me not to say anything about them to you."

"What do you mean?" Estrella huffs.

"I mean that while the black sky has conspired with the moon to swell our sleeping breaths in our narrow beds, Kit Hamilton has been having regular dates with me. Mostly, we just read tarot cards, study astrology charts, and smoke cigarettes."

Estrella ignores the pang of jealousy in her heart. "Okay then," she says, texting Yves. "We'll meet him in the city, during Tarts & Voyeurs next week."

• • •

"Well, now you know." Kit reclines in her gold and velvet chair and lights a cigarette. The wall behind her sparkles with jagged crystals. Water runs beneath her chair.

Estrella tries to hug her, but Kit is in another universe.

"Pay attention!" As Kit floats from her chair, Estrella smells Kit's Clive Christian perfume and the smoke of her cigarette. A chipped jade box glows from the library shelves behind her.

Now they're at the Guggenheim. They waft up the twisted ramp, stopping before a self-portrait of Andy Warhol in drag. "Do you think I look like him?" Kit asks. "I worry that I do."

"Umm..." Kit does resemble the regal portrait.

"I'm kidding." Kit sighs. "You took too long to answer, though." She waves her hand before the portrait; Andy Warhol winks. "Bring Margeaux and Yves here with you during the Tarts & Voyeurs trip next week. I have something to tell them. Ask Margeaux to bring a pen and to build up some

mental fortitude, for Chrissake. This is getting serious. Look at what happened to me."

What happened to Kit! This is her chance.

• • •

Estrella wakes with the question on her lips, but Kit is gone.

• • •

"Young people, this is 42nd Street." Dr. Anderson leads Glouton's freshman class past the theater district of New York City. "It's all nice and safe now, but don't be fooled—there used to be more whores and drunks on this street per square inch than they've got at the Kremlin."

The freshmen continue on, making their way up Fifth Avenue. Dim sun makes breaks in the steady clouds that float above Patience and Fortitude, the stone lions that guard the New York Public Library. Their bemused marble eyes follow the Gloutonites as they pass on their way to the Guggenheim, their last stop.

"An aptly named adventure," Margeaux says. She, Estrella and Amaka bring up the rear of the big group of freshmen. Amare and Adisa trail a few steps behind, both on their phones. "We saw it with our own peeping eyes, didn't we? Quite a lot of tongues and teeth. I must admit to a bit of jealousy. I feel I'll never be kissed."

"Who cares about that?" Amaka asks. "Where is this portrait? We must have a plan to get away from Dr. Anderson and Coach."

"Just because I told you about the plan, doesn't mean you're the boss now," Margeaux whispers.

"Of course I am the boss," Amaka replies. "And if I didn't rip that old, irrelevant map from your hands and demand to know what was in it, you would not have told me anything. It is lucky for you that I forgave your secrecy. Both of you." She looks at Estrella. "And when we return, you will tell me everything you see in your supposed map of stars. It is my continent, and I will learn everything this atlas is hiding."

"Okay, so I'm the boss," Estrella says. "And that was Margeaux's choice with the whole map of Africa. I can't read it either. Anyway, Kit said to build up our mental walls, so, *silence!*"

They enter the Guggenheim, minds empty. Amaka takes Estrella's hand, guiding her up the ramp, Margeaux right behind.

"Where are you going?" Amare's baritone reverberates behind them.

Amaka turns. "We all have women troubles. Because we are roommates, we are in sync. Please mind your own business and wait for us here."

Amare reddens, backing away, as the girls dodge into the bathroom, then back out the other side. They twist up the ramp to the top floor.

Yves sits on a bench, a copy of *The New York Post* folded in his lap. Its cover reads, "*Did the Butler Do It?*" The corresponding picture is of Yves and Kit.

Luckily, no one else is around, just a few blue-hairs moving slow as purgatory from one display to the next. The girls and Yves face Andy Warhol's *Self-Portrait in Drag*. Yves takes out an old-fashioned monocle from the breast pocket of his Tom Ford blazer. "In the dream she said I'd need this. It was in the safety deposit box," he looks at Margeaux, "with some items I have for you." He motions to the briefcase in his hands. Margeaux nods.

Yves says, "Looks a bit like Kit, doesn't he?" He situates his monocle.

"Now what?" Estrella looks to Margeaux, but her eyes are glassy, rolled back into her head. So are Amaka's. Estrella's own eyelids flutter.

Suddenly, Andy Warhol speaks in Kit's voice.

"Yves, in addition to those papers from Geneva, please give Margeaux the deck of cards that's hidden in the kitchen, at the back of the silver drawer. And Yves, I miss you so! Try to get on without me." Yves flashes a sad smile.

"Margeaux, I hate to have to tell you this, but you're going to have to make a real effort to silence your thoughts. Everyone who's ever taken a Mystery School class can hear them, and your life is in danger if the wrong person hears about the map of Africa." Margeaux puts her hands on either side of her head, as if to physically hold her thoughts in.

"Estrella, my dear, dear darling. My *God*, you were the cutest child. I'm proud of you for trying to help your mother, but you've got to get some rest—you're falling apart. And you'll need all the energy you can muster for what's ahead of you. Get Saul to tell you more. Tell him I told you it's time."

"Amaka, I'm not surprised that you've made your way here. You're definitely Babatunde's daughter—so powerful already. You've no idea what your father's given up for you and your mother. And by the way, that dress looks positively stunning on you—I can see why you're destined for Hollywood." Amaka nods.

"Oh no," Andy Warhol says. "You'd all better turn around."

Amare and Adisa meet their wide eyes. In the corner of the room, Estrella notices Dr. Anderson darting out of view.

Yves removes the monocle, nods to Amaka's guards, smooths his suit, and walks away without a word. He leaves the briefcase under the newspaper on the bench.

"Women's issues are very complicated," Amaka says to Amare, who frowns.

"Apparently so," Adisa replies, as Estrella picks up the newspaper and briefcase. "But we cannot have a human species without you, so we must adjust." He laughs as he and Amare accompany the girls back to the gift shop, where Coach and Dr. Anderson chat amicably by a table of jewelry.

...

Only one lamp light shines in the dusk-soaked dorm-room, though Marina's crystal catches Estrella's eye with its pink glow. "What do you think she meant about me being in danger because of the map of Africa?" Margeaux whispers.

"It is bizarre that only you can see the map as you do," Amaka whispers back. "Maybe there is someone who would pluck out your eyes to read it for themselves."

Margeaux covers her eyes with her long fingers topped by chewed fingernails.

"Amaka!" Estrella hisses. "No one's going to pluck out your eyes," she says to Margeaux. "But...why *are* you in danger? It's a great question, like what does Kit want Dr. Mather to tell me?"

"And what of my father?" Amaka asks. "What did he sacrifice for my mother and me?"

"Perhaps his sanity?" Margeaux retorts.

Amaka rolls her eyes. "Of course, Kit is right about Hollywood. I have determined that world-wide fame will be my next accomplishment."

"What do the papers say?" Estrella asks Margeaux, who looks at the seemingly blank sheets of paper that were in the briefcase.

"Hard to say," Margeaux replies. "Are they in Greek? If only you could see them, Estrella, you might know."

"Yeah, if only," Estrella says, feeling the prickle of fury in her belly. "Why *can't* I read them? WTF?"

A knock at their door makes everyone catch their breaths.

Alexis, the R.A. hands Estrella a gift basket. "It's from your butler," she says. "Well, I mean a delivery service." She doesn't move.

"Thank you," Amaka says, opening the door wider. "I think I hear someone calling your name from the kitchen. They said they were going to eat your cheesecake."

Alexis turns her ear down the hall. "That's from my mom. They better not." She walks swiftly toward the kitchen. Amaka closes the door.

Under boxes of cookies and crackers, wrapped in a silk Hermes scarf, is a deck of playing cards and a simple note that reads, '*From Kit's drawer.*'

Estrella hands the cards to Margeaux. "Can you see what they say?"

All three phones in the room light at once. It's a text from Dr. Mather. Just one word: Mueo.

"Silence," Estrella says. "Fine then, we won't talk about it. But that doesn't mean we aren't going to figure it out another way."

• • •

Estrella reclines on her bed in the empty dorm room. "Who will Kit talk shit about today?" She pushes the link on Kit's bracelet.

Quincy's squawk jolts Estrella upright. "You sure you want to do that?"

"Be quiet, Quincy," Linda's voice says.

Kit says, "Remember you have to follow the suit of the card that has been played."

"They must be playing bridge," Estrella whispers to herself, remembering the games Kit and Linda played every week with Yves and sometimes Evan.

Evan's voice says, "Who are you talking to, Aunt Kit? We all know the game."

At that moment, Amaka and Margeaux tramp into the dorm. Margeaux fishes Kit's cards from under her mattress and spreads them out. Estrella focuses all her concentration on planting Kit's words in Margeaux's mind.

"How funny! It's just like a voice popped into my head and said, 'Follow the suit of the card that has been played,'" Margeaux says out loud. "That's helpful, isn't it?" She looks at Amaka and Estrella's frowns. "Oh! My bad. Mueo, mueo mueo."

. . .

Estrella rests her greasy, pony-tailed head against a bookshelf in Kit's wing of the library, preparing for another session of searching for clues. She tucks her nose into the Bible. *Revelation.*

Margeaux darts in with the map of Africa.

"Something became clear once I figured out the cards," Margeaux whispers. "I know we aren't supposed to talk, but this is important."

Estrella holds her breath as soft rain dances on the roof.

"I think the papers are a list of *spells.* I believe they're written in a hybrid language of Latin, Greek and Sanskrit? And then a picture of something, like someone flying, or someone sleeping. Like I saw some words—one of them I know for sure was the Sanskrit symbol for Spring, because I recognized it from Shabad's tattoo, and then there was an image of a wolf."

Estrella nods. "Okay."

"And then I saw something in the map, in the stars, or whatever they are." Margeaux leans in close, pulling her black cashmere cardigan tighter around her. "It was Babatunde. And your father. Both of them, meeting again and again throughout time and space." The room grows darker by degrees as night descends. "They are protectors. Of North America and Africa."

"Protectors?" Estrella whispers.

"Of the crystals," Margeaux says. "They're in Mexico, Africa—all over the world, it looks like."

"Crystals? Like all the crystals in my dreams, and my Vision." Estrella hugs Margeaux and starts to cry. "I feel like I've been waiting to hear this all my life. It's like I can almost see the crystals under the earth, lining the ocean floors. What else do you see?"

"I can see the locations of the crystal clusters, like constellations, but inside the earth, and I can read the time of some events, and see certain people, dead and alive. Like Babatunde is standing guard over a cluster in Africa, and Victor used to be a guardian in Mexico, but now he's everywhere."

"What do you mean my father is everywhere?" Estrella stops herself from grabbing Margeaux by the throat to pull out her words more quickly.

"It's hard to explain. Victor was in Mexico until he died; now he is everywhere. That's all I can see. Maybe Amaka knows something."

Hearts beating fast, they abandon the library and their books, and all but run through the rainy dusk to Amaka.

•••

Amaka opens her eyes and unfolds her legs from the lotus position. "I could feel you coming," she says to her wet, breathless roommates. "It is about my father."

Her prescience renders them mute for a moment.

Finally, Margeaux whispers, "I know we aren't supposed to talk about this...oh wait!" She gets a piece of paper and writes everything she told Estrella.

Amaka reads the paper then burns it in Margeaux's Waterford crystal ashtray. "Perhaps the crystals are diamonds? I have long suspected that my father has a secret diamond mine on one of the tracts of land he owns throughout the continent. If so, I won't need a stupid rich husband; they're proving to be more difficult to control than I anticipated."

Margeaux shakes her head. "Definitely crystals."

Estrella watches Amaka do the math in her head and become disappointed. "So, you say my father, Babatunde Abioye, a man who only lives to enrich his family and his company, is protecting a relatively worthless crystal cave. And he was doing this with Victor Chavez, a man who gave his life for a worker's revolution?" Amaka paces the room while Margeaux and Estrella follow their roommate's every pivot on the carpeted floor until Amaka stops. "What do you want me to do?"

"Do?" Estrella asks.

"Search his private office, blackmail his top executives, break into his email server? I know he is hiding something from me now. He never mentioned knowing your father," she says to Estrella. "Even when I showed an interest in him after I Googled you before school."

An alarm rings on Margeaux's phone. "It's to remind me to meditate," she says.

"For now, I think that's what we all need to do," Estrella says. "Stay silent and breathe. Hopefully, we'll know what to do when the time comes."

• • •

Estrella writes out physics problems on her iPad from her unmade bed. Outside, the sun hides behind a thick coat of clouds. Her head throbs. She's exhausted—mentally and physically. Whenever she tries to rest, like Kit suggested, an image of her mother in jail develops in her mind.

Her phone buzzes with a kiss emoji from John. She replies with two kisses as, through the window, she watches Marc, Evan, and Tatiana walk toward the dining hall. She pops open another Red Bull. "If only I could go to sleep like Islid, the bear from my dreams," she says to herself. "Hibernate and wake up to a brand-new life. But I have to focus, now more than ever. I can't let my mom down."

She goes back to her work, not even looking up when Amaka and Margeaux sit together on her bed.

Amaka clears her throat and says, "Come to Mexico with us for spring break."

"What?" Estrella looks into two sets of sympathetic eyes. "I don't have time for fun now. You know that. Plus, my mom would never let me go."

"It's not for fun," Margeaux says. "We'll be in Cuernavaca, just outside Mexico City. It'll be like rejuvenating at a spa. Quiet. Relaxing."

"It is very beautiful," Amaka says. "And very safe. Amare and Adisa will be there. And we talked to Marina, who talked to your mother. She said you can go if you bring Marina to chaperone."

"You went behind my back and talked to Marina?"

"We wanted to ask her before we talked to you," Margeaux replies. "She said she could use a spa retreat as well. And your mum wants you to go."

Estrella imagines herself sitting by a pool, sleeping. "It does sound like heaven. And I know I've hit a dead end with finding Kit's murderer. Maybe a break will help me see things I might be missing. But I don't know."

"Yes, you do know—you just said it yourself," Amaka says.

Estrella smiles. "Okay, I'll go."

Amaka hugs Estrella and kisses her on her forehead.

"For all your talk of armies and power, Amaka, I swear your hugs feel like roses radiating from your heart," Estrella says.

"Well, isn't that poetic," Margeaux says. "I might use that in a song if you don't mind."

"This retreat will be just what you need: the City of Eternal Spring," Amaka says. "Complete rejuvenation. My mother has hired a new housekeeper. I will make sure she prepares everything and then makes herself absent. Housekeepers are so nosy."

Estrella blinks in surprise. "What did you just say?"

"It is true—I have never known one who wasn't," Amaka replies.

"No, I mean about eternal spring."

"I said you need a complete rejuvenation. You look terrible, frankly. Those circles under your eyes make you look like a battered wife."

"But you said it was the city of what?" Estrella asks, recalling the photo of her mom and Bill Hamilton with the words 'Eternal Spring' on the back, and the same words highlighted in Keats's poem.

"Eternal spring: that's what they call Cuernavaca because it's always so beautiful," Amaka says as she turns to Margeaux. "Pack sunscreen. Red skin will not complement your pink hair."

APRIL

Cuernavaca

Jacarandas bloom from the trees that line the long driveway leading up to Amaka's mansion. The blue sky caresses the purple flowers.

"This is the best place ever. Already, I never want to leave. Why did Mom take us to cold, boring Connecticut?" Estrella asks Marina. "We should've stayed here."

"She wanted to escape all the bad memories," Marina, up front with the driver, replies as she wipes the tears from her light green eyes. "But it is so beautiful, isn't it? The ranch where we were born is only about a hundred miles northwest of here."

"Memories of the fire?" Margeaux whispers to Estrella as their car passes through the gates of Montaña Árbol, Amaka's family vacation compound in the City of Eternal Spring. Amare and Adisa follow in a car carrying only them and everyone's suitcases, primarily Amaka's and Marina's.

"And her father's assassination," Amaka whispers to Margeaux, "But why would you bring up such a thing? We are here to relax and find peace."

Estrella's cells vibrate with power for the first time in months, like they did at the Vision Quest. "When I get settled, I'm taking a run," Estrella says as she disembarks, almost floating through the little purple petals that dust the awakening earth.

A yellow bird calls from a branch.

"*Welcome home, Little Star,*" it sings.

. . .

"I needed to relax," Marina chirps from her lounge chair by the pool as she slathers the world's most expensive skin care products onto her already flawless skin. "Celeste James swears by this serum. Estrella, will you go get me another daiquiri? These are so good! Great recipe, Margeaux."

The warm, dry sun sinks into Estrella's skin as she refills Marina's drink from the poolside bar. Amaka, wearing the newest one-piece, taps relentlessly on her phone. "I'm telling my Bimbo not to come and visit."

"Poor Bimbo," Margeaux says. "He doesn't yet realize that you are just using him for his vast wealth so that one day you can raise an army and conquer the world."

"Everyone has a purpose," Amaka replies, then says, "I see things are as I knew they would be...everyone's looking for me since I've gone off social media. Law Four: *Always say less than necessary.*"

Estrella sips on her daiquiri. None of them are supposed to be drinking but all of them are.

"Marina's not much of a chaperone, but she is a fun one," Margeaux whispers. "Like a modern Mary Poppins."

Amare, from one of the poolside tables, alternately looks at his phone and works on his homework. "Why is Amare basically the most serious and scary person I've ever met?" Estrella whispers to Margeaux. "We've been hanging out together for two solid days now, and he literally has not said a word. He's the real chaperone."

"Unlike Adisa," Margeaux says, pointing to the younger brother, who bounces on his chaise to the rhythm of the reggae beats coming from the speakers that surround the pool. Every now and then, he raps out a lyric and takes a sip of his drink.

The doorbell buzzes.

Amare looks up. "You are expecting guests?" he asks Amaka.

"No," she says without looking up from her phone.

"Get it," Amare says to Adisa.

Adisa takes another sip before he saunters into the house. He returns a moment later. "It is for you," he says to Amaka.

"Who is it?"

"An old friend from the neighborhood."

"Amaka, you are the most popular person I've ever met—you make friends everywhere you go." Marina says.

"It must be Señora Jimenez's daughter," Amaka says, wrapping herself in a silk robe and gliding into the house. She will be a fun addition to our party. She knows all the neighborhood gossip. Adisa, make her a drink."

Adisa dutifully heads over to the bar cart to begin blending.

"The youngest always gets bossed around, Adisa," Estrella says. "I should know."

A spasm wrings Estrella's stomach. "Dammit! Is that a cramp?" she whispers to Margeaux. "Of course I would get my period now. I'll be right back." She heads into the mansion, just a minute behind Amaka. Ahead of her, Amaka checks her makeup in the hallway mirror. Amaka opens the massive door, and a familiar male voice says, "Howdy, neighbor!"

Louis Washington.

Estrella ducks behind a huge flower arrangement.

Louis thrusts a bouquet of flowers at Amaka; she makes no move to take them. "We got a place just down the road," he says, leaning in for a kiss. Amaka backs away.

"Are you here with Miss Teen Mexico, El Presidente?"

He laughs happily at her reference to his Valentine's Day date. "You're a little jealous, I think. It means you care."

Amaka rolls her eyes. "Leave now. We came here to get away from stress, not to have it come knocking at our front door with bodega flowers." She takes the flowers and sniffs them as Louis moves closer.

Amaka steps back. "My information is that you were going to Haiti to volunteer with Médecins Sans Frontières."

"My information is that you and Estrella would be here." Louis grins. "Marc really wants to talk to Estrella. And I want to do so very much more than talk with you, Little Black Dove."

Estrella covers her mouth with her hand to keep from gasping.

Amaka begins to close the door. Louis talks in double-time.

"I *am* volunteering at a community center in the city, though, because you know I care about the people, same as you do." Louis winks. "We're staying at Christophe's aunt's second husband's estate down the road. And, we're having a little dinner party tonight. You can be the guest of honor. We can eat some food, listen to some music. You know—have fun together."

Estrella waits to hear Amaka's reply, thinking that a dinner party does kind of sound like fun.

Amaka glances over her shoulder, then whispers, "Tell Marc to stay away from Estrella. She needs to rest, and she has another boyfriend already. A better one. Tell him that."

Estrella smiles as footsteps squish on the floor behind her. She scoots further around the flowers and gets on her knees, so she's totally hidden by the table.

Marina, wearing only her bikini, joins Amaka at the door. "What's going on out here?"

Louis stumbles down the wide porch stairs.

"Marina! You look just...so, so beautiful." He jumps back up and extends his hand for Marina to take. Amaka slaps it away.

Marina giggles. "Just making sure everything is good," she says, sashaying back to the pool. Louis watches her walk away, mouth agape.

Amaka jolts him back to reality. "She is not interested in children. None of us are. Now go, or I'll call my guards."

"Adisa and Amare?" Louis stands taller. "How do you think I know you're here? They love me. Come on, girl. You've got to give me a chance."

"I will give you a chance to leave before I call the police. You know I'll do it."

Louis laughs. "I know you will, but in case you change your mind, we're just down the road." He gallantly bows. "Text anytime."

Amaka says, "I will not ever text you."

"Okay," Louis says. "But know this, Amaka. As beautiful as Marina is, you are more beautiful to me. And know that I mean it when I say, through the mask of Oberon, '*My Queen, we the globe can compass soon, swifter than the wandering moon.*'"

Louis trots out along the row of trees lining the drive, purple petals falling down around him. Amaka smells the roses once more, tosses them into the hedges and heads back to the pool.

Estrella pops into the bathroom before Amaka passes her. She rejoins the party in time to hear Amaka say, "It was just a lowly flower peddler. He had nothing I wanted."

Marina laughs while Adisa refreshes his drink.

• • •

Victor flies up from the ocean, Lupe by his side. He opens his arms and hugs Estrella. A feeling of joy spreads through her cells. Starlight shines from the robe of Mary of Guadalupe. "Paz," she says. Peace.

...

Estrella awakes thoroughly refreshed. She stretches her long legs and toes, as the sun peeks up from the East. The early spring mountain air carries in the thousand flower fragrances that ride on its light breezes. Birds sing outside the open window, "*Peace, peace, peace!*"

"I love this place," Estrella murmurs to herself. She closes her eyes and an image of her mother in jail visits her. She reopens them, a pang of guilt in her heart.

Margeaux rolls out of the facing bed of their suite and picks up the map of Africa from where it rests next to her. "I had a dream," she says. "Kit told me to look at the map right away." She opens the old book. "And here we are! It couldn't be more clear, could it?"

"Not to me," Estrella says as she cranes her neck to look at the map she cannot read.

"I'll check the cards anyway," Margeaux says. She shuffles the deck and pulls a card. "That's it, then. We are to go to Mexico City."

...

"What a fabulous idea!" Marina says, putting on her bejeweled tennis shoes. "I could use some walking."

"We can take the Montaña Árbol Mercedes," Amaka says, packing her Gucci cross-body bag with lip gloss and her chopsticks. "I have had enough of this relaxing. Perhaps we will see Carlos Slim, the wealthiest man in Mexico. My father knows him, but I have yet to be introduced."

"You know there are over eight million people in the city?" Margeaux says, patting sunscreen onto her freckled nose.

"Do not deny me my opportunities," Amaka replies. "I am capable of more than reason permits."

Amare and Adisa stride into the kitchen, both in designer joggers, t-shirts, and impossibly clean tennis shoes. "Shall we go?" Adisa asks. "I have researched the place to get the perfect taco. It is a hidden gem."

Estrella, Amaka, Margeaux and Marina crowd into the backseat, Adisa sits shotgun, and Amare drives the fifty-six miles on a smelly, four-lane highway, into the city.

. . .

A multicolored Oz, Mexico City teems with life. People swarm like colonies of bees; modern glass and steel skyscrapers joust with colonial churches and tiny stucco shacks. Loud buses and fast cars meld into a symphony with the calls of roosters, the laughter of children, and the hurried words of businessmen shouted into their phones. The saturated calm of Cuernavaca leaves Estrella alchemically—water into electricity. By the time they park in the overpriced garage, it seems everyone is buzzing, almost audibly.

A statue of Mary of Guadalupe brings back a flash of Estrella's dream from last night—her father flying up from the ocean.

"I want to move back here," Marina says as she twirls on the sunny street to the beat of a song blasting from a passing car.

"I do too!" Estrella says, swinging her hips through the jewel-toned, tree-lined streets of the oldest part of the city. Fragrant rices and nose-tickling chiles twist with the gentle wind. Somewhere nearby, a man is singing about an unrequited love.

The song reminds her that Marc's in Cuernavaca. Amaka hasn't mentioned her meeting on the porch with Louis, and Estrella hasn't mentioned that she overheard it from her hiding spot behind the plant.

The song of love grows louder as they round a corner, where a man plays an old guitar with an extra hole in its belly. He nods and smiles while he sings, motioning with his eyes to the hat filled with coins on the ground. Margeaux drops in one thousand pesos.

A sign with the word "*musica*" juts out from a dirty stucco building up ahead. "I've been wanting a nylon-string guitar," Margeaux says.

Guitars, violins, tambourines, and trumpets line the walls of the sunlit shop. Incense pours out from a room cordoned off with dusty, heavily embroidered drapes. Estrella walks past the room to bang on a drum she sees next to the guitars.

An arm reaches out and grabs her, pulling her behind the drapes.

Estrella squirms to break free of the strong grip. A tiny, withered woman lets go of her arm. "*Curandera*," she says, pointing to herself.

"Shaman," Estrella says, repeating the word in English. "Like my dad."

The woman motions for Estrella to sit in the chair across from her, and says in Spanish, "I read your fortune. One hundred pesos."

"Gracias, no." Estrella attempts to stand, but the woman forces her back down with a wave of her hand.

"One hundred pesos."

Estrella robotically pulls out the money from her Converse high-top shoe. The music from the other side of the drapes grows louder, lulling Estrella into a trance.

Quick as a leopard, the old woman leaps gracefully to Estrella's side, growing both taller and younger as she does. She anoints Estrella's forehead with oils in the sign of the cross.

Images, like a movie played under water, swim around Estrella. Islid, Dr. Mather, the elephant, a monkey, a whale, Kit speaking through Andy Warhol, Kit on the patio, blood trickling from her lips, a church in the desert, Mary of Guadalupe, Lupe, the wolf from the forest, a house on fire. Her father.

He stands before a deep blue lake, a spring bubbles in the distance. "*Come to the Lago Cristal.*" Light streams from his fingers. He points to Kit's locket. "*Everything you want to believe is true. You are truth. Believe. You know what you are here to do. You are the key. Unlock the power of The Cosmic.*"

Her father dissolves into water, filtered sunlight warms the dusty room. The old woman in front of Estrella says, "He is a tall man with much money. You will have many children. Your time is up now."

Estrella stands, her legs wobbly. Kit's locket tingles on her chest. She rubs her eyes.

"A tip?" the woman crows.

Estrella pushes a wad of money into the woman's hand. She stumbles, dazed, into the sun-drenched shop, where Margeaux and Amaka laugh and play with the guitars. Adisa and Marina bang on drums. Amare picks at a bass.

"What was in there?" Amaka asks Estrella.

"A fortune-teller."

"Good. I need some answers about my future. You can go first," Amaka says.

"What do you mean? I already had my fortune read. Didn't you notice I was in there for like, forever?" Estrella touches her locket. It's warm, and each beat of her heart is like an electric charge throughout her body.

Amaka looks closely at Estrella. "You were only there for one minute." She strides across the room and parts the curtains. Xylophones line the walls. No *curandera* anywhere.

Estella feels for her money. It's gone, too.

• • •

Estrella whispers to Margeaux and Amaka as they rifle through blouses in an open-air market drenched in sunlight. "I was hypnotized, I'm telling you. I saw my dad, and all these animals, and this place called the Lago Cristal. We need to find it."

"Sylvie will look beautiful in this blouse," Amaka says, holding up an embroidered top. "She should take more care of her appearance. This will be a start. And this turquoise ring will accentuate Zaharia's long fingers. I will say the gifts are from all of us, but you will each owe me a favor. As for your hypnosis and the Lago Cristal, I have never heard of the place."

Adisa approaches. "Do you hear this?" He touches his belly and squeaks out the words from the corner of his mouth, "I'm hungry. I need tacos."

Estrella laughs. "Me too. You said that place is close?"

Amaka pays for the blouse and the ring, Marina hands her purchases to Amare. "It's heavier than I thought," she says. Amare takes her packages with a bow.

They walk three blocks, where a line of people snakes around a tiny building.

"Wonder what's going on here?" Estrella asks.

"It is the taco restaurant," Adisa replies with a frown.

"Oh no way," Estrella says. "So much for it being a hidden gem. Where else can we go?"

"I have never waited in a line in my life, nor will I," Amaka says. "Find another place."

A clean shaven, heavily muscled man in a tight white t-shirt with earbuds and a holstered pistol on his hip approaches them where they linger at the end of the slow-moving line. Amare and Adisa step forward. "Can we help you?" Amare asks, in Spanish.

In English, the man replies, "Carlos Slim would like to offer you a seat at his personal table, if you would care to join him."

Amaka looks from Estrella to Margeaux with astonishment in her eyes, then focuses upon the man with the earbuds and the gun. "Please tell Mr. Slim that Babatunde Abioye's daughter and her guests would be delighted to dine at his table."

They follow the man into the noisy, humble restaurant. An old man with a closely cropped beard, smiling eyes and a portly frame stands from a table in the corner of the small room. He takes and kisses Marina's hand. "You honor me with your presence. Forgive me for noticing your radiance through the window—I have not seen such light and beauty since my wife passed away so many years ago."

Marina looks into Carlos Slim's eyes, where a shining tear forms. "You honor me with the comparison! Your wife was a great woman. She brought so much good into the world," she replies in Spanish. "But I cannot sit at your table until you give me a dance."

Carlos beckons to a man behind the counter, who turns up the soft music playing. The restaurant quiets. Carlos bows to Marina, leading her into the center of the few tables. "My Soumaya loved to dance," he says.

They complete the dance, a waltz, and the crowded room breaks into applause, most cheeks stained with tears.

•••

Adisa pats his protruding stomach as Amaka puts Carlos Slim's personal cell number into her phone. "I will give my father your regards," she says.

Estrella whispers to Margeaux, "I just felt a cramp. I'll be right back."

As she washes her hands in the bathroom sink, she notices the reflection of an old map in the mirror. She turns to examine the map.

"Holy shit!" she whispers to herself. "There it is! The Lago Cristal." She takes a photo of the map and rejoins her friends on the street.

• • •

"Olvídalo!" Someone shouts from a thick circle of mostly men on the street up ahead of them.

"That means 'forget it'" Estrella says to Margeaux.

"Wonder what they're forgetting," Margeaux replies. "Looks serious though, doesn't it?" They get closer. "Is that Marc Hamilton?"

Marc, Louis, and Christophe stand in the center of the circle of shouting men. Marc holds a small dog, a cinnamon-colored Chihuahua, who bleeds from a deep cut on its side. Three men yell at Marc in Spanish to give the dog back, or else they'll kill him and his friends—or worse. Several big mutts attached to makeshift leashes dot the angry circle of men. One has blood on its muzzle.

"Oh my God, it's a dogfight!" Margeaux whisper-shouts. "How did the lads get involved in that?"

Marc says it again, "Olvídalo!" He takes the little dog and tries to push his way out, but two men block his path. Christophe pushes one of the men, who pushes Christophe back. Louis attempts to broker some peace by pulling out his wallet and handing some money to one of the men with a big dog. The man swats the wallet to the ground, then kicks it away as Louis reaches for it. Louis straightens up, shakes his head at the man, and turns away, but the man pushes him from behind. In one motion, Louis punches the man right in the face.

"Holy shit!" Estrella whispers, as Amare and Adisa hand their wallets and watches to Marina.

"What are you doing?" Amaka says to Amare.

"Standing up for my friends," he replies, as he and Adisa run into the crowd, pulling men off Louis.

Estrella and Marc make eye-contact. Estrella pushes her way into the circle and takes the bloody dog from him, their hands touching in the exchange. Inside her mind, Marc's voice whispers, "*I miss you.*"

As soon as Estrella takes the dog, Marc drops into a fighter stance—Christophe does the same. Amare rolls up his sleeves, Adisa adjusts his brass knuckles.

Margeaux whispers, "This is intense."

Marina says, "We need to get out of here."

"But we cannot abandon them now," Amaka says.

As the circle closes in on her friends, Estrella sends light through her hands and into the little dog. The bleeding stops, the split skin draws back together.

A crowd gathers to watch the fight. A few of the spectators wear t-shirts with a photo of Alfonso holding his championship belt on the front, and a full-sized picture of Victor Chavez's face on the back—like Alfonso's tattoo.

"WTF?" Estrella says to Marina, pointing to the shirts as the dogfighters attack the Gloutonites.

• • •

"Never underestimate your enemy. It should be a Law of Power," Amaka says.

The half of the dogfighters who didn't run off in the first few minutes lay broken on the street.

"That was impressive," Estrella whispers to Amaka and Margeaux as the boys approach with proud smiles. "Obviously, the boys have gotten even stronger since the Vision Quest."

"Many thanks to your guards," Christophe says to Amaka as he takes a cigarette from Margeaux.

Louis struts over to Amaka. "Did you see how I just defended your honor? Anything for you, my queen."

Amaka rolls her eyes. "You fought for no reason," she says, then touches a cut above Louis's eye. "You must put some coconut oil on that, or it will leave a scar."

"Let it scar," Louis replies, "because that's the first place you ever touched me, and I want to remember it forever."

"You are ridiculous," Amaka says, blushing.

Estrella hands Marc the little healed dog, who licks Marc's face gratefully. "How did he get better so fast?" Marc asks. "I thought I'd have to find a vet."

"How did you kick all those guys' asses?" Estrella counters.

"Mike Hammersmark," they say together.

Marc pets the little dog, smiling at Estrella. "So, you, like, want to get something to eat? I heard about this great taco place not too far from here. It's a hidden gem."

Amaka appears at her side. "We have already eaten."

Louis stands right behind her. "Oh, come on. It's just a taco! One more won't hurt."

"No. We are going now," Amaka says, dragging Margeaux away from Christophe. "Where is Marina?"

Estrella scans the street for Marina and finds her and Amare huddled with a strange man, one of the ones wearing a t-shirt of Victor and Alfonso. Amare hands the man a black velvet pouch, then follows Marina back to Estrella as police sirens sound in the distance.

"Just a taco!" Louis calls to Amaka's back.

...

Back at Montaña Árbol, Marina dances with abandon and sings at the tops of her lungs as the golden light of the setting sun floods through the windows of the massive living room.

"So, what was up with you and Amare and that guy with the t-shirt," Estrella asks her. "And why did you know so much about Carlos Slim's wife?"

Marina kisses Estrella on the top of her head. "Please just let me have this moment right now," Marina replies. "I'm so happy! And life is so sad. I learned about Soumaya's philanthropy when I did research on all the billionaires for the Water concert. Isn't the Cosmic amazing? Look how it all worked out. Will you pretty please make me just one more little delicious drink?" She hands her empty glass to Estrella.

The feeling of a feather brushes Estrella's neck, and an image of Marc kissing her there sears her mind. She looks around, then focuses on imagining herself nibbling on his ear. "He probably won't even feel it anyway," she says to herself as she pulls the coconut puree from the fridge.

"The mountains are mesmerizing," Margeaux says from her perch next to Estrella. She motions to Amaka who taps on her phone. "She's got Bimbo, and you've got John. I wish there was somebody I liked who liked me."

"Amaka doesn't like Bimbo—she's just using him to raise her army," Estrella replies. Both girls laugh.

"Where is my drink?" Marina slurs from the massive living room. "But only virgin coladas for you virginal young ladies. Lucky for me, I am of age." She turns the music louder, waltzing with herself.

Estrella buzzes the drinks in the Vitamix, garnishes them with cherries and limes, and takes one out to Marina. "Will you dance these other drinks to Amare and Adisa in the pool house?" Estrella asks her sister. "I'll make something for dinner."

"Tacos!" Marina chirps as she heads to the pool house.

Estrella waits for the sound of Marina's stilettos to fade before she corrals Amaka and Margeaux into the kitchen, pulls out her phone and shows them the photo she took of the old map. She points to the lake. "We have to go there tonight."

"Why?" Margeaux asks. "Haven't we had enough adventure for one day?"

Amaka surveys the map. "This lake is in the mountains. How will we get there? And why do you want to go there anyway?"

Estrella lowers her voice. "The fortune teller told me to go there, I think. She channeled my dad or something. I need to go. I'll go alone if I have to but...I don't really know how to drive. I'm sure I could figure it out though." She looks at Margeaux, the only one of them who can drive.

Margeaux's posture straightens. "I don't have a license, but, as you know, I have driven on several occasions when mother was too drunk, and the chauffeur was out."

Amaka says, "Okay. We'll go. Margeaux will drive."

Margeaux puffs out a frustrated breath. "I will decide for myself if I'm going and driving, thank you so much. But yes, I'm in. All for one and one for all."

"Really?" Estrella lights up. "You guys are awesome."

"Of course," Amaka says. "Where the battle rages, there the loyalty of the soldier is proved. But what about Marina and my guards?"

"Oh, they'll be out in no time," Estrella says. "I put a little something extra in their drinks—some Rohypnol I bought at the bodega. They sell anything here, you know."

As if on cue, Marina stumbles back in. "Peace out, sisters," she mumbles. "I'm going to bed. That is one strong piña colada."

She staggers off to her room.

"Lightweight," Margeaux mutters under her breath. "Mother can take three of those and dance until sunrise."

They tiptoe after her, finding her passed out cold, her sleep mask half off, her sarong draped over her like a blanket.

They check the pool house.

Amare and Adisa lie on matching sofas and snore while the TV and the stereo blare. Amaka turns everything off and slaps each of her guards in the face. "Wake up!" She yells. She does it again, twice, but they remain still as stones.

"Look at them," Amaka says in disgust. "They have shown their weakness to me now. One pretty girl with a pineapple drink and the most feared warriors in my country are useless."

The silver of twilight replaces the gold of the sun. Estrella dangles the car keys.

. . .

A sliver of moon hangs low in the lavender sky, the air smells like honey.

The girls stifle their giggles as they put the Mercedes in neutral and push the big car down the driveway.

"As soon as we get it down the road, we will start it," Amaka whispers. "In case the noise of the engine wakes them."

A shadow in the trees catches Estrella's eye. "Look out!" She shouts.

Louis, Marc, and Christophe leap from the trees like monkeys and land on the roof of the car.

"Where are you little birds off to?" Christophe asks, climbing down.

Amaka, her composure already regained, says, "We're off to do woman's work. Not for you manly, street-fighting boys."

Marc steps toward Estrella. "We're coming with you, wherever you're going."

"No, you're not." Estrella steps away, squeezing the keys in her fist. As they connect eyes, she feels the feather of his lips on her neck. He touches his ear and grins.

"So, Marina, Amare, and Adisa are okay with you doing this?" Louis asks, eyeing the mansion.

"Go away now," Amaka says.

"Maybe I want to see Adisa," Louis says, making an exaggerated move up the darkening driveway, toward the house.

"Good luck with that," Margeaux murmurs.

Christophe suddenly shouts at the top of his lungs. "Amare, Adisa, Marina! Where are your naughty little girls?"

Estrella claps her hand over Christophe's mouth. "Shut up!"

"Naughty little girls!" Christophe screams it again through Estrella's hand.

"Okay, you can come, but be quiet," Estrella hisses.

Margeaux motions to Estrella for the car keys. Estrella tosses them to her, but Marc snatches them from the air.

Margeaux grabs Marc's hand. "I've been driving in the Alps since I was ten. I've got this."

Marc holds onto the keys. "I've driven through the Himalayas during a blinding snowstorm with a live yak in the car because Dad wanted to go snowboarding on untouched powder and broke his foot. I was nine. Plus, I'm the only one with an actual license. Let's go."

Marc pulls out of the quiet neighborhood and onto the highway. Estrella, riding shotgun, gives him directions from the map. They wind their way onto a mountain pass, the lights of the city fading as they drive. Soon, only the moon and their headlights cast any light.

"So did you see how we kicked those bad guys' asses?" Marc asks Estrella. "I think I'm going to name the dog Taco. I'm keeping him.

He's at the vet overnight getting fluids and shots." He glances at Estrella, who feels another feather on her neck. She blushes.

"I have so many ideas for fashion week," Christophe says. "Something with the images of Victor and Alfonso Chavez, but obviously different materials. And maybe a dog collar."

Margeaux gasps. "I love that! Does art imitate life or does life imitate art—that old, tireless question." She directs her voice to the front seat. "Quite the famous family you seem to have. Your father and Alfonso appear to be heroes in this land."

"How does Amare know Marina?" Estrella asks Amaka. "I saw them giving this guy, like, a little pouch—it was weird."

"I know less of those closest to me than I would like," Amaka replies. "What secrets do my father and Amare share, I also wonder."

"'*Come, my queen, take hands with me,*'" Louis quotes his lines from the upcoming play. "*And rock the ground whereupon these sleepers be.*" He adds his own words. "And together we can solve all your family mysteries."

Amaka rolls her eyes as she smiles. "Shuteth upeth."

"So, what are we doing, really?" Marc asks. "And what's up with Marina and the guys?"

"It's, you know, kind of a Mike Hammersmark situation," Estrella replies.

At the name, everyone in the back seat gets quiet and listens.

"To hell with this Mike Hammersmark," Christophe finally says. "To hell with silence. Mather can't hear us up here."

"Or can he?" Margeaux asks.

Out of nowhere, headlights flood the car from behind.

"Where did that car come from?" Louis asks, turning to look.

"There goes cell reception," Margeaux says.

The lights behind them draw closer; Marc speeds up.

"Turn right onto Brilla de Amo Road—here!" Estrella shouts.

Marc makes a direct right onto a narrow, zigzagging, unpaved road going straight up. On the right, the steep mountain drops into nothingness. A collective gasp sounds from the backseat. Marc slows down and turns on the brights.

"At least that car isn't behind us anymore," Christophe says after a quick check over his shoulder. "I almost thought they were following us."

The interior of their car lights up again. A vehicle snakes up the twisty road behind them, the same one as before.

Marc presses harder on the gas; a wheel spins but corrects itself. The car behind them speeds up, too, as Marc drops into second gear. Margeaux and Louis cover their eyes while Christophe hums a Russian fight song. Amaka sits like a steel rail, her eyes forward.

Estrella draws her finger along the photo of the map in her phone. "We'll reach Mesa Road in just a few kilometers. It'll be on the left."

The lights behind them get closer still. Marc accelerates; the Mercedes jumps forward. Rocks and dirt loosen under the wheels, the back end of the car swerves toward the side of the mountain.

Marc, his eyes firmly on the road, says to Estrella, "You know I really am sorry about your mom—I know she's innocent. I should've been a better friend these past few months." He gazes into Estrella's eyes.

"You can be a better friend now by not talking and watching the road!" Amaka shouts from the back as the lights get closer again.

A tug of evil turns Estrella's stomach. She looks behind her to find a pair of red eyes glaring into hers from the car behind them. Her body trembles, and in her mouth, she tastes invisible blood. She swallows her dread. "Go faster!"

"No!" everyone shouts from the back.

Marc rams the accelerator all the way to the floor, finally creating some distance between the two cars.

"Left! Here!" Estrella says, the evil whispering like spider legs on the hairs of her arms and across her back.

Marc cranks the wheel, turning sharply onto an even smaller road that leads to a forested campground, where he cuts the lights and pulls into a grove of trees. The moon casts little light here; only the uncountable stars illuminate the blackness.

They jump from the car and dive into the shadows. Seconds later, headlights shine, then tires crunch on the dirt road.

Four men get out of the car, each looking in a different direction. They sniff like animals, searching with their snouts. One turns his head toward Estrella. His eyes glow red.

Christophe shifts his weight and snaps a twig. All four men walk right toward them.

Estrella touches the bracelet Hugo gave her, silently whispering into it. On the other side of the campground, she can hear her own voice say, "They'll never find us here." The men run toward the sound.

The Mystery Schoolers silently high five each other as they ease themselves from their hiding spot. The lake shimmers in the distance.

Estrella motions for everyone to follow her.

The animal songs of the night grow louder, blanketing the mountain with sound, as the Mystery Schoolers slink through the tall grasses toward the star-sparkling lake, getting close enough to hear the water lightly lapping the shore.

Evil turns Estrella's stomach. Two red eyes, just a hundred yards away.

"Run!"

The Mystery Schoolers sprint, their powerful legs pumping with all their strength.

Suddenly, a wolf charges from the trees, rushing the men. Three hawks swoop from a treetop, joining the wolf in its attack. Red ants swarm up from their hills and invade the men's socks. Butterflies blind the men's red eyes with their silken wings. The screams of beasts fill the dark in brutal harmony with the screams of the men.

The Mystery Schoolers keep running and don't look back, not until the animal sounds are far-away moans and Estrella's sneakers sink into the wet sand that skirts the lake. Breathing hard, Estrella scans the star-tipped grasses behind them. The men are gone.

"Meet me back at the car," Estrella says, Kit's locket burning her chest. "I'll be alright."

"We can't leave you here," Louis whispers.

"Go!" The strength of her own voice surprises her.

"She will be fine," Amaka says, clear and confident. "The car is this way." She walks away from the lake.

"This is crazy," Christophe whispers as he follows Amaka. Margeaux gives Estrella a quick hug and follows, too.

"I'm coming back for you in twenty minutes," Louis says, falling in line with the receding shadows.

Marc hugs Estrella, squeezing her tight. "Be safe. We'll be right there for you." He releases her, then walks into the night.

Estrella listens to their quiet feet until the silence is so complete, she can only hear the soft music of the insects and night birds.

"Estrella, Child of Stars!" The waters of the lake call to her. The locket burns.

An owl flies by her shoulder and hoots. "Now, Estrella."

Estrella dives into the cold water.

When she emerges, she is one with the water, the forest, the animal songs. The locket opens, and a tiny shard of crystal floats from it into Estrella's hands, glistening like starlight. Pure joy pulses through Estrella's whole body. The music of the forest swells, a long note resounding as she opens her crystal eyes.

The spirit of her father shines in front of her, his crystal form reflecting pinpoints of light. "Daughter."

Estrella reaches out to the celestial form, he reaches back. They touch—starlight to starlight—levitating together above the water. "Child Angelai," he says, and a rainbow blossoms inside Estrella's forehead, right between her eyes.

Estrella's mind floats over the land. The animals of the forest, the mothers in the valley, the men in the city, the sick, the lonely, the wicked, the wasted—she feels the loving energy of her heart expand into theirs. The call of a whale echoes from thousands of miles away.

"My daughter!" Victor says. "I never meant to leave you like that. I'm so proud of who you've become. You must have faith that you can do what the Cosmic asks of you in this lifetime. We've all waited for eons for your birth. And now here you are, just perfect, my Little Star, Estrella. You are the key. The water waits for you to purify her, to set her free. The code you contain will remake the world. You'll have to be brave, my little daughter—braver than you ever thought you could be. But I'm always with you. Like Lupe—that was me—I was his spirit, here to protect you. It won't be easy, Little One, strong as you are. This is the Spirit War. Already, you have many powerful enemies, and they're so sneaky. Even now, you cannot trust one who you think you can. You cannot see through the mask."

An engine sounds. Victor's form begins to disperse; water swirls around Estrella's legs.

"Look for me in your dreams. You've got this, daughter. Just watch your temper—they'll use it against you."

"Wait!" Estrella cries, but her father disintegrates completely into the placid water, becoming the reflection of the stars.

The Mercedes rolls to the edge of the lake; Louis gets out. "I told you you had twenty minutes."

He holds open the door, waiting. The lake, void of her father, laps quietly on the shore. Tears of fury swell Estrella's eyes.

Thunder rumbles from the east. Lightning flashes.

. . .

"This is worse than driving up," Amaka says as the car crawls back down the treacherous mountain pass.

"At least we're not being followed," Louis offers.

Estrella looks through the back window. No lights.

Margeaux examines the blister on her heel. "Did you do what you needed to do, then?" she asks Estrella, sarcastically.

Estrella nods, too full of feelings to express them.

"So, are we going to talk about it or what?" Louis asks. "What the hell is going on? Why are we on this mountain? Who were those creepy-ass guys trying to kill us tonight? And what happened to us at the Vision Quest?"

"Don't look at me," Estrella says, because everyone's looking at her.

Marc slams on the brake.

Marina, in sarong and flip flops, stands in the middle of the dark highway. She throws open the car door and pushes her way in next to Estrella on the soaked leather seat. "Did you drug me?"

Estrella looks at the floor.

"Unbelievable!" Marina seethes. "You are too valuable to take these foolish risks, Estrella. How can I protect you if you sabotage me?"

Estrella keeps her eyes on the floorboards as they ride in uncomfortable silence to Montaña Árbol.

Marc pulls into the jacaranda-lined driveway to the sound of nightingales. In another hour, the sun will rise.

Marina is out first, her anger already subsiding. "Girls, come inside. Boys, go home. I'm going to check on Amare and Adisa." Her voice is strict, but she blows a kiss to the Gloutonites on her way up the mansion steps.

As soon as she's inside, the Mystery Schoolers huddle together in the driveway.

"That was the perfect end to a perfectly bizarre evening," Margeaux whispers. "How did she know where to look for us?"

"How did she walk up the mountain so fast?" Louis asks. "I was waiting for Nikki Kong to show up, and here comes Marina in her bathing suit. God is good.'"

Christophe laughs. "New York is Nikki's territory, it would seem. Marina takes Mexico."

Estrella glares at Christophe. "What do you mean?"

Christophe looks at Margeaux, then looks away. Margeaux bites her lip. "I might've told Evan about our night in the Bronx." She finally looks Estrella in the eyes. "And Christophe. And Sylvie and Zaharia too. I'm sorry but I was traumatized, you know."

Estrella shakes her head, and sneaks a side glance at Marc, who's suddenly checking his phone. "I told Marc," Estrella confesses.

"It appears I am the only one in this car who understands the meaning of the word 'silence'. It is why I will have the best grade in Mystery School."

"There are no grades in Mystery School," everyone replies together.

"Come inside now!" Marina shouts from an open window on the second floor.

"Good night," Amaka sighs. "I'll have to bribe Amare and Adisa to keep silent about this now. At least Amare understands the meaning of the word." She turns to Estrella and Margeaux. "Whatever I say when we go inside, back me up. I will tell the story. Estrella, you are taking the blame." She looks at Margeaux. "And you, too. It will make more sense if this is mostly your fault."

"*Then my queen, in silence sad, trip we after the nightshade,*" Louis quotes again from Shakespeare as he takes Amaka's hand and kisses it. Amaka pulls her hand away and slaps him with it. Louis touches his cheek. "I will never wash away this little love-touch."

Amaka rolls her eyes, throws back her shoulders, and glides into the mansion.

Estrella moves to follow her when Marc takes her hand. "Wait," he says, guiding her to the fountain, away from Margeaux and Christophe, who share a cigarette.

The fountain falls like rain; the crescent moon sets through the purple trees; happy birds whistle.

"Estrella, I can't stop thinking about you, even though I've tried. You're the coolest girl I've ever known." Marc gently lifts her chin to gaze into her eyes. "I don't know how we got so distant. And I feel like I let you down when you needed me most. But all I do is think of you."

Estrella blushes as she looks away.

Marc clears his throat. "*You walk in beauty like the night of cloudless climes and starry skies; and all that's best of dark and bright meet in your aspect and your eyes.* That's sort of a quote from Lord Byron that, you know, I read and thought of you. I hope I didn't sound like a..."

Before he can complete his thought, Estrella kisses him. "That was so beautiful," she says.

Marc kisses her back. Twice.

"I'm sorry too," Estrella says. "I think I've been acting out a little. Things are kind of overwhelming right now."

Marc gathers Estrella up in a long bear hug. "You're cute when you act out." He kisses the top of her head. "Will you go to prom with me? I love dancing with you."

Estrella smiles, giddy at the memory of dancing with Marc.

"I mean, you're not going with that military guy, John, are you?"

"Oh shit," Estrella says, remembering John. She pulls away from Marc. "I mean, we're not serious or anything," she says, not mentioning that she's going to Hargrave's end of year dance with John. "I guess I can't be serious with anyone right now. There's too much on my mind. I mean, he is really sweet, and he's very ambitious and everything."

Marc winces. "I'm sure he is. He seems like a great guy. I punched through the wall in my dorm the day he came to school."

"You did?"

Marc tosses a small stone into the fountain. "I can't compete with someone like John, Estrella. I'm not that salt-of-the-earth kind of guy." His eyes blaze. "I'll never have to work a day in my life. I can be lazy. I don't have anything in common with ninety-nine percent of the people—I know they hate me for who I am. I wish I could have a simple life, but that's not ever going to happen for me." He takes Estrella's hand. "I just like to be around you. I have since we were kids. Even tonight, getting chased around like that—it felt like fun because you were there."

Estrella kisses him again—the best, longest kiss of all.

"Inside—now!" Marina yells from the window.

...

Through the open window of her room, Estrella's eyes search the stars, every cell in her body pulsing. She touches her vibrating lips with her fingertips to feel the kiss again.

...

Roses fill the Basilica of Our Lady of Guadalupe to celebrate Easter Sunday. The Cathedral of the Assumption is grander, but Marina and Estrella wanted to be with Our Lady of Roses on their last day in Mexico, the mother of the land where they were born.

Estrella kneels on the foot bench and says her prayers while the choir sings.

Hallelujah, Christ is risen. Hallelujah, amen.

Next to her, Marina's knees lift off the bench and hover. Estrella swivels her eyes to the side; Marina is made of crystals; light radiates from inside her body. Estrella spontaneously levitates, too. She leaves her body and floats from the church.

In the square outside, Sunday shoppers, total strangers to each other, smile and hug. Beggars stand straight and comb back their hair. A restaurateur writes on his chalkboard that all who are hungry may come and eat for free.

Several blocks away, Margeaux, Amaka, Amare and Adisa laugh together for no reason until tears burn their eyes, and their bellies are sore.

. . .

At the top of the fifty-six stairs, the windows of the circular room open to the budding spring breeze. Dr. Mather's loose white linen shirt ripples in the lilting wind.

Joy illuminates the faces of the thirteen students with half-closed eyes—all but one. Tatiana glares across the circle at Marc and Estrella, who sit closer together than anyone else does.

Dr. Mather asks, "What is magic?"

Outside, the clustered pink flowers of an eastern redbud tree burst from their tight green buds and bloom.

...

"This isn't *The Millionaire Matchmaker*, kids." Coach interrupts Marc and Estrella who embrace beneath the flowering tree. "I'm watching you," he says as he lumbers off into the perfect spring afternoon.

Marc laughs. "See you tonight for dinner?"

Estrella confirms with a smile, Marc jogs off to basketball practice. Estrella's phone lights up with a text from John. It's a photo of a dress uniform and the words:

get your dancing shoes ready.

"Dammit!" Estrella grumbles. "How can I break up with him now?"

"Ready to study the great mysteries?" Margeaux playfully pulls Estrella's hair from behind, her backpack heavy with the map of Africa, the cards, and the papers from Geneva. "There's a beautiful alignment of Venus and Jupiter in Aries —perfect timing for new beginnings. We'll see all our challenges with fresh eyes."

They breeze through the library on their way to Kit's wing, where they toss their bookbags down, securing their favorite spot, back in the farthest corner. Within minutes, Amaka joins them.

"I only have five minutes. Let's debrief," she whispers. "Estrella, you have seen the vision of your father in the lake. Margeaux, you have a book of spells."

"Well, they're papers, actually. The book is an atlas of Africa..."

Amaka cuts off Margeaux. "The details are insignificant. Estrella can talk to animals, and she saw red eyes in the men who chased us—Margeaux and I cannot and did not." Amaka continues. "We have reason to believe that my father is somehow involved with crystal caves, and Estrella's father appeared to be made of crystal. In addition, Estrella has dreams about crystals. Estrella used one of the spells to fight the red-eyed men. In time, Margeaux will learn more spells. But will only Estrella be able to use them, or will I as well?"

"Or me," Margeaux says.

Amaka continues. "Kit Hamilton spoke to us and Estrella's butler, Yves, through the face of Andy Warhol. Yves used a magical monocle to see her, and it looked as though he was familiar with it. Make no mistake, I can see in Yves' soul that he is a haunted man, hiding an unbearable secret—at least one. Perhaps he knows what Dr. Mather knows about Estrella's father. Why won't he tell her what it is? What must be kept secret? Is it connected to Estrella's dreams of animals? Though dreams can be deceiving."

"My dreams don't feel like deceptions," Estrella interjects.

"Perhaps they are not, but as of now, only the three of us, Marc, Louis and Christophe are aware of any of this, and the boys only some. And of course, Estrella's mother is in jail, thus the Water Trust with its GDP of India, hangs in the balance. In the end, we will learn that all these pieces will lead us to money and power. Those men who followed us—I promise you they have something to do with the Trust. I must go to rehearsal—my understudy is looking for any opportunity to usurp me. Report back anything new you find this evening." Amaka glides from the library nook.

"How is she in charge of us all of a sudden?" Margeaux asks as she opens the old atlas.

"And she's not totally right," Estrella says. "Whatever is happening, it's not just about money and power. Like with my dad in the lake, and the animals. There's something cosmic going on—something spiritual."

Margeaux's phone lights. "Oh my."

"What?"

Estrella's phone lights too. It's a video from Zaharia.

I got this from my friend Eloise—her boyfriend is on the team.

The video shows Evan throwing the basketball at Marc's back—so hard that the force of it knocks Marc forward. He almost falls flat on his face while Evan says, "Maybe that'll jolt you into seeing that your wetback girlfriend needs to keep her money-grubbing hands off our bloodline. Her whole trashy family needs to be in jail, not just her mom."

Then Marc punches Evan right in the jaw.

Surprisingly quick for a man his size, Coach thunders onto the court. "Damn you, boys!" he shouts. "You're letting a woman get between family: one of the greatest families in the world. You've got to stick together." He looks up and zeroes in on the camera. "Give me that phone, dammit!"

Estrella and Margeaux watch the blank phone for a full minute. Finally, Margeaux says, "Notice how Coach blames women for the bad behavior of men. Pig."

"I know this sucks for you, Margeaux—Evan is one of your best friends. He used to be one of mine."

"*Words are easy, like the wind; faithful friends are hard to find*, as Bill Shakespeare would say, so I suppose I must make some sacrifices of ease to hold onto you both." Margeaux says as Estrella throws her arms around her.

Amaka Facetimes from rehearsal. "By now you have seen the sexist basketball video? Tell me that this isn't all about money. It is only money, the root of all evil on the earth, that can rip a family apart."

Tatiana, another star of the Glouton play, drifts into the frame of Amaka's phone, looking beautiful in her costume, but when she sees Amaka, she walks the other direction.

"Ha, ha!" Estrella says. "Amaka, you seem to be the one person on earth who Tatiana fears. Clearly, she's not worried about me. She tried to corner me outside the dining hall to tell me how her dad is going to win the presidential nomination and send all the greasy Mexicans back to Mexico. As if. I wanted to punch the bitch in the face, but instead, I said, 'Will you go there with Alfonso to have his greasy little Latin babies?'"

The girls laugh. In Cuernavaca, Marina told them that she saw Alfonso and Tatiana leaving a hotel together in the city just a few weeks before.

Amaka says, "She has reason to fear me—I have put a curse on her. But now I must go and perform as no other before me. The history and glory of cinema is mine to take." The screen darkens.

"Let's get out of here," Estrella says. "I need to see Marc."

She and Margeaux are skipping down the library steps when Dr. Anderson approaches. "Estrella Chavez, do you have a minute?"

Margeaux whispers, "Ugh. Authority. Ciao!" Before Estrella can blink, Margeaux's heading to the dining hall.

"Did you get my text?" Dr. Anderson asks.

"The Einstein quote?" Estrella replies. "*The difference between stupidity and genius is that genius has limits.* So true."

"Look at you, young lady—that trip to Mexico did you some good. You actually look a little happy. Of course, that whole Hamilton fight video must be a set-back. Damn that Coach making it sexist—I'll have to get an apology out of him now. Certainly not going to fire the man—has he done a great job with the football team this year or what? And so far, we're leading in basketball too—the sports angle is better for fundraising than blackmail. I would've tried it years ago, but I never thought Glouton had a shot, seeing as our student body is traditionally made of, let's just say, intellectual types. So, how *was* your trip to Mexico?"

"It was quite an experience. Really good. Relaxing," Estrella replies, as she thinks of the red-eyed men and her father in the lake.

"I suppose it must've been, down in the land of Eternal Spring."

Dr. Mather approaches. He looks smaller outside of Mystery School. He nods to Dr. Anderson. "Estrella, I need to see you right away."

"What's so urgent, Dr. Mather?" Dr. Anderson says. "Estrella and I were just catching up." Dr. Anderson looks annoyed.

"We have some Mystery School curriculum to discuss," Dr. Mather says.

Dr. Anderson half-smiles. "Well, I guess schoolwork trumps our chat. We'll talk soon, girl."

. . .

Estrella sits across from him at his messy desk. The kind, bleary eyes behind Dr. Mather's thick glasses begin to shine with crystals, like sunlight through an ocean wave. Dr. Mather's voice whispers inside Estrella's mind. *"Do you have the key?"*

It takes all of Estrella's willpower not to touch the locket that holds the tiny pink shard and pulses against her clavicle like a second heart.

Dr. Mather says aloud, "Things are getting quite serious." He points around the room, then puts a finger to his lips. Inside Estrella's mind, he says, *"There are dark, dark forces that know almost as much as I do. It's only a matter of time before they strike."*

"Yeah, no kidding," Estrella says aloud. "I think they already struck."

Dr. Mather raises his brows in worry, then again puts his fingers to his lips before he says aloud. "Have you been practicing your mental clarity?" He folds his legs into lotus, bows his head and begins the ocean breath. "You will find all the answers you seek within."

Estrella pushes off the academic journals that share her chair and joins Dr. Mather in his breath and posture. She focuses on her mind—the space between her eyes, the top of her head.

Suddenly, she's back at the Lago Cristal, receiving the key, then with the curandera, then at the Vision Quest, looking into the eyes of the wolf, then through her dorm room window into the eyes of Dr. Mather as he raises his hand, and she flies into the wall.

Estrella opens her eyes, her heart pounding.

"Things are more complicated than they seem," Dr. Mather says aloud. "*Trust me,*" he says inside her mind.

Estrella remembers what her father said about the mask, about not trusting someone you think you can.

"*You don't trust me,*" Dr. Mather says inside her mind, the sting of it showing in his eyes. She looks away. "*Did your father tell you about the Angelai?*" Dr. Mather's words sound inside her mind as he leans toward her.

Estrella shakes her head and looks toward the door.

Dr. Mather sits back in his big, cracked-leather chair. "*We never wanted it to be this way. All we've wanted is to keep you safe.*"

"We, who?" Estrella asks aloud, heat building in her palms.

"*Kit, Marina, your mother...the Angelai,*" Dr. Mather wordlessly replies. "*This is the Spirit War. We want to keep you safe, but we need you to fight. You are the key.*"

Tears roll down Estrella's cheeks. She wipes them away, sitting tall.

Dr. Mather speaks out loud, his voice tender with compassion. "You are confused. That's natural, I suppose. This is new for all of us."

"All of who?" Estrella almost screams, her hands and face burning with frustration. The papers on Dr. Mather's desk lift and flutter from a sudden wind that rushes through the room. Dark clouds gather outside the window, lightning illuminates the sky.

Dr. Mather breathes deeply until his office becomes the sound of the ocean.

Estrella's fists unclench, her jaw relaxes, and she cools. The swirling wind calms and then ceases. The sun relights the window.

"If you give me the key, I can keep you safe. You have to trust me now. If you don't, the consequences will be dire." Dr. Mather's unspoken words roll though Estrella's mind.

"I don't know who to trust right now!" Estrella bolts for the door.

• • •

Claws of anxiety pierce Estrella's heart and stomach as she walks with big steps across campus and pulls open the auditorium door.

Several production assistants brush Amaka's hair in the half-light, downstage right. Before Estrella makes it halfway up the center aisle, Amaka stops the brushing with a wave of her hand. She looks into Estrella's eyes. "You are not in a good place." She turns to her team of assistants. "Run my lines with my understudy." A petite girl jumps out from behind the curtain, a script in her hands.

Amaka puts her steady hand over Estrella's shaking one. "Let's find Margeaux and go back to the room. Just this morning, I received an order of those nut milk cappuccinos from Organic Avenue that you love."

They exit the dark theater into the cheerful sunshine and make their way, hand-in-hand, to the Music and Communications building. "Margeaux is here every day at this time for her hour of guitar practice, though she should be back in the library," Amaka says.

"Kit came to her in another dream and told her to study several source texts, including the Dead Sea Scrolls, and not to do it online."

"She never told me about that," Estrella says, as Amaka blocks Estrella with her arm. Evan plays bass with Margeaux in the tiny practice room. Amaka pulls Estrella away. "The last thing you need right now is more drama. We will go back to our room and relax. I will text her."

The door to their room is already ajar when they get there. "What the hell?" Estrella says, as Amaka pushes the door the rest of the way open.

All their clothes, books, and devices are scattered into disorganized piles, their mattresses piled in the middle of the floor. Marina's crystal egg above the door is gone, and Kit's cards and papers are scattered everywhere. The map of Africa lays open in the center of the room, right on top of the mattresses.

Amaka pulls out her phone. "How could Amare and Adisa let this happen? First the weakness in Cuernavaca and now this!"

Margeaux skids to a halt at the door, her jaw drops open. "Oh my God, we've been vandalized! Who would do such a thing?"

A moment later, Tatiana and her groupies appear. Tatiana brazenly picks up Amaka's nightgown and tosses it back down onto the littered floor. "My grandmother wears something like this."

Amaka lunges for Tatiana, but Estrella and Margeaux restrain her.

Tatiana unearths a guitar cord with her kitten heel. "This really isn't so bad, is it? Not when you consider what could have happened. At times like these, I like to count my blessings."

Amaka lunges at her again. Tatiana stumbles backwards and almost falls. "Do not come near me again!" Amaka shouts, "or I will see both your feet broken from your legs. You will stumble and fall all the days of your pointless life."

Amare, Adisa, and the campus police break through the crowd of girls that have gathered outside the door.

Officer Handy surveys the ransacked room. "Is anything missing?"

Estrella looks above the door, to the now empty place where Marina's crystal egg once sat, shining pink light, and somehow making Estrella feel safe.

...

For the next three hours, Estrella, Margeaux, Amaka, Zaharia and Sylvie piece the room back together, their phones exploding; everyone wants the inside scoop. Finally, the sun's oranges and pinks become purple and then gray outside the dorm window. Estrella's belly audibly rumbles. "Let's eat," she says. "We can finish this when we get back."

The dining hall empties as the girls eat the last scraps of food from the buffet. Louis and Marc carry their almost empty trays over.

"We wanted to come help, but we aren't allowed in the girl's dorm," Marc says then whispers, "do you think it was the same guys from Cuernavaca who broke into your room?"

Zaharia and Sylvie nod. "We heard of your mountain adventures," Sylvie says.

"But who exactly were those guys?" Zaharia asks in a whisper.

"Dark forces," Estrella mutters, recalling Dr. Mather's unspoken words from just a few hours ago.

Everyone eats without talking for a few minutes.

Finally, Margeaux puts down her shriveled burger, takes a sip of her Coke, and says, "I'll just say it, then, won't I? There's no other way. I'm going to prom with Evan. We're doubling with Tatiana and her rich, handsome date du jour. There. I said it." Her eyes search Estrella's for forgiveness.

But Estrella responds, "That's bullshit! I mean, I understand, but not really. You better not be nice to her the whole night."

Louis shakes his head. "You are too mean to Tatiana. She's actually pretty cool if you give her a chance."

"Tatiana deserves Estrella's condemnation," Amaka says. "Tatiana only shows you what you want to see."

Louis smiles. "So why not do the same for me? I want to see you on my arm all night long for prom. I know your date canceled on you so he could party with Victoria's Secret models in Madagascar. And I know you bought a dress." Louis gets down on one knee. "Please. Please give me a chance to see how beautiful you look in it. Come to prom with me. I've been saving up all year to take you out."

Eyes flashing, Amaka says, "Who? Who told you about Bimbo? Can nothing be kept a secret in this world?"

"Adisa. Who do you think?" Louis puts his hand over Amaka's phone. "Don't text him. He just wants the best for you, and he can clearly see that I'm it."

Everyone looks at Amaka.

"Will she turn him down yet again?" Margeaux whispers beneath her breath.

"Fine. I'll go with you." Everyone at the table bursts into applause. "But only because the dress is a vintage Valentino, and I don't have the time to find another suitable escort. But enough of these childish concerns. We must focus on the break-in, which is what we are *supposed* to be discussing in the first place."

Christophe falls into an empty chair. "Why the applause?"

"Louis got Amaka to go with him to prom," Marc says.

"Good for you, Louis. Now we just need to know who broke into their room. And who followed us up the mountain. And how Marina arrived so quickly. And...do you think your cousin would want to come to prom? I know he's in college, but..." Christophe slightly reddens. "You know, in a group—friends."

"Of course," Marc says. "Because you like girls." He winks at Christophe.

"I think he'd be open to it," Estrella says. "To say the least."

"So, what about the whole Cuernavaca drama?" Zaharia asks. "And the break-in? It must be connected to Kit, right?"

Everyone looks to Estrella. She swallows back sudden tears.

Marc puts his arm around her shoulders. "We can figure it all out later. You just enjoy the time with your mom tomorrow."

Estrella tucks her head into the nook between his shoulder and his neck. "I'm so glad you're all my friends," she says. "You're right, Marc. Together, we can figure this out."

But she remains silent about her conversation with Dr. Mather, and the vision of her father in the lake.

...

"What the hell is going on?"

Marina puts her brand-new Jag in cruise control. "Which part?"

"I saw you levitating in church."

"Okay. I saw you, too. We can levitate."

"I know I can levitate, but how come *you* can?"

"Do you remember when we were little together in Mexico?" Marina's light green eyes search her sister's.

"Not really. Just the fire, and Lupe in the car."

"Do you remember Dad?"

"What do you mean?" Estrella retorts, recalling the Lago Cristal.

"What did Dr. Mather tell you?" Marina asks.

"How do you know I talked to Dr. Mather?"

"Don't worry about it." Marina keeps her eyes on the road.

"I am worried about it. A lot. Things are getting really messed up, like someone broke into our room. And he doesn't tell me anything, except that I should trust him."

Marina's eyes deepen with love. "Then it's not time for you to know everything and you should trust him. You have to be patient and breathe and pray right now. And be *silent*. Focus on your mental clarity and listen to your dreams. Okay, hermanita? Things didn't go the way they were supposed to, to say the least. They never do. Trust me. All of this will make sense soon, I promise."

Estrella shouts, "I feel like I can't trust *anyone*, and I want to know what the hell is going on, dammit!"

They pull into the prison parking lot. Marina kisses Estrella on the forehead. "Mom will be so happy to see you. Don't mention anything about any of this, and don't swear, either. It's not pretty."

"I'd like to mention that I saw her in a picture with a man who looks exactly like Evan's asshole dad," Estrella replies.

"What picture?" Marina asks.

"Don't worry about it," Estrella throws back.

The sisters stop in front of the grimy glass doors.

Marina sighs. "Don't say anything that will upset Mom—nothing. She's been through enough. Just smile and tell her how much you love her and how good your grades are and all the fun you had with your friends in Mexico. But do *not* mention how you snuck out. When the time is right, you and I will talk, but this is not the time."

Marina wears the same ferocious expression that she did the night in Cuernavaca. Estrella seals her lips.

Linda beams when she sees her daughters.

They talk about Marina's upcoming wedding and Estrella's excellent grades. Estrella makes not one mention of levitation, the visitation from the angel of her father, romantic photos of Linda and William Hamilton, or the very real possibility that Linda may never again smell the April flowers that bloom outside the prison walls.

• • •

The ride back is uncomfortably silent. Estrella puts on NPR.

"Breaking news. Su Bang Bang's army has invaded Thailand through a coordinated attack of soft targets, culminating in the takeover of the presidential palace, and over one thousand miles of the Mekong River. Thousands of innocent bodies, including women and children, bloody the streets. The United States is expected to impose sanctions later this week. Su Bang Bang's primary ally, Russian Prime Minister Fyodor Markov, has released a statement condoning the palace coup as a necessary step toward peace. No comment as of yet from India or China."

Tears form in Marina's eyes.

Estrella's heart opens like a wound. "It's like I can feel the sorrow of all the people who are dead and bloody on the streets, and all the people who love them. The pain is almost unbearable."

"I feel it too, hermanita," Marina cries. "It's our grace and our curse, how we feel the pain and the love that moves through the Cosmic." She pulls the car onto the side of the road. "We have to pray." She takes Estrella's hands.

They bow their heads together and pray for the peace that war destroys. They pray until their hearts are fountains of love, washing away the worst of the sorrow. Marina restarts the engine.

"All this praying is great," Estrella says, wiping a tear from her cheek. "But I think this guy Su Bang Bang might require a more physical response."

"He's not the one," Marina says.

"What do you mean, he's not the one? Have you heard his speeches? He takes credit for everything."

"He does what he's told. They all do.

MAY

Thrown to the Wolves

Islid splashes out from the cold river; sunlight makes diamonds on the water. The bear, half brown, half white, stands tall on her legs.

"You are ready now."

Estrella dives into the water.

• • •

"Water; the lifeblood of all things."

Dr. Mather clasps his hands behind his back and spreads his toes in his socks. Birds whistle and chirp outside the windows, open to the first very warm temperatures of the year—the heat arriving earlier this year than last.

"Today's class, our last, will be a lecture."

Estrella and her fellow Mystery Schoolers make eye contact. Dr. Mather has never given a lecture.

"You can learn from books and from science, but you learn the most from time. And I have been here a long, long time. Here's what I know about water." He begins pacing, his head tilted down. "First—and we'll come back to this—water is the most abundant solid substance in space."

Estrella recalls the river from her dream, the cold of the water.

"If you're operating strictly from a chemical mindset, you downplay the truth of the most important element of our lives. Water is beyond science. Science can only glimpse at water—for water is life itself, the essence of spirit, of the Cosmic. But let's look at the chemistry anyway." He keeps pacing. "Water is burned hydrogen. When the Hindenburg exploded, it created little babies of water. Why? Because it was filled with hydrogen, and it burned when it hit oxygen. Ninety percent of the known universe is made of hydrogen. Seventy percent of the sun is hydrogen. The earth is sixty percent oxygen. Their union makes water. Father Sun, Mother Earth: their child is water. Seventy-one percent of the earth's surface is covered by water. Look at the Pacific Ocean. It covers over half the globe. We all live on an island on one side of the earth."

Estrella considers the immense part of the globe she never sees. Suddenly, she feels far away and small.

"Water does not conform to the laws of physics. We might say it is post-physics, or pre-physics. It is the only liquid mineral. In fact, just about all liquids, at their source, are made from water." Dr. Mather gives them a moment to absorb his words and continues.

"Only water can be any of the three states of matter: solid, liquid or gas. In fact, water can be in three forms at once: frozen on the ground, flowing beneath the ice in a river, and floating as the clouds in the sky."

Estrella glances at the clouds floating outside. Dr. Mather lifts his head.

"*We* are water. In Bruce Lee's final interview, he said we should flow like water. Only water can flow."

Estrella drops her jaw in awe at the Bruce Lee reference. Dr. Mather winks at her.

"Maybe life is water, and maybe we are different expressions of it. But where does water come from? Why is it here? We can look to Genesis 1:2 for a possible answer." Dr. Mather quotes the Bible. "'*And the earth was without form, and void, and darkness was born upon the face of the deep. And the spirit of God moved upon the face of the waters.*' No light, no earth, only water."

Outside, clouds gather and pass over the sun.

"What is the force that made us, that keeps us here? Only the earth, exactly where it is, the perfect distance from the sun, is within the water zone of zero to one hundred degrees Celsius. Temperatures in the universe range from absolute zero to four trillion degrees Celsius. What are the chances?"

Again, Estrella feels small and fragile, like a blade of grass.

"So, we are water. We are blessed. Water makes up the universe. One could almost say that the Cosmic itself *is* water. And here's something new: water carries crystals."

Estrella sees an image of her father in the lake, made of crystals.

Dr. Mather looks at her as he speaks. "Crystals are ions arranged in an organized, repeating pattern, a formation. From formation we get the word *information*. So, crystals are information. Computer chips are made of crystal. Crystals store and transmit information."

Dr. Mather's socks pad back and forth in front of the windows. "You can see the see the crystalline structure of water with your own eyes in ice, in snowflakes. Water is a liquid crystal. Estrella and Shabad have seen the beautiful patterns showing that perfect organization of water under a microscope. And through those experiments, they learned how we can either organize or disorganize the formations, or information. We disorganize water with heat when it then becomes steam. We can also, as they have shown, disorganize water using emotion. And, of course, we can disorganize water with chemicals, radiation, and the like. The acid. What is acidic destroys, just as what is alkaline heals. And we're a long way from alkaline."

Dr. Mather makes eye contact with each student before he moves on. "Our species evolved by drinking water that had never been disordered. Your ancestors had so much information in their water. They drank crystals, wild water."

At these words, a pure, electric charge travels through Estrella's cells.

"Spring water is the most ordered, the most crystalline. That's why people built communities around springs, why they still travel to springs for their healing properties. But what about the water *we* drink? Does our water have information in it, or has it been erased?" More clouds gather outside, the room cools. "Sure, sterilizing our water has short-term benefits. The bacteria we pour into the water from our sewage plants and industrial farms gets killed off, so no tummy ache. But it causes some pretty spectacular long-term problems as well." He doesn't look up as he paces. "Take chloroform, for instance. When chloroform is heated, it becomes a poisonous gas. You absorb more chloroform from the steam than you do from drinking it. Your shower can become a gas chamber. That's why all the showers at Glouton have filters. You can thank Kit Hamilton for that."

Estrella nods in agreement.

"There's more. Fluoride, a neurotoxin that's now in our water, was originally used in Russian and then German prison camps to make the prisoners more docile. How? Fluoride calcifies our pineal glands."

Shabad subconsciously touches his forehead, the home of the pineal gland.

"Rene Descartes called the pineal gland the '*principal seat of the soul, and the place in which all our thoughts are formed.*' Science says this isn't quite true, but it has proved that the pineal gland, located deep in the center of the brain, and also called 'the third eye,' regulates melatonin, which helps maintain circadian rhythm and regulates reproductive organs. Pretty important information, how to reproduce. And it's being lost, though not entirely, considering the world's rampant overpopulation."

A teetering laugh passes through the room.

"And, of course, there's money to be made in all this. The Pritta water filters that you buy at the grocery store to filter out the chlorine and the fluoride are made by Clorvox, the company that makes those same chemicals." Dr. Mather stops pacing. The clouds move away from the sun, the room swells with heat. "I think you all get the point now. Enjoy your summer."

• • •

Assume formlessness. The best way to protect yourself is to be as fluid and formless as water; never bet on stability or lasting order. Everything changes.

Estrella rereads Law 48, the final Law of Power.

Margeaux leans over the map of Africa, the cards, and the papers as cheerful rain bounces off the roof of the library.

Estrella strains her ears to hear what the information in the falling water might have to say. "If only I could hear the rain like I hear animals," she says. "Maybe the water could tell me who killed Kit, since it's literally everywhere."

Estrella writes out the few clues she has.

> *1: Eternal Spring—that turned out to be Cuernavaca and seeing my dad in the lake and being chased by someone with red eyes, like the man at New Year's Eve. So basically—still mysterious.*
>
> *2: Andy Warhol in Drag, a.k.a. Kit. She told Yves to give*

Margeaux the cards, and the papers from Geneva have spells, but I can't even read them. Only Margeaux. No idea what that's about. Not really. Also, Yves's magical monocle?

3: Marina levitating in church, and all her talk about listening to my dreams. Not a clue, exactly, but...

4: The crystal poison dart. Who took it?

5: The curare. Who ordered it?

6: All the selfies from the quince. Why is it that, out of thousands of selfies, not one shows anything to prove that my mom was somewhere other than murdering her best friend?

7: Mrs. Franks, the alleged witness. LIAR!!!!! What kind of idiot would invite such a traitor to her quinceañera?

Estrella makes her fingers into a gun and points it at her head. Margeaux looks up. "You alright, Star?"

"Just going over this whole situation. Mrs. Franks. Why did I ever invite her?"

"You had no way of knowing," Margeaux replies, her green eyes drenched with sympathy. "Have you learned anything else from the bracelet? I know you've been listening."

Estrella slumps against the wall and lets out a frustrated growl. "I've gone through all one hundred hours of recordings, but except for the conversations with Senator Clay and Dr. Mather, and the clue for you about reading the cards, I haven't heard anything significant at all. It's been mostly rants about Kit's numerous political enemies and what turned out to be the scene from *Gone with the Wind*, where Scarlett swears she'll never go hungry again. I have no idea why Kit would record that, or if Kit even realized she was recording half of what's on there."

"It's a horrible film," Margeaux says. "All white privilege and sexism."

"For sure," Estrella absently replies, as she picks up Kit's bracelet and pushes the invisibility function. The atomic mist vibrates around her for a moment. "Kind of fun," she says, setting the bracelet down. Kit's voice resonates from the library floor.

"It's worse than I thought," Kit says.

"What do you mean?" Margeaux asks distractedly.

"It's Kit!" Estrella says. "Shh! Somehow, I missed this part."

"I guess I'll have to be an atheist who prays, because only a miracle can save us all now. I've done everything I could, God knows. But it's almost hopeless. And what is Linda going to do when I'm gone? Or Estrella, for Chrissake? A child. She's strong-willed, that's for sure, but it'll take more than whatever power she has to get us all out of this jam. Evil. That's who's going to win. Wickedness. Greed. What chance do these children have in the face of such horror? Even the Scroll knows it's an open question. Will it be the Great Alkalinity or the Great Thirst? Ask me again in rhyming verse. In any event, I'm not long for the world; they're onto me. I can only hope that at least part of what I've come to believe is true, and there'll be a place for me in the Cosmic. Maybe I'll be of some help after I'm gone." A moment of silence and then, "Oh, Rhett, you whiny bitch, you do give a damn."

"How did I miss this part?" Estrella asks as she replays the piece of audio.

"Pretty dark stuff, isn't it?" Margeaux asks, the patter of spring rain tapping the roof above them.

Estrella recalls the part she still hasn't played for Margeaux where Kit says Margeaux can plan on a short life.

"I finally finished *War and Peace*," Estrella says, changing the subject. "It was the hardest out of all the books on Kit's list to get through, except the Bible. I haven't gotten through that yet, but I'm close. And *Ulysses*. All the answers to every question could be in there and I would never know. How is that book even popular? Worst book ever."

"Well, I loved *War and Peace*, but I'm waiting until I'm thirty-five to read *Ulysses*," Margeaux says. "I want to be able to appreciate it."

"*War and Peace* did turn out to be pretty good in the end, though," Estrella says. "Pierre and Natasha finally got together—I knew *that* was meant to happen. Andrei just wasn't right for her—he had to die. But, except for the words Kit underlined about the love of death, I didn't really see any clues. Thank God I'm not Russian, though. Christophe told me that all Russians read it several times in their lives. Once is definitely enough for me. One thing I did learn though; war is bad. Very, very bad. And peace is fragile. And temporary."

Margeaux stretches like a cat. "Su Bang Bang's from Indonesia, isn't he?"

"Mm-hmm." Estrella replies. "Su Bang Bang—talk about an asshole. Last week, he ordered the execution of three hundred *more* college professors. He said they were enemies of the so-called People's State. The United Nations imposed more sanctions, but Russia abstained from the vote. Dixon Duplessis says every country has a right to do what it wants."

"You know I don't really follow politics like you," Margeaux says, studying the map of Africa. "But Marut's from there too."

"Who's Marut?" Estrella asks.

"Dunno. Just now appeared in the map." Margeaux's eyes widen. "Look at all these names. They're from all over the world. Muriel, Munkar, Nuriel, and it looks like there are even more I can't quite see. Some are red and some are pinkish."

Estrella pointlessly looks at the map.

Margeaux continues. "What's really crazy is that most of the names are right here. Nine out of...twenty-six. One up by Alaska, two in Africa, one under the sea. Well, the Pacific Ocean."

Estrella thinks again about the vastness of the Pacific—half the world.

"That one's just moved a bit," Margeaux says. "Look—five of them aren't even on the earth. They're, like, stars or in the atmosphere or something. I really wish you could see this. It's quite extraordinary."

Estrella slams the Bible closed and whines, "That's great for you, Margeaux, that you can see all this, but it kind of irritates me that I can't. So maybe keep some of this to yourself, okay?"

"PMS?" Margeaux retorts. "Maybe keep that to yourself."

Estrella sticks out her tongue; Margeaux promptly immerses herself once more in the map. Both study a while longer, the rain tumbling like the high notes of a piano outside.

Margeaux breaks the silence. "You can help me with this one since you know Latin. What does '*volumen commendaverunt*' mean?" She writes the words in her notebook and slides it over to Estrella. "Maybe you can't read the map, but you do know Latin better than most."

"It means a scroll, or a book of commandments," Estrella replies. "Like Kit just talked about! And like I heard her talk to Marina about, before I came to school, and to Dr. Mather earlier on the bracelet."

Margeaux says, "Well, apparently, the Scroll is very close to here. I think it might have more information about all of this."

Estrella touches her locket. "How close to here?"

"Hard to say. Maybe in New York?" Margeaux puts her face right next to the book. "The closer I get, the less clear things look."

"Tell me about it."

...

A star marks the forehead of the elephant who blows water onto her calf; the savanna sun turns the spray into rainbows. The mighty beast becomes pink light and crystals; its pachydermatous form disappears into prisms of light.

"I am Zadkiel. Remember me."

...

Estrella wakes to Margeaux's electric guitar and plaintive voice.

"What are you singing, Pink?" Estrella asks, rubbing her eyes, still feeling starlight. She needed that nap. She still hardly sleeps at night; that's when she feels the most worry.

"She is singing about Zadkiel," Amaka says without looking up from her tablet. "For over two hours now."

"Zadkiel?" Estrella asks. "I just dreamed about an elephant named Zadkiel—and I've dreamed of her before, too, I think. The dream with the leopard." Estrella shivers, remembering.

"Zadkiel's one of the names on the map of Africa," Margeaux says. "I've decided she's a fussy, though actually very sweet, African princess, who, if only she would open her eyes, would find the true love of her life standing right before her. Though he is a peasant, he is the kindest, wisest man in the whole village. He saves her from a lion."

Amaka throws a sock at Margeaux. "My 'village' is home to over thirteen million people. And there are no lions there, nor kind, wise peasants. They are mostly con men and thieves."

Estrella asks, "What about elephants?"

• • •

"Now I go to conquer," Amaka says. "Soon, all the world will know my name, and the power of the land that made me."

"You know this play is turning into a pretty big deal," Margeaux says. "Both the theater writer *and* the movie critic from the *New York Times* will be watching, so I suppose all the world will know your name."

"Oh my God, what if I forget my lines?" A small bead of sweat glimmers on Amaka's forehead. "No, of course I will not forget; I am Amaka Abioye." She takes a breath and composes her face. "Estrella, will you please open the door for me?"

"Seriously?"

"Of course I am serious. My every move must now be that of a queen."

Estrella turns the handle as she says, "Anyone else, and they'd be opening their own door."

• • •

The foyer of the auditorium buzzes with excited voices. Bianca Wilder wears a dress small enough to miss but for the thousands of tiny Swarovski crystals that adorn the strip of fabric. She sniffs, rubs her nose, and talks constantly.

"She's on cocaine." Marc nudges Estrella and motions toward Bianca with his chin. "I see it all the time in Malibu."

Estrella's phone lights with a text from John.

Have fun! Wish I could be there.

Marc searches her eyes. "Who was that?"

"Marina." Estrella lies.

"She's coming, right?" Marc asks.

Behind them, an older woman says, "I've heard this Abioye is quite the star. My sources say she steals the show, even in an ensemble role."

"Holy shit!" Estrella whispers. "It's a movie critic, talking about Amaka!"

Estrella and Marc tilt their heads toward the woman, who says, "And, of course, Duplessis is rumored to be good. Acting runs in the family—like father, like daughter." The cameraman with the critic laughs. So do Marc and Estrella.

A stretch limo pulls up outside. "Who's that?" Marc asks, craning his neck.

Alfonso struts out, followed by a blonde woman wearing basically a bikini. Cameras flash.

"I didn't know he was coming," Estrella says. "I forget sometimes that he's sort of famous now."

Marc shakes his head. "Tat's going to be pissed that he brought that girl."

"Oh yeah. Alfonso and Tatiana have a thing," Estrella replies. "Gross."

"See," Marc says, "She's not into me—I told you. We just don't connect like that. Like us." He wraps his arm around Estrella's waist as Christophe approaches with Hugo.

"Stripper," Christophe, whispers in Estrella's ear, motioning with his eyes to Alfonso's date.

Hugo asks, "How do you know that?"

Christophe gives him a loving look. "I find your naiveté adorable."

Nadine, Colt, and some townies loudly enter the foyer. "What. The. Hell?" Estrella mutters. "Why is Nadine always bringing around her embarrassing boyfriend and his friends?" She pulls Nadine off to the side and whisper-shouts, "Why did you bring them? I told you just you."

Nadine rolls her eyes. "I mean, are you in an uptight contest? I crown you champion." She laughs. "Your friend Tatiana said the more the merrier. We all had fun at the Day of the Dead party, so relax."

Estrella's palms sweat with anger. The ticket table suddenly falls, causing Dr. Anderson to shout, "Clean-up on aisle four!"

Estrella refocuses on Nadine, spitting her words through clenched teeth. "You *know* she's not my friend. She's my *enemy*!"

Nadine smiles. "Relax, okay? Gabriel Estrada is your enemy. Tatiana's just a rich girl who's so much like you that you two butt heads. It's probably why I get along with both of you. Just let it go tonight and try to have some fun."

"I can't have fun when my mom's in jail!" Estrella says, even though she was having fun until Nadine got there.

Nadine gives Estrella a kiss on the cheek and a big hug. "It's all going to be okay." With Nadine's embrace, Estrella calms.

Adisa suddenly appears at Nadine's side. He and Nadine smile radiantly at each other. Colt leaves his friends and grabs Nadine's arm, glaring at Adisa. "Come on, Nadine. We need to get to our seats."

Marina and Nicolas walk in as the lights begin to dim. Marina magnetizes every single eyeball in the room. Suddenly, Octavio pushes out from behind the curtain, in full costume, and gives Marina an overly long, overly tender kiss on the cheek.

Nicolas is about to say something when Bianca Wilder grabs Octavio by the arm. "You're not supposed to be out here!"

"I heard all the rumors from Amaka," Christophe says as Bianca Wilder pulls Octavio backstage. "All the girls and boys in the cast and crew have professed their love to Octavio at some point during rehearsals. And of course, Octavio, thoughtful as he is, is now in relationships with three cast members and two members of the crew. During dress rehearsal last night, each of them learned about the others." He laughs. "Amaka says tensions are running high tonight, but Bianca says it'll be good for the energy of the show."

. . .

"What a show!" Margeaux coos, as the Mystery Schoolers cross the green through the lilac-perfumed evening to the after-party at Bianca Wilder's small campus cottage. "The Glouton youth and their director have done a fine justice to the Bard."

"Your performance sparkled like this champagne!" The theater critic says to Amaka, raising her glass in a toast. "And Bianca Wilder has job security at Glouton for the rest of her life if she wants it. I hear the live film will be edited and sent to all the festivals. Smashing success!"

Halfway through the party, Estrella notices Alfonso following Tatiana outside. Estrella sharpens her ears to listen in on their conversation through the open window.

"Leave me alone, you filthy Mexican loser. Go back to your whore," Tatiana says.

"You're my whore, you're my everything. I need you. You know I need you," Alfonso says softly.

The sound of a smashing glass interrupts Estrella's eavesdropping.

"We make only Greek toasts from now!" Christophe proclaims, draining his champagne and throwing his glass into the hearth of the little fireplace. "Opa!"

"Opa!" Nadine shouts, throwing her glass after Christophe's.

"Opa!" Bianca Wilder yells, smashing her glass.

Hugo gets a broom as more glasses smash.

A few feet away, Estrella hears Octavio say, "You are my soulmate, Marina. I will die without you."

"How many times have I heard a man say that to Marina?" Estrella says beneath her breath before she throws her glass into the hearth. "Opa!"

Marina gives Octavio a peck on the cheek. "I'm already in love with Nicolas, so you'll have to wait a lifetime. You're too young to know what love is, anyway. But you're very sweet and handsome."

Undeterred, Octavio cups the back of Marina's head and kisses her on the lips. Surprisingly, Marina surrenders to the kiss for a good while before she pushes him away.

"Now I can die," Octavio says.

"Isn't this a fun night," Margeaux says. "Though the lack of competent adult supervision is appalling. Opa!" She throws her glass into the fireplace.

Finally, the crowd begins to thin. Marina kisses Estrella goodbye with a champagne burp. The chauffeur comes back for Alfonso's date, but Alfonso and Tatiana never return to the party. Amaka and Louis, the only sober people in the room, lead the exodus of their intoxicated friends out of the cottage and into the heavy-mooned night.

. . .

The setting orange sun kisses the shadow of the moon, casting a glow on Amaka, Estrella and Hugo. The girls' dresses sparkle and shine, and Hugo cuts a figure in his tuxedo.

"Here they are!" Hugo straightens his bow tie as The Spirit of Ecstasy glides toward them from the hood of Kit's Rolls Royce. Yves, in a tuxedo and cap, lets out Marc, Louis and Christophe.

Marc kisses Estrella as she pins on his boutonniere. "This is going to be the best night of our lives," he whispers.

Laughter erupts the entire drive into the city. The moonroof stays open, music rattles the speakers, Christophe sneaks them sips from a silver flask.

When they walk into the restaurant, all eyes turn to them, all mouths smile with the memory of being young. Across the restaurant, Evan and Margeaux sit at a table with Tatiana and her date, as well as two other couples. Margeaux waves.

"She looks happy, for being a traitor," Estrella says.

"Just let it go," Louis whispers into Estrella's ear.

"You're right," Estrella replies. "I'm compartmentalizing tonight—no feelings except good ones."

The sensation of a touch of a feather brushes Estrella's neck. Marc winks. "I can't wait until after prom," he whispers. "Finally, just the two of us alone together." He holds up the keys to his father's New York apartment. "I know a great place for breakfast in the Village."

"We want everything on the menu!" Christophe says as he discreetly tips the maître. "And every bottle of champagne. I am an oligarch after all." The champagne arrives first. They laugh and raise their glasses in toast after toast.

Estrella Chavez.

A voice whispers inside Estrella's mind. She instinctively turns toward the bar.

A well-dressed, older man looks back at her, his creepy smile marred by deep scratches, like claws slashed his lips and cheeks. His green eyes turn red. Queasiness travels through Estrella's stomach.

Marc caresses her neck. "You alright? Who's at the bar?"

"I don't know, I think..."

Amaka puts her fork down and frowns. "Come with me to the ladies room," she whispers to Estrella. As they make their way through the restaurant, Amaka whispers over her shoulder, "When

I took that last bite of filet, I felt my dress pop in the back. Let us pray we can fix it."

Estrella walks closer to hide the wardrobe malfunction, searching for the man at the bar. "Oh shit, there he is!" Estrella whispers as they pass the man, who talks on his phone just outside the men's room.

"Who?" Amaka asks as Estrella shoves Amaka into the ladies room, where Margeaux, Tatiana, and Trixie, one of Tatiana's squad, primp in front of the softly lit mirrors.

Tatiana fakes a smile. "Hi, Amaka. Are you wearing a used dress?" She props her long, tanned leg up on a chair to touch up her toenail polish.

"Vintage, Tatiana," Margeaux says diplomatically. "Who did you tell me wore it originally, Amaka?"

"Liz Taylor," Amaka says as she applies some lip gloss, standing perfectly still. She makes no effort to secure the popped button. "Is that yet another Calvin Klein?"

Tatiana gives Amaka a dirty look, then turns her focus to Estrella.

"And you, little angel, you look pretty all the time now. You shine like a diamond for everyone to see." Tatiana blows on her toes, dabs on some lipstick, and winks at her, becoming who Estrella saw at the Vision Quest—red eyes, sickly green skin, slithering hair, bloody teeth. Estrella blinks, and Tatiana looks perfect as ever, her Calvin Klein dress floating over her creamy skin.

"Let's go," Tatiana says to her dining companions.

"I'll meet you at the table," Margeaux replies.

Amaka exhales as soon as the door closes. "Are you having fun with the Wicked Witch?" she asks Margeaux, before saying to Estrella, "Help me with this dress, Little Diamond. She was nice to you for once."

Estrella attaches the button with a safety pin from her handbag. "It's a trick I learned from Marina; always carry a safety pin. And lip gloss. And an extra pair of false eyelashes. Anyway, I don't think Tatiana meant to be nice."

"Well, she's got everyone else fooled," Margeaux says, applying more bright red lipstick and smoothing down her shiny pink hair. "Almost me. She can be quite charming. She has a great sense of humor, and both her manners and her French are flawless, of course."

"Drink the Kool-Aid, then." Amaka twists around to see the back of her dress in the mirror and smiles. "Liz Taylor, you had nothing on this." She turns to Estrella. "What man did you see?"

"I think one of the ones from Cuernavaca, but I'm not sure."

"Where?" Margeaux asks.

"At the bar, and then just outside the bathroom, but I might be seeing things."

"We see with more than our eyes," Amaka says. "We must be on guard."

"Watch me walk out then," Margeaux says, her eyes filled with worry.

Estrella opens the doors—no man in sight. "All clear," she says.

Margeaux exits, followed by Amaka.

Estrella straightens her dress, a few steps behind Amaka, when a feeling of wet fingers slinks down her back. She turns, to look into red eyes and a sick, claw-marked smile. A syringe gleams in the man's hand. He murmurs words Estrella doesn't understand and Estrella's limbs go weak. He backs her against the wall and raises the needle above her neck. Estrella tries to scream, but her throat is frozen.

As he thrusts the syringe downward, a drunk socialite staggers out of the bathroom, right in front of Estrella. The syringe stabs into her arm.

"Ouch." The socialite rubs the spot where the needle plunged in. "You mean man!" The woman slurs. "You need a spanking."

The man escapes into the men's room as the socialite teeters off toward her table.

Estrella rejoins her party just a few steps behind Amaka, her heart beating fast, her palms sweaty, blood roaring in her ears.

Marc rises when he sees her. "You still look hot." His eyes meet hers. "Are you okay?"

Amaka's voice sounds inside Estrella's mind. "*What is wrong?*"

Estrella puts a word into her mind. "*Evil.*"

Louis looks up from the remaining bites of steak he eats from Amaka's plate. In Estrella's mind, his voice says, "*Evil?*"

Christophe breaks from his tete-a-tete with Hugo to say out loud, "Did someone ask if the art here is medieval? It's dark, true, but the acrylics give it away."

"What?" Estrella, Marc, Louis and Amaka say together as the red-eyed man joins two others at a table. They only sit for a minute before they leave the restaurant, passing right by Estrella. She discreetly sticks out her foot, and the man trips. Estrella glares into his red eyes as he recovers his footing.

"Is that the guy?" Marc asks.

"*We must follow him!*" Amaka's voice whispers in her mind. She stands.

"Too late," Louis says aloud, watching the men get into an Uber through the candle-lit glass doors of the restaurant.

"It's not too late," Christophe says, checking his watch. "And it's prom, not the S.A.T. We can arrive when we like. Relax Louis."

Amaka sits. "We let him escape," she whispers to Estrella. "Now we are at his mercy."

"What are you talking about?" Hugo asks, finally breaking from his hour-long conversation with Christophe.

"Nothing," Estrella replies. "Just how good the food is."

On their trek through the restaurant, back to the limo, they pass the socialite who took the syringe for Estrella.

She's face down in her dessert.

...

Twinkle lights, neon stars, gold-lamé moons: the theme for prom this year is The Cosmic.

As Estrella stretches her long legs from the limo onto the asphalt outside the gym, Amaka whispers, "Who was that man in the restaurant?"

Estrella whispers back, "I'll tell you later. Let's just have some fun tonight."

Amaka raises her brows. "After your breakfast date with Marc?"

Estrella blushes as a limo pulls up behind them. Evan, Margeaux, Tatiana and her date step out onto the sidewalk.

Margeaux breaks the ice. "Hello, Marc. You remember Evan, right? He's your first cousin."

Marc puts out his hand for Evan to shake, then changes his mind and gives him a hug. "Let's forget about everything and have some fun tonight, okay, Cuz?"

Evan spins, lands in a split and jumps up, all in time to the music pouring from the doors. "Thank you, Aunt Kit, for making me take all those dance lessons," he says, smiling at Estrella. They attended them together. "Let's dance!"

Everyone enters the raucous gym together, their dancing shoes tied tight.

· · ·

Estrella kisses Marc on the cheek. "I'm thirsty and I have to pee."

He spins her once more. "Meet you back in here in ten minutes and then we'll make our exit." He grins nervously.

"Okay," Estrella says, her face reddening.

On her way from the loo to the punchbowl, she spies Louis and Amaka slow dancing to a fast song. "Ha! I knew it!" She says to herself, recalling the three nights she heard Amaka calling Louis' name in her sleep.

Shabad and Zaharia slow dance together as well, despite their families' differing religious perspectives. Princess Sylvie sits on the sidelines of the dance floor, her worshipful eyes turned to Octavio, who dances with Bianca Wilder.

"The only one of us missing is Nikki Kong," Sylvie says. "She took her finals early and is attending to family business in China. She plans to return to make her valedictorian speech at graduation."

"Such a mysterious badass," Estrella says, recalling for the thousandth time the night in the Bronx.

Across the room, Coach talks to Marc, waving his hands around and looking intense as usual. On the other side of the dance floor, Tatiana and Dr. Mather are locked in an animated discussion.

"What are *they* talking about?" Estrella wonders, focusing her ears to listen in. She gives up when, after three solid minutes of straining, she can't hear a word. "They must have their mental walls up," she says to herself. "Pretty smart, since anyone could be listening."

Dr. Anderson, who's tearing up the dance floor in a tight dress, catches Estrella's eye. She's half the size she was six months ago. Estrella waves. "So inspiring, how even old people can change," she says to Sylvie.

"Transformation," Sylvie replies. "Like the water you and Shabad made into crystals. With intention, we can change. It is inspiring."

Hugo taps Estrella on the shoulder. "Shall we dance?" He leads Estrella out onto the dance floor. "I've been dancing with every girl and all the boys who have come out—if only Christophe were among them." He looks longingly across the gym, where Christophe takes a selfie with a pretty girl. "I'm in love," Hugo says. "And I think you are too, with Marc. He's really nice Estrella, and I can tell he's into you."

"After this dance, we're going to the city together," Estrella replies. "Don't tell Marina or your mom. Ow!" Estrella doubles over in pain.

"What's wrong?" Hugo asks. "Don't worry I won't say anything— no need to be so over-the-top about it."

Estrella straightens, then doubles over again, her eyes blurring. A vision consumes her mind. The man from the restaurant turns into a snake; his fangs pierce her ribs. Her father, glowing like he did in the lake, opens Kit's Bible to Revelation; the wolf from the forest stands by his side.

"I mean, do you have cramps or something?" Hugo asks, looking around. "Try to be cool, we're at prom."

Estrella gasps, her brow wrinkled with anxiety and glistening with sweat. "I need to go to the library. Now. Come with me."

Hugo laughs. "To the library? What are you talking about? We're at the best party of my life right now. It's prom! You know I had to miss mine because I got into college early. Make Marc go, or just go tomorrow. I cannot believe how uptight you've turned out, though, I guess, you have always kind of been that way."

Estrella sharply inhales with another rush of pain. "I have to go *now*. We can get out and be back in just a minute—we're right by the door. Marc's with Coach. He can't get away right now. Come on!"

Hugo scans the room for Christophe, who balances a cup of punch on his head while performing an exuberant Russian folk dance for a cheering group of Gloutonites.

"Go by yourself."

Estrella digs her fingernails into Hugo's arm. "You owe me, remember? I'm the one who introduced you to Christophe at my quince. I might need some help, and you're coming with me. Let's go."

"Okay, fine. But we're coming right back. This *sucks!*"

Estrella clicks the invisibility link on the bracelet Hugo made her. In an instant, they're out the side door, making their way through the moonlit trees that line the way to the library.

"Why did God plague me with this weird-ass family?" Hugo asks the moon.

A man steps out from behind Methusaleh. His eyes turn red. Two other men emerge from the shadows next to him.

"Run!" Estrella screams as she grabs Hugo's hand. The man lunges, his meaty hands grazing the back of Estrella's ankle.

Steps from the library door, Estrella waves her hand like she did that night she broke into Kit's, simultaneously uttering a silent prayer that it'll work again.

The door unlocks and opens.

Hugo and Estrella leap over the threshold and slam the door behind them. The sound of three bodies slamming into wood and steel echoes in the barely lit library, its shelves shadows, its air dusty and still.

"What the hell?" Hugo asks, panting. "Do you know those guys? How did you open the door like that? We need to call the police."

"Shut up and run," Estrella says, already up the stairs on her way to Kit's wing.

The door bangs open; footsteps thud on the floor below them. She runs toward Kit's Bible—the one her father was reading in her vision.

Estrella turns to Revelation. Her finger lands on 12:7:

And there was war in Heaven. Michael and his angels fought against the dragon, and the dragon and his angels fought back.

The page dissolves into a vision of the wolf, who's winged and flies above the forest. He beckons to her, his eyes sparkling with crystals.

The thundering sounds of the men's footsteps get closer.

Hugo glares at her. "I'll be honest," he hiss-whispers. "I'm super pissed right now. You dragged me away from prom with Christophe so you can read the fricking *Bible*, which is actually the word of men and not God, by the way—you're so brainwashed by the patriarchy. And who are those guys?"

Estrella puts her finger to her lips and whispers. "We need to get out of here."

"No shit." Hugo whispers back, as four Italian leather men's shoes appear through an opening in the stacks.

Estrella presses her bracelet and holds onto Hugo. The microwaves bend around them, and they run as quietly as they can. The man from the restaurant sniffs the air as they pass. He lashes out his arm, just missing them. They keep running for the stairs, and almost get to the bottom of them, when they see the third man, an enormous mountain of a man, stationed there, holding a gun. They automatically back up the steps.

"Lucky for you, I'm a genius," Hugo whispers. "And I think I know how to get us the hell out of here." He takes out his phone and begins tapping the screen. "Where's the tech wing?"

They scuttle through rows of books, crouched low and barely breathing, silent as ghosts. In the far corner of the Tech Wing, a form materializes from thin air.

A motorcycle manifests before them.

"Damn," Estrella whispers. "I know you've been pushing 3D to its limits at MIT, but I had no idea you'd gotten this far."

"I'm talking to BMW," Hugo whispers with pride, still working his phone. "It's basically a complete prototype. I just need to work out a few kinks."

"Come out, come out, little kitty." Heavy footsteps grow closer.

"What kind of kinks?" Estrella nearly gags on the approaching smell of rotting flesh and bleach.

"The engine has trouble starting," Hugo says. "And running. But I've updated the code."

The outlines of two men shadow the wide entrance of the Tech Wing. The man from the restaurant licks his reptilian lips with his slimy, forked tongue as his green eyes turn red and ooze blood. Worms and spiders cover his serpentine body. He raises his sinewy arm, stretching his filthy claws toward them as he incants words Estrella doesn't understand. He keeps coming.

Crippling fear tightens Estrella's belly with every step he takes and each syllable he utters. Hugo keeps tapping.

Estrella screams, "*Halemos vaporios!*"

Pink light radiates from Estrella's palm, knocking the men onto their backs, and causing Estrella to fall backwards from the force. "Holy shit!" Estrella cries as she and Hugo jump on the motorcycle. Hugo pushes a button on the control panel of the bike.

Nothing happens.

The men climb back to their feet. Estrella holds out her palm again, bracing herself for the power. This time, her pink light is met with red, and it takes all her strength to resist, as if she's pushing against a concrete wall. "I won't be able to keep this up for long," she says as Hugo taps his screen furiously, then jabs at the control panel on the motorcycle again.

Suddenly, the roar of the engine fills the library. Estrella holds Hugo tight as they charge straight at the men, who dive out of the way. They bump down the stairs, toppling the mountain with the gun. With a wave of her hand, Estrella opens the door, repeating the motion to close it.

Hugo skids to a stop on the sidewalk and turns in the direction of the gym. He's electrified. "We have to get back and call the cops. Wait until I tell Christophe. He's going to be so impressed. The motorcycle worked! We'll have to take it for a midnight spin."

Estrella sees the winged wolf in the forest behind her eyes. "I need you to take me to Glouton's cabin in the woods. Now."

Hugo looks at Estrella with complete incredulity. "What is *wrong* with you? Does Marina know about these people you're messed up with? And that you can shine light from your palm and open doors with it? If not, she will, because I'm about to tell her." Hugo pulls out his phone. "Plus, we need to call the cops on those guys in there."

Estrella puts her hand over his. "Please."

"No. No way. Absolutely not." Hugo crosses his arms over his chest.

"Then get off the bike and I'll go myself."

"You don't know how to ride a motorcycle."

"I can figure it out. I have to go now. This is a war, *the* war."

"What war? Oh my *God*!" Hugo yells to the stars. "Why is this my family?"

"Please," Estrella cries. She clasps her pounding, aching chest.

Hugo spins the motorcycle around and sighs. "Fine. I'll help you with your insane war, because you're family, but you owe me sooo big. You'll literally never be able to repay me." He revs the motorcycle. "Let's see how far this bike can go."

• • •

The black night hugs the road, the wind unravels Estrella's coiffed hair, her dress trails behind them. She holds onto Hugo with one arm, and with the other, she texts Marc. Immediately her phone lights up.

I'm on my way.

• • •

"So, we're here to wait on a wolf to come and tell you something?" Hugo paces the shadowed main room of the Water Woods cabin. "Why are we here, *in the woods*, while everyone else is at *prom*? This is such bullshit!"

"Oh my God, is this all bullshit?" Estrella replies, looking past her doubting expression through the windows of the cabin into the dark, empty woods. "Maybe I'm actually crazy. All these dreams and visions—what if they're actually hallucinations? I'm so sorry, Hugo."

Hugo softens. "Well, I mean, in fairness, those men in the library weren't hallucinations. And we're family, so of course I'm here for you even if you do need mental help."

An owl hoots. *Go outside!* It calls to Estrella.

She opens the door to find the wolf from the Vision Quest, bigger and stronger than half a year ago. His golden eyes connect to Estrella's. "*Angelai*," his voice says inside her mind as he nuzzles her hand.

With his touch, a vision comes to Estrella: a whale, Islid, Zadkiel, her father, Marina, Dr. Mather, and Kit, all floating in the ocean around a table in Kit's library.

"There it is!" Estrella gasps aloud. "The Great Tabernacle!" The tiny crystal key at Estrella's throat heats the gold of the heart that houses it.

The wolf's ears stand up; he faces the road.

An evil red feeling crawls along the skin of Estrella's arms.

"*Demonai*," says the wolf.

Hugo screams behind her. "Wolf!" He huddles behind the open cabin door.

"It's okay," Estrella says as a black Mercedes climbs over the hill, descending toward the cabin. The three men from the library jump out. One carries a steel pipe.

Hugo's eyes dart from Estrella to the wolf to the three men closing in on them.

"I'll go for the one with the gun first," Estrella says. "You take the guy with the pipe." She drops into horse stance and kicks off her heels.

"We're going to fight these guys?" Hugo asks, taking off his tux jacket and flinging his bow tie to the ground. "This *sucks*! Instead of dancing the night away with the most handsome man who's ever lived, I'm about to get killed out in the middle of nowhere. Fabulous. See you in hell." He puts up his fists.

The wolf charges the men—leaping, snarling—so fast he is almost flying. A hawk attacks from a nearby tree, pecking at the eyes of the man with the gun. He screams and drops to the ground, curling into a little ball while the hawk pecks and claws at him, even after his eyes are bloody holes.

Estrella sidesteps the man from the restaurant, kicking him in the back. He stumbles forward and quickly recovers, spinning around to kick her in the face.

"That's all you've got?" Estrella asks, surprised to find herself still standing.

She summons all the energy she has within, focusing on her hands. Pink light flies from her palm, meeting the red light of her opponent.

Headlights cut through the dark, a car door slams. Marc runs to Estrella.

The hawk carries the blinded man's gun away by the trigger guard as the man stumbles away, back to the Mercedes.

The wolf plunges his fangs into the third man's rib cage; the man screams once before he passes out. Hugo stomps on his chest and stands over him. "I dare you to get back up!" he yells.

Marc chokes the man from the restaurant from behind as heat moves from Estrella's belly and up her spine, through her arms, and out her fingers. A white light flashes from her hand and hits the man in the chest. He falls, unconscious.

The man on the ground knocks Hugo off him, stumble-running after the man with the bleeding eyes. But the wolf catches him by the back of his neck and drags him toward a thicket of trees. The man's screams recede, then suddenly stop altogether.

"Help me get this guy inside," Estrella says.

They drag the unconscious man into the cabin, where Hugo finds duct tape. They bind the man's hands, watching him until he suddenly wakes. He tries to lunge at Estrella but finds himself taped to a chair.

Estrella punches him in the face as hard as she can. "Who are you?"

Silence.

"Who sent you?" Silence.

"What do you want?"

He laughs. "How about I ask you a question, little Angelai. Where is the key?"

Marc punches him, but the man laughs.

Estrella asks, "What key?"

He springs up from the chair, his hands free, the duct tape torn. He reaches for Estrella's neck. She kicks him in the chest; he flies back into the fireplace. Blood gushes from his head and onto the stones. He looks surprised as the color leaves his face. Blood trickles from the side of his mouth.

"You can't kill us like this," he says through a bubble of blood. "I will see you soon enough. We will have the key."

A red and black cloud floats out of his body, through the ceiling, toward the moon.

Hugo breaks the silence. "Girl, I don't know what kind of candle-lighting, weird black magic drama you are into, but this is way too much for me."

Estrella stares at the body as it grows cold. "*Michael and his angels fought the dragon*," she mutters. "A casualty of war."

"What do we do with him?" Marc steps out of the way of the blood that runs from the bricks onto the floor.

The wolf howls outside.

Hugo, Estrella, and Marc make eye contact.

"Should we...you know," Hugo says.

Wordlessly, they strip the body and throw it to the wolf.

• • •

The barest hint of light softens the night that hangs around the cabin. Marc lights a fire to burn the bloodstained rug and the man's clothes while Hugo finds a bucket in the kitchen to wash the gore from the fireplace bricks.

Estrella looks through the dead man's wallet. "Stanley Crouch. New Yorker. February thirteenth, same day as Zandra."

"Stanley Crouch? That's the name of Dad's accountant," Marc says. "I've never met him, but he calls Dad all the time. He's from the city. Wonder if he's the same guy. Probably just a coincidence."

Hugo says, "I'll see what I can find on him. A guy in my dorm just hacked the FBI. It's super easy."

The room grows lighter as Marc extinguishes the fire. Hugo dusts off his newly purchased jacket and bow tie. "Maybe I can catch Christophe for breakfast."

Estrella hugs Hugo. "You're the best cousin ever." She looks around the room, then studies his face. "You know not to say anything about any of this, right?"

"No one would ever believe me anyway, so no need to worry."

"What's your story then? About tonight?" Marc asks.

"Okay, let me think," Hugo says, cracking his neck. "How about, I got bored and went back to Boston on the motorcycle that I broke into the library to make? So, I guess I'm taking the blame for that, and I *won't* be having breakfast with Christophe. More bullshit." He glares at Estrella. "You owe me so big right now that you will never, in your entire life, be able to pay me back. You owe me for three lifetimes." He revs up the motorcycle. "And we all should probably contact an attorney. Just in case no one buys our ridiculous stories. Who gets bored at prom?"

He spins out of the long drive and is gone.

Marc hands Estrella her high-heeled shoes. They laugh together, but abruptly stop. Marc puts his arm around her and guides her outside.

"No trace of the wolf or the body," Estrella says. In the breaking daylight, she can fully see Marc's car. "What's this?" She points to the cherry red Ferrari.

"It's my car. I got it for my sixteenth birthday."

"I thought you'd drive something more understated, like a Volvo or something."

Marc shrugs. "Why? The great thing about having a lot of money is having a lot of money. Carpe diem."

...

"Why are you wearing those ridiculous clothes?" Amaka asks as Marc and Estrella put their trays overflowing with eggs, toast, fruit, pancakes, oatmeal, and coffee onto the dining hall table where Amaka, Louis, and Christophe sit. Louis and Amaka hold hands beneath the table.

"It's true," Christophe says, his eyes concealed behind over-sized sunglasses. "Your outfits are ridiculous. And not what you were wearing just a few hours ago. I'm angry at your cousin, by the way. He left and didn't text until just an hour ago. He said he was bored. I have been accused of many things, but never of being boring."

Estrella smooths down the front of her New York Giants sweat-suit, Marc stretches out the tight collar of his. They bought the sweat-suits at a gas station, where the put their bloody, tattered formal wear in the dumpster out back and poured a quart of oil all over them.

"Later," Marc says as he and Estrella funnel food into their mouths.

Amaka whispers intensely to Estrella's bowed head, "Why haven't you answered my texts? Everyone is looking for you. Dr. Mather, Dr. Anderson, even Coach. I think they might have called the police. They are very..." Coach's red face, a blue vein throbbing at his temple suddenly comes into view. "Angry."

"In my office. Right now," Coach sputters. Estrella and Marc look longingly at their trays, as, still chewing, they follow Coach from the dining hall and into his office, where they sit on uncomfortable wooden chairs in front of his desk.

"Where the hell were you two?"

Marc says, as planned, "We wanted to be alone together, so we took a drive into the city."

"Is that where you got these Giants getups?" Coach yells.

Marc shrugs. "You know I've always been a fan."

"No, Marc, I know that you're a perpetual loser Jets fan. But I guess what I really want to know is where have you been? It is one hundred percent against Glouton's rules to leave the property without permission, and we have searched every inch of this property looking for you two."

At that moment, Dr. Mather opens the door. "Thank God, you found them," he says to Coach, then addresses his students. "What the hell were you thinking?" At the same time, his voice whispers inside Estrella's mind. "*Is the key still safe?*"

"Everything is all good," Estrella replies aloud.

Coach almost explodes. "No, Estrella Chavez, it is *not* all good. In fact, from where I'm looking right now, it's all bad. Very, very bad. You'll likely be suspended or expelled." He glares at Marc. "You, too, Mr. Hamilton. You're not immune." Coach points to the door. "Get out of here. Dr. Anderson and I will determine your punishment and be in touch with your parents. For now, you are not to leave your rooms."

• • •

"Looks like we're in some real trouble now," Marc says, holding Estrella's hand in front of her dorm building. "Funny how, in the past month, we've faced a gang of dogfighters, been chased through the mountains by creepy dudes, and accidentally killed a man and fed his body to a wolf—yet *this* feels like real trouble."

Estrella laughs.

In a soft voice, Marc asks, "What exactly are we involved in?"

Estrella looks into Marc's endless brown eyes. "I don't actually know, but I think the answer is locked in a box in the library. I have the key. I'm going back there tonight."

Marc squeezes her in a hug. "Then I'm going, too. If a box in the library can tell us what the hell is going on, I'm in."

He holds her hand tighter. "And, I mean, things definitely went another direction, but...I was going to ask you if you want to, you know, be exclusive. I think I'm in love with you."

Estrella's mouth drops open in shock.

"You don't have to give me an answer right now. And you don't have to say it back. But I'm so into you. Like, I know I'll never have these feelings for anyone else, especially after what happened tonight. Whatever this life brings, we're in it together."

...

Midnight birds make an occasional whistle as Amaka, Margeaux, and Estrella sneak across the deserted Glouton lawns. They meet Louis, Christophe, and Marc in the darkness behind the library.

"We are as one army," Amaka whispers. "We will use our collective powers to defeat our enemies." She pulls out a small canister. "Pepper spray. I took it from Adisa."

"All for one and one for all," Christophe says.

"Amaka and I will stand guard outside," Louis says. "Margeaux, Marc, and Christophe will go into the library with you, Estrella. Do what you have to do and come right back."

Estrella nods as they round the library and approach the entrance. "What the hell?" she whispers.

Tatiana reclines on the broad library steps.

Christophe steps ahead of the pack. "Hey, Tat, what are you doing here?"

Tatiana rises. Her eyes glow red, her hair writhes with snakes and worms, spiders pop out from beneath her scaly skin.

Terror grabs Estrella's heart. She tries to run but can't move her feet.

Tatiana waves her hand. *"Austavalem instipedid!"*

. . .

Estrella blinks open her groggy eyes, bringing her fingers to the deep scratches and painful bruises on her neck and chest. In front of her, Tatiana's rancid form grunts as it throws books from the shelves. Her back is turned.

Estrella quietly lifts to her feet and taps Tatiana on her reptilian shoulder.

As Tatiana turns her rotted head, Estrella punches her with all her might, straight into her yellow, jagged teeth.

Blood gushes as Tatiana becomes her human self. "You bitch!" she shrieks, her two front teeth falling to the marble floor. "I'm ruined now." Tatiana's pretty-again hands cover her mangled face.

Estrella settles into horse-stance. "I've been ready all year to beat the shit out of you, you fake-ass bitch," she yells, lifting her fists.

Tatiana mumbles unintelligible words through her bloody gums, turning half-way back into a monster—scales appear on her arms, a spider skitters from an eye, but she struggles to gather strength.

Estrella punches her again, in the same bloody mouth. Another tooth falls. Tatiana bends to pick it up, but Estrella kicks her in the ribs, knocking her across the library floor. Estrella lunges toward her, but Tatiana pushes herself off the floor, screams and runs away.

"You better run, bitch!" Estrella shouts as she picks up one of Tatiana's teeth from the floor. "This is a souvenir I'll enjoy for the rest of my life." She pockets the tooth, then walks along the shelves, stopping at the books she filed on the Yin Dynasty. "There it is!"

She opens her locket, removing the tiny pink crystal shard, and placing it into the tiny, chipped hole in the unassuming jade box that glows before her: the one she dropped in Kit's bedroom, back in August.

The top of the box opens; something shines inside. Estrella reaches in.

The tiny box feels bottomless until her hand bumps something hard. She pulls out a long, pink crystal sword. Ancient symbols adorn its hilt, it radiates soft light. A flood of love, a memory as old as the stars, washes over her.

Sudden wind breezes behind Estrella. A feeling of evil grips her heart. She turns to find Dr. Anderson in front of her, holding a black crystal sword. Estrella relaxes. "Dr. Anderson. You scared me."

"Good." Dr. Anderson's eyes turn red, her skin rough and green, her fingers purple. Her hair crawls with worms. "Drop your sword, Angelai." She advances, sword at the ready.

"The mask!" Estrella mutters to herself. "Definitely not Dr. Mather." She straightens her back, bends her knees, lifts the sword over her shoulder and says, "*Michael and his angels fought against the dragon.*"

Dr. Anderson strikes Estrella's sword with her own. The impact launches Estrella back into a bookshelf. Her sword scuttles across the marble floor, far out of reach.

"*And the dragon and his angels fought back,*" Dr. Anderson replies, reaching for the box and key.

From the floor, Estrella kicks Dr. Anderson's legs out from under her, dropping her to her knees. Estrella rolls toward her sword. "You may have gotten fit, but I'm strong, too." She lifts her sword. "And younger."

Dr. Anderson shouts, "*Atuniarum!*"

The sword flies from Estrella's grip as Estrella freezes, unable to move.

Dr. Anderson licks her wormy lips, then raises the black sword above her head as she screeches, "*Abio!*"

The black sword meets the pink one just above Estrella's neck, as the library lights up in pinks, greens, reds, and blues.

Marina, shining like diamonds in the foam of the ocean, leaps and suspends herself in midair. She gives Estrella a wink as Dr. Anderson sails backward from the unexpected force of Marina's sword against hers. Marina uses her advantage and slices open Dr. Anderson's throat.

Green and black pus oozes from Dr. Anderson's monstrous neck onto the library floor. Marina grabs Dr. Anderson's sword, then flies to Estrella.

"*Remundus!*"

Estrella unfreezes as Marina throws down the swords, gathering her sister up in her arms. "Hermanita! It's okay. I'm here now."

Estrella buries her head in Marina's shoulder, the force of her returning breath causing her to heave with each inhale.

With a sucking sound, the molten form on the floor rises onto her scaly elbow. Before Estrella can move, a dagger flies from Dr. Anderson's claw, into Marina's back. The monster convulses, bubbles, sizzles, and finally falls still, a cloud of foul smoke drifting from the rotten flesh.

Marina lurches forward onto Estrella's shoulder. She smiles as she speaks. "She can only kill my body without the sword. I'll always be here for you, I promise. You'll know me."

"No, no, no, no, no!" Estrella screams as she feels the life leaving her sister's body.

• • •

Starlight fills the dark room of the library where Estrella holds Marina's corpse, and Dr. Anderson's bloody body stiffens on the floor.

Dr. Mather materializes from the light. "I wanted to get here sooner, but Maalik imprisoned me with a sleeping spell."

"Who's Maalik?" Estrella asks, too trauma-shocked to ask anything more.

"Tatiana Duplessis. Maalik has made his mark on this world, I'm afraid. His power is strong, stronger than mine was tonight."

Estrella briefly smirks, touching the tooth in the front pocket of her jeans, then bursts back into tears.

Dr. Mather kneels by Marina. "Arariel loved being Marina." He waves his hand; the blood disappears.

"How did you do that?" Estrella asks. "And did you, like, *fly* here? Like Marina and Dr. Anderson? And Who's Arariel?"

"Arariel is one of us: an Angelai, like you and me, and your father, and nine others you will come to know in time. And yes, I can fly."

"An Angelai. Like the wolf called me. But what do you mean, she liked 'being Marina?'"

"Arariel has a playful spirit. Being in the body of a beautiful woman is a source of constant delight for her."

More tears barge through Estrella's eyes. "Who's this, then?" She points to the decomposed monster.

"Up until the day before your quinceañera, it was Dr. Constance Anderson, one of my dearest friends. What a great woman. The day before your quinceañera, she suffered a heart attack. That's when Azreal came in."

"Who's Azreal? Kind of sounds like Zadkiel, the elephant from my dreams."

"Azreal is, or was, a Demonai, like Maalik. He's been a merciless terror for ten thousand years. Thank God, he is gone forever now. He met the sword. And Zadkiel is one of us, too, in an animal form, for now."

"Did she, I mean he, kill Kit?" Estrella asks.

"Maybe. One of them did, or more than likely got someone to do it for them."

Outside the window, Estrella's bird sings, "*Morning comes soon. Say goodbye to the moon.*"

"We have to act quickly," Dr. Mather says. "This never happened."

Estrella shakes with shock as they roll Dr. Anderson in a carpet, and carry her, light as air, across the green to her desk. Estrella looks around as they make their trek, wondering for the first time what happened to her classmates, and considering that she is disposing of her second body in twenty-four hours.

"No one can see us, Estrella, don't worry," Dr. Mather says. "We are invisible to the world."

"How?"

"We Angelai have many powers, Estrella. Through our lifetimes we learn to control them. You will have to learn very quickly if we are to save the water. Right now, I am redirecting our light waves, but no one is watching anyway."

"Huh. So, Hugo's technology is a kind of magic. Cool," Estrella replies.

"Na clausvara!" Dr. Mather incants as he waves his hand over the open gash on Dr. Anderson's throat. The wound closes, leaving no scar behind. "This will look like a heart attack now, how she really died."

"What about Marina?" Estrella asks, bursting again into uncontrollable tears as the moon drops further toward the morning's horizon.

"Take my hand." Dr. Mather holds out his hand. Estrella takes it, and they dissolve into the black clouds. The sky becomes Kit's wing of the library.

"How did we get back here?" Estrella rubs her eyes.

"You probably won't have time in this life to learn all the tricks," He replies as he waves his hand over Marina, who lifts from the cold floor and begins to float through the shelves toward the stairs.

"Let's go. I'll fill you in on the drive." Dr. Mather places both swords, black and pale rose, in the tiny jade box. He pulls out a thumb drive and a letter. "These contain all the information you need to get your mother out of jail. The Scroll is in there too, but it only comes out to speak when *it* chooses."

. . .

Marina floats into the trunk of her Jaguar that's parked on the library lawn. Dr. Mather passes his hand over the vehicle and murmurs, "*Raksalu,*" before he takes the wheel. They head toward the city.

"Alright, we're safe from detection—I put a security spell over the car. Ask me anything."

Estrella's heart pulses like an open wound, her throat tight from holding back tears. "Can you please bring back Marina? Please? I've done it with a bird, and I think a dog. Please bring her back, I beg of you." Sobs heave through her whole body.

Dr. Mather shakes his head.

"I'm so sorry, Estrella. So sorry. Maybe if I got there the moment Connie threw the knife. We are powerful, but not omnipotent—the Cosmic has laws. But you have to understand, Arariel is still alive—only Marina's body is gone. Like with your father."

"My father? I mean, I did see him in the lake, but I thought maybe it was more like a vision."

"Your father, Nikki, me, Sylvie, Shabad, Babatunde, and the others that live in the Cosmic, living as pure love, like Marina is now. In fact, when we're unembodied, truly we're more powerful, but sometimes, we have to take a form to have the greatest influence."

"Nikki, Shabad, Sylvie and Amaka's dad?" The surprise of the information stops Estrella's tears.

Dr. Mather gives her a serious look. "You can never, never let on that you know any of the Angelai. Keeping it a secret is essential. It's bad enough that at least Maalik knows you're Angelai. And who knows who he or Azreal told. Secrecy is essential—we need every advantage."

"You mean, like to fight the Spirit War?"

Dr. Mather turns onto a deserted highway. "It's not so much a war as a balancing. But right, the very essence of the Demonai, with all their evil—their acid—makes it a war. Greed, ego, wanting more and more, never being satisfied. And all the cruelty and the like. It wasn't always that way. We used to all roam the earth together, as spirits, or embodied—whatever the Cosmic commanded—but the power to create, to own, to rule, it corrupted a few of us, then a few more. We actually made the first sword, with the ancient crystals, as directed by the Scroll. But then, of course, the Demonai stole the concept—they're thieves by nature."

Estrella drinks in his words as they follow the darkened, twisty road.

"And then they really took the weapons game to a new level when they stole the body of Archimedes. In fact, it would actually appear that they're winning at this point. But with the birth of you, and now that Azreal's extinguished, and we've got *their* sword, we might have a chance to keep the water wild and save all of the creatures of the Cosmic in the process."

"With the birth of me?"

"Yep. You're a Newly-Born. It's been about ten thousand years or so since we've had a newcomer. You're a big deal."

"So, can I fly and stuff?"

Dr. Mather chuckles. "You have to learn these things just like all the rest of us, through lifetimes of trial and error. But your newness contains a seed, a key, a code. You contain the pure, creative spark of alkalinity. Of wildness. Of love. Map Readers have been prophesying you for a long, long time."

"Kit was a Map Reader?"

Dr. Mather nods.

"And now, Margeaux? That map of Africa? She can see all kinds of things in it."

Dr. Mather nods. "She has much to learn as well. If only Kit was here to help her."

"But what about my mom? Does she know how to read it? She and Kit were so close. Or Yves? He could see Kit when she was in that Andy Warhol portrait at the Guggenheim, with that monocle. Maybe she taught him how to read it."

"What? Andy Warhol at the Guggenheim? A monocle? Yves?" Dr. Mather lets out a tense breath. "From now on, you'll have to communicate this type of information to me immediately. I had no idea. In fact, I've been suspicious of Yves for some time. Just a feeling. I could never get a read from him—which is suspect in itself. Kit never told me what she shared with him. And now, apparently, he's got the Eye—the monocle you saw him use. It's been supposedly missing since the Austro-Prussian War."

"You're not the only one," Estrella says. "Marc and Amaka think Yves is suspicious, but...I don't know. I just don't think he killed Kit. And it wasn't my mom either."

Dr. Mather clears his throat, keeping his eyes on the road. "It's important to trust your instincts—most of the time. As for your mom reading the map—she and Kit were very close, but only the Map Reader can read the map. And your mom's not entirely on board with the concept of angels and demons, though, from Victor and Marina and Kit, and even witnessing your powers as a child, she knows there's something greater at work. She's certainly on board with the Remundus—she and Raeesa."

"Raeesa Gajani? The kidnapped activist? And What's the Remundus?"

"We must be very careful about what information to share with your mother," Dr. Mather says. "I know it will be hard for you, but you've got to keep some things from her. Like who the Map Reader is now. I'll tell her what she needs to know when she needs to know it." He takes a long breath. "Anything else? Any brushes with danger? Anyone else who might have seen your powers at work?"

"Nikki saved us from a gang of guys in the Bronx during Parent's Weekend."

Dr. Mather nods. "She told me about that. She said you worked with her brilliantly."

Estrella's heart lifts with pride. "And, in Cuernavaca, three other guys, one with red eyes, followed us, but, actually, the animals took them out."

"The red eyes—a Demonai," Dr. Mather says. "I wonder which?"

"No idea," Estrella replies. "It was dark."

"Anything else?" Dr. Mather asks.

Estrella recalls her recent accidental murder of Stanley Crouch, and her accomplices, Marc and Hugo. It's not just her who could get into trouble.

"No. Nothing else. But what do you mean about my code? It's more than just my Mayan gift? And what about Raeesa and the Remundus?"

Dr. Mather smiles a little. "The Mayan healing gift thing—Marina decided that would be a good way to break you in gently to your powers. Honestly, if it weren't for Marina and Kit, I would've told you everything the first day of school, but they wanted to do it at your quinceañera—Kit said the map told her it was better timing, and Marina just wanted you to have a bit of fun in life before we broke the news. And then, after everything that happened, Marina insisted that I say nothing until everything was straightened out with your mom."

Dr. Mather continues, "But as to your code, there are two forces—acid and alkaline. We got into it a bit in class last week. In its most basic, physical sense, acid is heating, alkaline cooling. But, like everything in the Cosmic, it's deeper than that; metaphor is reality. Acid symbolizes anger, greed, hate, ego, decay, and domestication, whereas alkaline symbolizes kindness, selflessness, compassion, love, purity, and wildness."

"So, *I* contain the seed of love?" Estrella asks. "And purity? But, I mean, how does that help the water? And, like, what am I supposed to do? What about how I get so angry sometimes, even when I'm trying not to? I mean, I don't always feel loving."

"Well, Estrella, you'll have to grow, to transform. There's nothing easy about being embodied. You'll have to put in the work. Now, as to how that will happen, at this point, your guess is as good as mine. That's a big challenge for us when we become embodied—we have a mission, and we know what it is, and what we're supposed to do, but only because the Cosmic makes it clear to us one day at a time. For instance, I know that my mission in this life is to teach Mystery School, and to show the power of words, vibration, intention. I got the call from the Cosmic, I looked around, and I saw a couple in Long Island who would be loving, supportive parents of some means, which I knew would be important—it's much harder to achieve anything in an earthly life without money—and in I went."

"Like, into your mom's belly?"

"That's right. There are two ways to become embodied, for Angelai and Demonai both; through birth, like you, me, and Marina, or through the moment of death, like Dr. Anderson."

"Did you know how to fly when you were a baby? Like, have you always been aware you were an Angelai?"

"Yes, I have. You might have been aware too, but the trauma with your father set you back."

"The trauma with my father?"

Dr. Mather's eyes brim with compassion. "You see, even though we're Angelai, when we become embodied, we take on the Genetic Code of Karma of the body we inhabit. We take on all the history of that flesh. So, when you were born to Victor and Linda Chavez, you became all of who they were, and who their ancestors were. Those bonds of flesh run deep, let me tell you. Over lifetimes, the cells of our bodies are remade again and again, but they remember. They recognize those they've loved. We call it chemistry, but it's much more than that. And sometimes, the chemistry is so strong that it overrules logic and even the spirit."

Estrella shakes her head in disbelief. "I just have to say, Dr. Mather, that all this information is kind of blowing my mind right now."

Dr. Mather chuckles. "The cellular bonds to our children are usually the strongest, but sometimes, a friendship or a true love can have an even stronger pull. That's why I don't have any kids, and why both the Angelai and Demonai can be stronger when they don't take a human form—cellular bonds can weaken the spirit essence. But to get stuff done, a lot of times, the Celestials have to take a human, or even an animal form, like Zadkiel, or Islid."

Dreams of Islid and Zadkiel flit through Estrella's mind as Dr. Mather continues.

"And the Genetic Code of Karma isn't just between people. It's in our personalities, too. Like if someone really likes music or art or science, or even drugs. Or if you're prone to anger or sorrow. It runs deep. Like when my mother died, even knowing all I know about the Cosmic, about eternal life, about the water that runs through the universe and through us all, I was a wreck. I couldn't leave the house for weeks, the grief was so consuming. Sometimes, the flesh is stronger than the spirit. And that's how it was with you. When your father was assassinated, the pain of his loss set you back. Up until that time, you and Marina were making real progress. But your father's murder was a cataclysmic event for you."

"Is that why they killed my father? They knew about me? Is Gabriel Estrada a Demonai?"

"If they knew about you or Marina, you would've both been dead long ago. They killed your father because of his potential political power—he was really getting a movement going. He was a protector of one of the crystal caves, the one in Mexico, near Cuernavaca. Like Babatunde is in Africa, on the western coast. But no one's made a play for the cave yet, so I don't think they know about it. And we don't know too much about what they have going on either. Kit was getting some good information, but..." Dr. Mather wipes a tear from his eye. "Damn them! We Angelai count on our Map Readers, and Kit was a great one. God bless Margeaux Prince. Talk about a life-challenge. Plus, Map Readers are mortal, which gets a little tricky, because they never truly believe the way we do. Same goes for the entire Remundus. And I'm pretty sure that Gabiel Estrada, while utterly corrupted by evil, is not, himself, a Demonai."

"So, what is the Remundus?" Estrella asks again. "Mundus means 'world' in Latin, so like a new world?"

"The Remundus is our team, so to speak, our earthly workers in the Spirit War. They're very loosely aligned with the Pythagoreans, though it's become much larger and more diffuse since then—talk about herding cats. Everyone has their own agenda, but overall, there is a group of good-hearted, well-intentioned, committed people out there who are on our side. Unfortunately, so do the Demonai, though they're far from good-hearted or well-intentioned, and, even more unfortunately, they're a bit better organized. One might even call them a cult at this point. The Proletum."

"Letum. In Latin that means 'violent death'," Estrella says. "Like these people are for it. Creepy."

"They are aligned with the aforementioned Archimedes—the father of modern war. Charming. Sadly, he has quite a following."

"Was he a Demonai?"

"No, not him. He worked for one, and then they took his body. You'll often find that's the case. Basically, the simple rule is, the one with all the money is the Demonai. Then they can pay for all the horrible things their worm-infested hearts desire."

Estrella takes a deep breath. "Okay, so we're in the Spirit War, and our endgame is to purify the water. I have the code for that. We're fighting a bunch of monsters and their army of assassins. On our side, we have a disorganized group of do-gooders. But now we have an extra sword, at least. And no one has any actual idea how I'm supposed to carry out my mission, but it will become clear one day at a time. Like the Cosmic will tell me, like through dreams of animals? And Margeaux will give me directions from the map and cards that only she can read?" Estrella shakes her head. "Our situation sucks."

Dr. Mather laughs. "It's not great right now, that's for sure. But the good thing about the Demonai is that they're just as awful to each other as they are to everyone else. Their lust for power knows no bounds. They often end up defeating themselves, though we certainly don't want to count on it."

He pulls the car to a stop at a hairpin turn. "And the number one thing is that you've got to turn all your thoughts, emotions, and actions into a force for good, for love. In this love, you will find powers beyond the limits of your imagination. You've got to learn to transmute your anger. It can be a very destructive and counter-productive force." He pops the trunk. "And don't forget, that at the bottom of that bottomless box you hold, you have the Scroll. It's the voice of the Cosmic, the will of the water. When the time is right, it'll come out and help you. And there's only one Scroll...the Demonai don't have it, just us." He opens his door. "It's time."

Estrella bursts into heavy sobs as they put Marina's body in the driver's seat. She kisses her sister one final time.

Dr. Mather waves his hand, and the car races at full speed into a tree, bursting into flames.

Crystals and pink light rise from the fire into the night sky. Flowers burst into bloom on the nearby trees, the moon brightens.

Dr. Mather takes Estrella's hand. They fly over the turning earth, where in the city below them, babies in the hospitals are born laughing.

• • •

Estrella slinks into the early morning dining hall to find a ragged crew with faces drawn from sleeplessness.

Marc jumps from the table and meets her at the door. "Are you alright? We were freaking out. I looked in the library for you—where were you?"

"I'll tell you all about it later," Estrella says, following Marc back to the table and taking a bite of egg from his plate. "Right now,

I have to go to the city. Alone." She surveys her fellow Mystery Schoolers. "What about you guys? What happened?"

"No one can remember what happened," Louis says. "We woke up in the bushes about an hour ago."

"You can't go to the city now," Margeaux says. "We have finals, and you'll get expelled for sure."

"Think about your future," Amaka commands. "We can fight our enemies again tomorrow. For now, our battle lies within the class-room walls."

"I am thinking about my future," Estrella replies.

"Can I give you a ride?" Marc pulls his keys from his pocket.

Estrella shakes her head, knowing that, from now on, she will have to keep certain secrets from Marc.

Marc caresses Estrella's tight neck. "At least to the train?"

• • •

Memories of Estrella's childhood wash over her as green trees turn into cement buildings through the windows of the train. Tears es-cape her eyes behind the expensive sunglasses Marina gave her for Christmas. The lilting bells of Marina's laugh ring from the front of the train. Estrella twists toward the sound to see crowns of pink light radiating from the passengers on board, who suddenly laugh together for no reason.

Estrella deboards the train and climbs up the subway steps, becoming part of the sunny downtown New York morning. Crowds of businessmen and women push past her; a hint of a sea breeze tickles her nose. She navigates the throng, her mind focused on her plan.

Finally, she stops in front of a sleek skyscraper, dropping her head back to look at the top floor: her destination. She touches the thumb drive in her pocket and breathes—in through the nose, out through the nose—the first lesson of Mystery School.

She presses the link on Hugo's bracelet, then walks right past the two broad-shouldered men with crew cuts in navy blue suits bursting at the seams. She slips into the elevator through its closing doors, then waves her vibrating hand over the coded keypad. The elevator launches up to the penthouse, where she strides out of the elevator into an open office.

A supermodel receptionist with a French accent gives her a tight-lipped smile, then stands and nearly shouts at her to stop as Estrella marches past her, into the glass-walled boardroom. The receptionist, on Estrella's heels, apologizes rapidly. "So sorry, ladies and gentlemen, she rushed past me, I have alerted security."

William Hamilton fixes his gaze on Estrella. Worms and open sores dot his scaly skin. Estrella plugs her nose.

The Water Trust board members at the long, modern table look from Estrella to William to the receptionist. Estrella recognizes a few as acquaintances of Kit and her mom.

William's handsome facade covers him as he smiles his warm smile and tells the French receptionist, "I've got this." He turns to Estrella. "Shouldn't you be in school, Miss Chavez?"

Estrella consolidates her energy and says, "We need to talk."

He asks gently, "Can it wait, Estrella? We're in a meeting at the moment."

The board gives a little uncomfortable laugh.

"Now." Estrella's cells vibrate from inside her bones.

William's eyes narrow and flash red with anger. "Give us a minute," he tells the wide-eyed professionals gathered around the table.

The members of the board dutifully pick up their papers and file out of the office. One, a hippie-like man, says as he passes, "We miss your mother here."

Estrella nods, knowing that without her mother's leadership, soon, no water will be free. It will all be for sale, at the highest price. And it will be filthy. But if all goes the way she plans, her mom will be at the head of this table next week.

"What are you doing here?" William hisses.

"You know exactly what I'm doing here. I have the swords. You must have felt the loss of Azreal. If not, let me be the first to tell you. It was Arariel with the crystal sword in the library." Estrella smirks.

"Marina?" Bill softens, concern showing behind his hazel eyes. "Is she alright?"

"She's dead." Estrella breathes into the anger she knows will weaken her, then inserts the thumb drive into the laptop at the head of the table.

Bill wipes a tear from his eye, his beastly appearance dissolved into his human form, the horrible smell gone.

Numbers, words in Spanish, and maps of Mexico flash on the white wall behind the desk. Then William, as a young man, shakes hands with a man in a Mexican army uniform and an eye patch.

Bill transforms again into a monster. "What do you want?"

The board members aren't even pretending not to gape through the glass walls.

Estrella breathes and recenters herself. "My mother goes free and runs the Trust again. Now."

"You know I'll never do that."

"Look, that's you." On the white wall, an old video starts playing, featuring young William and a group of men sitting at a table in a dimly lit room, where William reaches into a bag and pulls out several stacks of American money. Then he presents a photo of Victor and Linda to the men sitting across the table. The men nod as he slides across several more photographs of different faces. One is Babatunde, Amaka's father. Another wears an eye patch.

When Estrella reviewed the footage with Dr. Mather just a few hours ago, he told her that the photos are of the leaders of the Water Trust who died in a plane crash on their way home from Victor's funeral. Only Babatunde survived.

Dr. Mather also told her that the man with the eye patch is known to be the Demonai's top assassin, one of the Proletum.

"Who made this?" William asks. Estrella can see him mentally going through his long list of enemies, trying to recall who else was there that day and could have been recording the meeting.

"That's a great question, *Barachiel*," she replies, emphasizing every syllable of his Demonai name. "It would appear that someone in the room was keeping a record—an enemy on the inside." Dr. Mather said he had no clue who sent Kit the thumb drive.

William blazes. "Why don't you just go to the police?"

"Or the FBI, or the CIA? Come on—those are your guys. We're taking this to the media. It'll make a great story. The good part, where the drug lords come in, and you guys all act friendly and give each other money and drugs is in ten, nine, eight, seven..."

Bill picks up his phone; Estrella pauses the video.

"Hank. You need to tell Scott to drop all the charges against Linda Chavez immediately." A panicked muffle comes from the phone against Bill's ear. "Just do it," Bill says. "Now." He looks at the image frozen on the screen. "And make sure the pathway is there to reinstate her as chairman of the Trust."

The voice on the other end of the line says, "What the hell are you talking about? Have you lost your mind?"

"Make it happen!" William says, slamming down his phone.

Estrella's jaw drops as she realizes the extent of William Hamilton's power. Just a phone call, like Dr. Mather said.

"By the way," Estrella says, feeling her own power, "We obviously have this information in many trusted hands. With one click of a button, it goes viral. And you don't want your own child to know who you really are, much less all your shareholders. Did I mention that we have your sword?"

She enjoys the sound of her voice, even though Dr. Mather told her that ego weakens Angelai.

"Don't you wonder, Angelai, if your mother *is* guilty? She certainly has a way of getting what she wants." William's words hit Estrella in the chest. On her spreadsheet of most likely suspects, Linda never fell from the top spot on the list. Estrella breathes and pushes past the doubt. Doubt, she also learned, is one of the great Demonai weapons.

"It doesn't matter, does it?" she says. "We go forward from here." She's almost to the glass door, when she turns back to face him. "How can you be so horrible? How could you murder my father and burn our ranch to the ground? You deserve to be a monster."

Steam comes from Bill's scaly skin. "I'm glad I killed Victor. He stole what was mine. And I'll be glad to kill you too, the living embodiment of him. I think I'll dismember you and feed you to my bird. But perhaps you should ask if you, too, have an enemy on the inside. I would never destroy Linda's home. It was precious to her."

His words surprise Estrella. "Why would you care what's precious to my mom?"

William laughs. "You have no idea who I am, or what I'm capable of doing." He slips back into his carefully maintained cover with ease. Gone are the scales and worms. Only the smell remains. "We will have our sword back soon enough. And yours. Did you really think you were the only Newly-Born of this epoch? We too have a map, and someone who knows how to read it. And yes, Angelai, now we have a child of our own."

Fear cuts through the center of Estrella's body, but she breathes into it, focusing on love. She smiles. "Thanks for the info about the

Newly-Born. Can't wait to tell the others. You should really practice the part about being silent. There's a reason for that, you know."

She flings the glass door open, her head held high, her chest lifted with light as the board members file back in.

Behind her, she hears William say, "Kids—they never change. Shall we resume?"

JUNE

Angelai Dominai

The small, blue-collar church bursts with mourners. Estrella looks out over the despondent crowd from behind the pulpit. Though she knew everyone loved Marina, she didn't realize her sister had made an impact on so many lives. Estrella clears her throat to deliver her eulogy.

As she speaks, a wave of crystals and light swirls around the chapel. Behind the altar, Estrella's feet lift an inch from the floor. Through Estrella's teary eyes, the walls of the church dissolve; the mourners become prisms of light.

· · ·

Estrella and Linda sip coffee in the little kitchen heavy with the absence of Marina.

They sit in hollow silence for many minutes until Linda puts her cup firmly down, takes a deep breath, and lets it out slowly. "William told me you went to see him in the city."

Estrella spits out her coffee. "William Hamilton? When? Why?"

Linda says, "He called to talk about Marina."

"He called to talk about Marina?" Estrella enunciates every word back to her mother, as if Linda was hard of hearing.

"I know everyone says that he's a wicked man, but she is still his daughter," Linda replies.

Estrella rubs her ears until they pop. "What?"

"William Hamilton is Marina's father," Linda says. "Your father, Victor, my dear friend, married me to preserve my honor when William had his accident. Bill was my true love."

Estrella stares at her mom for a moment before she speaks. "How is this possible? So, Marina is Evan's half-sister? And Marc's cousin?" She shivers. "I'm not his daughter though, right?"

Linda semi-smiles. "No. Don't worry. You are one hundred percent mine and Victor's."

"But you do know who Bill Hamilton is?" Estrella asks, recalling his smell.

Linda sighs. "I know he's been seduced by money and power, the same as most men in his position. I know that Kit said she thought it might be more than that, that he might be like...like you and Victor and Marina, but evil instead of good. Frankly, it all seems a little woo-woo to me, but I know you *do* have powers, like Marina did and your dad. I've seen them. Back in Mexico. But I don't think Bill is Satan, just corrupted. And even Marina and Kit said that there's hope that even the worst of us can change—just like Jesus said."

Estrella examines her mother. "Oh shit. Mom, you really don't get it. It's just like Dr. Mather said, the Genetic Code of Karma stuff, and mortals not being able to see who the Angelai and Demonai really are."

"Yeah, well, I take everything Dr. Mather says with a big grain of salt and I think you should, too," Linda replies. "Everyone has an agenda."

Estrella's eyes open wide. "What agenda? To purify the water? And I *know* Bill Hamilton is a demon—I've seen it myself!"

"You've always had quite an imagination," Linda says. "I think we're going to need to agree to disagree on this. The one thing we all agree on is that we want to save the water—let's stick to that."

"But you do realize that Bill Hamilton killed my father and put you in jail? Right? Like, you have to admit that's evil. And he probably killed Kit, too."

Linda rolls her eyes. "He didn't kill Kit," Linda replies. "And he would've gotten me out of jail as soon as he quashed the Species Extinction Report and took control of the Water Trust. But, thanks to you, I'm out early, and still have control. Excellent work, by the way. Even Bill was impressed with your confidence as you blackmailed him." Linda takes a sip of coffee. "But I don't believe he had Victor killed. He swears it just looks that way on the video you showed him."

"Here's the video," Estrella replies as she pulls up the file on her phone and plays it for Linda. "You can decide for yourself."

Linda stands from the table, her chair clanging to the floor. "It's him!"

"I told you," Estrella says.

"Not Bill," Linda says, trembling. "The man with the eye patch. That's the man who killed Victor." She retakes her seat. "Where did you get this?"

Estrella takes her phone from Linda's shaking hand. "Someone gave it to Kit, but Dr. Mather doesn't know who. And you can see that Bill hired him, right?"

"Kit saw this?" Linda drops the phone. "This whole time, she knew." She breaks into fresh tears. "Damn him! Damn the Proletum that made him do it. That pack of jackals and freaks, with their blood sacrifices in the woods. Damn his father. *He's* the devil! Look what he did to his son—to my Bill!"

"Blood sacrifices in the woods?" The image of the leopard from Estrella's dream makes her queasy. "And what do you mean about Bill and Kit's dad?"

Linda blows her nose into a tissue. "William, Jr. What an *asshole.* If the demons are real, it makes perfect sense that he was one of them. He was dying from cancer—so he drove himself and Bill off a bridge. He killed them both to take his son's body." Linda looks to the heavens and shakes her head. "It sounds ridiculous just to say it. Kit was only ever partially convinced herself, but that's the story she read in the map. One thing's for sure, Bill changed after that day. He broke off our engagement and within three weeks, he was planning a wedding with that pill-popping Barbie doll."

Estrella shakes her head. "So, I'm going to tell you again—it *is* all real. Like super-real. Bill Hamilton is a monster, like he looks like a sick reptile and smells even worse. Dr. Mather and I can see the monsters and you can't—that's why he says you aren't really on board."

Linda glares at Estrella. "Is *that* what Dr. Mather says? That I'm not on board? On *board*? Oh, I'm on board. In fact, I'm the captain of this cursed ship. All of your angels and devils aside, I know the stakes. I know what your father lived for, and Kit, and even Bill before he turned. The water. *You*, Estrella, and all your friends. I will see to it that you inherit a fertile earth, a living earth, with clean, free water. I've sacrificed my entire life for the water. I've lost everything." She sucks in her tears as she says, "And now even my Marina is gone, my *child*."

"She saved my life, Mom," Estrella sobs. "From them, from one of them. You have to believe me, they're real."

Linda holds Estrella as they cry together. "Okay," Linda finally says. "I'll believe you. At least most of it." She gently tilts Estrella's chin to look into her eyes. "And you believe me—I will prevail. The Proletum thinks they have all the power, but, thanks to you, the Remundus is back in control. And we have a plan and the financing to keep power for the next century—long enough to ensure the purity of the water."

"So Amaka was right," Estrella says. "It *is* all about money and power."

"Of course it is," Linda replies. "You are aware that we're here on planet earth. This is a land of hungry beasts known as the human race— cursed with both a sinful nature and free will." Linda pours herself a third cup. "It all starts with the Species Extinction Report and securing Paul Phillips as president. And finding Raeesa. Which is why I need to know who the new Map Reader is. Kit said she had already made contact with her, someone at Glouton. Do you know who? Maybe one of your professors?"

Estrella looks down. Dr. Mather told her not to tell her mom anything. "No. Nope. No idea," Estrella lies. "But let's get back to the part about William Hamilton being Marina's dad, and thank *God* not mine," she says, turning the subject. "Does Aunt Zandra know?"

"I think she suspects. But she loves you and Marina so much, she would never say anything."

"Hmm. I can't believe Aunt Zandra could keep a secret. But then again, she never told anyone that she was standing over Kit's dead body out there on the patio. And you never said anything about it either—even when you were facing the electric chair."

"We're not going there, Estrella," Linda replies. "The judge declared a mistrial, since the defense's star witness, Ms. Franks, went missing. Why would you invite her, anyway? But thank God it's over. Time to move on."

"You're the one who wanted a lot of guests," Estrella retorts, then asks. "What about Marina? Did she know Bill was her dad?"

"Yes, Marina knew—she guessed it. She said when she looked into Bill's eyes, she saw herself. She was about thirteen—right after the fire. I had to tell her. And she and Bill always had a connection. He even gave her a family necklace for her quince. He's as devastated as I am."

"I doubt it," Estrella replies. "I mean, he had you put in jail just to keep the Water Trust from releasing a report, so that his companies can keep destroying the water. He's a total dick, Mom. And a literal *demon*. Don't be fooled."

"Believe it or not, he's not the worst of my enemies," Linda replies. "He told me that he had me arrested to keep me from being killed by any number of his charming Proletum friends. If not for Bill, I'd be dead, so remember that when you pass judgment on the man." Linda bursts back into tears. "I know he's not perfect, and maybe you're right, maybe he's a demon, but the bonds of the heart are strong, stronger than the devil sometimes. I haven't stopped hoping that he'll change. Marina told me that it's happened before. We prayed the rosary every day for him. I will keep praying."

Estrella remembers how William looked human again in the boardroom when he asked about Marina. Dr. Mather said the highest power of the Angelai is to transmute wickedness through love. Though the sword is usually necessary.

"Either way, you're in for the fight of your life," Estrella says to Linda. "We all are. We can't lose. The water must be free."

Linda holds up her fists like a boxer's. "Oh, I'll keep fighting. I'm getting good at it."

Estrella's phone lights with Hugo's face.

"You're never going to believe it! Celeste James's plane crashed outside Vegas. Marina's idol! She's the only survivor. It's a miracle! If only Marina was still here." He breaks into tears. "They're having an Instagram Live celebration for Celeste later today—I'll send the link."

Estrella walks outside with the phone, waiting until Linda can't hear her to whisper, "What happened with the library thing?"

"Oh," Hugo responds, his face changing from sorrow to fury. "You mean the library at Glouton that sent me a bill for $10,972 for the damage I confessed to doing at prom? I'm borrowing it from Alfonso while the lawyers settle Marina's will."

"So sorry again." Estrella says.

"Even if I do get money in the will, you better pay me back," Hugo hisses. "And as for Stanley Crouch, before we fed him to a *magical wolf*, he was indeed Nelson Hamilton's accountant. I did some hacking, and I found out that the FBI and the local police are looking for him. Actively. So basically, once we've had some time to mourn, which will never be enough time—*ever*, you and I are going to have a long talk, because I deserve to know what the hell is going on with you and your witchcraft and whatever else you've gotten me into."

• • •

Yves pulls Kit's Rolls to a gliding stop in front of the Water Woods cabin. "Shall I wait?"

Estrella surveys the grounds while she and Margeaux slide out of the car. She notices no sign of the wolf or any other evidence of prom night.

"No, we're good. Thanks for the ride," Estrella replies. "But come back in two hours—that's when Dr. Mather said we'll be ready."

Yves slightly bows his head. "At your service."

He drives back out the windy dirt road as Nadine's new Jetta approaches. Nadine bounds out of her car and wraps Estrella in a tight hug. "Weren't expecting me, were you?"

Estrella pushes off her small friend. "What are you doing here?"

From the late morning summer sky, points of light like stars fall to the warm earth. Dr. Mather, Nikki, Shabad, and Sylvie take form from the lights.

"I forgot to tell you, Nadine's Angelai," Dr. Mather says. "Let's do this inside before everyone else shows up."

Shabad smiles wide at Estrella as Sylvie holds Estrella's hand and guides her inside. Nadine shoots a palm of light at Nikki, electrifying her hair for a moment. Nikki waves her own palm, and Nadine bumps into a forcefield.

Margeaux, her mouth dropped in shock, looks at Estrella with questioning green eyes. Estrella shrugs.

"This is the first, last, and only time we'll meet like this," Dr. Mather says, his voice echoing in the large room of the cabin. "To say this is kismet is an understatement. In a thousand years, we've never had so many of us all together. Kit did a great job in interpreting the map and cards to get us here, and of course, we all heard the call of the Cosmic." Dr. Mather proceeds.

"Margeaux's the new Map Reader. If you had a hunch, you're right. The news came to me in a dream, and I know Nikki had a vision during class of Margeaux with the atlas. Margeaux, I'll be your only line of communication, and I'll tell you when the conversation will be safe. Never speak of any of this to anyone, ever. That's how we've managed to avoid extinguishment all these millennia—we've trusted the voice of the Cosmic to guide us and kept our own voices silent. I'll make sure everyone knows what they need to know. And of course, we can always connect in the dream state, and in mutual meditation. Any questions or thoughts?"

Sylvie takes Margeaux and Estrella's hands. They all lift a few feet from the stone floor. "Know that we love you, and we're here for you," she says as a rainbow appears over their trio. Shabad, Nadine, Dr. Mather, and Nikki join hands around the three, and also levitate. Estrella's heart opens with a feeling of joy so big she could never have imagined it. She notices tears of joy flowing from Margeaux's eyes as they all touch back down.

Tires crunch on the dirt road outside. The rainbow dissolves into the shadows and summer light of the cabin.

"They're here," Dr. Mather says. "God help us all. If I didn't trust Kit so much, I would never let this happen. But no matter what she said, I just couldn't bring in Evan."

Nikki nods then says, "But Amaka's quite good."

"She *is*," Nadine agrees, as Sylvie and Shabad nod their heads. "So strong! If only Babatunde would relent and transmit his power to her, she could be almost as powerful as we are."

"He might yet," Dr. Mather says. "He knows the water's desperation."

Amaka walks in first, followed by Louis, Marc, Christophe, and Zaharia. "I am three minutes early," Amaka says. "Why are you all here before me? Margeaux is never on time for anything." She looks around the cabin. "And I sense that you have been here for some time."

All the Angelai laugh.

"Everyone sit," Dr. Mather says, cutting them off.

Marc makes eye-contact with Estrella, then they look together at the fireplace bricks. Estrella notices the slightest discoloration where they scrubbed.

Dr. Mather paces the cabin as the Mystery Schoolers—minus Tatiana and Evan and plus Nadine—take their places on the warming stone floor and twist into lotus.

"You are not the same as you were when we first came to this cabin. And it's not just the so-called 'powers' you've developed since then." The lilting June breeze lifts the curtains of the open windows as Dr. Mather speaks. "Your innocence is lost. We've attended not one, but three funerals this academic year. How many thousands have died in that time at the hands of Su Bang Bang and his army? How many tons of acid poured into our dying rivers, oceans, and streams? These are the casualties of war. Our war. The Spirit War."

Amaka looks right at Estrella and mouths the word, "war."

"In our first class, I asked, why you? Why this particular group? Every year, I select students who I believe will benefit the most from the unorthodox curriculum, sure. Those who will take their knowledge and hopefully do good with it. But I didn't select you for this class. Kit Hamilton did."

Marc and Estrella meet eyes again.

"Each one of you was a dot on a map that only she could read. We saw what happened to her for this extraordinary ability. Bad news, Margeaux—you've got the gift—but we'll get into that in a minute."

Everyone looks at Margeaux, who smiles in spite of Dr. Mather's ominous words.

"So, you were dots on a map. And all of your dots appeared on the same day. November eleventh, fifteen years ago. Anyone know what that day is?"

"It's the day I was born," Estrella says with surprise.

"That's right. That's the day Estrella was born: the first Angelai to be born in over ten thousand years. An Angelai is a spirit with the distilled powers of the Cosmic who takes a human form. I'm one and Estrella is one. There are others, but they can't be revealed—for your safety and for theirs. Truly, it's unimportant. What *is* important to note is that there are also Demonai, like the man who chased some of you in Cuernavaca. And they're all out to kill me and Estrella, and any of the other Angelai their Map Reader can locate."

Dr. Mather pauses, his audience rapt.

"Kit knew that each of you was meant to be in the council of this brand new Angelai, that you were the ones who would be able to help her achieve her earthly mission. You are here to free the water." Twelve sets of wide eyes follow him as he paces. "All these human wars, they are distractions. They use religion, or economics, or whatever, to mask the truth of the Spirit War. Water—life itself. Bad news: we're losing. We lost Jerameel back around the Industrial

Revolution. Barachiel drew and quartered his earthly body with the Moon Sword. Good news: now we've got the Moon Sword *and* the Sun Sword, and Azreal is out of the picture. And with Ambriel—or should I say Estrella—on our side, we're in much better shape."

Estrella blushes.

"That's what happened at the Vision Quest—it was as it was meant to be. Estrella was initiated into the Angelai. When this happened, you, her earthly tribe, received the powers you will need to fulfill your mission. There are only three ways someone can receive Celestial powers: direct transmission, dedicated study, or birth."

Dr. Mather stops pacing and takes a deep breath of the forest air drifting through the open window. "Of course, the powers are strongest in the very few who are born with them, like Estrella. But you have direct transmission of these powers. With continued, dedicated study, you'll be surprised at how powerful you can become. I'm proud to say you've been developing these powers appropriately with perhaps a few exceptions—a.k.a., the sports field."

Everyone giggles.

"Some of you have been putting in significant study, and it shows." He looks right at Amaka, who, like all the assembled students, has barely blinked since he began speaking. "Each of you will be tested, tempted, and pushed to your limits. Some of you will likely not live long. Remember, this is a war. If the Demonai don't already know about you, it won't be long. You must constantly refine your powers to accomplish your mission and stay alive. And, above all, as from our first class, keep *silent*. Your power to *not* speak may be the one that saves your life."

Dr. Mather restarts his pacing. "Also, you have a network of helpers—a loosely aligned group of various politicians, business leaders, and activists called the Remundus. The Remundus first sprung up from the teachings of Pythagoras, thousands of years ago, and have been passing down their knowledge and doing mostly good works on the earth ever since. They passionately believe in living in harmony with nature, which is great, though they sometimes miss the mark, and get caught up in the minutia of the world. Remember—your mission is the *water*. Purifying and setting free the water. Rewilding her. It is, above all, a *spiritual* mission. The Cosmic will always be there to guide you, but, in the end, you'll have to rely on your own powers of intuition and discernment to know who to trust and how to proceed.

"Because there is another group, the Proletum, who cleave to the mathematics of Archimedes. So basically, they're all about the machines of destruction and war. The Demonai, a very smelly, ugly band of immortals, has got them convinced that their mission is to control the water, everywhere it flows—including the water inside our very bodies. The Proletum believe that nature is to be subdued, exploited. They've bought into the Demonai lie of scarcity, and sadly, they're quite an effective cabal. They're tricky—often well disguised as friends. Or even family."

Estrella looks at Marc, and thinks of his uncle, Bill Hamilton III.

Dr. Mather stops pacing and claps his hands together. "Okay! So that's that. Before we get to the fun stuff, let's talk about the summer plans Kit saw for you all." He nods in Christophe's direction. "Christophe, you're going to make a map of all the water in your homeland, so the Water Trust can make a bid for as much land, and the clean, cold water that flows through it, as they can get away with. Make it look like you're working on your Trans-Siberian railroad redesign project."

Christophe nods. "Luckily, people are easily bribed."

"Shabad," Dr. Mather says. "You've got to get back to the Ganges, and remain there for the foreseeable future, putting all the force of your love into that sacred river. She's already nearly lost—poisoned, blocked, choked. In two years, the stars over the Ganges will be ready for Estrella to purify them. But quite a few other things need to happen first, and still more will need to occur after."

"In August," Dr. Mather says, "Estrella, Nikki, and Nadine are to go to Iran to break Raeesa Gajani from her cell. Raeesa is currently the leader of the Remundus. One day, it will be Zaharia. But Zaharia, you are to spend the summer as you normally would. Raeesa will communicate with you when the time is right. And— my personal vision about this was very clear—you'll need to bring Adisa, Amaka's friendlier guard."

Zaharia's face lights, but Amaka looks angry.

"Amaka," Dr. Mather says, meeting her fiery stare, "You will study a network of caves near the ocean with your father and Amare."

Amaka nods, but she's clearly not thrilled with her assignment.

"Everyone else, just do what you normally would. Have fun, go to parties, live your best life. But do it with your mental walls strong, and don't forget to meditate every day. Okay, now for the good stuff."

"Margeaux, please rise." Margeaux stands, a little shakily, and walks to Dr. Mather who removes the little jade box from his sportscoat. "You have the map and the cards already, and the earthly texts. In this box is the Scroll, the voice of water itself. When it decides to speak, it will be you who will best know how to interpret it. Only you can read the map and cards, as you have been given the generational gift of sight. Happily, you can also read the Demonai map, should you discover its location. Sadly, the Demonai Map Reader can also read ours, should they learn where it is. I've put a spell on it to keep it safe for now. You must continue to study and learn as much as you can without Kit's guidance. Have faith that The Cosmic will bring you what you need to know. Your first challenge will be to find the Demonai Newly-Born. If he's real, that is. But we do have reason to believe we might have a new Demonai on our hands. Good luck." Margeaux's face becomes anxious.

"Marc, Amaka and Louis: rise."

Dr. Mather pulls three pink crystal knives from the box. "You are entrusted with The Cosmic knives. These knives cannot kill a Demonai. None of these weapons can—only the sword—but these weapons can diminish their powers. If you must use them for defense or to advance your mission, be certain of your heart's righteousness. Karma is real.

"Christophe." The young man steps forward to receive crystal darts. A black dart glistens among the pink ones, along with a pink crystal tube. "You are now the guardian of the celestial plumbata. As you can see, I was able to pick up an extra at the police station—the one found in Kit Hamilton's neck. The Demonai have one of ours, so we're even. The tube is for launching them." Christophe bows and retakes his seat.

"Sylvie, Zaharia and Nadine." The young women step forward. Dr. Mather pulls out three crystal bows and three quills of arrows. "Now that you are entrusted with these celestial bows, you'll want to join the archery club. Of course, these bows are much more powerful than anything you'll ever use in the club. These weapons come with a charm." Dr. Mather raises his hand and incants, "*Cessuros!*" The bows and arrows shrink to the size of a doll's toy. "*Cresco!*" The weapons expand to their original size. The young women bow and return to their cushions.

"Octavio and Nikki Kong." The Kong twins rise and bow before Dr. Mather. He reaches into the jade box and removes two crystal ninja stars. "You will find, if you should ever be inspired to use them, that these shuriken seem to have a life of their own. You throw them as much with your mind as you do with your hand." The twins bow again and rejoin the circle.

All the weapons pulse with pink light. Dr. Mather surveys his class. "These weapons were made by the Angelai and have been in human hands since the days of Pythagoras. To say that you are being entrusted with the most important things you will ever receive is a shocking understatement. Use them wisely and hide them well. That you will be caretakers of the Angelai's most precious tools is in itself an indication of how desperate our situation has become. Already, this class has lost a combined four phones this year."

Marc, Christophe and Margeaux cast down their eyes. Margeaux and Marc each lost two phones, but Dr. Mather is unaware of Margeaux's second loss.

Dr. Mather pulls the Moon Sword that Dr. Anderson carried from the box. "Shabad."

Shabad bows to Dr. Mather. He holds the sword and chants, "*Saucha, saucha, saucha.*" The sword turns from black to gray, and finally to rose, shining with pink light. Dr. Mather puts it back in the box, then pulls out the Sun Sword.

"Estrella."

Estrella's feet don't touch the floor as she joins Dr. Mather at the front of the room. Instinctively, she takes the sword he extends and raises it over her head.

"Angelai Dominai!" she roars. The class jumps to its feet.

"Angelai Dominai," they yell back, their weapons raised and ready.

...

"Well, isn't this something. We're all part of a secret rebel group in a war between angels. Estrella's our leader, I'm our scribe, of sorts, and it turns out, Estrella's fun friend, Nadine is on our team. We may not win, but we'll surely have a good time. Make a wish!"

Margeaux says, blowing the top off a dandelion in the long dirt driveway outside Water Woods.

"Ha!" Nadine says. "They still don't know who I am; that's how good my charm is. Not even Tatiana, that snake in the grass. It must've killed her pride when you knocked her teeth out and she had to miss graduation because of her big, ugly mouth. I can't wait to keep working her like I'm a first-generation immigrant. Sorry, Estrella, no offense. You know what I mean."

"How can you be an Angelai when you say dumb things like that," Estrella replies. "Not to mention all the gambling, drinking and drugs. You don't really seem angelic, no offense."

"I'm an angel, not a saint. And neither are you," Nadine replies. "Oh, and look, here comes Marc Hamilton right now to prove it."

Marc approaches from under a fragrant pine tree, where he and Dr. Mather were talking, just the two of them. He picks up a dandelion on the way, presenting it to Estrella. Estrella takes it, blushing as their fingers touch. Nadine says, "I'll bet you two want to be alone." She sticks out her tongue and moves it around it in circles, then grabs Margeaux's arm. "Come on Lady Di. Let's go see your friend Mussolini, I mean Amaka."

Estrella collapses into Marc's strong embrace, allowing him to hold her as the sun and breeze tickle her through the treetops. "This is wild, right?" Marc says. "You're an *angel*." He squeezes her a little tighter. "And I'm here to protect you, to be by your side. Like, it was prophesied. I knew it. There's always just been something about you. You're irresistible to me." He kisses her neck, then takes out the crystal knife he just received. It catches a glint of sun. "Pretty badass." He looks into her eyes. "You're going to be okay. I know you've been through more this year than a person can handle. But you can handle it. *We* can handle it, because I'm here with you. Not just, like to back you up with the knife, but...my heart is here for you. I can take all your sorrows. I know you're still in shock about Marina. I swear, Estrella, I love you so much."

Estrella breaks free of his embrace enough to tilt back her head and kiss him. Twice. "I love you too."

A few hundred feet away, where the other Mystery Schoolers gather, applause breaks out. Estrella and Marc both laugh. "I guess this means we're exclusive now," Marc says, as Kit's Rolls comes up the dirt road.

"Yes, of course," Estrella replies, kissing him again as she and Margeaux climb into the door Yves holds open. Nikki and Sylvie push in next to them.

"Shabad's riding with Zaharia, of course," Nikki whispers as Yves closes the door. "He needs to be careful about falling in love with a mortal. And so do you, Ambriel."

"Don't worry about my love-life—I know what I'm doing," Estrella replies, as a text comes in from John.

Thinking of you constantly. Can't wait to see you back at home.

Three heart emojis.

• • •

The last day of school looks much like the first. Fancy cars congest the parking lot. Butlers, parents, and luggage line the dormitory halls. The only difference is that now Estrella has a butler with a fancy car, too.

Yves packs up Estrella's clothes, her single plant, and her computer, then gives her a formal nod. "I'll drive these to your house and see you in the morning."

As soon as the door closes behind him, Amaka who applies La Mer to her face and hands, as she does every night, says, "This Spirit War will be a bloodbath. Estrella, what is your plan?"

"What do you mean? I don't need a plan. Dr. Mather said my mission will become clear day by day. Personally, I plan to work on flying this summer. It must have something to do with the center of the body and deep breath—like levitating..." She gathers together her center, lifts a few feet off the floor and flaps her arms.

Amaka shakes her head. "You look ridiculous." Estrella lowers to the floor. "You must determine your mission, day by day—you cannot wait for the clouds to part and a voice to tell you what to do. If you are our leader, you must have a plan, a strategy. You've succeeded in getting your mother out of jail—she is an ally, but what else have you got?"

"Well, I mean, like Dr. Mather said, we all have our missions this summer," Estrella replies. "And remember, I'm on a spiritual mission—we all are supposed to be. If you want to know about a plan for the Remundus, Raeesa's in charge of that, so once I rescue her, she'll tell Zaharia, and you can ask her."

"It is I who should lead," Amaka says, "Everyone knows that."

"Perhaps the Cosmic wants a gentler hand to lead humanity," Margeaux says.

Amaka narrows her eyes. "Then the Cosmic is impotent! A gentle hand cannot fight."

A sound of thunder cracks through the dorm room; the little jade box on Estrella's bed pops open. The tattered scroll unfurls.

> *I am The Cosmic*
> *This is my Scroll*
> *You are my servant*
> *I guide your soul*

I am Water
I am Day
I am Night
I made the beginning
The Sound
The Light
From Suns
From Void
From Tongues
I am employed
I am Truth
You will know Me
By my words
Here unspooling

"Holy shit!" Estrella's eyes open as wide as her jaw. Margeaux grabs her hand, she grabs Amaka's. The scroll keeps unfurling, its disembodied voice an echo, like if the moon could speak.

Ambriel, the Newly-Born
Holds the sun
The code of crystals
Ready, set, run
To oceans
To lakes
To rivers
To seas
I am the ocean
Water sings me
Like Aawough
Queen of beasts

I am a weapon, a strengthening
Meet your mirror, Estrella
Islid you will see
Make your first quest
The ursa of your dreams
Then to mighty Zadkiel
Keeper of memories
Is the Genetic Code of Karma
Greater than alkalinity
Is Pythagoras less than Archimedes
Do you leave a remundus or an acid earth of mines
Tick tock tick
There flies the time
Amaka goes to the caves
With Adisa and Babatunde
Margeaux goes to play
Maps, cards, guitars
She reads the stars
Like Jia and Marie
All animals of the Maikoh desire peace
But the birds carry war on their breeze
For the hands that Hanuman lost
Beware the fury of such costs
Raeesa, Amare, Su Bang Bang, China
Where goes the pure waters of Russia
And what of Alfonso
Child of Zandra
Victor held his head
Beneath the crystal water
Bequeathed the crystal power
Does he rise to the moments of his hour

> *For the Demonai*
> *Yes*
> *Possess a Newly-Born too*
> *Who seeks back their sword*
> *Nakir, made of moon*
> *Sun Sword*
> *Moon Sword*
> *War*
> *Peace*
> *The games of my children*
> *Where do they lead*
> *I am water*
> *I will be free*
> *Through flood*
> *Through quake*
> *Through eruption*
> *For my own sake*
> *Remundus will be*
> *With or without*
> *You and your kin*
> *Now I finish*
> *Where you must begin*
> *Angelai*
> *Demonai*
> *Array my battlefield*

Another clap of thunder shakes the dorm room as the Scroll rolls itself back into a brittle tube and jumps into the jade box.

Estrella takes a deep breath—she didn't realize she had been holding hers. Margeaux's green eyes sparkle with tears. "That didn't sound very good, did it? All that talk of war."

"And what was that about Alfonso?" Estrella asks. "It all happened so fast."

Amaka looks at her phone. "Child of Zandra...Victor held his head beneath the water, bequeathed the power...will he rise to the hour...I wrote as quickly as I could. I didn't get every word."

Estrella throws her arms around Amaka. "You're awesome!"

"I am winning this war by any means," Amaka replies. "I have also recorded it." She puts her phone between the three of them and pushes a button.

The sound of waves rolling into and pulling back from the shore. Then a river rushing over stones. Then rain.

Water.

"I had a feeling that the words of the Scroll would be impossible to record. We must rely only on my notes. Thank God I am an excellent note-taker. Now to the work of reviewing the words of this cryptic scroll. Margeaux, put on a pot of tea. Dr. Mather said you were the one who would interpret it best. Perhaps we can make sense of it before we must leave tomorrow."

• • •

Mary of Guadalupe balances on the crescent moon, her robe of stars spreading through the night sky. Below her, a whale swims in the ocean, an elephant trumpets, a wolf howls, a monkey swings through palm trees, a bear splashes into a river.

A fragrance of roses seeps into Estrella's skin.

"Exire!"

• • •

"Go forth." Estrella murmurs the translation of exire as she wipes the sleep from her eyes and answers the door.

Yves' face is a January day: lightless and lonely. "The police were around last night to ask a few pointed questions about Kit," he says. "We'd better move quickly this morning." He picks up Estrella's suitcase and waits in the hall while Estrella, Margeaux and Amaka hug goodbye.

"I will communicate as much as possible without words," Amaka says. "We must be careful of the words we speak. We cannot know who is listening."

On their walk to the rental car, Estrella touches the tooth on a belly chain that rests on her hip bone. Right before she fell asleep last night, just a few hours ago, she read Tatiana's Instagram, finding nothing since a post a few weeks ago, when Tatiana posted a closed-mouth smile photo and a caption about how she's spending a month in a convent praying for her father's victory. "Yeah right," Estrella says to herself, recalling the post. "The convent would explode—she's obviously getting her teeth done. Dixon Duplessis has less than no chance of winning anyway."

Estrella's phone lights with a text from Marc.

Four hearts.

Estrella replies with five hearts as her phone lights.

Can't wait to see you!

"John. Shit," Estrella mutters as she walks to the car. She still hasn't told him about her and Marc. She's waiting for the right time.

Nikki meets Estrella and Yves at the car.

Originally, the three of them planned to travel together, but it's too risky now. Yves's presence will draw attention to Nikki and Estrella.

They drop Yves off at the airport first. He applies his fake mustache, reviews his fake passport, gives the women a lonely smile, and pushes open his door.

"You look hilarious, Yves," Estrella says. "See you in Rome."

Estrella meets Nikki's eyes with her own: crystal to crystal. The compass on the dashboard points northwest.

They're going to find Islid, like the Scroll, the voice of water, told them to do.

ACKNOWLEDGMENTS

Thank you to Marvin Marks Matherne, Jr., Jordan Rosenfeld, Erin Sinclair, DartFrog Books, Tami Hotard, Erica Cross, Daniel Vitalis, Momma, Loyola, New Orleans, the Cosmic, and all my many dogs.

You all kept me going, all these years and re-writes, giving me suggestions, ideas, and support, sometimes from the beyond. Without you, Mystery School would be mere air, a breeze upon the water.